Cather

Life in the South

Vol. 2

SALZWASSER
VERLAG

Catherine Cooper Hopley

Life in the South

Vol. 2

Reprint of the original, first published in 1863.

1st Edition 2022 | ISBN: 978-3-37500-108-7

Verlag (Publisher): Salzwasser Verlag GmbH, Zeilweg 44, 60439 Frankfurt, Deutschland
Vertretungsberechtigt (Authorized to represent): E. Roepke, Zeilweg 44, 60439 Frankfurt, Deutschland
Druck (Print): Books on Demand GmbH, In de Tarpen 42, 22848 Norderstedt, Deutschland

LIFE IN THE SOUTH.

VOL. II.

LIFE IN THE SOUTH;

FROM THE COMMENCEMENT OF THE WAR.

BY

A BLOCKADED BRITISH SUBJECT.

BEING A SOCIAL HISTORY OF THOSE WHO TOOK PART IN THE BATTLES, FROM A PERSONAL ACQUAINTANCE WITH THEM IN THEIR OWN HOMES.

FROM THE SPRING OF 1860 TO AUGUST 1862.

IN TWO VOLUMES.

VOL. II.

LONDON

1863.

CONTENTS.

CHAPTER I.

CHAPTER II.

CHAPTER III.

CHAPTER IX.

CHAPTER X.

CHAPTER XI.

CHAPTER XII.

CHAPTER XIII.

CHAPTER XIV.

CHAPTER XV.

CHAPTER XVI.

CHAPTER XVII.

CHAPTER XVIII.

CHAPTER XIX.

CHAPTER XX.

LIFE IN THE SOUTH.

CHAPTER I.

Return to Richmond—Suspense and Suspicion—A Supposed Spy—The Battle of Manassas—The Plan of the Battle—Unequal Forces—Feats of Daring—Incidents of the Battle—Sunday after the Battle—The Congregation on that occasion—Cause of the Panic—The Union Prisoners—That Letter—A Sensitive Trio—Who become very excited—The London Correspondents.

CROWDS of new faces greeted me on arriving at the American Hotel, late in the afternoon of Saturday, 20th July. By the eager groups gathered on sofas and in corners, I conjectured that exciting news was rife; but I knew no one, and could ask no questions.

After being in my room a short time, Mrs. Ayres, the landlady, tapped at my door, and on entering, kindly welcomed me back, and sat down to hear an account of my trip. It has been already stated that hotel-keepers in America enjoy a very respectable position in society; and this lady, brought up on her father's plantation, had married and lived in the country until within a year or two, when from some fancy, her husband had become the proprietor of a city hotel. The change of habits did not suit her taste; but with a good housekeeper, and a numerous establishment of servants, very little trouble devolved upon herself. Before my departure to the Peninsula, she had conversed with me occasionlly in the drawing-room, and I found every reason to believe her a true Virginian lady. Her manner was exceedingly mild and kind, and, in my present position, gratifying. "Have you heard of the great battle?" was one of her first remarks; and then she told me that another was anticipated shortly, because the two armies were so near. Afterwards she made some inquiries concerning myself, my occupations, and intentions, which I excused, as reasonable enough; and on hearing of my disappointment in not having been able to accomplish my journey Northwards, and my doubts as to future arrangements, she told me that her eldest daughter had just returned home from her summer vacation, and that she should like her to go on with her music, and read French for an hour a-day, if I were inclined to instruct her. Indeed, under the existing state of my finances, with no probability of receiving any remittances whatever, I was only too glad to accept the proposal. Mrs. Ayres' private sitting-room was very near to mine; and she left me, with an invitation to come and bring my work and sit with her, whenever I felt disposed. I must say, the protection of her society and acquaintance was quite a relief to me.

All that evening busy whispers and much anxiety

were visible in the countenances of those down-stairs. Arrivals were more numerous than ever, and I saw the servants preparing beds in a large adjoining sitting-room. Many, it seemed, were going off again; and, from what I could gather, were proceeding to the battle-field.

Sunday-morning. A lady sitting near me whispered to another, though not so low as to prevent my hearing her, that all the doctors, who could be spared from the city, had been ordered to Manassas. Evidently another battle was either raging, or at hand. All that day the streets were more than ever full of bustle and confusion. Troops were arriving and departing continually. It was a time of fearful, restless suspense; anticipating one knew not what. About three o'clock P.M., the trains from Northwards arrived, bringing news that a dreadful battle was being fought, and that President Davis was commanding in person. Oh! how I wished that I knew some of those strange faces, and could ask them the particulars.

That afternoon Mrs. Ayres sought me, and again questioned me respecting my visit to Yorktown. Her questions and manner differed from last evening, and I was puzzled to conjecture her motive, but frankly told her all I had seen and done; and using no disguise, informed her of my intentions to raise a subscription for Miss Gibbon's own disposal, as she required so many articles that would be more difficult and tedious to procure through the usual sources.

I also showed her my list of commissions, and, thinking her curiosity proceeded alone from sympathy in the cause, was as communicative as she could desire.

She left me, to return again shortly. Something perplexed her. What could it be?

"Miss Jones, you will excuse my asking you, but will you object to tell me what you took those sketches of the fortifications for?"

Ah me! the truth was out; and the ubiquitous Captain Jones instantly recurred to me.

"Certainly, Mrs. Ayres; but I have not sketched any of the fortifications, which did not strike me as being particularly interesting. I sketched James Town as I did before the war was thought of, and as I always do wherever I see any object worth remembering."

"Oh, then you did *not* draw a plan of the fortifications on the river; you *will* excuse me, will you not?" said she, kindly placing her hand on mine, "and you will not feel hurt if I tell you—but, I knew it was not so—and I—told Mr. Ayres it was all nonsense—but—"

"Do, pray, tell me what all this means," I exclaimed, half frightened, half amused.

"Well, if you are sure you won't mind it; but three gentlemen of this city have waited on Mr. Ayres this afternoon, to tell him there was a lady in the house whom they thought was a Yankee spy, who had been down to Yorktown making drawings of all the fortifications. And a gentleman on the boat had watched you tracing something after you had been talking to Captain Meade, (he had been making a plan of the battle of Bethel for me), and he saw you take down all the batteries at James Town."

It made me laugh, but I did feel rather indignant. What is the use of taking any interest in these people? I thought more than once; though, after reflection, I forgave the suspicion, which really seemed somewhat justifiable, and, as in Mr. Quence's case, attributed their conduct to the necessities of the war. Still, I might be in danger by such suspicion, and asserted my British blood and privileged neutrality somewhat warmly. That little incident gained me one safe friend in Mrs. Ayres, who delicately endeavoured to heal any wound her information might have occasioned, and, as if to convince me of her confidence, at once headed my list of intended subscribers with five dollars.

This encouraged me a little, and I wrote notices of the purport, and placed them in conspicuous positions about the rooms. That was merely a little interlude to the events of the day, which was passed by everybody else in a state of feverish excitement and restlessness. Every arrival at the hotel caused increased bustle and commotion; each arrival announced fresh news, each more momentous than before, and thus did the public agitation increase until the evening, when the news of the victory brought it to the culminating point.

How shall the tidings be described? Shall we begin with the telegraphic despatch—those few concise words that President Davis sent to his wife from the battle-field on that eventful Sabbath evening? "July 21st, 1861.—We have won a dearly-bought but signal victory; night closes on the enemy in full retreat, and we in full pursuit."

Oh! how that information spread like wild-fire through the large and crowded hotel. And then amongst those awe-stricken faces, what varieties of expression were to be seen! Between kindred love and patriotism, what a tumult of feeling seemed panting for utterance! Those who had no near relatives in the engagement (though such were few) disguised not their loud rejoicings. But, "Oh, my only son!" "My husband!" "My brother!" "My two sons!"—and then the fearful suspense of the speakers, the rush to the telegraph-office, the craving for more information, the eager looks and restless fever of impatience cannot be described.

Who can ever forget the scenes of those two following days! the sending and receiving of telegraphic messages, the hurrying off of mothers, fathers, and sisters to the battle-field; the impossibility for all to go, owing to the crowds who were hastening to the relief of the wounded; the agonies of those who were compelled to wait; the constant tide of fresh information rushing in to the relief of some, and the alarm and consternation of others; the horrors of many who were yet uncertain; and the shrieks of those to whom sad losses were suddenly revealed. Added to all this, the flood of arrivals by every train, of persons from all parts of the Confederacy, who had just received the tidings. Next came the bringing in of the wounded soldiers, and their disposition in hospitals, almshouses, and a large empty hotel, to say nothing of private families, who, whether for relatives or not, threw open their doors to receive and nurse the brave sons of the South, who had willingly resigned their homes of plenty to set off for Virginia's protection. Never was more bustle and business got through in the whilom quiet city of Richmond, though it all tended to one result—the business of war.

A great amount of self-gratulatory sentiment escaped from every Southern tongue, and took deep root in every Southern heart, though but little outward rejoicing had been displayed. A few cheers greeted their President on his return from the battlefield; otherwise the feeling seemed too deep to be expressed by much outward demonstration, even by a most demonstrative people.

Among the few of my last winter's friends still remaining in the city, was a married sister of Mrs. Castleton's, of whom I had seen but little, owing to the oppressive heat that rendered walking almost impossible. That week a storm cooled the air for a time, which enabled me to visit her, and I found her occupied in nursing two wounded soldiers, one belonging to the "Hampton Legion" of South Carolina, and the other to the "Washington Artillery" of

New Orleans. There have been such innumerable varieties of anecdotes related concerning this battle, that the reader may be already tired of reading of them; yet I must repeat a few of those told to me by persons upon whose veracity one can rely, and by those who themselves took a part in the fight.

I will detain my readers a few moments, in order to simplify to the best of my ability, in untechnical language, the plan of this celebrated battle, which will be rendered more intelligible by tracing the two roads, with the river crossing them; dotting the localities of Centreville, the bridge, and fords, as described below.

The city of Alexandria, near the southern point of the district of Columbia, and just within the borders of Virginia, is the great south-western outlet from the United States capital. From it, two important roads run nearly parallel, rather south of westward: namely, the Alexandria and Orange County railroad, through Manassas; and three or four miles to the north of this, slightly diverging from Alexandria, the Warrenton turnpike road, which runs through Fairfax Court-house, Centreville, over the Stone Bridge and Bull Run, towards Warrenton, sixteen miles further west. The reader is already acquainted with the character of Virginia roads, and must here picture to himself a hilly, wooded, and very rough country, with masses of rock jutting up even in the roads, in comparison with which, the common at Tunbridge Wells would be pronounced almost a level plain.

The stream, or, as it would be called in England, the river, of Bull Run flows in a south-eastern direction in a very winding course among these hills, crossing both the turnpike and the railroad, and on to the Occoquan river, with which it unites, and thence into the Potomac. These rivers vary materially in different seasons, and from the nature of the country; sometimes being almost dry at certain fordable places and at others deep and rapid. From the larger streams diverge those smaller branches, known as Cub Run, Cedar Run, Little River, Young's Branch, Broad Run, &c., with rough by-roads, crossing them at the fords.

It is well understood that the object of the "grand army of the Potomac" was a triumphant march through Virginia, to capture the capital. Smaller collections of Federal troops had already been defeated in this attempt at Aquia Creek, at Fairfax Court-house, at Vienna on another more northern line of railway, at Harper's Ferry, Winchester, and also on the Peninsula. At this time the "grand army," under General McDowell (whom the Confederates invest with higher military qualities than most of the Federal Generals), was massed in great force at Centreville, six miles eastward of the Stone Bridge, on the high road from Alexandria. Superior numbers gave confidence to the invaders, whose anticipated result was "to crush the rebellion" in "one decisive blow."

To defeat this object, General Beauregard had concentrated his forces at Manassas, on the line of railroad above described, whence important routes branched off into the interior of Virginia. Bull Run was the great barrier between the two armies, encamped on each side of it, within a few miles of each other, extending their pickets and reconnaissances to the various fords in their vicinity. General McDowell's first attempt to cross was about six miles below the Stone Bridge at Blackburn's and Mitchel's Fords, in front of the army at Manassas. This movement was defeated on Thursday, in the battle of the 18th July. Another feint of attack was made at those points on the 21st, in order to disguise his real intentions, and detain the main body of the Confederate army there, while the Federals should effect a crossing about six miles above the Stone Bridge, at a ford near Sudley church. This *détour* of the Federal army was intended to have been accomplished before break of day on the Sabbath, when General Beauregard, had he not received timely intimation of the movement, intended to have rested his army, and afforded them opportunities for religious services at their several camps. Owing to the roughness of the roads, the difficult passage of the *détour* through the woods, and the narrow passes being blocked up by the vast moving columns of his army, General

McDowell's troops did not effect the crossing until daylight revealed their course. General Beauregard had fortunately thrown out a division of his army in the direction of Sudley, and other companies were deployed along the stream to guard the fords, so that the Confederate troops were scattered over a space of fifteen miles, their chief strength lying in the right wing at Blackburn's ford, where the battle was expected to take place; the scattered regiments of the left wing extending to the upper ford at Sudley, where the Federals were effecting their flank movement in great force, and with their heavy artillery were occupying a commanding position along a ridge of hills. It was against these powerful forces that those few Southern regiments marched with such heroic valour, in spite of a disparity of one to five. Parts of the 4th Alabama, the 8th Georgia, and the 2nd Mississippi, stood their ground for an hour in the face of leaden hail and powerful batteries; not yielding an inch. When greatly reduced they were joined by the 4th South Carolina, part of a Virginia regiment, and the Hampton Legion, until the Federal batteries of Heintzleman, Sherman, the Rhode Island, and Hunter's division rolling down upon them in a cross-fire, compelled their retreat amid such fearful odds.

One of my informants, who was for a long time exposed to this cross-fire, said, "When I think of that tremendous host of 22,000 men arrayed against us, and our insignificant body of 600 men, it seems nothing short of a miracle that we were not annihilated. This was the company from South Carolina who begged so hard of General Beauregard to be placed in the front ranks, in order to have the "first fire" at the enemy, that he is said to have altered his arrangement of troops in order to oblige them. So death-like was the conflict in which this little band was engaged that when one of their officers fell, and some of them were about to remove him, the Colonel exclaimed, "Fire away, boys! we cannot spare the sound ones to attend to the dead—the wounded must see to that." So six wounded men were appointed to carry off their officer, one of whom, injured in the eyes by the bursting of a shell, survived to tell me the circumstance.

The 8th Georgia regiment was for a long time engaged against a very powerful force, who were advancing upon them from the ledge of that hill above. At one time they were almost overpowered by sheer numbers, and the day seemed gone. Col. Bartow succeeded in rallying them, and was soon after wounded by a shot in his foot. He then seized the flag and sat upon a fence, crying, "Never retreat boys! I'll sit here and be shot to death before I retreat." The little band, however, became sorely reduced, and hope was departing. "Oh that the ball in my foot had gone through my heart, and that I had not lived to see this defeat!" cried the Colonel, in utter anguish. The brave, though too reckless man, had scarcely uttered the distrustful wish before a second ball pierced his heart, and he fell,—too soon, alas! to learn the glorious news that his brave "boys" were reinforced, and to hear the shout of "victory." He was only about thirty-three years of age.

One of those Georgia "boys" was shot in the arm, rendering it powerless, but it did not arrest his ardour. By resting his gun on the trunk of a tree he managed to reload it, and with *one arm* shot and killed successively three men, whom he had marked as having fired upon three of his friends. Another similar spirit was displayed by a comrade whose leg was broken by a cannon-ball. Crawling to a tree, and partially shielding himself behind it, he loaded and reloaded his gun, and continued to fire till his powder was exhausted, each time "picking out his man" and sending him to his long account. Another wounded Georgian, whilst lying on the ground, saw his own two brothers shot down. Marking their murderers, and with an almost superhuman effort, he raised himself, faint with bleeding, upon his elbows, took aim, and revenged himself of their death by bringing both of the Federal soldiers to the earth, one with each barrel of his gun.

Such feats of daring were terrible in their ferocity. There is no yielding, no "give up." If an officer fall, the men still fight, often separating themselves and wandering off in pairs, or singly, to pick out their men and shoot them down.

The reader will now comprehend the retreat of the Confederate left wing, in order to concentrate their force, and form a new front to meet the advancing enemy, whose lines extended on two sides of them, towards the middle of the day.

A young lad at the hotel that week, who had just come from the army on a few days' furlough, told us scores of these incidents, and not with any attempt at boasting, or as if it were surprising, but only a matter of course. I asked him how many he thought he had killed in the fight. "I cannot say exactly," he replied, "but I seldom miss my game when I take a gun in hand." Many of the "boys," when armed with more than one weapon—and some had rifles, revolvers, swords, and bowie-knives—would have recourse to each in turn, not stopping to reload, but dashing with savage fury at the invader.

They talked of shooting their fellow-creatures as they would of blackbirds. Every day one heard of the number of captives as "bagging game," and they spoke of "best shots," and how many were fired, and the amount of "game" disposed of, as if the victims were no better than partridges at a *battue*. It was more like a game of marbles, or, at best, an archery party, with all the rivalry of securing prizes, and how best to obtain them.

Bowie-knives, guerilla warfare, "aim at the helmsman," "picking off captains!" What savage demons do even our best friends appear, even those we have so well esteemed and loved, when possessed and transformed by the passion of such a hate as this!

And yet, though so fierce in their hatred on the

battle-field, they had no sooner ceased to fight than the tenderest sympathies replaced the fierceness of their fury, and to the fallen and wounded enemy I heard of many instances of almost brother's care.

During the winter I had, through my old friend Mr. Tyler, become acquainted with an intelligent and gentlemanly young man, who, like everybody else, had afterwards joined the army, and was now *aide-de-camp* to one of the generals. That week he also re-appeared at the hotel, and informed me he was corre-sponding with one of the Southern newspapers, indeed one of the best conducted and influential of all the Confederate papers. His *nom de plume* was a very modest one, but he shall here be called Rebelfield. It was pleasant to see an old acquaintance, and fresh from the battle-field too, for I knew that I could depend on all he would tell me. A misfortune to him was the cause of my gaining a great deal of interesting information from a "very reliable source." His right hand had been slightly hurt, too much so to enable him to hold his pen; and when he re-gretted his inability to furnish his regular commu-nications to the press, I volunteered my services as amanuensis, which he accepted readily; thus his dic-tation answered the purpose of a mutual advantage.

I will trouble my readers with only one or two more of those instances of bravery, which may be taken as the characteristic of the Southern soldiers. An Alabama "boy," really a boy in this case, of scarcely seventeen, but tall and robust, had passed himself off as much older in order to be accepted as a volunteer. A Federal Zouave took him prisoner, bound him tightly with cords, and left him lying by the edge of a field to be carried off by-and-by. It did not suit the Alabamian temper to lie there idle, and with a good set of teeth, he gnawed asunder the ropes around his wrist, cut with his penknife the rest of his fetters, took a musket from a dying man, and marched off to join his regiment. Soon another Zouave approached, at whom the "boy" took deliberate aim, and shot him dead. By-and-by a colonel of dragoons rode up, but not suspecting the boy to be an enemy, approached quite near. Alabama presented his musket and ordered him to surrender. "Who are you?" said the Colonel. "I am an Alabamian, and you are my prisoner. Come down." So, like Captain Smith's squirrels, down came the Colonel. The boy mounted his horse, and conducted his prisoner to the General's tent.

General A. M. Jackson, since known as "Stonewall,"* received a rifle-ball in his hand early in the day, but in spite of a very painful wound remained on the field until the close of the engagement. "Don't waste your ammunition, boys!" he exclaimed,

* The singular prenomen of "Stonewall," was acquired by this celebrated General at the battle of Manassas, where he occupied an important position with his brigade near the Henry House; and for a long time held it against vastly superior forces; afterwards being complimented by General Beauregard, who said he had stood his ground like a *stone wall.* His brigade thus earned their character and title.

in the hearing of my informant, "and don't fire unless you are sure of hitting them. We may want all the powder we have to pursue them to-night." Another "boy" shot a wild rabbit as he marched along that darted from its lair—poor terrified animal! and his game was carried with him throughout the remainder of the day. When firing he laid it down, then carried it on again, saying, "I shall want a good supper to-night after this day's work;" and he saved his rabbit and enjoyed his supper. It is a well-authenticated fact, that at the close of that hard-fought battle, many of the Confederate troops had not three rounds of ammunition left in their cartouches!

Towards the end of the week a comparative lull succeeded, though groups at every corner and at every doorway, both out of the house and in it, ceased not to introduce fresh news, and also "eye-witnesses," from whom every incident of the battle was received with re-awakened interest.

It was a solemn service at St. Paul's church, Richmond, the Sunday after the battle of Manassas. Congress had appointed a general thanksgiving for "a great and important victory," and the lessons and psalms were selected to suit the occasion; especial prayers were offered, and the whole tenor of the worship might be comprised in the few words, "Give God the glory." The President with his family occupied their usual pew, about the middle of the church. General Lee was also present, and sat where our Prince of Wales had done, less than one year before. For the first time I had an opportunity, irresistible in spite of the time and place, of seeing and observing the new President of the Southern Confederacy. Character is stamped upon his features. A broad, full, prominent forehead, nose somewhat aquiline, lips thin, firm, and delicate. Mildness and gentleness are the prominent expression; kindness, benevolence, then a touch of sadness strikes you: the least shadow of bitterness melting into sorrow: and had he not sufficient cause? But there is plenty of resolution, and dignity combined with conscientiousness; and you feel that words from those lips would not fall light and powerless. He is said to be a devout Christian, too; meek devotion marks his bearing in the presence of the Almighty; nor was the father buried in the patriot, nor the parent's duty sunk in individual worship. Frequently he shared his book with his young son by his side, quietly pointing to direct the eye, or guide him in the chants.

And here it may not be out of place to observe, that in few churches of the States is the manner of the congregation marked by more attention, devotion, and stillness, than in St. Paul's church, Richmond. Ever since the visit of the Prince of Wales to that city, the people have not ceased to regret the confusion, ill-breeding, and interruptions, that disturbed the sanctity of the place on that occasion. Crowds of country people flocked in and occupied the seats of the regular congregation, or even choked up the aisles, to the exclusion of devotional worshippers. The Castletons' pew was quite near to that occupied by the Prince, and Mr. Castleton had informed me that he saw persons pushing their way up the aisle, until they came in full view of him, when they would stand with folded arms, and survey him with close scrutiny, oblivious to all around, until their gaze was satisfied; then they would effect their exit as they had their entrance. Others stood upon the seats to behold him, resolving, as they had never seen a "live prince" before, and might never have so good an opportunity again, that they would make the most of it. But this is their way of paying "homage." Many miles had the majority of them travelled for this very purpose, and it was not likely they would be easily baffled.

But to return to the church on this particular Sabbath—28th of July. Another thing which struck me was the crowd of grave subdued persons there assembled, although the services were for special thanksgiving, and the large number of wounded soldiers interspersed among the congregation. There they were in all sorts of dresses and uniforms; in all sorts of bandages and plaisters; arms in slings, and bound-up heads, but calm and devotional, seated with the families at whose houses they had been received and tended during the previous week, and allowing no trifles to prevent their attendance at the house of God on that great and solemn occasion.

Rebelfield described some most harrowing scenes that he had witnessed at the hospitals. In spite of "all the doctors" being summoned to the battle-field, there were not half enough. To one small country church such crowds of wounded men were carried, that they lay on the floor closely packed, while *one young student* alone was there to perform the operations. Piles of limbs! yes, piles of human limbs—were accumulated in one corner, amputation being the speediest method of cure! The little communion table of Sudley church became the patients' couch while the butchery was carried on.

But blame not that young doctor, and blame not the remissness that led to such horrifying necessities. Scarcely three months before, these 150,000 men of the Southern army had been lounging at their own firesides, or rambling over their cotton plantations. The country was blockaded when wholly unprepared for such emergencies. We have seen the life of the doctors of the South. What sort of experience could they have had in army surgery, and what instruments and appurtenances had they at hand? The few experienced practitioners from the cities could accomplish comparatively little, and here were hundreds of wounded men, who, not until several days elapsed, were all discovered and carried to the surgeons. And oh! the sickening effects of that hot July. The lists of sufferings are too dreadful to place before my readers, but it is very certain that hundreds on that scattered battle-field lingered in the broiling sunshine, tormented by thirst and insects scarcely less intolerable than their wounds, until a merciful death relieved their agonies. For miles around every dwelling became a hospital; and renewed exertions on the part of the women, renewed contributions on the part of the men, were offered promptly: no entreaties were necessary to extort them; every one hastened as if for their own blood relatives, to send comforts and luxuries; which after all were but too few!

In looking at the results of that terrible slaughter, the battle of Bull Run, one can scarcely fail to recognize a signal Providence in the remarkably abundant preparations made by the Federalists for their expedition to Richmond, and the wonderful panic that seized them, causing all these provisions to fall into the hands of the very people whom they were blockading, and endeavouring to deprive of the necessaries of life; well-supplied medicine chests, wine, clothing, even ladies' apparel, and dainties of every kind. The Southerners had often said, "The best way to provide ourselves with arms is to fight for them," and so it proved then, and so it has proved throughout the whole campaign. There have been various attempts to account for that panic, but the most prevalent idea is, that it was caused by a shout of triumph at the capture of Sherman's battery, that, during the whole day, had been so strongly contested; captured and recaptured again and again. More than one person described that shout as something more overpowering than the cannon's roar. It was taken up, and carried along the line for several miles, and they heard the uproar rolling along in its approach like an avalanche of thunder. The enemy were not aware of the cause, and were in their turn overpowered by terror. One frightened company infected the rest, and the result is known. Afterwards I visited the battle-field, and heard that race described by the wives of the farmers who lived close by. It was almost as fearful as the battle itself. All Monday, Tuesday, and Wednesday were the poor terrified, tattered, and starving fugitives passing by from their hiding-places; at first rushing madly on, trampling each other in their speed, or dashing themselves against trees and fences as they turned in dread to gaze behind them; then staggering in their fatigue and hunger, lifting their poor hands in entreaties to the cottagers in mercy to point the way to Alexandria, but *not to tell the* "*Secessioners*" which way they had gone. However, that early failure to the Federalists taught them a useful lesson, while, sad to relate, the success to the Southerners caused them to relax in their exertions.

Amongst the arrivals of the previous week had been the "Yankee prisoners." Upwards of a thousand had been sent to Richmond alone; of whom nearly a hundred were wounded, and were disposed of in a large, commodious, brick almshouse, where they received the same care and treatment from Southern doctors, as the Southern soldiers they had come to fight. Indeed, so far have Virginian hospitality and honour been displayed, that, in spite of the scarceness of medicines, the Northern wounded prisoners (and there were at least 500 in the State) positively shared the scanty supply in common with the Southerners, who, as the unhealthy season approached, risked death for the want of them: while the North, even to cure their own men, would not permit a supply to cross the borders. From an army physician I was told that though he had not enough quinine for his own men, it was being administered to the "Yankee" prisoners.

Several persons were admitted to visit these prisoners, among whom were ministers of the gospel, to give them spiritual comfort or counsel. The majority of them seemed deeply impressed with the kindness of their conquerors, and were surprised and amused at the cheerful gaiety and independent manners of the negro attendants—those "manacled slaves," whose condition seemed so much more enviable than their own just then. With a few exceptions, they expressed regret that they engaged in the war at all, assuring the Southerners that they had either been deceived in their ideas of them, or bribed to come without any other alternative than to starve. Many very interesting though sorrowful incidents were related by some of the wounded, of their experiences on the battle-field: one of which, however, will convey a fair idea of the whole.

A clergyman addressed a man who was lying moaning in great apparent distress, asking him if he suffered much? "Yes, my wounds pain me sorely," said he, "but my heart pains me still more sorely, to think I have sacrificed so much to take up arms against such a people. While our men were escaping, they ran past me and over me, and I lay tortured in the sun's heat. I tried to get them to stop and move me out of the way, and procure me some water to drink, but none would stay to listen. When the crowd had passed, and I was expecting to lie there all night, a Southerner came and spoke to me; then he fetched me some water, and called to a friend to help him to lift me out of the way. They put me on a blanket, and did the best they could for me, while my own people had left me to die. And now I am here, and better cared for than I have been ever since I left my home, and by the very people I came to fight against." Many declared nothing should ever induce them to take up arms against the South again, and that if ever they reached the North, they would tell their own people how deceived they had been.

After the excitement of the battle had somewhat subsided I bethought me of *that letter* written from Milbank, and resolved to make inquiries at the Post-office department, to see if perchance it might still be in the State. An official wrote down my address, promising to institute a search for it; I having also given him a description of the despatch, and the name of the person to whom it was addressed; and I left him, with very little hope of his ever thinking either of Miss Sarah Jones, or her letter again.

That was the letter that Mr. Quence had been so desirous to have published in the "Richmond Enquirer," and I asked Rebelfield, who knew every one connected with that paper, if he had ever observed such a communication; for we had received the newspapers so irregularly at Milbank, that it might have easily escaped notice, and now, as people were taking so much trouble to watch me, and judge harshly of my actions, such a correspondence might be the means of protecting me from very unpleasant consequences, and this made me rather more anxious about it. Rebelfield asked to whom the letter had been addressed.

"To Mr. Tyler, one of the editors."

"Oh! He is Col. Tyler now, in the Wise Brigade, and has gone to Western Virginia."

My friend promised to inquire at the office, and find out what had become of the letter.

And how was the subscription for Miss Gibbon succeeding all this time?

Not at all. There were three ladies, who—of all that great hotel full of guests,—made themselves more conspicuous than the rest by dress, manner, and conversation, and the three were on intimate terms with each other. One shall be called Mrs. Graigh, who came from Mobile, accompanied by her husband, a very wealthy merchant, and some extravagantly attired, bejewelled daughters. Another was Mrs. Greene, a silly, affected, hysterical lady, always in tears over her departed (not dead) husband who was in the army somewhere. The third was Mrs. Gen. Henningsen, a fat, fair, and (not) forty, but fashionable lady, who had lately arrived by a very circuitous route from New York; and had met with many adventures on the road, being a well-known Secessionist and Southerner, also a Georgian: she had, in spite of her trunks being searched at three or four different places, succeeded in bringing a quantity of quinine, four or five revolvers secured under her hoops, and a model of a submarine battery; which achievement, as many similar ones were, had been duly but incautiously announced in the Richmond papers; rendering the lady, for the time being, quite a lioness, and keeping her well occupied in relating her adventures to every fresh comer. It was surprising to find how much harm was done at that time to the "rebel" successes, by the indiscreet notices in the papers. If a ship ran the blockade and brought a valuable cargo into port, the fact and the name were immediately published, rendering a capture certain by the Federal gunboats which would await her departure again. Those escapes from Maryland, the smuggling of goods, and every trifling success were publicly spoken of; and I sometimes thought that if newspapers had been tabooed for a time, it would have been greatly to the advantage of the Confederate States. A suspension of their publication was imminent, when printing ink became exhausted, and the type of some of them so much worn that the readers were fed by promises for several weeks; while the papers were almost unreadable. That "the blockade was going to be raised" so soon, was a great impediment to enterprise, the people arguing, "It is of no use to invest capital in such a manufacture, when it is quite understood that the blockade will be raised by the first week in September."

But to return to the three ladies. After the notices in behalf of the Yorktown hospital had been seen in the Hotel, some of the guests naturally inquired who was collecting the subscriptions; and on discovering that it was a stranger whom no one knew, and who had no ostensible occupation, or reason for residing alone in a country from which strangers were gladly escaping, they seemed more disposed to resent as officiousness, if not worse, any effort to collect funds over which they would have no further control. Some very harsh and unjustifiable remarks were audibly expressed in my presence: which might have been taken as highly insulting; but again I was induced to summon all my philosophy and forgiveness, in order to excuse the speakers, who I knew had so much reason to suspect black sheep among them. Poor patriotic sufferers! Were not their hearts' best instincts lacerated daily by the sufferings or massacre of their nearest relatives; and were they not witnessing their beloved country devastated and desolated by a futile war!

Mrs. Ayres had pointed out Mr. Graigh to me as a wealthy and liberal man, and I had ventured to introduce the subject to him. His manner had not been very encouraging nor polite, but he had promised to promote the object, and would "hand" me a sum of money by-and-by.

The next time he appeared I summoned my very best smile to ask him if he had thought of Yorktown, when he curtly replied that he had given twenty dollars, to a gentleman *whom he knew*, for that same object. Such conduct was too marked to be misunderstood; and feeling too much pained to disguise my sense of the indignity, I hastened away to Mrs. Ayres to tell her my troubles. She excused the Graighs, and endeavoured to soothe me by saying, "Those Southerners are very different from the Virginians—they are so impetuous," &c. However, I sent one of the children to take down the notices, and thus ended my collections for Yorktown. Only mine, however; for I must do the people the justice to say it was the stranger and not the cause that induced their refusal; the contributions were merely passed into another channel.

At that time some of Mr. W. H. Russell's letters from Mississippi had just found their way into the Richmond papers, which the public were in their over-sensitiveness construing into injurious misrepresentations of their institutions and country. Though it was evident to an English reader that those letters were conscientious descriptions of events and customs that could in no way injure the Confederate cause, but rather the contrary, and that the few objectionable comments would have no weight in the great balance of English opinion, the too tenacious slaveholders were violently indignant. They were particularly angry at an account of a little negro boy at a hotel in (I think) Vicksburg, or somewhere near the Mississippi, who had, when Dr. Russell asked him if he were happy, turned round to see who was listening before he gave his cautious reply. "What *gentleman* would question another gentleman's servant in that manner?" and "Who ever saw a negro boy act with so much caution? why, he would have burst out laughing without knowing what to answer to such a question." "If the 'Times' reporter had given him a plate full of molasses, he would soon have seen whether he was happy or not." And that poor little negro boy, at the hotel where "negroes of all shades and complexions" were to be seen, was dragged time after time into the Southern newspapers long after the republication of the unfortunate letter. Another offence of Dr. Russell's was some remark he made in Washington about the battle of Manassas, eagerly caught up, with probable exaggerations, by the Northern press, and afterwards recopied with bitter animadversions by the Southern papers.

"What did *he* know about it, when he was never near the place, and ran faster than any of them," &c. &c.

When those three ladies, Mrs. Greene, Mrs. Graigh and Mrs. Henningsen, discovered that Miss Jones was also a "British subject," it did not, under the present irritability, tend to improve their opinion of her; and to make matters worse, they had observed Mr. Phillips Day, who had called to kindly show me an English paper, and those ladies, with less politeness than usual in their countrywomen, had listened to our conversation and watched us in no very flattering manner. The next morning I was sitting reading the newspaper on a sofa, when they all entered the room and seated themselves very near me. They were talking in so loud a tone that it was impossible for me not to hear their conversation, which turned pointedly upon "that reporter" of the London 'Times.' "And now we have another of these English abolitionists in Richmond, I suppose he will be talking about our servants next." Several of such tenacious and pointed remarks were uttered and caught up by each of the three ladies, with some very mistaken and unjust reflections on Mr. Russell, particularly the following: "These itinerant reporters, of whom no one has ever heard before, come and partake of our hospitality, and then——."

The Englishwoman was also over-sensitive and impetuous, especially where her country was concerned; and if Mr. Russell were mistaken in his observations of Southern institutions, it was very evident that these ladies knew little respecting the character of the London press.

"Excuse me, ladies, for interrupting you, but Dr. Russell, of the London 'Times,' is——."

"No, we don't excuse anybody who listens to our conversation, and interferes with us," said Mrs. Graigh: "we wish people would just let us alone; we can fight our own battles, and don't want anybody to keep watch over *us*." Both she and Mrs. Greene burst out, in a manner so violent and unladylike, as well as abusive, that to argue or even continue the conversation was impossible; therefore I merely bowed, and apologizing briefly, went on reading my paper.

The paragraphs in the daily journals then gradually changed their tone, when mentioning the, at first, "distinguished correspondents." Soon one saw such notices as these :—

"MR. RUSSELL.—We observe that the notorious correspondent of the London 'Times' expresses the opinion that the North can easily subjugate the South if she puts forth her strength. Mr. Russell's letters from the United States thus far have not, &c."

"RUSSELL AS A REPORTER.—We give to this individual, says the Atlanta 'Intelligencer,' everything that is due as a reporter of the English press. We have, however, some knowledge of his *antecedents* that may be interesting to our readers. In the great struggle for the rights and independence of Ireland, he, this man, *Russell*, was the hired reporter of the London 'Times,' when, &c."

"THE ENGLISH PRESS ON AMERICAN AFFAIRS.—The comments of the English press on American affairs are the most amusing reading of the day. The combination of extraordinary ignorance and magnificent assumption is perfectly overwhelming."

Nevertheless the Confederates were watching eagerly for any measure that might lead to a cessation of hostilities. The least fragment of comfort that could be sifted from the Northern or English papers was ardently grasped; and they indulged in strong hopes that the recent successes at Manassas would both convince the Federal Government of the inutility of the war, and bring about the anticipated "recognition" by the European powers.

CHAPTER II.

The Campaign in Western Virginia—That Letter again—Ingenious Contrivances—Habitual Extravagance—Zeal and Munificence—The Five Honourable Judges—The Prisoners' Hospitals—"Exonerated in the eyes of Government"—Preparations to Winter in the South—The Yellow Bridesmaid—Hatty requires a Carriage to Herself—"Writing" Pictures—An Affecting Incident—Professional Correspondence—A Tempting Speculation—The Negotiations are tedious—The Consul is expected to do everything—Another "Distinguished Visitor"—The Underground Railway—Expectations and Disappointments—Necessity is the Parent of Invention—A Shoemaker's Charges—An "Early Engagement" is expected — Willing Sacrifices for Liberty—Procuring my Passport — Mrs. General Pegram's Family—Departure of Messrs. Mason and Slidell.

MRS. GEN. HENNINGSEN appeared to think that her two friends had not demeaned themselves in a very becoming manner, and, as if anxious to mollify their offence, made overtures towards my acquaintance, and introduced herself afterwards by saying, "My husband is an Englishman, and I like English people very much." She went on to say that she had had such and such English acquaintances, who were all "so intelligent," or "so sensible," or "so" something else, all of which was very amiably intended; and in the desolate life I was then leading, any such indications of kindness were only too welcome to be rejected.

Mrs. Henningsen was truly a woman of the world —clever, shrewd and fascinating; a great talker and a greater diplomatist; but withal possessed of one of the kindest hearts and most generous dispositions in the world. She knew everybody, and was constantly surrounded by a circle of political, military, and social acquaintance. She never was alone, never quiet; and besides entertaining a constant reinforcement of visitors, she devoted herself so zealously to the sick and wounded, that one would have thought her sole education and existence had been occupied in nursing.

When she could spare a few minutes to converse with me, she invariably imparted news from Western Virginia, where her husband, General Henningsen, was on active duty as Colonel in the Wise Brigade. From her I learned much of those frightfully hazardous and laborious campaigns, that have been described by so many writers, as to render detail unnecessary here. Mrs. Henningsen was not discreet in her comments upon those terrible slaughters, nor sparing in her censures of the Government for not reinforcing General Wise. Generals M'Clellan and Rosencranz were then on the Federal side in Western Virginia, and the Confederates were indebted to the habitual caution alone of the first-named General, for retaining as much as they did of that part of the State; for the number of the Southern troops was always overrated. Heartrending tidings, one heard, of the sufferings of the soldiers, many arriving from that section, charged with letters or messages to Mrs. Henningsen. One man who came, related how his son had marched eighteen miles without shoes, having nothing to eat for four days but birch bark; another man tasted no food whatever for forty-eight hours; another had nothing on his feet during a seventy-six mile march, during the latter part of which they were blistered so sorely, that the soldier toiled along in anguish; and these were only a few of the thousand cases of suffering. With a poor population in those mountainous districts, and with roads, if roads they can be called, consisting of alternate steps of solid rock two or three feet deep, with pools of water lying between them, mud and fallen trees (it rained incessantly all that summer), the sufferings and hardships of the soldiers can perhaps find no precedent in ancient or modern times. After a few months' campaign, the country became so devastated that no food could be procured; the inhabitants of the farm-houses had fled their homes, and often it was necessary to travel miles and miles to find fodder for one horse. I heard a man from there declare that on arriving at the end of his journey, he was obliged to proceed eight miles further, in order to procure a meal for his famished steed. One of the companies in General Wise's brigade did not, for the space of three months, encamp more than two nights in one place, and during that whole time was accomplishing forced marches, in climbing hills and rocks, working at entrenchments, and sleeping in wet woods, with empty stomachs! An old and experienced European soldier, who had joined that expedition, assured me that he had never either seen or heard of such a trying campaign as that. One of the Baltimore regiments, in that suffering army, was resting at night, after a toilsome march, near the banks of a stream, which, owing to heavy showers, so suddenly overflowed its banks that the soldiers were awakened from their hardly-earned slumbers in an almost swimming condition, all their clothes and much baggage having been washed away. Those devoted Marylanders, too, who were cut off from all friends and means of replenishing their stock of clothing! Many, many members of that regiment died amongst those mountain torrents, and their friends will never know where their bodies lie. Those same floods left them in so crippled a condition that half of them were afterwards incapacitated by "chills" and cramps. Governor Wise started with 120 men, rallying raw recruits as he proceeded; but, owing to sickness, not the half of his men were ever in active service at the same time. At one time he was within five miles of the Ohio river, and could have secured the valuable salt-works in the Kanawha valley but for want of reinforcements and provisions. The incapacity from sickness in that portion of the Confederate army, at that time, was appalling. No medicines, no brandy, very little food, continual rains for thirty days, and consequent freshets; footsore soldiers, campless and blanketless, glad to gather the raw corn as it stood in the fields; while the deaths, in one regiment only, numbered eight or ten a day. Every horse and waggon was pressed into the service, and crops were rotting in the fields for want of hands. Quinine, so largely used in the aguish symptoms that predominated, had already doubled its price in Richmond, and other medicines were becoming equally choice. Many valuable medicinal drugs are indigenous to the Southern States, but as yet the people had not begun to prepare them; and the phantom of "raising the blockade" was again the enemy to enterprise. An enormous change had, it is true, been already achieved, and important factories had been established throughout the South; a most salutary effect had been wrought in developing its resources, yet during the continuance of the war, with every available man called to the battle-field, it was and will be impossible to meet the demand for the thousands of articles that never were manufactured there, and never will be.

But what about *that letter?*

The next time I saw Mr. Rebelfield and asked him, he said, "Oh! I quite forgot to inquire." The usual excuse! When again I saw Mr. Mortimer, he promised to have it sought for; and after becoming tired of waiting for people who had all more business on their hands than it was possible to accomplish, I decided to write it over again and present it elsewhere. It might be foolish to care so much about such a trifle, but under the peculiar circumstances of my position, pardon the weakness, kind reader.

The anxiety my friends had expressed added to

my uneasiness, and I used every effort to have letters conveyed to them. "Why do you not ask the Consul?" said one. That I knew was useless. "If I had known of it I could have sent them for you yesterday," said Mrs. Henningsen; "a gentleman left here for Baltimore, and carried a large packet of letters for us." Still I persevered, and prepared a great budget both for England and the North, in readiness for some fortunate opportunity, which at last appeared. My kind friend in time of need, T. H. W., happened to meet me, and learning my anxiety, assured me he could send it "easily;—oh, directly; and as large a packet as I pleased!" No one, who has never been similarly circumstanced, can imagine the happy relief of such a privilege. My pen, as if alive, positively refused to stop. There was so much to tell, both of public and private matters, and it was hard to add the *last* word to that goodly packet of letters, papers, and sketches. But *that letter?* Yes, that letter, and more on the same subject, were written again and again.

By this time my Richmond acquaintances were increasing fast, and among quite a different circle. It was interesting, though painful, to hear about the battles, and blockade, and the determination of the people; and to watch the changes that were taking place in their habits and customs. Instead of lounging in their rocking-chairs, in dreamy listlessness, the ladies were plying their crochet and, knitting-needles in such good earnest, that soon I heard them say not another skein of wool or ball of yarn was to be procured in the city. They had "bought up" all that was to be found, and even made excursions to Petersburg to do more shopping. They were preparing for the soldier's winter comforts. Then Mrs. Henningsen brought home dozens and dozens of yards of cotton sheeting, which she set every one to work to prepare for a new hospital recently established. By this time many "stores" were emptied of goods, and closed; and what articles remained increased in value daily, so that it became quite a matter of importance to the public to ascertain where such or such things could be procured, and the papers were full of advertisements to say that at such a place a cargo of this or that had just "run the blockade," or otherwise been smuggled over from Maryland or through Kentucky. In order to stop the intercourse between North and South, nothing less than a Chinese wall from the Atlantic to the Pacific—and not even that—would prove effectual, while diving-bells beneath the waves, and balloons above, could be available; and where, as I said before, the all-powerful magnet of affection influenced the agents, they would find means to communicate with each other. The more severe the proclamations of President Lincoln, the more inventive did the Southerners become in their plans to defeat his frail attempt; the tighter the rein was drawn, the more did they rear and plunge under their intolerable restrictions. At one time the Marylanders made a large kite of Northern newspapers, with wings and tail of letters and messages, and, watching the wind, sent it across the Potomac, where it was secured by the happy rebels. It is impossible to relate one-hundredth part of the feats of those ingenious but unconquerable people, who, in spite of all their deprivations, continued to wear the same light-heartedness and confidence. One could not help thinking that if the Northern President could take a peep at Richmond some fine day, he would think he had not yet made much progress towards "subjugating the South." The streets and park were thronged with cheerful faces, and groups of soldiers everywhere lounging and laughing. Let him peep in at the hotels of an evening and listen to the music and mirth within, and serenades without. Let him gaze upon the well-stocked tables, and visit the markets, and he would have been inclined to give up the task as hopeless. Above all, let him hear a few sentiments expressed by some of the slaves, and he would find his own toiling, starving poor, more worthy objects of his chivalry.

With the exception of some imported items of food and luxuries, the usual articles of consumption were still abundant; and the guests at the hotels drank the tepid and muddy water of the James river with great contentment. Iceless, however, it required intense thirst to accomplish this. 'Tis true we began to find substitutes for coffee recommended; and inducements to establish salt works along the little inlets of the shore, where it was impossible for ships to enter. But ah! the fatal European promise of not recognizing "an inefficient blockade," again came in the way of enterprise; and though some few people did manufacture salt in insignificant quantities, not anything like a staple was produced. Paper of all kinds was becoming very scarce and dear, and people were experimentalizing in the manufacture of ink, but not at first succeeding very well, as those English dispatches proved, for it was doubtful whether they could be deciphered after all. Unused to save, or economize in any way, the majority of people had no idea of taking care of trifles; and in spite of threatened scarceness, I used to observe the negroes every week sweep away enough of rags and sheets of writing-paper to furnish at least a day's newspapers to the hotel. Once I could not forbear to ask one of the servants why she did not pick up those sheets of paper, which some departed guests had left upon their tables. "La, Miss Jones! I haint got no use for them: what's the good?"

It will be seen by the following paragraphs that a good deal of the "trade element" flourished in the South, though these extortioners were generally known to be "Northern men with Southern sympathies" (for Southern dollars), or German Jews.

The Government authorities used every effort to have the war conducted in an honourable manner, and such extortions were condemned. Governor Moore, of Alabama, in his message to the Legislature, after condemning the extortions that have been practised upon the Government and people of the

Confederacy, makes the following recommendations:

"Merchants and tradesmen, in common with persons engaged in every legitimate pursuit, are entitled to the fostering care of the Government; but when so forgetful of social duty, and regardless of the interests of their country, as to monopolize the trade in those commodities most necessary for the comfort and subsistence of our soldiers and citizens, it becomes the duty of the Legislature, as the public guardians, to adopt such measures as will prevent, as far as possible, the State and the people from becoming the prey of such harpies."

Parched corn, rye, potatoes, and a variety of "substitutes" were recommended in lieu of coffee, or to mix with it; and here is another new substitute for coffee. The Shrevesport (Louisiana) "Southwestern" says:

"Lately we have read many recipes for making coffee, but we see none come up to the one we offer: Throw away the coffee-pot, substitute in its place a bowl or deep plate full of milk and mush.* It is far better, more nutritious, than the best of coffee. We have tasted it, therefore can speak advisedly of its merits. We go in for home consumption."

Liberal support to the war was still frequent in munificent gifts and personal sacrifices.

"THE SPIRIT OF THE SOUTH.—A Mr. Watson, of Mississippi, has raised, at his own expense, a company of Light Artillery, and has turned it over to the Government fully equipped, with all the materiel required by rule.

"The battery is composed of six guns, and no horse belonging to it cost less than 250 dollars. Everything connected with this corps is of the best description, and was procured without regard to cost. The outlay in cash amounted to 60,000 dollars. Having

* "Mush" is made of Indian-corn flour or "meal," after the manner of oatmeal porridge.

completed his arrangements to his satisfaction so far as he could, Mr. Watson notified General Twiggs of his action, and desired him to select officers for the corps, stating that he wanted the *best* that could be got, as his men and materiel were of that character. The General made the selections, and that battery will prove a thorn in the sides of the Yankees whenever opportunity offers.

"Mr. Watson is a private in the ranks."

Just about that time the Hon. Roger A. Pryor, of Virginia, a Colonel in the Confederate army, sent an order to the committee for the relief of the hospitals, that his salary, as a member of Congress, was to be drawn from the Confederate treasury, and appropriated to the use of the wounded. A noble example, followed by others in many similar acts of munificence.

Next to munitions of war, few things seemed more important than quinine; but I often heard of facts like this, viz.:

"Mr. Heidrick, who arrived at Cincinnati a few days ago to purchase quinine, was unable to obtain any for the Southern market, as it was *contraband of war*."

While I have been rambling over all the efforts and contrivances of the Confederacy, in as hurried and confused a manner as we used to do everything in those anxious times, *that letter* has been lying on another editor's table for many days, because he also had gone to the mountains; so growing very bold I regained possession of it, and becoming quite impatient of the many little annoyances of my hotel life, I took it to editor the third. He was not there.

Would I leave it? Oh no, that would be equally useless. Mr. Moseley, of the "Whig," was the last to call upon, and he was visible. I told him the whole truth; that it had been written last April, and sent with other similar communications of the same kind to England *several times*, and that being now alone in Richmond, &c., &c., as the reader already knows.

Would I leave it?—he would look over it.

"Oh no, Mr. Moseley; if you please just glance at it *now*. In a moment you can judge; or let me read it to you quickly."

He took the letter, and before he got half through the first page, exclaimed, "This is just what we want your people to understand: I hope that communication arrived in England and got into print. Yes, I am very much obliged to you for bringing it here, and I shall be glad to publish it directly." And he immediately called to some one and ordered it to be put into "to-morrow's issue," while I thought that the London Press would not be quite so ready to be troubled with all the letters which I, whom nobody ever heard of, chose to write for them.

Rebelfield saw one or two descriptions I had written, and insisted on running off with them for his own paper after that; and although my signature did not appear, Mrs Henningsen and Mrs. Ayres knew that they were of my scribbling, and soon informed others of the fact. Poor Mrs. Graigh, and Greene! I was really sorry to see how mean they felt themselves at having treated me so rudely, and then finding I had spent so much time alone in my room exerting myself for their cause.

One day, not long afterwards, a large official-looking envelope was brought to me, having printed on the outside—

"CONFEDERATE STATES OF AMERICA.

"*Post-Office Department.*"

What could it mean—addressed to "Miss Sarah Jones?" Lo! it was *that letter* from Milbank. It had never gone beyond Richmond, but had been opened, and the enclosure opened too, and read, of course; and the gentleman who had promised me to "institute a search" for it, had caused it to be found, and sent it to me. Well! now the authorities themselves had read it; and that perhaps accounted for the very polite note with which it was forwarded. Mrs Ayres congratulated me on its recovery, but I should have felt more satisfied had the letter to my mother found its way to England in time! That it did not, was Mr. Quence's fault.

Among the regular boarders at the hotel, were several members of Congress, five of whom were judges, from the States of Alabama and Georgia. Mrs. Henningsen always endeavoured to gather the guests together in the evening for music, and sometimes dancing, or whist, because, she said, it was the duty of every one to try to make the furloughs of the soldiers cheerful and pleasant for them. The hotel was never free from soldiers.

And thus the judges and I became acquainted. I wish I could repeat all the conversations that passed between us on the subject of slavery; but a few items I must mention. One of the judges said:—

"Thirty years ago we were very nearly abolishing slavery, because it is the most troublesome and expensive kind of labour; but the Yankees began to abuse us, and impose upon us, and therefore we were put upon the defensive, and compelled to uphold an institution, in order to self-justification, that we would gladly have been rid of."

I boldly presented the objection to the excessive ignorance in which negroes were forced to remain, and the impossibility of human progress so far as they were concerned; which was a melancholy contemplation at this era of civilization; while it was evident that some of them had both capacity and ambition to learn. One of the gentlemen in reply assured me that masters generally were far from objecting to the instructions that negroes might receive, and mentioned many cases where they were regularly taught by their young masters or mistresses. "The present ignorant condition of our servants is a thing that will no doubt be remedied before long. It is very probable that a law may be passed soon for the education of negroes to a certain extent. They make better servants, are more attached and faithful, besides giving far less trouble. The condition of our negroes will improve materially as soon as the war is over, and we are left to ourselves. It must be a work of years to fit them for a new state of things. At present only the authority of a master is sufficient for them, and compulsory labour."

I know from many persons, as well as from observation, that the condition of the slaves has become worse and worse for several years, on account of increased rigour; but that previously their condition had been gradually improving for the last fifty years; just as we find an improvement in the discipline of institutions and asylums in England. Just as gentleness has taken the place of strait jackets and chains in lunatic asylums; and the amusement and occupation of infants and idiots have superseded rods and dark closets. Intercourse with the polished world beyond, and the improvement of the country by commerce and travelling, will do more towards the amelioration, or the abolition of slavery, than a twenty years' war, and all the Proclamations of all the Presidents that may be elected, so long as the Federal States continue to exist.

Mrs. Henningsen was permitted to visit the Yankee prisoners who were in a hospital; she was also allowed, or at least she did, whether by permission or not, often carry them delicacies and comforts. Occasionally she recognized some whom she had known in the North: clerks, waiters, or mechanics. On her return from the hospital one day, she spoke warmly of the injustice of the Northern press in representing the cruelties and indignities the prisoners were said to suffer in Richmond. She said the Southern doctors were then attending them, and administering expensive medicines, while they did not know where to look for more when they were gone. Indeed, kind-hearted as she was, she could not forbear from complaining grievously, and said, "A poor soldier died in this house last week for want of the very medicines which that doctor was giving to the prisoners; and if Lincoln will not allow medicines to be brought here for his own army, *they* ought to suffer for the want of them, and not our people." She also told me that on leaving one of the rooms she had said, "Is there anything you want that I can bring you the next time I come?" All said no, but one prisoner, who asked her, "Do, please, madam, bring me some pound cake—that's all I want." The next day she took the cake. Instances of great ingratitude and bad conduct were spoken of on the part of these men. Some of them had insulted their nurses so much as to necessitate their removal; and one man, who had been wounded by a bullet in the arm, though not much injured by the accident, after having it extracted, cried out, "Doctor, hand me that bullet, will you? I have not done with it quite so soon." He then put it in his pocket, and with a frightful oath exclaimed, "—— but that shall go into into some rebel's heart yet." And it was a Southern doctor who was curing him.

Another of those judges, sitting next to me one day at dinner, said, "I am glad those letters of yours were published, because it has exonerated you in the eyes of the Government."

"'*Exonerated*' me!" I exclaimed, and, I am ashamed to say, in a tone so sudden and distinct, as to cause people to look round; but my English blood was boiling. "Why should I be 'exonerated?' Who dared to suppose it necessary to exonerate *me?* I don't understand. I did not know the Government was even aware of my existence."

"There are many ladies who have been the means of doing us great harm, as well as great good, during our present troubles; and we are obliged to keep our eyes open. We have been at a loss to account for the means by which the enemy has become acquainted with some very important measures that have been passed lately, and," he added, confidentially, "we are watching some persons in this town pretty closely."

"There are some persons in this house who can worm themselves into everybody's confidence, and who are receiving much attention upstairs in the drawing-rooms; but who require to be watched much more closely than I do."

The fact is, the Southern people are not diplomatists. Honest and straightforward themselves, with no disposition for intrigue, they are slow to detect those qualities in others; while a plain, open spoken body, such as myself, who did not disguise that I took an interest in all that was going on, was more likely to be suspected of sinister designs.

"To whom do you allude?" said the Member of Congress.

"That you must excuse me in not stating, but I have good reasons for doubting the sincerity of two or three people here, who nevertheless enjoy the indiscreet confidence of those who go into the sitting-rooms, and converse without reserve, imagining only friends are present. One is even in a Government office."

There were two persons whom I had frequently mentioned to Mrs. Henningsen as being very doubtful to the cause of the Confederacy; who I knew were in constant communication with the North, and who nevertheless had always assigned some trifling excuse when I had asked them to forward letters for me. Mrs. Gen. Henningsen had however not suspected them, and mentioned several acts of liberality they had displayed towards the hospitals, and the army generally. That might be, but those Pennsylvanians did not please me somehow.

Soon after my good friend T. H. W. had forwarded that great budget of news to England for me, I saw that a Southern mail of about fifteen hundred letters had been seized at Louisville, Kentucky, and knowing that the secret agent had made that neutral point the depository of his dispatches, his arrest gave rise to sundry misgivings; for it would not be very agreeable to have my letters detained for examination at Washington.

What with "keeping up with the times," through a daily perusal of the papers, the early walk, the evenings down stairs, and the hour or more for Miss

Ayres' French and music lessons, together with writing and drawing, the days soon rolled away. I had remained at the Hotel from week to week, like Mr. Micawber, in expectation for something to "turn up," and now began to anticipate the time when the young ladies of the Confederacy might feel disposed to resume their educational pursuits. Colleges and academies for boys were becoming a matter of history. It was common to hear fathers assert that it was useless to attempt to confine their sons to study. Those who were old enough to enlist, enlisted; those who were not, were wishing to be; and "too much excited" to settle down to books. Such was not exactly the case with the girls, whose schools and colleges were announced to commence in September and October, as usual. There was no choice but to become reconciled to another winter in the South; and in order to be as speedily settled as possible, I sent early advertisements to the papers.

Among my now numerous acquaintances, private recommendations would have proved sufficient, but experience had taught me to depend on no one. Full of kind intentions and willingness to serve a friend, the people were living in such a rush of excitement, that "I quite forgot" appeared to be a perfectly justifiable excuse for every remissness.

An advertisement was a business-like mode of proceeding that was more likely to command attention. I desired not to lose another opportunity of wending my way Southwards; the interior would be safer, and also new ground to visit; had there been no other pupils in the Confederacy, I had determined not to return to the incompatible Quences, and had not even apprized them that I was still in Richmond.

References and introductions were more important than ever at this time, and in looking round for some reliable person, Senator Hunter recurred to me. Dr. W. of Essex had referred me to him before I came to Virginia: and he had, from Washington, promptly and politely written to encourage my acceptance of the "position" at Forest Rill. I knew his family, and also his relatives in Richmond; and as he was now Secretary of State, his introduction would be very valuable to me.

He received me most kindly, and remembered my name, which was gratifying in the midst of his weighty public occupations. I made known my present position and wishes, and obtained his cordial acquiescence.

During the few minutes of our interview the frequent notes, messages, and personages handed into the office suggested the importance of not intruding too long on the Secretary of State; and merely stopping to learn that all of his own male relatives, as well as those of the W.'s, were in the army, I took leave, much encouraged by his kind reception.

The General Garnet who was killed in the battle of Rich Mountain was a relative of the Hon. R. M. T. Hunter. He was at Font Hill on the day that I had been there, when in Essex, and had been introduced to me as "Major Garnet" then. Such a polished gentleman, and he gone too!

There were among the servants of the hotel several who exhibited their peculiar characteristics under new phases, but I fear to weary my readers of the genus negro, and will only introduce one young lady, a "yaller gal," as she was called by the rest, but on account of that very tint, usurping an extra amount of airs and graces, being the privileged belle among the chambermaids, and belonging to the "drawing-room floor" besides.

There was a wedding among the negroes of the establishment. A dining-room servant of our hotel was about to take unto himself a wife from another part of the town, and many of his fellow-servants were invited. The negroes marry very young generally. They entertain no anxieties regarding the support of a wife and family, that responsibility not devolving upon them, and no fears of poverty or pauperism, such a condition of things being unknown among them; therefore they have only to obtain their master's consent and "get married." Hatty, our damsel of the bilious hue, was to be one of the bridesmaids, and some of the ladies of the hotel had lent their aid and taste in furnishing her toilet. The wedding was to take place in the evening, and to be followed by a dance and supper. I was sitting in a cool corner of the drawing-room, absorbed in the newspapers, when a great deal of rustling and giggling on the stairs, and in the hall attracted my attention; and looking up, beheld a troop of negro damsels all attired in white, profusely relieved by flowers and ribbons.

"Do come out here and see the bridesmaids," exclaimed several ladies.

The coloured belles were all really well dressed in good materials; but Hatty, being the especial favourite, attracted the principal attention, therefore we will allow the others to pass down the stairs, our private stairs, "the ladies' entrance" positively, where two hack carriages are awaiting them; while Mrs. Henningsen, Clara and Amelia Graigh, and two or three others, are turning Hatty round and round, putting the finishing touches to her evening costume. I carefully noted the dress, and give it accurately to the reader. Clear white muslin, fancifully tucked to the waist; bouquets of white roses on the boddice and sleeves; white kid gloves; wreath of white roses around her head of wavy, not woolly hair; gold watch and chain, lent by one of the ladies; gold bracelets; blond lappets from her wreath, drooping below her waist; besides which an abundance of very rich white satin ribbon trimmings with flowing ends were supposed to set off the whole. An embroidered pocket-handkerchief and gaudy fan complete the bridesmaid's toilet. "My ladies helped to fix me up," said Hatty, as she strutted up and down the hall, with her head tossing, her fan fluttering, and her ribbons flying. "Mrs. Alaba lent me dis heah watch an' chain, Miss Clara gin me dese heah flowers, Miss

Mealy lent me dis bres' pin (brooch) and dese heah beads" (a necklace).

"And who gave you the dress, and gloves, and lace?"

"Why I bought 'em wif my own money, sure." Highly indignant, Hatty swept along the hall and down the stairs to the street door, where a great deal of loud talking and arguing was heard. We all ran to the balcony to see what commotion disturbed the bridesmaid, and saw her put her foot on the step of the carriage and bounce back again, vociferating loudly—What! mus *my*self in dat carridge! I ain't a going to do it. Folks expects a great deal from de American hotel belles; an' I'd like to know what they'd think to see me come out all mussed up like that!"

Some voices within the carriage were heard to expostulate and coax the American hotel "belle;" and somewhat soothed, Hatty, with another bounce, essays to enter, bringing her head in violent contact with the roof, equally to the discomfiture of her wreath and her (coloured) temper. Down she came more wrath than ever. "I ain't a goin' to get into no sech carridge as *that!* If they want me to go at all, they've got to send another a purpose for me." The united persuasions of the three already seated, with those of the coachman and groomsman, induced a more yielding but less responsible "belle" to resign her seat to the expansive draperies of Hatty, under the promise of the carriage being sent back for her immediately. So Hatty, taking possession of the whole of the back seat, consented to shed the light of her smiles on the wedding party.

One day, when I was occupied in finishing the sketches for T. H. W., Cornelius, my smiling Mercury of the dining-room, tapped at my door to bring a note. The door being partially open, he saw my occupation, and making an excuse to lay the note on my table, he stepped in to observe the process.

"Oh *my!* what's that you're doing, Miss Jones? Mayn't I jes' come in an' see?" advancing as he spoke. "Why that's a pictur' you're writin,' ain't it, miss? What city is that, mam?"

"That is a village, Cornelius, and a river; it is Yorktown."

"That's where you went to, ain't it, mam? It does look natrel. Tre—e—s, an' hou—ses, an' bo—o—ats; an' them's sojers, ain't they? Oh my! an' them's the camps, too. You do that *all* the time, don't you, Miss Jones?"

"Do *what*, Cornelius?"

"Write picturs, mam? I wish you'd write me one; jes' a lee—tle one, Miss Jones (coaxingly), to put in a looking-glass frame I've got; else gim'me *this*. Oh, *do* gim'me this, *please* mam.

"Oh, I cannot spare that, Cornelius."

"Then do write me a little house, an' some flowers, an roses, an' such like, all round it; jes' a leetle one, *please*."

Several times after that, while Cornelius was waiting upon me in the dining-room, he asked—"Miss Jones, mam, have you wrote me that house yet?"

So at last Cornelius had his house and garden, with a coloured lady going up the path, which delighted him "mightily."

"That will do for your wife, Cornelius."

"'*Tis* mighty like her, sure," said he.

"Like her! What! are you married, Cornelius?"

"Yes, mam, I bin married dis long time. My wife lives up to Mrs. Pegram's; she b'longs to her."

The boy did not look more than eighteen.

I don't know how many requests that I would "write" pictures were proffered me after that, and it was quite difficult to excuse myself from such an influx of business.

Richmond began to be very full of prisoners by that time, and it was considered expedient to "divide the honour of entertaining them" with other cities. About 150 were sent down to New Orleans one day, and Petersburg, Lynchburg, and Charleston each had their complement. It was a painful spectacle when they passed up the street to the railway depôt four abreast, guarded by a double row of soldiers. What a diversity of expression there was to be perceived among them. Some marched in pride, and others slouched along, looking from under their brows as if disturbed by an evil conscience. There was the incorrigible "dare-devil," who looked as if he would leave no means untried to revenge himself upon his captors. There were the better class, who kept their eyes upon the ground, mortified at their own position and that of their companions. Some, quite young lads, looked wistfully around and up to all the windows, as in the vain hope of discovering a friend or one sympathising glance, poor boys! and others gazed about with cheerless indifference. Some few philosophic spirits as much as said, "Prisoners or not, I'm bound to see all that is to be seen, and find out what sort of a place this Richmond is."

One of those affecting incidents occurred at their departure that, whether concerning friends or foes, must have moved the stoniest heart. A gentleman who had seen them go, related the circumstance to me. A young lady, of Northern birth, who had been for some time a resident in Richmond, and, having a lucrative occupation, preferred to remain after the war broke out, discovered, by some means, that her brother was amongst the prisoners. She had made several ineffectual applications and attempts to see him. Owing to the necessity of military law in such a case, her most urgent requests had been refused. For some weeks the poor girl had been too unwell to leave her home, but was recovering, and sitting at her window just as the prisoners passed by on their way to the depôt. An impression seized her that her brother was amongst them, though a separation of several years, and the difference of dress and circumstances, rendered recognition difficult. A misgiving, however—one of those impulses of the heart that are not to be stifled—caused her to start to her feet, and hastily throwing on her shawl and bonnet, she summoned a friend and hurried to the depôt. There the guard was so watchful and the line so strict, that she was unable to approach within ten yards; but with straining eyes and anxious love, did the poor girl endeavour to scrutinize each probable form, until a mutual gaze met hers, and revealed the object of her search. Her brother recognized her. Pushing her way to the front, but repulsed by the guard, each precious moment threatening to sever them, perhaps for ever, who can judge of the agony of the poor stricken sister! Some of the bystanders became interested in the scene, and used their influence to permit a message to be conveyed to the prisoner. "Oh! is there anything I can do for him, —anything he wants?" she exclaimed. But the wants of the prisoner were few. With loss of liberty, what else could avail him. "Take him this," said she, "it is all I have in the world." And she handed a small, a very small packet. So they passed to the prisoner a few dollar bills, with some small change, not knowing whether the poor boy would ever find any need for it, or an opportunity of spending it.

Soon the cars were ready. Open freight cars, with benches arranged upon them, and a boarding round the edge for security. He took his seat with the rest, in full view of his sobbing sister, and the cars began to slowly move. With an irresistible impulse she darted forward. Sympathy governed, stronger than law, the crowd who were watching the departure;

an opening was made through the guard, and she reached his hand. One grasp, so firm, so tight, of those clasped hands, that she was drawn along the track as the quickening motion of the engine was bearing her long-absent brother yet further from her presence; and not until her arm was well-nigh strained from her body, and the poor prisoner, as he leaned himself towards her, was in danger of being dragged from the car, could that long, loving grasp be loosened.

Ah! how many of such sorrows were rending the hearts of tens of thousands, both North and South. If those who prosecute this merciless war did but reflect upon sorrows such as these, and even worse bereavements, must they not pause and question that fanaticism and that anomalous "philanthropy" at which they are straining as an excuse for fighting?

My advertisement was bringing me a large correspondence in the shape of applicants. Some of the letters were of so singular a character that I must transcribe a few of the expressions, which at least afford a proof of the trustful, though unbusiness-like customs of the majority of Southern people.

Those that were best written and expressed were also of the most business-like nature, and were generally summed up with a list of questions, viz.:—

"How long have you resided in the South?"

"What part of England do you hail from?"

"Can you give references in the South?"

"What is your age?"

"How long have you taught?"

"Where have you taught?"

"To what religious sect are you attached?"

Many of them consisted chiefly in recommending themselves and neighbourhood, thus:—

"We live in a healthy and refined neighbourhood, handy to Presbyterian, Methodist, and Baptist churches." Or,

"We cannot help thinking you will be pleased with our part of the country and with the people of this section. We have already a countrywoman of yours not far off, who has remained among us many years, being so pleased with her present home. We have an episcopal church at a convenient distance, and churches of all denominations in our neighbourhood, which is a very healthy one."

One of them in a postscript added:—

"We wish for a person who is fully qualified to teach what she *professes* to teach ACCURATELY; which will be ascertained by acquaintance and observation, and if need be by examination by MYSELF."

"There! it is of no use to try and impose upon *me*," thought the good gentleman; "I have had enough of that."

Here is quite an original style:—

"Miss L. M. N.,

"From an advertisement in the 'Richmond Enquirer' of to-day I see you want a situation as teacher.

"I am in need of a teacher" (so the writing indicated), "and one of the qualifications you mention in your card of the Enquirer. (?)

"I live in four or five hours' ride of Richmond, and if you will come up to my house I will engage you at $25 per month" (it was quite kind of him to wish to lose no time), "and if you like it you can continue the year.

"The school will be a small one; my three daughters, a little son, and probably a few of the neighbours' children.

"Please address me at, &c. &c.

"You can refer to our delegate on the Legislature, X. Y, Z., &c.

"Please reply by return of mail, and oblige, yours truly,

"A. B. C."

Subsequent events caused me to congratulate myself in not having accepted this prompt invitation, as all that "section" fell into the hands of the "enemy" the following spring.

The next was still more pithy, written on a little square piece of paper. Writing paper was running very short by that time.

"Miss, (that was an excellent supposition,)—

"I saw your advertisement a few days ago, wishing a situation as teacher. I know of a gentleman who wishes to employ a Teacher to teach" (it reminded one of our nursery poems, 'A twister in twisting, he twisted a twist,') "French, music, and the ornamentals. If you can recommend yourself" (that expressed great confidence in my judgment) "*as* A FIRST-RATE PERFORMER on both piano and guitar, also a good Singer, he would like to get you." (Really.) "Please answer this by the first mail, stating your Salary.

"Yours, X. Y. Z."

This specimen was underlined to an enormous extent.

It was impossible to discover whether the writer, so partial in his or her capitals, was a gentleman or lady; nor did he or she state why the gentleman who "wanted to get me" did not write his own letters. Perhaps he couldn't. Several merely stated their terms, and wanted to know when I could be at such a place, where a carriage would meet me, generally adding that one or more churches were within reach, and perhaps in a postscript saying, "The qualifications you advertise are those we wish."

One gentleman, a "Professor" in a college in the cotton States, said that, owing to the scarcity of money, he expected to be paid in cotton the next term, and therefore could not promise the precise time when he would be able to remunerate me, though I might depend on receiving my entire salary some time or other, because his "patrons" (as the parents of pupils are termed) were of the "first class and very wealthy." This was honest of him; and could I have been sure of running the blockade, a thousand dollars' worth of cotton might have been no bad investment. He offered me $1000 per ann.

Before the war, 1,500 dollars for nine or ten months' instruction in the "ornamentals," was not an unusual salary. The remuneration varies from about 75*l.* to 120*l.* generally. Sometimes 200*l.*, or even more, may be obtained, and some hundreds of "Yankee girls" are thrown out of excellent homes and ample opportunities of their favourite dollar making, by having become obnoxious to the South.

The advertisement had been published early in August, and the letters came dropping in for many weeks. Among them three or four were selected for negotiations. Those at the colleges offered the most liberal remunerations, but I felt a dislike to the position. One of the last was from the Governor of Florida, and this turned the scale of my plans. Mrs. Henningsen and others were consulted. The former said she knew some of the leading people of Tallahassee, the capital of Florida, and would give me letters of introduction. "Judge Baker of Florida knows the Governor; ask him to write for you."

Judge Baker did so, and showed me the letter, which was flattering, as regarded certain points, but ended with, "Miss Jones *is a close observer* of the events now harassing our country." That seemed a strange sort of postscript; and coming from a remarkably cautious man, who had shown himself studiously reserved towards myself, was rather too pointed; and I told Mrs. Henningsen, the letter was, on the whole, no recommendation, but rather the contrary. One of my correspondents had said, "If you are not disposed to favour our institutions, or if you have any Northern proclivities, our correspondence had better cease at once;" and I was becoming quite discouraged at having the same ground to go over, again and again. One of the pleasantest writers was the Professor of a College at Warrenton in Virginia, to whom I had been introduced irrespective of the advertisement. That negotiation progressed more rapidly than any of the others, and the parties were very desirous to engage me. I disliked the idea of a school, and they were Baptists again! If I must enter a College, it might as well be in Alabama or Mississippi, in both of which States there were negotiants. Florida however took the lead. The "land of flowers and orange groves" presented such charming pictures to one's mind; but the weeks rolled away, and the Governor did not write. Judge Baker said, "Perhaps he has gone to his plantation, which is beyond Tallahassee: there have been very heavy rains lately, and in such a case the mail is apt to be delayed." I thought of that week at Milbank, but five weeks were ample for rains to fall and evaporate two or three times over. October was drawing near; courtesy, health, finances, all rendered some decision necessary. The Professors of Alabama and Mississippi were almost as tedious in their negotiations as the Governor of Florida. Mississippi was most promising, but Tennessee was so torn to pieces by the battles and skirmishes of almost daily occurrence in Kentucky and Missouri, that a journey through that State presented many dangers; and the end of September arrived.

Richmond was the last large city in the Confederacy to issue its own postage stamps. New Orleans, Memphis, Charleston and others had long ago adopted them, but at Richmond we still prepaid our letters, and in specie too. Everybody was complaining. A friend at Fredericksburg wrote that she had, in September, received a letter written in Richmond on the 22nd of August, and post-marked "Richmond, August 23rd, 1861." "Sixty miles only from Richmond, and yet a letter, bearing date August 22, not received here till the 11th of September!"

No wonder then at the tediousness of a correspondence of six and eight hundred miles. The newspapers, particularly the 'Examiner,' were loud in their murmurings against the "Government" for this as for all other remissness. If everybody else in the Confederacy had worked half as hard as the "Government" they would have designed and printed stamps long ago. "Good old slow Virginia" was not apt to take the lead in anything, except in the confidence and respect of her sister States. "Shall we chronicle the arrival or the failure of mails as a noticeable event?" said the 'Examiner.'

Quite a number of events interesting to me occurred during the last two weeks of my stay in Richmond. Unexpectedly I met some of my Essex friends, who wondered very much to hear that I had spent all the summer in Virginia and had not been to visit them. They told me of the W.'s, and of Cinta's improved health, but how the war had unsettled them for everything, and rendered them in constant dread of invasion from the Rappahannock River. We English people do not like to make conveniences of our friends' houses; and, thinking it probable that the W.'s were from home, as usual, in the summer, I had foreborne from telling them of my detention; much as I should have enjoyed a sojourn at Forest Rill.

The forty days allowed for the departure of "alien enemies" were clearing the Confederacy of many disaffected people at that time, but *they* were not to be intrusted with letters. Mr. Phillips Day had left for England, and taken charge of despatches for me; every opportunity of sending was a boon, and in the uncertainty of transmission, the same subjects must be recapitulated continually. Like the "rebels" in their endeavours to overcome the blockade, the more obstacles that presented themselves, the more one felt a desire to write. An English gentleman and lady were sojourning at our hotel for a few days, making great efforts to leave Virginia. Alas! how I wished to accompany them! but the means were then wanting. "Why don't you borrow money of your Consul?" people said. Mr. Cridland was not a banker, and I knew that he had already been applied to by more than one British subject, less able to support themselves than I was, and he had only lately told me of a man of wealth, an Englishman, who, cut off from his remittances from abroad, was, with his family, suffering the severest deprivations; indeed almost starving! Only one business was thought of—the business of war; and I had esteemed myself most fortunate to meet with the success that had saved me so far from positive distress. Many persons were known to proclaim themselves as alien enemies for the mere privilege of departing; but the couple mentioned above, said they were *not* enemies and not hypocrites, and did not wish to report themselves as such. On the other hand the Government was becoming somewhat impatient of the delay of the promised "recognition." The first week in September had come and gone, and the blockade was not raised. "British subjects" now began to find themselves at a discount. The "higher powers" did not scruple to tell those who applied for passports that, "if England were to recognize our Government, her subjects here would enjoy their proper rights and privileges. England does not recognize you and protect you as her own subjects; why should we do so?"

The removal of our Consuls was even agitated by some of the leading papers, who thought it "unbecoming in an independent and self-reliant people" to permit agents to remain among them who were not accredited to the "Confederate States of America."

European news was anticipated with more earnestness than ever. When the comments of the victory at Manassas began to find their way into the Southern papers, "It was evident," the people said, "that the British authorities are meditating the acknowledgment of the independence of the Southern Confederacy." Great confidence was also placed in an official report of Admiral Milne, that "the blockade is totally inefficient," which buoyed up the hopes of all who were wont to respect "the integrity of England." There had been notices of the arrival of some half-dozen ships, lately, at "Southern ports," and a list published of as many that had reached Liverpool from the South. The prospect of a "cotton panic" in England was used as another strong argument, that the ports must inevitably be opened soon; and the recognition of New Grenada as an independent Government, that the "stronger claims" of the Confederate States must quickly be acknowledged.

Another event tending to excite the sanguine expectations of the Richmond public was the arrival of Sir James Ferguson just then; especially as he was said to bring with him "official communications" to President Davis, General Wise, Ex-President Tyler, and others. The arrival of "his Lordship and suite," as the people said, created quite a stir in official and other circles.

The sovereign people of the American republic do not make titles one of their especial studies; and are therefore apt to confuse terribly the degrees of rank with which every one in an aristocratic community is cognizant. I used to see the "Lordship" applied indiscriminately to the Prince of Wales, and downwards. Mr. Grantley Berkeley was "his Lordship" when he said anything to please them.

Watching as eagerly as the public generally, for any promising signification of a better state of things, I set off forthwith to the British Consul, to inquire the truth of the statement regarding Sir James Ferguson's official visit. Mr. Cridland, who was always ready to excuse one's troublesome anxiety, informed me that Sir James Ferguson's letters were simply introductory ones, that he had submitted to have all his baggage searched on his journey, and that his visit was wholly an unofficial one.

I asked Mr. Cridland if Sir James would not experience some difficulty in getting away again, owing to the recent refusals to grant passes, and mentioned the case of Mr. and Mrs. English at the American Hotel; with whom he was also acquainted. He could afford neither information nor assistance, he said. Indeed the Consul's own position was somewhat anomalous, accredited to a country with which no communication could be obtained. If that Mr. English could get away, he should become the bearer of despatches for him, he said, but then he must not carry letters for any one else. I felt very desirous to see Sir James Ferguson; the pleasure of meeting an English gentleman was so great in those troublous, cruel times. My wishes were scarcely expressed before they were gratified, for in he walked, and the Consul immediately introduced him to his fellow-countrywoman. To be living in the midst of such harassing and all-absorbing events, tended greatly to remove the barrier of conventionalities. English reserve did not exclude the congeniality of a common nationality, and it was a happiness even to open one's lips to a personage just arrived from England. He told me that his stay would be short, and that his friend, the Hon. Mr. Bourke, had proceeded further South; that England remained entirely neutral on the subject of the war, and there was no prospect of any immediate improvement in the condition of "British subjects" who chose to remain in the country.

So we parted; and I also took leave of Mr. Cridland, telling him of my intended departure from Richmond.

My readers will, I fear, become quite wearied of Sarah Jones and her adventures, but I must just mention another circumstance or two that were curiously linked together. One of the members of Congress stopping at "our hotel," was Judge Wright of Georgia, since then a colonel in the Confederate army. He was a friend of that Mrs. Greene who had been, and continued to be, so uncourteous in her manners; that is to say, he came from the same town, and considered it incumbent on himself to exercise acts of politeness and assistance to her, in the absence of her husband. Towards myself he behaved with much courtesy and kindness, and among other things promised to try to have some letters conveyed beyond the borders for me; saying he knew parties belonging to the Government who might be able to send them by the "underground railway;" and he carried off a good-sized envelope filled to its uttermost. Another member of Congress, Judge Clitheral of Alabama, undertook to send one *viâ* New Orleans for me, —that was another chance; but then it was so uncertain whether they would ever reach their destination! Judge Clitheral maintained that it was very easy to run the blockade at New Orleans. "I will tell you how we manage it," said he. "You know there are more mouths than one to the Mississippi River: the other day, when the blockade ships were just outside, we sent out two old hulks quite good for nothing; and while the gun-boats were chasing them, some fine cargoes of cotton sailed out in another direction." In that case there seemed a fair hope of my letters escaping in the same manner.

Judge Wright was personally acquainted with President Davis, and used to relate instances of his domestic life and his affection for his children; and how they came into the dining-room when company was present, and climbed upon his knees for dessert, and all that sort of thing. He said I ought to go and call on the President before I left Richmond; but I had never felt disposed to appear at the weekly or the evening receptions; and thought unless I could enjoy an especial salutation, and exchange of cordialities, there would be very little gratification in looking at him in a crowd, which one had often done as he rode about, or in church, as has been seen. "What should the President care about a stranger who went all alone to the receptions?" Judge Wright insisted that I should visit the Presidential mansion, and wrote a note to Mrs. Davis to say that "he hoped to have the pleasure of introducing an English lady who," &c. &c.—using some very complimentary expressions; and "would she mention an hour when the President and herself would be disposed to receive us." That promised to be just as I desired, and a great deal of pleasure was anticipated; because, as the gentleman at Milbank had said of the Queen, I "felt great respect for" President Davis. Unfortunately, as my readers may remember, the President was very ill at that very time, so ill indeed for several weeks, that his life was despaired of, and the Northern newspapers even went so far as to bury him, write an obituary quite flattering, for an enemy, and appoint his successor. He left the city, however, for change of air; and subsequently Mrs. Davis and Mrs. General Johnston were thrown from their carriage, the former hurting her arm quite seriously; then it was time for my departure; and I never shook hands with President Jefferson Davis!

One thing more before I go. Another large official envelope was brought to me, with a message that a gentleman was waiting down stairs. The name on the card was T. S. Bledsoe, a person of whom I had never heard; but on going down I found a pleasant-looking man, rather past middle age, who said he had brought some letters that had been left at his office by Judge Wright, to be sent abroad, but he knew of no means of forwarding them. Mr. Bledsoe was in the War Department, he told me, and conversed on several subjects for some time. He was a man of reflection, and apt to go off into a train of thought in the midst of a conversation; his face wearing a placid satisfied expression, that informed you his meditations were not unpleasing. His brow was massive, but benevolent; and without knowing anything of my visitor, it was evident to me that he was a character. He called several times, but always seemed rather more inclined to sit quietly listening to others, and indulge in his own reveries, than to be very communicative himself.

General Henningsen had returned home from Western Virginia with General Wise; and again one heard of the calamitous sufferings of the army on those mountains. With the rough roads of deep clay, clogged with fallen timber, and with the mountain torrents rushing down the gorges, the difficulty of transporting baggage had been insurmountable. What with losses by floods, and losses by retreats, an army prostrated by sickness, with no means of replenishments, they had latterly lived upon the scantiest rations. With the General's staff of twelve, their cooking apparatus consisted latterly of one frying-pan, one tin cup, and a pewter spoon, while the equipments of the dining-table were not much better. Then there were private differences and rivalries among the Generals. One was considered untrue to the cause, and another was a drunkard, and Mrs. Henningsen was proud to assure us of the confidence that Governor (General) Wise had always placed in "*my* General." Again was the Government bitterly condemned, by the constant grumblers, for not reinforcing the army there, while others said it would do Western Virginia good to let the inhabitants know some of the discomforts of war. The whole force of fighting men in that campaign had never exceeded 10,000! Poor President of a new Government! Who can wonder at his being ill? I had seen his face and form grow gradually thinner, and the lines deepen week by week.

Here are further indications of a striving country. Not only "wooden shoes for the army" were suggested, but—

"VARIOUS SUBSTITUTES FOR LEATHER.—There has been received at the Clothing Bureau here, about 5000 pairs of shoes, the upper part of which are made of superior canvass, so prepared as to be impervious to water. We understand that they are very comfortable and durable shoes. As leather is both scarce and high, we have no doubt that shoes of this description will, if they are found to answer a good purpose, be very generally worn."

"COAL.—The price of common ordinary coal in this city now is $6.50 per load, an increase of more than one dollar over former prices. The poor, as usual, will be the chief sufferers by this rise, for which we take occasion to say there was no necessity, unless it was found convenient to follow the fashion now in vogue, with all who have anything to sell, to 'make hay while the sun shines.'"

"TESTING CANNON.—Some forty old iron 4-pound cannon, recently resuscitated from among the rubbish of the State Armoury, and rifled at the Tredegar Works, were tested on Tuesday, and found to work with admirable effect."

The corners of some of the principal streets in Richmond were guarded by posts formed of old revolutionary cannon, partially buried; these, among other cases of practical economy, were dug up and converted into use; pity as it was, to destroy such old relics; but the Southerners had not then fought battles enough to supply themselves by capture.

Speaking of leather reminds me of how I got a pair of walking-shoes mended in those "hard times." Having sought, in vain, for a man whom I had employed the previous winter, and finding nothing but knapsacks and cartouches being made where he had worked, I tried to prevail on another workman to repair the shoes. "It isn't of any use to send them here, madam, for we have nothing to repair them with. We don't find anything to work with, to make such things now a days; there's nothing called for but knapsacks, so we've taken to make them instead." This was said at every *ci-devant* shoemakers. It so chanced that I had by me some scraps of Spanish leather, that had been procured for another purpose long before, and I thought possibly the man who had "nothing to repair them with," could make these answer the purpose. But he declined to spend his time on them, so great was the demand for his oilcloth knapsacks; and I went to four or five places before I could persuade any one to undertake the work. At last a German was a little more obliging, but he wanted some binding, none of which could be procured in the city. As good luck would have it, I had a whole piece of binding, having supplied myself amply with all sorts of haberdashery in London the year before, knowing the usual dearness of every article in the South, and I returned willingly to fetch it. On promising the man the scraps of leather, and all the remaining binding for his own use, he undertook to repair the shoes. How pleased he looked as he examined his acquisitions! "He didn't believe there was any like that in the whole country," he said, and told me how much he had paid for the last few yards he bought. At which rate I had paid him the value of some six or eight shillings for a little job of work that came to pieces the third time of wearing.

While we have been talking of the President, the Judges, the Generals, and the cobblers, Mr. and Mrs. English have been waiting to go to England, but are still refused their "passes." Governor Milton of Florida has not answered my letter, and whether to attribute the fact to the irregularities of the Post-office department, of which daily complaints are heard, or to his unwillingness to permit those "close observations" to be made over the State of Florida, or to any other cause, it is impossible to determine. The Professors of the Georgia and Alabama Colleges are almost as tedious, and while they are waiting to ascertain whether I "favour the South," the Baptist

Professors at Warrenton write to say that "the Seminary will open next week;" and "a definite answer is urgently requested." Perhaps the irregularities of the mails might prevent those letters from ever reaching me, even if written.

Complaints of the Richmond Post-office extended even to Alabama and Florida; some one from the latter State admitting it to be presumptuous to expect a letter from Richmond "more than once a week!" Judge Baker said, "It is all new work to our people, as we have generally employed the Yankees in our post-offices."

Something must be decided forthwith. Courtesy, health, and finances all demand that. In spite of my prejudice against Baptists and Colleges, Warrenton was noted for beauty and healthfulness, in the midst of mountain scenery. The very thought of it rendered me impatient to get away from the crowded, dirty, wearying excitement of Richmond; and yet it was a great disappointment to give up the Southern scheme, particularly Florida. Candour appeared to be the safest method of dealing with the parties, therefore I informed them of the uncertainty of my other, though prior correspondents, and arranged to accept the appointment under a certain proviso, in which they acquiesced, and "the die was cast" once more.

I will not detain my readers with the detail of all those events, which by that time began to find their way to England, and occupy the public mind there as they were doing at the scenes of action. There were all the complications of the Confiscation and Sequestration Acts, and the intricacies of deciding between loyal and disloyal citizens, who might have their business in the North, and their property in the South, or *vice versâ;* some with partners or agents at the same time in New York, New Orleans, and Charleston; some with their cotton plantations in the Gulf States, and their villas on the Hudson River. Hundreds who had been carrying on their business in both North and South at the same time. In fact, the perplexities of this war, between personal interests and family ties, are inappreciable, inexplicable.

Miss Catherine Gibbon and I had exchanged several letters. Once she had "run up" to Richmond to buy what could be bought, and told me she had accompanied "our regiment," as she called that from her native county, further down on the Peninsula, where General Magruder had been throwing the gauntlet to the Federal forces in vain, and "the boys" were becoming impatient of their idle life—scarce other than perpetual drill.

The same complaint was audible from Manassas, where the oft-repeated assurance that "an early engagement might be expected" caused the impatient public to indulge in some not very gentle sentiments, and the ladies were almost disposed to go themselves and take Washington by storm. Rebelfield had returned to head-quarters there, and whenever you saw a soldier take leave of his friends at the Hotel, he was sure to be "going to Manassas."

The reader has heard all about the "shin-plaisters," of which there were enough to wrap up the whole city (exclusive of the Post-office, however). Silver only was available there, and the much-tried public were compelled to purchase that scarce commodity at 15 per cent., and to keep a store of small coin for the express purpose of stopping to pay the postage on every letter to be mailed: not that there was an increase of clerks for this business; and you would think that the reduced corps already engaged had nothing else in this world to perform or think of, than stamping letters, had you witnessed their slow movements, while the crowd outside were awaiting their turn to hand in their five or ten cent coins. Had such a trial of patience ever fallen to the lot of Job, he never would have acquired his character. A long time must elapse before you can induce the Southerners to be in a hurry. You never see a negro in a hurry, and the master and mistress are inured to slowness. They are reared and educated in slow movements; and can you expect the "gentlemanly Southerners" to be rushing about like "Yankees," or brisk Englishmen in the City? Are they to move with more celerity, or less dignity than their slaves? Even the clerks in the stores are too well bred to be in a hurry, whatever their customers may be.

The arrival of a cargo of blankets through the

blockade towards the end of September, was announced with comments in all the papers, as an auspicious event for the Confederacy. At that time all those battles at the different Lexingtons, Columbus-es, Springfields, and Beauforts were being fought; and as a great many of these towns are too small to be printed on English maps, I will refer my readers to a short table appended to this book, of the localities of some of those perplexing places.

To fully chronicle the occurrences during my sojourn at the hotel in Richmond, would wear out the reader's patience. There were refugees from all parts of the *ci-devant* United States, each relating something linked with the civil war and all its horrors. One feature was remarkable. Persons who had forsaken their homes with merely the clothes they wore, those who had sacrificed all to the war, whatever at another time would have been pronounced a dire misfortune, was now not thought of. No one was singular in being homeless, and no one ashamed to own his losses. A mutual confidence engendered a mutual sympathy. One heart, one mind, one cause was apparent, and this union of sentiment continued to strengthen, and will continue to strengthen, as the Confederacy is sifted from its foreign population. It was common to hear persons who escaped from the invaded districts say of their desolated homes, "We had already devoted all we had to the war, and our property without liberty is valueless to us." A gentleman from Louisville in Kentucky, who had come to join the Confederate army, said in my hearing, "I have left my wife and child and 150,000 dollars' worth of property, but if they will only allow me to have my wife and child, and let the State secede, they are welcome to the property."

Just before I left, I encountered Cornelius scampering down the stairs in a tremendous bustle, decked out in smiles and shirt collar.

"Why, Cornelius, where are you going in such grand clothes?"

"Oh, Miss Jones, I'm sick; I'm going home for a few days."

"Sick!" I am sure his appearance rather belied his words, and with all those smiles and studs and shirt-bosom.

"Where do you mean, 'going *home?*'"

"Home to Petersburg, ma'am, that's whar my home is, whar I b'long to. Judge Tullen, he's my master."

"Well, good-bye, Cornelius; I am going away too, and shall be gone before you come back."

"An' you hain't coming here again, Miss Jones?"

"Oh yes, perhaps; but I cannot tell."

"Good-bye, ma'am; I reckon 'tis time the cars was a goin'. Pleasant journey to *you*, ma'am. Thank'ee, ma'am."

And away ran the "sick" Cornelius, looking as ready for a holiday trip as any one would wish to see.

Poor slaves! how little they knew of war and trouble!

It was necessary that I should procure a passport, in order to leave the city. Who will go with me to the War Department? "Oh, ask So-and-so to get your pass for you." But So-and-so was not to be found just then. "Mr. P. or Q. will go with you." Mr. P. and Q. both readily promised. One of them would be in the drawing-room at such a time. But he wasn't, and when he appeared in the evening, of course he had "quite forgot." Ah well! there is a civil war going on.

The next morning I resolved to go myself. It was not very agreeable to push one's way through that crowd. Dear me! how many soldiers! Two other ladies though, one in tears. Poor thing! her son not expected to live: she was asking for a pass to the army, and did not hope to find her boy alive. Oh, what trouble everywhere!

I presented my request.

"*Warrenton?* that's too near to the fighting; we can't allow anybody to go so near as that."

"Oh, I am not afraid."

"Perhaps not, madam; it is not a question of *your* fears; but it is too near the enemy for us to issue passes there."

"But I am going to live there; indeed I must go."

"*Must* go? Have you any friends in the army at that point?"

"No, not any. No friends at all in the South," I added mischievously.

Of course the official began to wear a very uncompromising look; but I had caught sight of my friend Mr. Bledsoe, and knew I could obtain the pass from him.

"What is your purport in going to Warrenton?" asked the gentleman, in a rather exacting manner.

"I am going to reside in the College there, as *Professor of Music*" (said the applicant, with an air of great self-importance). "Ah, Mr. Bledsoe! good morning: and Colonel Este too—How is Mrs. Este?"

Mr. Bledsoe had approached on seeing me, and of course asked where I was going; then he added to the official, "This lady is safe enough, you need not be afraid of her." Addressing me, he said, "Here we have had two of your people coming to us day after day, trying to persuade us to give them passports. Why did they not leave during the forty days' grace, had they wished to go at all? It looks rather strange to want to go now."

"If you allude to Mr. and Mrs. English, it is because they are *not alien* enemies, but warm friends of the South. If you will permit me to say so, Mr. Bledsoe, those are the very persons to whom you *should* give passports, and allow them to go home and proclaim the truth about the Confederacy."

"Well I think so too, I think so too—I'll see about it," said the kind old gentleman.

The Colonel Este whom I saw, and his wife and sister, had been recently found, but to me, very pleasant friends, residing in Richmond. Germans, and excellent musicians, some agreeable evenings spent at their house had been among the few enjoyments of that dreary summer. The Colonel was in the Wise Brigade, a Prussian by birth, and an accomplished soldier. Mrs. Este had given me a pressing invitation to spend the following Christmas holidays with her, which was something pleasant to anticipate. The one theme of war, however, prevents my speaking of half the persons with whom I became acquainted; not even of Mrs. Pegram and her charming daughters, who were also kind and agreeable friends; and from whom I learned many circumstances of the Rich Mountain battle, where Mrs. General Pegram's son, the brother of those young ladies, Colonel Pegram, was taken prisoner, as my readers know. But Mrs. Pegram told me he was very kindly treated in the North, and even permitted to go to the Springs in Pennsylvania to recruit his health. "He has so many friends in Washington they will be sure to take care of him," she said, "and General Scott is related to us."

Mrs. Pegram had spoken also of a Federal officer, a former friend of hers, then imprisoned in Richmond; and whom she had been permitted to visit frequently and supply with comforts, in return for the indulgence her son was receiving in the Northern prisons.

What a strange, strange war!

Tolerable ink, Confederate States envelopes, and very indifferent writing-paper, with many other articles of home manufacture, continued to be advertised.

In purchasing a fresh supply of writing materials,

I found that "Southern enterprise" had as yet produced only a rough light-brown specimen of writing-paper at about fourteen-pence a quire, and envelopes of the same (which no English tradesman would use for enclosing pence), at eightpence a packet. "A very superior article" was advertised from a new paper-mill at Knoxville, Tennessee, but it was not forthcoming at Richmond. As for drawing-paper, "Government had bought it all up for the Departments," also water colours; and I even ventured to present a few cakes of the latter to an "official," who most graciously accepted the gift "in the spirit in which it was offered." Other newly-established factories were one for glass in South Carolina; one for shoe pegs in Georgia; and some home-made lace from Memphis.

The subject of writing-paper reminds me of Mr. Cridland again. "See here," he had said: "imagine a British official using such paper as that, which I am economising as if it were made of gold; and these envelopes at 25 cents a packet." Not even excepting the President and his Cabinet, I do not believe a person in the South worked so hard as our acting Consul at Richmond, in spite of which his salary was quite inadequate to the enormous expenses of living.

Besides enterprise there were other effects of the blockade equally common in their way; viz., a young gentleman said:—

"'Sambo, I want you to come up to our house and play the violin.'

"'Yeas, massa.'

"Now, don't forget it; for we are going to have a wedding. So here is your dollar in advance. Now, be sure and come early.'

"'Dolla won't do me, massa; dese hard times; mus hab more money 'n dat.'

"'Why, I thought your price used to be a dollar. How much do you charge now?'

"'Well, de fac is dis, massa, I used to play for a dolla. But since de ports hab been blockaded de price ob rosum hab riz, and I can't afford to play for less dan one dolla and a half; fac, massa.'"

Northern and English news continued to be of the first interest next to the detail of battles; many people were, however, becoming impatient of the subject, and declared the blockade to be the best thing that could happen to the South.

According to the usual indiscretion of the daily journals, the contemplated voyage of Messrs. Mason and Slidell was announced half a dozen times, and various routes designated. Charleston, Tampico, and even the names of vessels about to run the blockade were published.

"COMMISSIONERS TO EUROPE.—Messrs. Mason and Slidell, Commissioners to England and France, left the city a few days since for their posts. They were accompanied respectively by Mr. Macfarland, of Petersburg, and Mr. Eustis, of New Orleans, as secretaries."

CHAPTER III.

Despondencies—A Disconsolate Journey—Relentless Sufferings—An Invigorating Change—The Walk to the College—Several Prospects for the Future—Mrs. McGee—A young Refugee from Alexandria—Substantial Objections to Exercise—The Heads of the College—Mountain Scenery—The Underground Railway.

THE day previous to that on which I left Richmond was excessively warm for the beginning of October. Towards evening a thunder-storm occurred, the air was rapidly cooled, and the rain continued to fall in torrents.

The daily report of the "early engagement" at Manassas, and the "onward movement" to Washington, that all the world was watching for, had received additional weight by an order, considered significant, from General Beauregard, to remove the sick and disabled from the camps.

In the drawing-room was a party of the grumblers inveighing bitterly against the "neglect of the Government" in not providing accommodations for the sick soldiers, a whole train of whom had just arrived in the city, and were lying about on the "sidewalks" and steps of the hospitals, in the pelting rain, while arrangements were being made to receive them. "Government" had to bear the blame for everything, whereas perhaps the chief cause of half the discomforts and miseries of the country might be attributed to the "Institution," which renders labour derogatory, and the white class dependent.

It was heartrending to hear of those poor sufferers, many of whom never could, and never did recover from that untoward thunder-shower.

Dismal as the great crowded hotel was, I was departing with many misgivings. Of all the letters that had been despatched, one could not be sure that any would reach their destination; nor could I tell the misery my absence might be causing to my anxious relatives. In spite of my prejudice against Baptists, I was going amongst them again, to be shut up in a seminary with a troop of silly girls, where one might never hear of what was going on, instead of figuring in the first circles of Florida. All these discontented and desponding reflections did not tend to raise one's spirits, nor did another little occurrence, which I must here mention.

Mrs. Ayres had been aware of the circumstances of my detention in Richmond. I had long before given my "purse of gold" into the keeping of the hotel safe, reserving to myself only just enough for positive necessities. The lessons to Miss Ayres, T. H. W.'s pictures, and a trifling sum for an occasional contribution to a newspaper, had enabled me precisely, and only just, to meet my hotel expenses; but that was more than many could say.

After retiring to my room, Mrs. Ayres and Mrs. Henningsen came to take leave of me, and, with the greatest delicacy and affectionate thoughtfulness, put a twenty-dollar note into my hand, "to purchase a remembrance" of them. This kindness quite overcame me, and a thousand conflicting emotions rushed through my mind. A would-be independent English woman to receive such a gift from a people in need of every sympathy and assistance themselves! And yet it was as welcome as if from one's own relations; for I had indeed only just enough for my journey, and that was all. Such unlooked-for appreciation of my position told me, moreover, that I was again leaving friends for uncertain strangers, which added additional regret to the parting.

The battles of 1862, to the north of Richmond, have brought those lines of road through Culpepper and Gordonsville before the reader repeatedly; and it will be readily understood that, between the Confederate armies then massed throughout that region, and the capital, the traffic was immense. We had not to set out on our journey so very early on that route—eight o'clock, if I remember correctly—but still too early for the appearance of the hotel guests, and, excepting one more adieu at the doors of Mrs. Ayres and Mrs. Henningsen, I was alone, and left the house alone.

It had rained all night; it was raining still: everything around was depressing. The depôt was one pool of mud; the difficulties of collecting and securing the luggage were awful. The crowds of soldiers and rough people; the uncertainty of the time of starting, the impossibility of reaching the ticket-office through that swaggering crowd; all was depressing. My turn arrived, or nearly so; two or three pale soldiers were still before me. "*Thirteen dollars* for one day's leave of absence!—there goes *my* month's pay," said a melancholy-looking man. Poor fellow! it did seem hard.

At last my ticket was procured, and I had found a seat. The car was full of soldiers. One woman with a baby, probably going to visit her husband at Manassas too. Every other passenger looked a soldier. Pale men, some of them so thin and delicate, I wondered to which of the hospitals they could be going that way. One man stood up close by me; he could not find a seat, and I asked him which hospital he was going to.

"Lord bless you, ma'am! I've been these ten weeks at the hospital, and have just come out, and glad enough too. I'm going to join my regiment now."

I am sure *he* did not look fit for fighting.

"And those others there, they do not look strong enough to go into camp yet?"

"They'll soon be all right when they get out in the air; they are all mighty glad to get out of the hospitals."

Poor fellows! with their haggard eyes and wasted forms! Everything is depressing.

Just before we started I saw Sir James Ferguson pass by on the platform. There was no room in the car in which I was sitting, so he could not come in there. It was the 7th or 8th of October, and I had heard he was intending to visit Manassas. How I wished he had come into that car! Not that there was the least fear of a lady suffering the slightest annoyance from Southern soldiers, but it was dreadful to sit alone there in such a crowd. He had just come from England, and was going back again. What an opportunity to inform his country of the real sentiment of the South! A man of influence, too; and who would care what any Miss Jones might say? I felt an irresistible desire to converse with him, and entreat him to use his present experiences in endeavouring to put a stop to these fruitless miseries. My heart seemed bursting, yet I was afraid to trust myself to move or speak. And then he had not observed me; and what would he think of my presence there, alone in such a crowd?

The cars began to move, and I sat still. The rain still fell in dismal drizzlings, and we had not proceeded far before we arrived at a "switch"* in the road, where were waiting, without any engine, a train of baggage cars, or rather cattle cars, ordinarily used for stock, but now full, quite full, of emaciated, prostrate soldiers. The doors were

* See "Webster."

open or broken away, the bars, or air-holes, were broken too, and the insides of all, with their helpless freight, exposed to view. There they were, lying on sopping straw, or what was used for such, being the dried leaves of the corn or maize. There they had been all the night in that pouring rain. Some few were standing, leaning their wasted forms against the openings, or hanging their poor heads from the windows, their clothes worn and damp, and quite insufficient for that wretched weather. Six or eight car-loads of this suffering humanity!—upwards of a hundred there must have been; and half at least doomed to an early grave—some perhaps already dead from this pitiless exposure! And I had left the negroes fat and happy in the crowded city, and my countrymen were harping on the miseries of slavery! Was there no help for these their suffering masters? would my philanthropic country never learn the truth? and could we look on continually at these things and offer no relief? More cars were passed, and more sick and dying soldiers, too feeble even to move themselves away from the drenching rain that poured upon them through the shattered cars. Oh, it was too terrible! Showers of tears burst through the flood-gates of my overburdened spirit. The pent-up feelings could find no other relief. It mattered not; my fellow-travellers were probably too inured of late to notice grief, and too full of their own sorrows to observe mine, and my tears flowed unrestrained; they must find vent.

It was past mid-day when we arrived at Warrenton junction, where the line branches off. Here the business of war, the miseries of the blockade, and the difficulties of transportation were more than ever apparent. A great deal of confusion had delayed us both at Gordonsville and Culpepper, two small, shabby villages, crowded with soldiers, where changes of cars, and changes of passengers, some of the soldiers joining their regiments there, and others from the hospitals returning to Manassas, had delayed us considerably. At the Manassas junction the confusion increased ten-fold, and I suspect that owing to the scarcity of railway carriages and engines, the non-military passengers were detained, while the long train from Richmond was being emptied by detachments to the army at Manassas, and returning thence with fresh cargoes of living freight for Richmond. While waiting at that point for above an hour, "Manassas! Manassas!" seemed to be the cry whenever a train started off, and they were unceasingly moving to and fro, keeping one in a perpetual fever of alarm lest that, by which I intended to continue my journey, should depart without me. It was useless to ask; no one knew how, when, and which train was going forward or back. No porters, no office; afraid to lose sight of my luggage, and yet not knowing where it was to be conveyed for the next starting-point. There was only a crowded dirty platform, with no waiting-room for ladies, none whatever, in fact. Negro servants were handing to the travellers trays of refreshments that were enough to take away whatever inclination for food one might have felt; and yet the soldiers devoured them greedily. At last the crowd diminished, another long train had started for Richmond and a short one remained in sight.

By mere chance I found myself once more seated in the right carriage. Not until the conductor came to inspect my ticket was I sure that it was the proper train, so confused and uncertain had been the information amidst the all-absorbing Manassas.

The branch to Warrenton is only a short one; and the weather was clearing up when we were traversing those twelve or fourteen miles. The leaden atmosphere assumed a bluer tint, and the outlines of the "Blue Ridge" were discernible. Only a few travellers were in the cars, the crowds having gone "to Manassas." On reaching the termination of the branch line, those few passengers soon alighted and disappeared. There was no station, only a small platform; my luggage was deposited upon it, my ticket was given up, the engine was "unhitched" and steamed away. "No road nor path could I descry," and not a human being. By this time the sun was shining, and a certain purity in the atmosphere refreshed my worn-out spirits, so that the dilemma was rather amusing than not. I looked about, and saw a negro turn round the corner of a building that might be a storehouse. Calling to him, I asked him which was the way to Warrenton.

"Dis heah's Warrenton, mistus."

"But where is the town? and which is the way to go to it?"

"Dis heah's *dee*po; thar's the Court-house up yon."

"Where is the Ladies' College, and how far?"

"Wa-ay up yonder; mile, may be."

"Is there no hack-carriage about here, or any one to carry my trunks?"

The negro said he would fetch a waggon for the trunks, or a carriage for myself, or both, according to my wishes; that he would carry the "baggage" at so much each piece (which, as there were four pieces, would amount to half-a-dollar), or he would carry me, baggage and all, for "half-a-dollar."

That was a close calculation of his; and as he did not seem to understand the "distinction without a difference," I merely asked if there were a path to the Seminary.

"Sort o'; mighty bad walking tho', mistus."

I felt inclined to try it, however; and having learned my way, told him to bring the carriage quickly, and that I would walk on until he overtook me.

Waiting a little while until the vehicle appeared, rumbling and tumbling over the rocky road, with my coloured friend and another one on the box, and making sure that the luggage was safe, I walked quietly up the hill. The path was "mighty rough" indeed, if that could be called a path which consisted of stepping-stones of solid rock, planted in stiff clay; but one could traverse them tolerably, and a few leaps, after that dreadful day, served to revive one's drooping spirits.

Reaching the top of this "street," I found more of a town than the style of the depôt would lead one to expect; and as the negro had pointed out the direction of the College, I had only to proceed. The carriage full of luggage soon overtook me; but all the time the stepping-stones rendered walking possible, that was more agreeable than being jolted over the still larger rocks of which the streets were composed. It is of no use to state how large some of these rocks were, nor what kind of slants and mud-holes the carriage overcame, because I am quite sure the reader would not believe it; but I thought, if this be a specimen of mountain-roads—"*streets*," in a good-sized town, too,—Heaven preserve the poor soldiers over roads which even they call "bad!" Suddenly, for it was a short half-mile, we came to a street opening on to fields and the distant country, about four hundred yards down which, a very pretty, large modern residence of dark brick, with ample piazzas, stood in a field thickly planted with young trees of many varieties. The negroes pointed and nodded for me to turn that way, and down I went through a gate to a private path; a carriage-drive opening from another gate a few yards further on. This house stood alone on the slope which I was then descending; in the hollow, some little distance beyond, ran the railroad, and again beyond that the ground arose in undulating woody hills and cultivated land. To the right lay the village or town, the houses being interspersed with thick groves of trees, wearing their first tints of autumn. Two pretty church-spires rose from the midst; and the back-ground was formed by the far off spurs of the Blue Ridge, behind which the sun was just disappearing. A thousand times in my wanderings in that Western world, when depressed by grief, or lonely amongst the crowd of strangers, have I blessed the Almighty for the appreciation of his works that he has implanted in me. A thousand times has the pure influence of nature refreshed the wearied mind, and averted the thoughts from scenes of care and sorrow. So it was now. I stood at the gate, rivetted by the beauty of that landscape and the long-desired contemplation of that mountain-scenery.

On a flight of steps and piazza round the entrance to the mansion, stood an old gentleman and some half-dozen girls, in friendly chat. But they were Baptists, and the view was more agreeable to contemplate; so I did not hurry myself. I have often wondered they did not hate me for the *brusque*, ungracious manners, which must have been too evident to them on my first appearance.

The old gentleman was quite blind to my uncouthness; it was entirely lost upon him. He expressed regret that I should have had the trouble of finding my way alone. He had been to the train yesterday to meet me, and Professor Latham had gone there now; he wondered the latter had missed me. I told him I had enjoyed the walk, and he conducted me into the house, and sent for his daughter.

That lady, Mrs. Latham, appeared:—a tall, strikingly elegant person, with a great deal of character stamped upon her handsome sprightly features. After the usual courtesies, she took me up stairs into a large room looking out upon the same lovely prospect, now tinted with the gorgeous colours of an October sunset. A young lady was busy at a sewing-machine; her sister, "Miss Bacon," and two sweet little girls, of three and five years old, were playing in the room. Soon an energetic, bustling little lady entered in her walking dress. "Mrs. McGee, Miss Jones."

"Oh, Mrs. Latham!" said Mrs. McGee, "I don't know what you will do for butter. Mr. Stillman says he cannot depend on having it, for as soon as the country people bring it into town, it is all bought up for the hospitals or the camps."

"I hope we shall not starve you to death here, Miss Jones," said Mrs. Latham, archly, "but I fear there is quite a probability of it; we find it almost impossible to get anything to eat. The soldiers consume everything."

A pleasant, neatly-furnished little room, appropriated to my use, looked out, by one window, on to that same pretty village, with its spires and background, and by the other, over the railroad and distant country. A table only was wanting among the furniture, and that was an article I never had found in any room, until asked for. American ladies do not employ themselves much in table occupations. When they do write, they take a sheet of paper on a book on their knees, generally dispensing with ink, and using a pencil. Even before the blockade that was the custom, and, indeed, in the North as well as the South. But a table was soon forthcoming, and with a drawer too, quite *à propos*.

At the evening meal the Rev. Dr. Bacon appeared at the head of a long table, with some ten or twelve young girls ranged on each side, Mrs. Latham presiding over the tea equipage, Professor Latham and Mrs. McGee sitting near me, by Mrs. Latham. The girls all looked bright and happy, and under no restraint whatever. The conversation was general, but the Professor appeared to be an absent-minded or a very reflective personage. Family worship followed the evening meal, at which I saw no lack of butter nor of any other commodity, and which was relished by the traveller more than she had relished a meal for many a week.

After prayers we all ascended to the drawing-room, girls and all. Dr. Bacon conversed with some of them about their brothers, who, it seemed, were in the army, and the same theme, the "early engagement" at Manassas, was ever on the tongue. On the ringing of a bell the girls retired "to study," I was told; and then the Professor mentioned that he should be obliged to go to Richmond on the morrow, to apply to the "Departments" about something or other, which was soon explained to me by Dr. Bacon. The

Provost Marshal, I believe it was, had sent a demand to the Doctor that the seminary should be given up as a hospital. The parties concerned were now obliged to appeal to Government, and bring proofs that the house and grounds were private property, and for this purpose the Professor was intending to repair to Richmond. No wonder he had looked thoughtful. Not a word was said to me about pupils, or professions, or any other business. A few general matters were introduced, and the first evening among the Baptists was chronicled as a thing of the past.

The next morning I was told the "classes were not organized," and the studies not sufficiently regulated to commence the music lessons, so I had nothing left me but to settle myself in my room and enjoy my view. Mrs. McGee came to visit me there, and told me, among other items of information, that her little girl was one of the pupils, and that during her husband's absence in the army (he belonged to the "Warrenton Rifles") she was boarding at the Seminary, and as Mrs. Latham was in delicate health, she was glad to assist her in her household cares, "because," she said, "it affords occupation for me, and I do not feel so nervous about my husband. His regiment is at Centreville now, and they are expecting an advance every day." She was a nice sensible lady, that Mrs. McGee.

My engagement was merely as the teacher of music, and until the pupils had all arrived, two or three hours each morning sufficed for my share of the duties. Not a word was said about any other classes, though the Doctor, the Professor, and Miss Bacon were occupied constantly in the class-rooms. The Professor returned from Richmond with a load off his mind. The Seminary was not to be given up, and other buildings in the town were to be appropriated as hospitals instead.

When the music pupils had been appointed their regular hours for lessons, and I had taken my seat at the piano, the first pupil made her appearance. A plump, pretty little girl of about eleven years old, with a happy face and little pursed-up mouth, came and seated herself upon the music-stool, folded her little fat fingers on her lap, and looked straight before her, as if sitting for her portrait, not attempting to move or speak.

"Have you no music?" I asked, after waiting in vain for a sound or a movement.

"No, m'm." (promptly.)

"Have you never learned music yet?"

"Oh yes, m'm, a long time."

"Where is what you have learned then?"

"It's in Alexandria; we left it there when we came away."

"That was a pity. Why did you not bring it with you?"

All this time she had looked straight before her, not once turning her head, but now she turned towards me quickly and fired up, but not rudely:

"Humph! we couldn't; we all came away in the middle of the night. Mamma had begun to have some things packed, and then we heard that the Yankees were coming, and the servants got us all up, and dressed us, and we only brought away some of our clothes. Mamma sent *us* off, and thought she would stay and have the furniture packed up, but she didn't, for the people said the Yankees were coming, and all she brought away was just some bedding for the children; not half enough though. The little ones sleep upon the floor, and they have such fun," said the child, bursting into a laugh at the remembrance of some of the "fun." "It is so funny not to have our things, and I don't know what mamma will do when the winter sets in. *All* our winter clothes are in Alexandria." She told me all this by degrees, prompted by remarks and questions from me. It might be funny enough to her, so far, but perhaps the mother did not see the joke. By degrees I learned that Josie's father was a very wealthy Southerner, and the house in Alexandria was a large, newly-built family residence, elegantly furnished, the beautiful piano and collection of music being mere trifles, among the rest of valuables, that were left behind in the care of one old faithful slave.

"Can't I have Beauregard's March to learn, if you please, ma'am?" said my first pupil.

Here was another difficulty. A great number of national songs, marches, and anthems had been composed for the Confederacy and published till the stock of music paper had become exhausted. Johnston of Richmond, and Blackmar of New Orleans and of Vicksburg, became the chief music-publishers of the South, and those popular airs, on poor thin paper, were caught up as fast as printed. I wanted to persuade my present pupils to turn to the standard composers, of whose compositions an abundant supply remained. But no, nothing would satisfy them but the Dixie's and Confederate marches, Beauregard's, President's, and Palmetto waltzes, songs, and quicksteps. If I presented a good composition for their practice, it was learned only with a sort of proviso, that "when I have learned this, may I learn the Jeff Davis waltz?" or some other equally popular melody.

Josie was not the only one who had left Alexandria in the night, nor the only one who came away without her music; and what with the mania for poor compositions on bad paper, the difficulty of procuring even these, and the aversion to classical music, of which there was an abundance in Richmond, the music lessons were not very satisfactory to the teacher, whatever they might be to the pupils. Among the juvenile musicians were several Mollies, and Sallies, and Bessies. A taste seemed to prevail in that part of Virginia to give children old-fashioned names with new-fashioned terminations, and scarcely six girls could be selected among the three dozen whose names did not end in *ie*.

Our early hours afforded time for a charming run before the morning studies, and I tried to persuade some of the girls to accompany me. Neither the Doctor, nor the Professor, nor either of the ladies ever said a word about the walks, unless I proposed them first, when they received it as a great kindness in me—the invitation to the pupils—and used their influence to persuade the girls whom I invited, to take exercise.

"I can't go out," said one of the Mollies. "It will wear out my shoes, and what shall I do for more when these are gone?"

"Which way are you going, Miss Jones?" said one of the Betties.

"Whichever way you like, where the roads are dry."

"*I'll* go, if you will walk along the railway, then we can keep on the wood-work without hurting my shoes."

So with every one of my young pedestrians. One had been waiting nine weeks, and had but just got her new shoes. Another had sent to Nashville* for some. Others had promised to walk as soon as they could procure any. When fine and dry, and we could venture on the grass or railroad, I had sometimes six or seven companions, but rarely was I accompanied by more than one or two, if by any. So much for shoes and music during the civil war and blockade.

Some of the pupils came from Culpepper County, some from Fairfax, some from near Leesburg, and one from Rappahannock (county) amongst the mountains,

* Tennessee, above 500 miles.

where the river of the same name takes its rise. A tall handsome girl this latter, vigorous with the pure mountain air. Two of her brothers belonged to the Stuart cavalry, that has made itself so famous during the war. Warrenton, in Fauquier County, is celebrated for its "springs," its scenery, and healthfulness, and besides this for its being the native place of many old Virginian families. Ex-President Tyler, Ex-Governor Smith, known by the *soubriquet* of "Extra Billy" Smith, and Captain Marr, the first victim of a battle on Virginian soil, were all natives of Warrenton. The Black Horse cavalry was equipped by the patriots of Fauquier County. On first volunteering, that company had resolved to ride only black horses, but as these died off or were killed, and it became difficult to replace them, the "Black Horse" title died with the devoted steeds.

The "Warrenton Rifles" have distinguished themselves in many engagements. They alone preserved Fairfax Court-house against the Federal attack on the 1st June, and were foremost in the battle of the 18th July, Blackburn's Ford, and were engaged again on the 21st, Bull Run.

I never was so agreeably surprised, or had my prejudices so quickly cleared away, as by that family at the College. Dr. Bacon was a Baptist, but an unbigoted one. Scarcely ever, even in England, have I met with a man of so much general information, combined with such simplicity of mind and manners: a thoroughly educated gentleman besides; and learned in classics. He was a member of a Greek society—I forget the name—of one of the New Haven (Connecticut) colleges; or rather he had been, before the war and separation. For eighteen years he was President of a college in Washington, and had returned to end his days in Virginia. His daughters united the amiability of the Southern character with much of the energy of the North; and were intelligent, accomplished women, as well as delightful companions. The eldest was married to a Virginian, Professor Latham of the University at Charlottesville, a scholar and a gentleman. My duties there proved exceedingly light and agreeable, not occupying me at the utmost four hours of the morning. All the afternoon I could employ myself by my beautiful window, and the evening passed pleasantly in music, chess, and conversation. The attentions of the united family were equally flattering as gratifying. The conversation of the two gentlemen afforded both pleasure and instruction. Dr. Bacon had travelled much in all the States, and possessed a fund of information and anecdote; lately he had been over the battle-grounds of July, and perhaps no one had bestowed more care in ascertaining facts, and in comprehending the position of the troops than he had. He promised me a trip to the battle-field, and spared no pains in describing the localities beforehand.

The pupils were amiable, unaffected girls, kind and respectful towards myself, and their lightheartedness and buoyant spirits were refreshing to contemplate.

It made one feel like a school-girl oneself to be amongst them; and especially when we assembled at meals, always rendered agreeable by cheerfulness and conversation; added to this, the mountain air gave me so excellent an appetite, the dinners being well cooked and hot, with the comfort of a neat and well-appointed table besides, that I fed and flourished rapidly on the wholesome viands which were always present in abundance.

Mrs. Latham often apologized for the little variety displayed upon the table, and recounted the troubles of marketing, where an army was so near. The table was liberally supplied, I thought, and must have been sumptuously so before the war, or what would have been considered so in England; but schools and colleges for Young America are expected to furnish the luxuries of home, especially in the South. I remember one day hearing Mrs. Latham, in great tribulation, discussing the weighty matter of a substitute for butter at the tea-table, after Mrs. McGee had been walking and driving here and there in vain endeavours to procure some. Honey and preserves were on the table, "but without butter what would the girls do?"

Warrenton is not on the mountains, nor even near them by comparison. The Blue Ridge does not rise abruptly from a plain, the whole country consisting of hills and valleys, increasing in altitude and depth from the Potomac westward. Warrenton, notwithstanding, lies at a considerable elevation. Even from the railway, running as it does between high ground, one obtained a view of great extent; and from the higher points a vast expanse of undulating hills and richly-wooded country, even to the Potomac itself. We looked over lines of hills to others yet further off, until they all seemed level in the immense distance. On certain days of peculiar clearness, we could distinguish the camps of Manassas and Centreville; and the people told me that on the day of the "great battle" of Bull Run, with the assistance of a telescope, they had watched the whole proceedings.

What magnificent scenery that was, looking from the College Hill on the October afternoons! Perhaps not one-tenth part of the State of Virginia was cleared from timber before the war; there were hills beyond hills all thickly wooded.

The maple gum, varieties of oak, with the abundance of sumach, cause a brilliancy of tint of which no English eye, accustomed only to English autumns, can conceive; and over the whole was thrown the veil of the glowing sunset atmosphere, from the golden fading into red, and thence from crimson into purple, till the deep blue settled over the distant expanse.

Scarcely a day passed that we did not see some one from Centreville where the great body of the army was then stationed. Dr. McGee (Lieutenant) came several times to see his wife and little Lizzie, and always had something amusing to tell us of the soldiers. Nearly all the pupils had brothers or relatives in the army, and seldom an evening passed without some guest, who kept us "posted" in the annals of the camps. Lieutenant McGee was a Baltimorean, and his wife a Pennsylvanian, though I believe as sincerely "Southerners" as any born in the Confederacy. Dr. McGee's brothers were, if not in the Confederate army, in the service of the Government, and their feats in running the blockade of the Potomac were a constant boast. I heard of one gentleman who in four trips to Baltimore made 15,000 dollars clear profit. One of the articles in greatest requisition was shoe thread; and even the Southerners were known to thrive on the misfortunes of their neighbours occasionally, as well as Yankees. One man purchased a large stock of shoemakers' thread at 25 cents per lb. in Baltimore, and sold it at Richmond for four dollars per lb. These speculations showed poor patriotism, for gold was necessary to pay for articles beyond the Potomac, and this perhaps has been one reason of the scarcity of specie in the Confederacy.

One evening a gentleman called who had just come from Alexandria. He had made his way there on foot, walked about, and got through a tolerable day's shopping, filled his pockets with shoes and other articles, and walked back again without molestation; having passed the Federal pickets twice.

One gentleman, whose name would be well known were I to mention it, made his way from Richmond to Baltimore, so disguised that his intimate friends there did not recognize him. He inquired for, and heard reports of persons whom he had left in Richmond, and stayed four days at an hotel where he, in his own identity, was well known. He conversed with many who asked him about himself, and returned to Virginia quite safely, bringing the welcome news that a regiment called the "Union Regiment" was being organized in Baltimore, who intended to join the Federal army until they should be sent on picket duty: when they would come over bodily to Secessia. That "Union" regiment performed their feat successfully from Alexandria, in the December following, bringing with them a quantity of valuable baggage. It was said at that time that there were at least 8000 Marylanders in the Confederate army, and as many more ready to take up arms. Every person who came from the camps brought information of deserters from the Federals: the usual excuse being that they were tired of fighting; and not being permitted to resign, and go home, determined to go somewhere; and therefore came over to Secessia. Oh, the blessings of governing a "sovereign people!"

The Doctor and the Professor sometimes gave utterance to their expressions of astonishment at "the temper and disposition of the North," which were slowly and startlingly developing themselves to the mind, awakening in the beholders a consciousness of facts that only one year ago would have been pronounced impossible. It had been thought that of all the nations of the world, America would be the last to encourage a civil war. That she would shrink from this catastrophe as a cruelty and fratricide. It had been expected that with her boasted liberties and prosperity she would have looked with horror on a national debt; whereas now behold her encountering an enormous debt, and dragging her people into taxes and poverty. It was thought that there continued to exist in the North a conservative element which would oppose the war to the utmost; but in spite of the disgraceful defeats, they were rushing madly on to still greater schemes of subjugation and tyranny.

"It is the trading element of the North," said the Professor, "that persists in a war which would appear to be quite in opposition to their commercial and peaceful occupations. It is a speculation they have entered upon, a bargain which they are resolved to pursue to the last end; a singular predicament, in which they find themselves in pursuit of a rainbow with a bag of gold tied to one end, which, at whatever sacrifice of time and labour, they are resolved to obtain."

We all wondered—every one did wherever two or three were gathered together—how long this fruitless chase would continue; and it was evident that, chivalrous as the Southerners are by nature and education, they were all heartily sick of the war. Forced into it contrary to their inclination, they were ready to accept peace upon any honourable terms: and yet they would throw their very life into the battle, rather than yield to unjust demands.

CHAPTER IV.

Excitement in the vicinity of the Army—Federal Rewards to the Army—Chausseur—Home Effects of the War—Marketing Excursions—Free Negroes—A Slave who belonged to no one—Hopes kindled, but suddenly extinguished—The inexorable Consuls—Practical Results of the Blockade.

WE lived a life of as much excitement in the neighbourhood of the armies at Warrenton, as we had done at Milbank, so near to Acquia Creek, where the first "road to Richmond" was attempted. Now, however, we had become accustomed to the war; sad as it was to feel so. The many successes of the Southern arms inspired the people with a confidence which, together with the phantom of "recognition," have since proved baneful to them.

One Sunday, after the morning-service, an immense commotion disturbed the town. Some one from the camps had arrived to say that the place was to be "vacated immediately," by order of General Beauregard; that the Federals were approaching, "and overwhelming numbers," were on their way. Another rumour said that the Yankees had possession of ——, a little village a few miles off, and were advancing rapidly. At one of the churches the order was even given out by the Minister, seasoned with appropriate exhortations to trustfulness in Divine aid, with "long suffering," and devotion to the cause.

"What shall you do?" I asked Mrs. Latham.

"Stay here; and if they come, they come. They will make but a very short stay, with our army so near at hand."

I resolved to assert my neutrality as a British subject, and thought my position in a ladies' seminary about as safe a one as could be found anywhere else; though of course one felt a little tremulous at the prospect of a battle so near.

It was surprising, and yet amusing, to witness the fearless indifference of the girls at such reports. One would not have been very much astonished had several of them gone off into fits and hysterics, accompanied by shrieks and other tragic demonstrations. Nothing of the kind was ever seen. They treated the matter more as a joke than anything else. Some of them, whose parents resided in the vicinity of places where skirmishes were often occurring, looked a little pale and anxious until correct information could be obtained; but, on the whole, such a company of juvenile heroines can scarcely be imagined.

Somehow or other—perhaps because the order came upon the Sabbath-day, or lacked authority,—but on this occasion no one did evacuate Warrenton.

Towards evening the message became perplexed with other tidings; and the next day we learned the "reliable" part of the story.

The little village, whose name is forgotten, had been, during the summer, desolated by the Federal army, all the houses but three having been destroyed; the which three were now taken possession of by three old Union men, whose "loyalty" was thus rewarded, no doubt. So the place being occupied by "Unionists" was literally correct; but the three aforesaid Unionists had more to fear than to hope in their new homes, and the story "founded on fact" reassured the peaceful inhabitants of Warrenton.

It was common to hear of those acts of Federal liberality towards the loyal citizens. Before the war commenced, or rather before any positive engagement had taken place, the Southerners were accustomed to hear that the Northern volunteers were bribed by the prospect of a "Southern farm." "Yes, they all shall have a farm in Virginia: it shall suit them exactly—a farm six feet by two, for each of them." Too true, alas! for thousands.

However, the Federal officers were not ashamed to boast of the magnificent keepsakes they often sent to their wives and lady-loves at home. Pianos, books, a wardrobe, anything to be captured, was permitted to be appropriated. "Indeed it is doubtful whether a Yankee would engage in any occupation if he did not expect to 'make' by it," said the Professor.

As the days grew shorter and cooler, the blockade began to be felt more severely in its effects. Such trifling articles of household requirements as matches, soap, candles, starch, glue, &c., were becoming exceedingly scarce. All of them could be produced at home; but it seemed no one's business to begin. Southern extravagance and affluence had never thought of saving grease for soap, any more than rags for paper, or hides for leather. The bugbear of "raising the blockade" impeded speculation; and by slow degrees, and in scanty quantities, these things found their way into the market.

We had already begun to drink rye mixed with our coffee, though indeed it was scarcely apparent to the taste; and Mrs. McGee, who entered heart and soul into the all-important supplies for the table, amused us highly with her adventures in search of eatables. Tea was then three dollars and a-half per lb., and began to be used as an occasional treat. An abundance of delicious milk, however, was always at hand; and this is so usual a beverage, that the tea was not much missed. Coffee had risen from ten cents to seventy-five cents a pound. Salt, as a great favour to "such a good customer," was purchased at three dollars and a-half per sack. There happened to be a supply at Warrenton just then, because at the same time it was selling at twenty-two dollars per sack at Lynchburg, and eight, ten, or eighteen dollars in different other places, according to the supply on hand. These unequal supplies gave rise to very inconvenient speculations. Once when the pupils and other persons had learned that a good supply of certain articles of clothing were to be found at such a store, they wrote home to their parents for money for the purchases, all resolving to avail themselves immediately, on the principle of "first come first served;" and such was, in fact, the case, for by the time the funds arrived, the disappointing intelligence was received that a merchant from Richmond had been up and "bought the whole stock!"

The greatest patience had to be exercised about the *chausseur*. The mud of Warrenton surpassed all other mud, in quality and quantity, that I ever saw. To walk without "overshoes," as galoshes are called, could scarcely be attempted. I had sought for a pair at every store at Richmond in vain, although these articles are considered so indispensable in America, that they are usually to be met with everywhere in abundant supplies; then I heard by good luck that some were to be purchased in Warrenton. Hastening to the place designated, I found three pairs. Such pairs! such a size and pattern! no one could guess where such singular-looking articles could have escaped from within twenty years. Two sizes too big, too; but that was better than two sizes too small, and I bought a pair, and had good reason to congratulate myself on securing them.

"Who lives there?" I asked, as we passed a beautiful modern residence.

"Mrs. —— *did* live there; but the house is built to be warmed by furnaces, and as she could not procure any of the proper coal, she left the house, and she and her family are boarding with Mrs. N."

Perhaps a dozen large family mansions in the town were in the same condition, and obliged to be vacated.

The large school-room at the Seminary was ordinarily warmed by a stove, which consumed a certain kind of coal, not now to be had, and the Doctor was very much concerned to find a substitute. As is often the case in the American autumns, a sudden "spell" of exceedingly cold weather will visit us for a few days, and be then succeeded by very warm weather again. It was the case now, during the middle of October, after which the Indian summer set in; and I noted particularly from the 5th to the 10th of December some very lovely weather, when we once more discarded furs and fires, and sat out on the verandah by moonlight, until quite late, without even a shawl being necessary. But at this time the Doctor and Professor were nearly beside themselves to supply the house with fuel. It was built entirely for coal fires, and no coal was to be had. No stoves for burning wood could be procured in town either; and what was to be done? Every girl expected of course to have a fire in her own room; we know how lavishly the Virginia fires were piled up on every chilly day, and the poor children, accustomed to such comforts, were shivering about the house, causing much distress to their kind Professor and his wife, who were driven to their wits' ends to meet the difficulty.

I had the advantage of them in one respect, which was in being able to get warm by exercise, in which they were afraid to indulge for fear of wearing out their only shoes. My purchases in London the year before had saved me from all anxieties, *de quoi s'habiller:* that was an immense comfort. At last one stove for burning wood was hunted out from some warehouse, and burnished up for the College drawing-room, which forthwith became the crowded resort of all those shivering daughters of Virginia. The next difficulty was to find a certain kind of wick, to be burned in the lamps throughout the house, and we all contented ourselves with miserable experiments of home-made candles, which were managed with the utmost economy, and lighted one from the other, because the matches were "all used up."

For want of oils and wicks, and other requisites for lighting, evening-services at the churches were suspended, and the shops all closed at sunset. "No more" of such or such a thing began to be a common piece of information; and if perchance a fresh supply of any article were heard of, the probability was that it was either "bought up for the hospitals," or the soldiers had secured it by paying an exorbitant price. The country-people soon found that the soldiers were good customers, and charged outrageously for their farm-house dainties.

Lieutenant McGee never came home without bringing some amusing anecdote of the Warrenton Rifle-Corps. One day he told us that a countryman had come into camp with a quantity of "blackberry pies." Blackberries in America are a much finer fruit than those ripened by our faint English sun, and are quite popular in their season. The huckster's pastry was not altogether palatable to the soldiers' taste, and the man was threatened with the loss of his customers if he did not bring a better article on his next appearance. The following week a fresh supply of pastry was brought into camp,—a great deep basket, piled up with another edition of blackberry pies. They were tasted, pronounced excellent, paid for, basket and all, and the farmer made a hasty retreat with his money.

The "excellence" lay solely in the upper stratum of pastry; beneath appeared another description, made with bad butter and filled with bad fruit. Basket and contents were placed aside, awaiting the return of the dealer. On the reappearance of the unfortunate vender he was cordially grasped by the hand, and then by the collar, and the gallant 17th tied him safely to a tree. Then reproducing the basket of still sourer and still more ancient pastry, and placing themselves at a respectful distance, they practised the innocent sport of making the poor man's face a target for the flying pies; and such a pied pastry-merchant was never seen before: nor did he ever venture again to bring his uneatable merchandize to the "pious 17th," as the Lieutenant termed his regiment.

In spite of the dearness of provisions, our table was always well supplied. The heads of the establishment had no idea of diminishing the comforts of their inmates to increase their own profits or save their purse-strings. The only anxiety seemed to be that they should not find enough to eat; and Mrs. McGee, after engaging a carriage several weeks beforehand, went on a foraging expedition around the country, to try and persuade certain farmers to reserve their poultry, eggs, and butter for the use of the College.

Even those rides of hers belonged to the war. Her carriage broke down, and the horses were worn out, and, poor lady, at one time she had a narrow escape from passing the night in a mud hole by the road side, into which the carriage sank, and the united efforts of driver and horses could not drag it from its bed. Other travellers finally lent their aid, and released both lady and horses.

The prices then paid for country articles were, for butter, from 40 to 60 cents per pound, instead of 12 or 15 cents; eggs from 40 to 60 cents per dozen; a turkey, the usual price for which had been one dollar, was now two dollars and a half; and chickens one dollar and a half per pair instead of thirty cents. "I declare it is too ridiculous of those negroes," said Mrs. McGee; "it costs them nothing in the world to feed their chickens, and they are pretending that the 'hard times' compel them to double their price: what do they know of hard times, I wonder!" Wood for burning was eight or ten dollars a cord, or load, instead of three dollars. "The wood waggons have grown wonderfully short this year," said our indefatigable *ménagère;* "the cords are not two thirds their usual length, but more than three times their usual price." The difficulty of transportation, and the want of men to cut it, caused this price in a country so covered with timber, that at other times persons might procure as much as they chose, and be almost thanked for doing it. We heard of much suffering among the poor as soon as fires became necessary, and much inconvenience was felt by others who either could find no stoves, or no dwellings, and where families accustomed to spacious houses were crowded together to share their fires and apartments, and assist each other in "enduring all things" in the same cheerful contented hopeful spirit, which was a marvel to contemplate.

One of the servants at the College was a nearly white free negro, who had lived in Philadelphia and Washington, and was in her own estimation a person of vast importance. There were a great many free negroes at Warrenton, and also white negroes, the latter to be attributed to a sin, which must be declared the worst evil of slavery, if it were confined to slaveholders alone.

There is a sort of gipsy beauty in the nearly white negro. The large dark eyes retain their brilliancy, while their form is improved; a rich glow in the cheeks, a well-formed nose and full rosy lips, with glossy black ringlets, are good artistic features to begin with. Add to these an expression mild and pensive, but full of feeling, with a smile lingering about the mouth, ready to burst forth at a word of encouragement, and display the dazzling and well-formed teeth. The Almighty seems to have compassionated the grim ugliness of these human monkeys in their savage state, and compensated their natural hideousness by a rapid development of beauty and improvement in amalgamation with the white race. It belongs more to statistics than to the present history, to declare how far their mental and moral progress keep pace with their physical bleaching.

But the free negroes, so numerous, gave me an opportunity of observing and comparing the difference between them and the slaves, which was very striking. They are, on the whole, an impudent, unprincipled race, with no attachment to, and therefore feeling no interest in, their employers. They belong to no one. With no laws to protect them, no affections to influence them, and no hopes to stimulate them, free negroes seem to be the most pitiable class of people in the world. I used to feel sorry even to look at that girl at the College, with her sour, unhappy, bad, yet contemptuous countenance, in spite of quite good features. Whenever anything was missed in those scarce times, and that was by no means unfrequently, Rosa was certainly the guilty party: but it was no less certain to be denied with her accustomed insolence. I often felt inclined to talk to her, and try to soften her disposition, but it was useless. Her character was hardened. She had found herself one of a despised race in the North, and enjoying fewer privileges in the South than even the slaves themselves, without any of the comforts and protection secured to them. With but few exceptions, you may always perceive a self-assuming, put-on-the-defensive impudence expressed in the countenance of a free negro. But there was another negro woman who was a great favourite in the house, though she did not belong to the family, but was hired.

Poor Aunt Peggy! I found out her history in a conversation with her after she had accomplished her morning's sweepings one day, and appeared with a frontage of armour, or rather a breast-plate, composed of scores of pins darned in and out all over her boddice.

"Why, Aunt Peggy, you have quite a stock of pins now."

"Yee-ees 'm, I picks em all up, a sweeping the young ladies' rooms. Pins is high now, an' skeerce, an' I nebber throws nuffin away when I sweeps."

"That's right, Aunt Peggy; the servants waste a great deal that might be useful. You don't burn up your rags now, do you, Aunt Peggy, for they are wanted to make paper?"

"But you ain't got no use for paper *now*, has you mistis? you can't send no letter any whars."

"Oh yes we can; besides, we want paper for newspapers, and a great many other things."

"But you can't send no letters North now, ken you, miss?"

"Not very easily, but people don't want to send many letters to the Yankees."

"My mistis is North, an' *she* ain't no Yankee; she's as good a mistis as ever lived, *she* is," said Aunt Peggy, vehemently, "an' I wish she could get back, I do."

"Where is she now, and why does she stay there?'

"Jes' afore dis fuss broke out she went to Phillidelphy to visit her parents, and then she stopped there. My master's dead, an' she ain't got no home down heah, but she wrote an' sed she'd come back jes' as soon as she could. She's lef' all her servants, an' all her property down heah, an' they won't let her come back heah."

Poor Aunt Peggy looked very sorrowful, and added, with a great sigh, "I hope she'll get back afore I die; she's a mighty good missus to me, an' I thinks a deal on her, I does."

Mrs.Latham told me that Aunt Peggy had been left with the rest of the negroes belonging to an estate, by their mistress, as she had herself informed me; and that now the poor servants, without any protector, were suffering sadly. Peggy was hired to this family by a gentleman who pretended to have some management of the estate, but his was not like the care of the mistress, and poor Peggy's comforts had been quite neglected. She had only lately come to the Seminary, and as yet had not received any addition to her wardrobe, which was by no means in a very attractive condition.

After hearing of this, I said to her one day, "Aunt

Peggy, I must try and find you another handkerchief to wrap round your head while that is being washed. It does not look very neat, does it?"

"De Lord bress you, mistis!" said Aunt Peggy, throwing herself back, until her waist was almost at right angles, and bursting into a hearty laugh; "'tis jes' all I got. I haint the smallest bit o' rag to wear 'ceptin' dis heah. Dese heah close is all I got neither. Nebber *was* so bad off in all my life. I tell ye, mistis, I'se mighty 'shamed to go so, but I ca'an't help it, to save my life."

She looked mightily amused at her rags, nevertheless.

"How is it, Aunt Peggy? Don't those you belong to give you clothes?"

"Why, mistis, I don't belong to nobody, an' that's jes' how 'tis. Ye see, mistis, my master's dead, and he lef' word in his will dat noffin' wasn't to be disturbed for two yeahs; and we was all to stay on de place jes' the same. Den my mistus she went off to Philli-delphy, and can't get home, that's how 'tis I'm so bad off. I was hired to Mr. S. for six months, an' he never gave me so much as a rag, when he'd ort to a giv' me a whole suit at Christmas; and then I was hired to Mr. T., an' he didn't give me noffin' but one pair o' shoes, an' 'spected me to clothe myself; but laws bress you, mistis, I can't make no money now to buy clothes. Time's is too hard, an' I busy at work all de time. Humph! I tell ye, mistis, I never was hired out in all my life afore, and here's I in my forty-five, an' the mother of eight children and fourteen gran' children, an' nebber was away from home in my life before: nebber expected to be, neever. Here we're all knockin' aroun'—some here, some thar, and my mistus wa-ay off among de Yankees, an I heah wif no body to care whether I goes naked or not. My poor mast'r nebber meant for us to be knockin' aroun' like dis heah; an' dat's why he lef' word we wasn't to be disturbed for two yeahs; and now maybe we shan't have no home afore Christmas. Goodness knows whether we'll have any Christmas or not dis yeah, wif my mistus all among de Yankees."

A negro will never stop talking all the time they can find a listener, and as I liked to hear their quaint remarks and genuine sentiments, I had nothing to do but to set them going and then continue my occupation and listen. So these were Aunt Peggy's ideas of home and owner.

Before I had been many weeks at Warrenton the good news caught my eye, that British vessels of war were in future, by consent and arrangement, to keep up communication with Her British Majesty's Consuls in blockaded States.

Very soon a goodly packet of letters was confidently forwarded to Mr. Cridland, intreating him to admit of no delay in dispatching them by this new and most welcome arrangement. Oh, hopes departed!—hear the Consul's reply:—

"The communications to which you allude are to be confined strictly to the business of the Consulates.

The regulations in regard to letters are more stringent than ever, and Lord Lyons has positively forbidden any and all the Consuls to receive, forward, or transmit any letters from or to private individuals residing in the seceding States. He cannot allow Consuls to evade the non-intercourse law for any one. I regret extremely that I cannot relieve your anxiety, and oblige a lady and a friend."

He added that Mr. and Mrs. English had succeeded in getting off. That Mrs. English had appealed to the President in person, who of course could not refuse her: and that they had sailed in the Asia from New York, Sir James Ferguson and Mr. Bourke being also in the same ship.

It was too bad. I could endure such suspense no longer. More than six months had elapsed since one word had reached me from England, and sometimes I thought, winter or not, nothing should detain me any longer in such a situation. I requested Mr. Cridland to forward my packet of letters to Charleston, and resolved to appeal to the Consul there, Robert Bunch, Esq., in behalf of British subjects generally, and myself particularly; I even went so far as to address a letter to Lord Lyons to explain the condition in which the war had found us, and forced us, and enclosed the same to Mr. Bunch. It happened that I had been acquainted with a gentleman in the North who, I knew, enjoyed the personal intimacy and friendship of Lord Lyons; and this gentleman resided in the same town with some of my relatives. So I conceived the notion of writing to him through his lordship, and of requesting him to communicate the contents of the letter to my friends there.

Mr. Bunch replied with promptness and courtesy, endorsing Mr. Cridland's information, and informing me that he was "most strictly enjoined not to violate the rule," and that "the United States Government has a distinct right to interdict the correspondence of private persons," &c. &c. He however promised to forward my letter to Lord Lyons: we had of course a right to address the representatives of our own country.

In acknowledging his letter, I requested Mr. Bunch to deliver my packet into the hands of a gentleman in Charleston, whom I had met in Richmond, and who had kindly promised to use his endeavours in getting some communications through the blockade for me. This anti-neutral fact it was thought better not to confide to the extremely conscientious Consul; and certainly it would have been more agreeable to send one's letters in a straightforward manner, as a British subject ought to do. It was, however, a matter of too much moment, to neglect the least hope of success. So that the letters went, no matter how to me.

The subject of letters repeatedly will weary the reader; but it is one of the characteristics of the war. Other British subjects, I saw, by singular advertisements, were contriving ways and means to communicate with England. For a time an agent travelled all the way to Tampico. No stone was left unturned by the semi-imprisoned "neutrals," thus cut off from every privilege and protection.

The appropriation, for the Government and army, of lines of railway, horses, waggons, and mules, enhanced the price of fuel in a manner as to cause much apprehension for the poor. That is, the *white* poor.

Contributions for the army seemed to increase rather than diminish, and especially for the Maryland and Alexandria regiments; they being cut off from home assistance. One gentleman wrote word through the "Enquirer" that he had three sons and one son-in-law in the army; and if it should be necessary for the old to enlist, in order to "drive the invader from our soil," he was ready to go himself. He enclosed with the letter 500 dollars "for the Maryland regiments." Another gentleman sent 250 dollars for the same object; and in one week of October, nearly 200,000 dollars were received for winter clothing for the army, from various Southern contributors.

The anticipated "raising of the blockade," though an impediment, was not an entire check to enterprise. Never was the fact that "necessity is the parent of invention," more adequately proved.

As the resources of the South were developed by degrees, so were the wants of the young and struggling nation. Among other things, people were experimentalizing in bank-note paper. This again demanded engravers and their tools, and among one of the most serious losses by sea just then, was the capture of a ship containing all the essentials for lithography.

"WHO WILL MANUFACTURE COTTON CARDS?

"TO THE EDITOR OF THE ENQUIRER.

"*Jacksonville, Ala. Nov.* 1, 1861.

"GENTLEMEN—What is to be done for Cotton Cards in our Confederacy, there being no factory of the kind south of Baltimore? Men we have in abundance to fight our battles, and munitions of war also are doubtless on hand, and being provided. But soldiers must be clothed. This can be done by our noble women, if they can get *cards*; but without them "country" jeans cannot be made, and all know that without these "country jeans" our soldiers now in Virginia, would be destitute of clothing to a great extent, indeed.

"Richmond is becoming distinguished as a manufacturing city. Can she not add, to her present establishments, one for the manufacture of cards, both for factories and the hand? The proprietors of such an establishment would doubtless realize largely on their investment, and contribute much, also, to Southern independence."

The daily advertisements in the papers gave more signs of the stimulus that invention had received, particularly in the production of war materials. "Confederate cloth," for army suits, "Confederate boots," Confederate matches, paper, ink, and a dozen other things began to be circulated, though in small and inefficient quantities.

Though in common justice to the slaveholders, one is compelled to testify to the comparatively happy condition of their negroes, one is equally bound to condemn the consequences of the Institution in the slow development of progress among the poorer white class. One observed the evils of inactivity in a hundred ways where the energy of the "smart Yankee," would have overcome difficulties in an incredibly short space of time. Here were thousands and thousands of uncleared acres of timber. The cries of Richmond and other large towns were loud for fuel; much suffering existed as winter approached, and more was anticipated, while thousands of capable but indolent men pleaded "no waggons," or other foolish excuses to supply the market. "I feel inclined to set about making waggons myself," said Dr. Bacon, who had none of the distaste for labour entertained by the less intelligent. "Our Yankee enemies would have made a road, and invented a carriage to run on it while our own people are freezing to death," he generously admitted. To show how far this disinclination to exertion is carried, I cannot withhold a remark I heard an Alabamian soldier make, in spite of the bravery displayed by his State when aroused in battle. "I'll tell you what," said the soldier; "when I got home, and had nothing to do but to sit in the rocking-chair, and call to a nigger to bring me a cigar and a glass of water, I felt very little disposed to come back to the ranks."

CHAPTER V.

Leesburg and Evansport—Arthur's appreciation of Yankees—Criticisms—A Trip to the Battle-ground—The Battle-field—The Graves of the 8th Georgia Regiment—The Henry House—A Desolate Picture—The Road to Centreville—A Fresh Dilemma—The Absent Husband—Supper in the Camp—A Hurricane in the Encampment—A Glance at the Hero—Indulgences to the Sovereign People—The Cotton Correspondent is Urgent—I decide upon Florida—A Temporary Supply of Fuel—Warrenton Cemetery—Capture of Messrs. Mason and Slidell.

THE two great events of the Southern army in Virginia, during October, were the successful closing of the Potomac against Federal ships, and the terrible slaughter called the battle of Leesburg. We had heard reports of cannon for many days, which had kept us all in a fever of excitement; thinking the "onward movement" had really begun. Sometimes we heard the fearful booming, booming, from one quarter and sometimes from another; the reverberation among the hills often deceiving us as to the direction. It had been whispered for some time, that grand preparations were being made on the banks of the Potomac, where those immense guns called "Long Tom," and "Long Sam," captured at the battle of Manassas, were being placed in position. A battle at Evansport, a little village near which they were stationed, was one of the daily expectations, "because," the people said, "the Yankees will bring all their force to open the navigation of the Potomac," but, after all those great preparations, no very important result to either side ensued; provisions, fuel, and fodder commanded an enormous price in Washington for a time, but in a country where no one feels it a disgrace to labour, and the enterprise of the people is unbounded, the Federals overcame the obstacle by promptly inaugurating fresh lines of traffic elsewhere. They were *harassed* by those vast preparations, and that was all.

We used to hear of artifices, at once savage and ludicrous, provoked by the tyranny of the oppressor over a people whom they only aspired to subdue "by force of numbers!"

Within the range of Federal pickets, or at least of their telescopes, the Confederates left two or three old waggons loaded with fodder, apparently, but the fodder hid from the distant watcher some good pieces of artillery, and the tempting prize enticed within the fatal shot the too unwary pilferer. Many such artifices, while the army was at Centreville and on the Potomac, caused not only desertions but frightful loss of pickets on the Federal side; tending greatly to the demoralization of their army at that time. The prisoners taken during October and November by those means amounted to hundreds, and they all agreed in declaring that it was almost impossible to get their men to go out on picket duty, as "they scarcely ever returned."

A dining-room servant at the College belonged to an officer stationed at Centreville, and his master removed him from his engagement, in order to take him into camp to wait upon himself. One day Arthur came back to see the Professor and "Miss Adie," his late mistress. He came "fixed up" in a new grey suit, faced with red, and never was vanity more pompously displayed than in this imitation military individual. He had a new cap of blue cloth, also relieved with red, the front being embellished with the brass letters W. A. R. What the initials signified, neither he nor any one else could divine.

Arthur said he had a holiday, and came "jes' to wait on de young ladies once mo!" He insisted on waiting at the dinner table, though perhaps the display of his "uniform" was the greater inducement of the two.

"Why, Arthur, where did you get such a good cap?"

"I bied it off one o' de Yankees, dat came into *our* camp."

"What did they come there for?"

"Humph! them's prisoners, sure."

"Don't they want their caps?"

"Yankees care for money more'n *caps*, missus. Said dey got no use for 'em now; an' I giv a Yankee ten dolla's for dis heah."

"Not a bad bargain for the prisoners; their caps cost them nothing, and they can procure more at the same rate, as soon as they go back again," said the Professor.

There were two sisters, Allie, and Susie at the College, who came from near Leesburg, and the anxious faces of those two girls were sad to contemplate, while the rumours and booming of that sickening slaughter were flying through the air. As my readers know, the battle occupied two days. Leesburg was about twenty-three miles to the north of us, and in the stillness of the autumn air, we heard the awful cannonading which at times seemed to shake the very ground we stood upon. Those poor children were ashamed to display signs of fear; their fortitude and hopefulness were wonderful; yet the pale faces and compressed lips plainly told of the inward terror they suffered on behalf of their homes and parents. Brave little heroines! their suspense was soon relieved; a messenger from the place came to detail the whole affair. The battle had been eight miles from their home, and the result was in the Southern favour; but, oh! what heart-rending scenes were those described! How the Yankees had "retreated," or rather fallen headlong down the banks into the Potomac, rushing and tumbling pell-mell, like sheep or swine, with the Confederate muskets "picking them out," even as they plunged in their terror-stricken panic into the river. How they cast off their clothes and endeavoured to swim across, but how the cold temperature of the water on their heated bodies caused them to sink immediately. How they tried to escape on rafts, or crowded into boats which sank with their weight of living freight. It was indeed an awful battle, attended with a panic, equal almost to that at Manassas.

In nearly every engagement during that first summer campaign, we invariably heard that the Federal shots were ineffectual on account of their being aimed "too high." The Confederate losses in Western Virginia were mainly attributable to diminished and inferior forces, and the reckless daring of young officers. There, as elsewhere, the tops of the trees sustained the principal damage, and the newspapers commented upon this so freely, to the great provocation of the more discreet, that the improvement in the firing of Federal soldiers was soon apparent. In Leesburg, however, the Southern losses were insignificant, for the Confederates were well practised in their aim, and quickly dispersed their terrified opponents.

Not only the shooting, but the riding, of the enemy elicited considerable amusement to the Confederates, who are accustomed to mount into the saddle as soon as they can run alone, and to hold a gun from eight years old. "When they attempt to gallop, they tumble over and roll off their horses like ten pins:" said the Southerners of their enemies. "Ten pins" being a sort of grown-up game of nine pins. The poor Yankee soldiers in their dread of the "Secessioners" at Leesburg, and after their general experience of the summer campaign, had recourse to all manner of manœuvres in order to escape death or imprisonment. One poor man was found leaning against a tree apparently in his last gasp. "You wretched sinner," said a Confederate soldier, "it looks as if it would be a mercy to put an end to your sufferings," levelling his musket at the man.

"Oh mercy, mercy! don't shoot me!" exclaimed the feigner, leaping to his feet, with not a wound in his body, and dodging behind the tree.

"You lying scoundrel! what did you try to deceive me for? Run for your life, you contemptible Yankee!" So he gave the poor wretch a start of ten paces, and told him to escape if he could, but ere two more were accomplished, the fatal rifle brought him to the earth!

Many, many such anecdotes, too sad to relate, were told by the glorying Southerners, who week by week were goaded on by deeper and deeper provocations, to reduce the enemy by a system of savage warfare, against which their souls would have recoiled on first entering the ranks.

The propitious arrival of the Confederate steamer "Bermuda" was announced with great exultation. The author, in sad disloyalty to her Queen, was unneutral enough to rejoice immensely over this piece of good luck for the South; because that very polite and obliging gentleman at Charleston, (not the British Consul,) had just written her word that "the packet she had done him the honour to forward," had just left the harbour in charge of a gentleman who had sailed in the "Bermuda." That was very happy news, and of course I was pleased to know, or to suppose, that the "Bermuda" had not only brought in, but carried out, a valuable cargo. Other valuable freights, published as "an important event in the campaign," ran the blockade at the time: also coffee, immediately "bought up" by Government for the army.

For several weeks Mrs. McGee had been endeavouring to secure and engage a carriage for our expedition to the battle-ground. The Doctor and the Professor had made diligent inquiries, but with "the army so near," every kind of vehicle and animal was monopolized by the one great business.

The summer days were fast departing, and no time was to be lost. At last a carriage was procured, and the following Saturday decided upon. It proved too rainy, and in consideration of our repeated disappointments, the Monday or Tuesday of the ensuing week was fixed upon. These days, however, would deprive us of the pleasure of the good Doctor's company, as he objected to give up his classes: and this would be quite a drawback to our pleasure, for to me his information and intelligence were always welcome. Dr. McGee, however, promised to meet us at a settled point; and glad to make sure of carriage and horses while they could be hired, we set off, at dawn of day, on a fresh, clear, beautiful morning, towards the end of October.

Bessie, of Rappahannock county, and her friend Mollie, of Loudon County, were to accompany us, as both of them had brothers in the army at Centreville. Pencils and provisions were all prepared, and a rare treat was in store for one, at least, of the party—perhaps two, for Mrs. McGee had been over the battle-ground several times already, and the two girls were thinking much more of their brothers and cousins, than of the historic interest and opportunities of seeing a veritable battle-field.

It is sufficient to say of the roads that they were worse than any that have been yet described. No English person would ever have thought it possible to go up, and down, and over those masses of rock. Neither would any English horses have attempted to descend those steps of rocks; but Virginian horses are used to it. Mrs. McGee said that among the mountains (this was comparatively level), when the horses came to a great smooth slab of rocks of some two yards square, and at an angle of say 30°, they put their four feet together, throw themselves back upon their haunches, and let themselves slide down with the carriage or waggon after them. What cultivated intelligence!

Sometimes we were unexpectedly jerked into each others' laps, and then immediately pitched back again by a deep rut on the opposite side; but this gave us exercise and variety, and we got on pretty well at the rate of three miles an hour, walking up the hills sometimes to rest the not-too fresh horses.

We had been thoroughly jolted for about five hours, when after passing through continuous woods, we turned abruptly round an angle of the road and the *battle-field* was evident, at a moment's glance. We came suddenly upon the brow of a hill, which descended into a level, where the stream called Young's Branch crossed the road below. On either side was a range of higher ground, as it were facing each other. On the hill at our right were several buildings, or what had been such, but, even at that distance, were seen to be mere shells. The sky and the light shone through them, and every step of our approach began to reveal the havoc of cannon balls and rifle bullets. A scene of desolation whichever way one turned. Cleared, yes, frightfully cleared land—a sort of amphitheatre of desolation. As we descended the hill, prostrate fences, singed and blackened rails, and stems of broken trees were scattered everywhere. Trampled fields, and what might have been luxuriant harvests, waste and desolation, met our view.

We left the carriage at the farm-house of Mr. Dogan, which had been the head-quarters of the Federal General McDowell on that memorable 21st July, and near which the Rhode Island battery had been stationed. Passing from thence along the ridge of hill nearly parallel to the road, we traversed the chief line of the Federal positions, where the celebrated batteries of Sherman and Heintzelman had first opened fire. It was in the face of these tremendous batteries that a few of the Confederate regiments had made desperate charges from the opposite range of hills, to check their advance; among which the 4th Alabama, 2nd Mississippi, and the 8th Georgia, won to themselves such undying honours. But the Federal batteries ploughed down the ranks of the desperate Southerners, and took fresh positions as the already insignificant forces of their enemy were weakened; the latter contesting step by step of ground, backwards down the hill, across the road, and up the hill in their rear, only reinforced by slow and small detachments, until 4 o'clock P.M. Sherman's and the other batteries had been captured and recaptured repeatedly, and at last effectually. It was in the little yard at the back of one of those frail dwellings that Sherman's battery fell finally into the hands of the exulting Confederates. And it was then that a shout rent the air, taken up, and carried on along the lines for fifteen miles; inspiring the one side with the hope of victory, and the other with that sense of defeat that caused their panic, and the, to them, appalling result.

Perhaps there never was a battle fought by such unequal numbers as that of Bull Run. The Confederate troops were so divided, and at different times exposed in such small numbers, that it was like a succession of little battles of one or two regiments against a vast army. To show the desperation with which it was fought, I may mention that in one narrow space, without moving two yards, Dr. Bacon picked up a whole handful of bullets. This was in a little ravine where two men of the 4th Alabama regiment lay motionless, while the enemy passed over them, feigning death in order to escape it; but who afterwards succeeded in making good their retreat, and in joining their regiment. Another man near there stopped to wash the blood from his face; he was alone, and became immediately a mark for his enemies. He said the bullets were flying thickly about his ears, and he thought every moment would be his last; so falling prostrate, he also feigned death, running and crawling as he watched his opportunity, and then lying still again, until he at last escaped, and joined his comrades in safety.

Making our way along the same ridge of hill which had witnessed the opening of the battle, we came to a farm-house occupied by people of the name of Matthews, of whom several brothers cultivated farms in the neighbourhood. These people were said to be traitors to the South, and were suspected of having assisted the Federal army across that part of the country, which enabled them to get so far in the rear of the Confederates by the ford near Sudley church as the position they held on the 21st. We asked those people where they were on the day of the battle, in the midst of which stood their uninjured dwelling. The woman said she had "just happened to have started off in the morning, early, to visit somebody at a distance." How her house escaped as it did, when others so near were entirely destroyed, was a very marvellous occurrence. If her family had been the means of betraying the position of the Confederates, they suffered a retribution for their treachery, though in a horrid manner, for an immense pit near to their dwelling having received about one hundred and fifty of the Federal dead, their remains tainted the springs, to which they were accustomed to resort, so that the water had since been quite undrinkable.

Close by that house were the graves of some of the 8th Georgia Regiment, who had been buried by their devoted comrades exactly where they fell. A heap of fence rails and branches marked each resting-place, a small stake bearing the soldier's name.

While we were rambling among these graves, gathering relics, transcribing the names, and making a rapid use of our pencils, a misty threatening rain began to fall. The beautiful morning had terminated in a dull dreary day, befitting the harrowing scenes by which we were surrounded. Dr. McGee had not made his appearance at the appointed place of meeting, and his wife was straining her eyes this way and that in scarcely a mood for enjoyment. Whether his absence was to be attributed to some mistake in the day, or the locality, or whether to the "early engagement," which was "certainly to take place," she could not conjecture.

Bessie and Mollie were also becoming very anxious to greet those same cousins and brothers, who were to have accompanied the lieutenant, and though too polite and goodnatured to wish to hurry me, were, it was evident, very impatient to be off. Mrs. McGee said that if she did not find her husband at the ruins of old Mrs. Henry's house, she should lose no time in proceeding on to Centreville, only six miles further; and that, as there was a nearly full moon, we should be able to reach home without risk, even were it past sunset. The battle-ground was sixteen miles from Warrenton; and six miles further over such very rough roads, followed by the twenty-two miles home again, seemed a rather severe day's work for the horses; but husbands, lovers, and brothers, weighed down the balance of prudence: and I, nothing loth for adventures, had only to yield to my three companions.

Making our way back to the carriage in the drizzling rain, we descended the narrow hilly lane forming part of the road from Sudley to Manassas, where the contest had been so deadly, and drove along the turnpike road and over Young's Branch, fordable at that part, that had been so oft-times crossed and recrossed by the conflicting forces and crimsoned with their blood; and where scarcely a broken tree stem, or a standing post, did not bear marks of bullets. We passed "the Stone House," also rendered historic, and where now not an entire window pane or undefaced space was to be seen. We then ascended to the higher ground on the right, held from the first, and maintained by the Confederates, where their Imboden's battery and Washington Artillery had also mowed down the ranks of the enemy on the opposite hill.

Perhaps old Mrs. Henry's story may not be unwelcome here, although it is so well known to many. She was a very old woman of some eighty or more years, living in the little cottage with her daughter, who was turned of sixty, and an old negro servant.

The sudden appearance of the enemy, and the rapidity with which the battle had commenced, rendered it impossible for these three old women to leave their house. There they were, on the ridge of a hill between two armies. The poor daughter ran out, distracted, to find means of escape, but was driven in again by the soldiers, who said the danger was greater without than within. Her poor bedridden mother could not be moved without a conveyance and assistance, and where were those to be found while cannon-balls and musket shot were creating storm and tumult all around her! One of those formidable missiles soon terminated the existence of poor old Mrs. Henry. She was shot in her bed, and died without a struggle. The providential escape of the other two is nothing less than miraculous, for the house was literally battered to pieces by the cannon-balls. But the two terrified women had piled up all their furniture, poor things! as if chairs and tables could protect them against cannon balls, and crouched down between it and the chimney, where the wall was thickest; or rather where the only thickness was, for the cottage was a mere wooden shanty. The old negro woman was injured in the foot by the bursting of a shell in their room; but the daughter escaped unhurt; and the poor scared mortals were discovered in the evening half dead with terror and hunger, and, nearly beside themselves in their awful situation, afraid to venture forth. That they did come forth from their cramped-up corner alive, is among the wonders of the war. The old lady was buried in her little garden close to the window where she was lying, and where she met with her death. Her grave was covered over like the others with fence rails, looking like a heap of faggots; and within a few yards, under a couple of trees, the scattered bones lay bleaching of the horses that fell in that deadly conflict,—that final conflict over Sherman's battery, where it was captured, and the tide of battle turned by this event.

By the time we reached this deeply-interesting spot, the rain was falling fast, and the wind was sighing among the broken pine stems and whistling through the roof of the shattered dwelling. Not far off in front of it, was the little marble shaft that marked the spot where the gallant Colonel Bartow received his mortal wound. The place where General Bee fell was within a hundred yards, and not far off 250 of the Federals lay buried. In another spot on the opposite hill another heap of invaders were placed beneath the sod. Many other places we visited, all so frequently described that my readers need no repetition of the scenes.

Several parties were inspecting these historic grounds even on this dreary autumnal day, and we were informed that not a day had passed since the engagement but a score or more of persons had visited those battle-grounds. But no Lieutenant McGee, nor soldier brothers and cousins were to be seen, and, already past midday, we must hasten on to Centreville.

"Just one minute more, pray, allow me," I cried to the disappointed ladies. Not to transcribe that—of all interesting points, the most remarkable feature of the battle-field—to my sketch-book, was out of the question. And I perhaps the very first British subject who had enjoyed the privilege of going over that celebrated ground, and who perhaps might be the first to transfer its scenes to England! That was a distinction highly gratifying to the ambitious blockaded subject.

Every mile of our progress now displayed more and more the devastations of contending armies. At that time the Federals had not obtained possession of any points westward or southward of the battle-ground, but they had held Centreville and much of the intervening country; and no army could exist without leaving its traces wherever the camps had been pitched. Everywhere now were to be seen comfortable homes despoiled and deserted, or half in ruins, affording a scanty protection to the teamsters who seemed to spend their days in trudging to and fro between the camps and the nearest town, or railroad depôt; here and there pickets hovering near the heap of damp green logs that they vainly endeavoured to kindle into a fire; a company on march, or a regiment just ordered off, with stray soldiers going and coming in little parties, were the only passengers that greeted you as you proceeded mile after mile through that beautiful but desolate country.

No one who had once seen it could ever forget the view that meets your eye on reaching the ridge of hills that overlook the valley around Centreville. This place had been chosen on account of its elevated and admirable position for defence. It seemed, indeed, a natural fortification, commanding a wide-stretching valley on all sides, especially westward, which, on gaining the hill as you approached from the Stone Bridge, lay spread before you dotted—nay, covered—with camps. To the right and left, and on the slopes of the opposite hills, camps lay everywhere. Among the woods, between and beyond them, on the open glades, glistening in contrast to the glowing tints of autumn, beautiful in the distance, yet sad to contemplate, we beheld the winter dwellings of tens of thousands of the devoted Southern soldiers.

From showers, the rain became continuous; and our progress was slow and precarious. Mrs. McGee did not express any misgivings, but I could see that she was becoming anxious. The two girls thought only of seeing their relatives, and anticipated no danger. It was not exactly danger either that I feared, but here we were, twenty miles from home, in the immediate vicinity of an army, prepared for a momentary advance or attack. We were not sure but we should find them fighting when we arrived, and more than once stopped the carriage to listen for the reports of cannon. I began to inquire if there were a dwelling near, where there might be a probability of securing a night's lodging. But, dear me, we had only to cast our eyes on the desolate, ruined homes that were already passed, to imagine what prospect was in store for us.

"It would be nonsense to turn back now we are just there, and not see the Doctor," said the disconsolate wife.

"Oh, Mrs. McGee, do let us go on," exclaimed the girls; "we don't care if we pass the night in the carriage."

Neither the arrangement nor the result of the expedition rested upon me, and reckless as the project seemed, I could not oppose it, and on we went. After the extensive view we had caught from the top of the last hill, we had to descend into a long valley before reaching the village of Centreville. As we were tumbling over the huge rocks, and dipping into the holes of water and mud that were all the deeper from the weight of the many vehicles that had pitched into them as we were now doing, the driver all at once came to a halt, and alighted from his box to gaze mysteriously and in apprehension at one of the back wheels.

"What is it, Tim?—what is it? Speak: what

is the matter?" vociferated Mrs. McGee, in great alarm.

"Dis heah pin, 'twon't hold on I reckon. Dis heah wheel 'll be off, afore we gits many yards furder, I reckon," said Tim.

"What on earth are we to do now?" said Mrs. McGee, in undisguised alarm.

"My goodness!" exclaimed Mollie.

"Goodness alive!" said Bessie.

"How long will it last, Tim?"

"Pends, missus, on how we gets 'long."

A very lucid definition, truly.

"Will it last till we get to the camps, do you think?"

"Pends on how far dey is, missus."

The absurd stupidity of negroes was always amusing in the midst of the most alarming situations; at least to me, and I could not help laughing, 'to save my life,' in Virginia phraseology. Sorry as I was to laugh in such a predicament, it had the effect of restoring the courage of my companions, in a small degree, and Mrs. McGee told Tim to drive very carefully to the first encampment. We had got over one dilemma wonderfully well. This was in being permitted to pass the pickets without any written order. Having depended on her husband's pass and protection, Mrs. McGee had not provided this important key for our party; but her name, and that of her husband's regiment, and the names of the young ladies' brothers and cousins, weighed so far with the natural politeness of the Southern picket, who in defiance of the most stringent laws could scarcely refuse the request of a lady, that he had permitted us to pass—as far at least as the pickets were concerned. We were still directed to go to such an encampment and apply to a General or Colonel whose name I have forgotten, for permission to approach the town; and after a tedious, cautious, nervous jolting, every instant expecting to be tumbled over, we arrived at that important place, obtained the pass, and also some rope, with which the wheel was secured for the remainder of the distance.

Thus strengthened and encouraged, up the hill to Centreville we toiled. Such a desolate, ruined, miserable place! There was the little church which had been so desecrated by the profane and obscene inscriptions of the Federal soldiers; and there was the house that had been the head-quarters of the Federal officers, and where their sumptuous meals had been prepared when the awful chase began.

"Where is the encampment of the 17th Virginia regiment?" asked Mrs. McGee.

"It's just beyond the church." "It's three miles further on." "They are all out on picket duty." "Don't know where it is *now*." "They *were* camped next to such an one." These were the conflicting instructions; every fresh question producing some more perplexing reply.

Another hour of traversing and questioning and the day was fast declining.

The "17th Va." was discovered at last, and we found that we had already passed it twice; but in the secrecy and discipline necessary in camp life, we learned that the soldiers were often ignorant of the name of the regiments, even in their own immediate vicinity. They are coming and going, ordered here or there on pickets or skirmishes, and each man has too much of his own business to attend to, to keep account of his neighbours. Bessie and Mollie were just as much teased in discovering the whereabouts of their brothers; and I did not even attempt to ask for my acquaintances, though several whom I had known at Richmond, it would have been pleasant enough to see again. But if my companions could only find their relatives, that would be all we could expect.

"How do you do, Colonel—Captain—Lieutenant—Mr. B—?" cried Mrs. McGee, as, one after the other, she recognized the Warrenton volunteers.

"This is a great honour, to see you here, ladies," said the officers of the gallant 17th. "McGee has gone to meet you on the battle-ground, but he did not tell us we were to have the pleasure of seeing you in camp."

"Doctor McGee gone!" cried the astonished wife; "this is the second time, I have come to Centreville for nothing."

"Got leave this morning; got his pass, and that's the last we have seen of him."

That "misfortunes never come singly," was a true

statement of our expedition to the battle-ground. Wet weather, no escorts, a broken carriage, and now benighted in the camps. Not a habitable place within miles; the attack imminent. Impossible to venture home on a dark night in a broken carriage, and equally impossible to get another. The elder lady husbandless, the young ones brotherless, the Englishwoman friendless. Perhaps not that exactly with so many kind people surrounding her.

"Well, there is the Doctor's tent at your service, and a capital stove in it too," said the Colonel. "He is the only man who has been able to procure a stove for his tent, lucky fellow!—the only one in the whole regiment."

To repeat all the conversation; the arguments, objections, persuasions, disappointments, and final surrenderings, would be too tedious. It ended, however, in the determination to stay all night in the Doctor's camp—Lieutenant McGee's, of the 17th Virginia regiment; the "Doctor" belonging to his civil, not military profession.

"If we are not safe in the midst of an army of soldiers, I do not know where we should be so," said Mrs. McGee; and as no one else thought of being afraid, of course I did not.

The carriage could not be repaired before the morning, and there was no choice but to make the best of it. And how delighted and proud the soldiers were to wait upon us! They made up such a roaring fire, and brought blankets—new ones, not yet given out to the men, beautiful new blankets—and piled them on the baggage to make comfortable seats. One arranged a cloth upon a large case for a table, and a capital supper soon appeared, cooked by the gallant 17th, of course. If any one of them should ever see these pages, they will remember that day, as we shall ever do. There was a plenty of fresh beef in camp at that time, and an abundant supply of everything. A few weeks before there had not been three days' rations in the army; it was just about the time when the stove-pipe "batteries," and painted logs on Munson's Hill had created such alarm in the Federal camp. We were visiting the army at a more fortunate time, and our supper consisted of excellent beef-steaks, fried potatoes, omelettes, hot rolls and bread, good butter, and hot coffee, the latter not even mixed with rye nor any other substitute. This was officers' fare, but every one will allow that it was a sumptuous supper for a blockaded army; and the breakfast was a repetition of the same viands. The girls were immensely delighted, for they found some acquaintances, though not their brothers. Mrs. McGee, poor thing, was too disappointed, and wondering concerning the fate of her husband, to enjoy herself at all. It was a circumstance in one's life, that night in the camps; but whether the American "armies of sovereigns" are treated with unusual indulgence, or owing to the mutual sympathy engendered by this particular war, it was by no means uncommon for ladies to visit their relatives in the camp; and Mrs. McGee, Mollie and Bessie, were as much at their ease there as anywhere else; excepting that the former turned her anxious eyes towards the entrance every time the canvass was moved on one side.

The soldiers contrived to bring three camp bedsteads into that tent; Mrs. McGee firmly refused to retire to rest, and persisted in sitting up, "in case the Doctor should arrive."

Some very sound refreshing sleep did three of the party obtain in the camp of the army at Centreville, in spite of the biting, penetrating cold and frosty night that set in after the rain, so that we were roasted by the stove on one side, and frozen through our wall-less tenement on the other.

The first thing in the morning Mrs. McGee asked, "Is the carriage mended?" It would be ready by eleven.

A beautiful bracing morning visited us after the yesterday's rain. The Colonel and the Major came to pay their respects to the ladies, and offered to conduct us to see the fortifications; and while the breakfast was being prepared by the soldier cooks, I made a good use of my pencil in sketching the novel and amusing scene. The anticipated attack had not yet been made, and the soldiers said the "Yankees would not make it either."

They amused us with an account of a late gale, which had played sad havoc among the camps.

"The first thing I knew," said one officer, "was the

camp tumbling about my ears, I inside of it: there I was, all in a heap, and could neither find my way out, nor get any one to assist me, so I concluded to lie there till the rain was over." Several others shared a similar fate. One man, after calling in vain from beneath his superabundant covering, managed to slit a small aperture, through which he could peep at his neighbours, and beheld them, some dragged headlong while endeavouring to keep their tents together, some extricating themselves from the soaking folds, and others lying in a heap, tents and all, like himself. "We were ordered off on picket in the midst of the storm," said one company, "our tents were falling and being blown away, but we could not stay to fix them, and found them all of a heap when we returned, three days afterwards." Those who were on picket duty at the time returned to find their tents blown to the breezes, or torn to shreds, and of course with a loss of many valuables besides. One gentleman assured us that his clothes were wet through for three days and nights, adding, goodhumouredly, "It's nothing when you're used to it." Another declared he could now lie down to sleep in a pond, without injury!

More able pens than mine, and more able pencils too, have described all those fortifications at Centreville, over which in such good and *unsuspicious* company I was conducted, and permitted to sketch as much as I pleased. All that autumn the certain set, who expended their patriotism in smoking and grumbling, were loud in their complaints that nothing was done, and the soldiers were "rusting in the camps." There seemed very little indication of rusting in idleness when one contemplated those mounds of batteries and breastworks, and other military arrangements, whose names I scarcely remember. It seemed impossible to take that place, with the guns pointing in every direction. All through the country too, and all along the Potomac, the Southern army had held their ground, and kept back the "grand army of the Potomac" for six months, and yet were "doing nothing." Besides these strong defences, the first policy, approved by all the world, of the Southern President, had been "a defensive warfare," and it has been only by slow degrees, and frightful provocations, that the character of the war has changed, and that a less humane policy has been thrust in self-defence upon the Confederate Government.

Mollie's and Bessie's brothers and cousins were not to be found; they had either been ordered elsewhere, or they were on picket duty. Doctor McGee had not returned, and his wife was impatient to get home.

The repaired carriage duly arrived, and we bid adieu to our kind entertainers of the gallant 17th. There was one lion that we had not seen, the lion in fact of the army at Centreville then. But we caught one peep at him as we were returning home.

Just as we were descending the rocky street of

the village, a horseman appeared. "There's General Beauregard!" I cried inadvertently, quite forgetting that the window was down, and really not intending to speak so distinctly. The General heard his name, and thinking no doubt that he might be sought for by some one, considerately stopped to allow his horse to drink some water from a muddy pool.

"Where is he?" exclaimed Mrs. McGee, putting her head out of the other window, "for I want to ask him——."

"Here, this side—here he is," we whispered.

But the General's horse did not relish the muddy water, and was impatient to be off, therefore he reared and plunged and showed off his rider to great advantage, whose grave, reserved, reflecting, and somewhat sad face commanded deference and sympathy. The General, by this time thinking that after all he was not required, gave one glance at the carriage and rode quietly away. In the meantime Mrs. McGee in a great flurry, with her head out of the other window, was looking this way and that to find some one to tell the General she wished to speak to him; and by the time she had obtained a listener, General Beauregard and staff had ridden beyond reach of ear or eye. It was something even to see him, although I lost the pleasure of an introduction; and I knew him instantly, from the excellent likeness published of the Confederate hero.

The fine weather, on our journey homewards, enabled us really to enjoy the scenery more than it had been possible to do the previous day. An abbatis still surrounded the stone bridge, having been cut away only along a portion of the road; the beautiful woods were fast being cleared in the vicinity of the camps, and it was melancholy to reflect on how many, many miles of the noble "Old Dominion" had been already laid waste by the devastating armies. Fording the stream by the old Stone House we could look up to the ridge of hills on each side of us, and better comprehend the destructive fires of the two opposing lines of batteries.

Several little villages along that road have since taken their place in the history of the war as being the scenes of skirmishes and raids, namely, Gainesville, near where the Manassas railroad crosses the Warrenton turnpike, which consists of only three or four houses and a little tavern; Grovetown, and New Baltimore; the latter being somewhat larger, with some pretty residences near it.

Mrs. Latham had not been in the least alarmed at our absence. She knew we were safe with Mrs. McGee, she said. All the family clustered about us to hear of our adventures, and as for poor Mrs. McGee, after straining her eyes over every road and field, and stopping the carriage at least a dozen times to ask the passers by if they had seen the Doctor, behold the lost Gilpin sitting in her own arm-chair with his little Lizzie on his lap. Mrs. McGee vowed she would never make an appointment on a battle-field again. Of course he had mistaken the place, or the time, or both; and thinking the rain must have prevented our coming at all, he had availed himself of his leave of absence to go home at once; prudently resolving to remain there until the reappearance of his wife. He rather exceeded his "leave," but that was not an uncommon case. "French leave" was, perhaps, more often obtained than that of the General's; but one saw again the "sovereign people" through all these customs. The army of sovereigns had volunteered so willingly, that a great many liberties were winked at. In this case the truant said, "We have just returned from picket duty, and I knew our regiment would not be required again just yet. As for the Yankees, they know better than to attack us, and if I thought we were going to make an advance, I should not have come away in this manner."

Dr. McGee was the First Lieutenant, and generally acting Captain, as his Captain had somehow or other been absent in all the actions in which his company had as yet been engaged.

At the battle of Blackburn's Ford on the 18th July, which was really the opening of the battle of Manassas, the Captain early in the day "sustained a scratch on his ankle," as the First Lieutenant described his wound. It was sufficient to cause him to quit the field. The 1st and 17th Va. regiments had been ordered to the Ford to prevent the crossing of the Federals, but owing to the number of their sick their ranks contained only 1500 men against 5000 of the enemy. It was at this point that the Confederates were engaged, or rather threatened, during the Friday and Saturday, while the main army of the Federals was crossing above the Stone Bridge. Dr. McGee was an intelligent man, and one who had studied human nature. He described the daring courage of many of his men, and yet related how much appalled and paralyzed some of them had been at the opening action. He admitted that the cowards were not all on one side. Lieutenant McGee said he had been astonished to find those whom he had expected to prove the bravest in action—always ready to fight at home, and celebrated among their comrades for courage—seem completely unnerved and lost as soon as the fighting commenced; while others whose fortitude he had doubted, showed themselves the coolest and bravest on the battle-field. One man in his new experience had stood cramped up behind his musket, or crouched upon the earth, sometimes hiding his head, then clasping his hands, exclaiming "Oh my God, my God! I can't stand this!" trembling and crying like a child.

One day four young ladies came to visit at the College, of whom Mrs. Latham afterwards informed me that the two younger had been pupils the previous spring; and just before the summer vacation, that the two elder ones had come to visit in the neighbourhood, their parents intending to follow them and spend the summer at the Springs. They were all residents of Maryland. Hostilities had commenced, and the lines of railway were so suddenly destroyed one after the other that the parents had been defeated in their project, and severed from their children. Here were the sisters visiting about from one family to another, homeless and moneyless, but in excellent spirits. They lived in hopes of getting across to their parents soon, but it was no easy matter at such a time to convey and protect four young girls across the borders into an enemy's country.

After giving up all idea of hearing any more of my Mississippi correspondent, another letter arrived, expressive of a desire that the engagement should be concluded and that I should proceed "immediately" on the journey. "Immediately" was not now so easy to comply with, and the family at the College were treating me in so kind and congenial a manner, that I thought I could do no better than consult them frankly. Dr. Bacon said he knew that part of the country, and the people, and that he was sure I should not find myself agreeably placed there. "Mississippi is one of our Western States, you know," said he, "and the inhabitants of many portions of it continue to dwell almost in the roughness of pioneer life. It is only at such places as Vicksburg and Natchez on the river, where frequent intercourse and commerce have introduced modern refinements, that you will find anything like congenial society. Dr. Bacon said he felt very constrained in offering advice, which might not appear altogether disinterested.

He did not disguise the fact that my services were appreciated. Indeed, many of the parents had called upon me, and invited me to their houses, thanking me warmly for the interest I had manifested in their children, in persuading them to take exercise, &c.—Dr. Bacon very kindly said my sojourn at the College had already been of advantage to the institution, and many more equally gratifying things; which I mention only to show how very much appreciated is even the "taking an interest" in one's occupations, and pupils; so accustomed were the people to have about them those whose interest had been confined to dollar-making only. I am sure I took very little trouble, and led, on the whole, quite an agreeable life; which made me look with regret upon the idea of leaving them. The Doctor and the Professor, while they left me perfectly free to go or stay, proposed to make my salary equal to that offered in Mississippi, should I choose to remain. On the whole, I thought it best to decline Mississippi.

Two days after the resignation had been sent, a letter from the Governor of Florida arrived. He had been one of the first with whom I negotiated, and here was the end of October. It was quite an unbusiness-like letter. Not a single question was answered that I had asked, no information given me respecting his family, his wishes; nothing stated at all; quite a short letter, to say that he would transmit the funds for my journey to Judge

Baker at Richmond, and that he should expect me the first week in January. Was ever any negotiation so strange? One thing more he added in a postscript. "You shall be paid in specie, if you shall desire it in lieu of our Confederate notes." That prospect was more practicable than to be paid in cotton, and as I should possibly require it for travelling, it was an important acquiescence to a request I had made.

Florida had always possessed such attractions that this was a great temptation, and to leave the College at Christmas would not appear so abrupt as to leave it immediately. The Doctor and the Professor admitted the prospects were too favourable to attempt to persuade me to stay, although their friendly manners made me more and more indifferent about leaving them. Therefore I promised that if they could find another pianist to take my place I would resign it at Christmas, and wrote to His Excellency the Governor to tell him to depend on my presence at the appointed time; but in order not to tie myself to a long engagement, I also told him that "in case of the continuation of the war, it would be necessary for me to use every effort to leave the country on the approach of summer." Then I requested him to send me instructions for my journey; for beyond Charleston in South Carolina, it was impossible to learn anything of the route at that distance of nearly a thousand miles. Other business questions were asked, and the letter despatched.

The weather was now setting in with hard frosts, and the difficulty of procuring fuel was very great. The good Doctor had given up his own study, for which a stove could not be found. Other economical and unaccustomed arrangements were obliged to be made throughout the house, and the pupils were shivering and crowding round the drawing-room stove, to the entire exclusion of the two gentlemen, who pretended to be extremely warm rather than disturb the chilly damsels.

One morning as we were walking along the road some little distance from the town, we met three or four waggons loaded with wood evidently cut for sale.

"See those good loads of wood, Miss Jones," said Josie. "Oh *my!* would not Professor Latham be glad to buy them?"

"Let us run home and tell him," said Sallie.

"Where are you going with those loads?" I asked the first driver.

"Gwine into town, mistus; sell 'em."

"Are they for any one in particular?"

"Jes' who wants to buy em, ma'am."

Here was good news. Not engaged for the hospitals or any one.

"Oh *my!*" said Carrie; "if Dr. Bacon would buy all those loads, could we not all have fires in our rooms!"

I told the men where the College was, and gave them to understand that they would be paid a good price for their loads, there; that it was nearly the first house they came to, which would save them the trouble of going all the way into town.

They promised to take their loads as directed, but I had not much confidence in their looks; and we turned homewards, keeping a-head of the waggons. As soon as we arrived at the gate, the girls ran off to inform the Professor of the warmer prospect in view; and looking round I saw waggon the first proceeding straight into town instead of turning down our road. Running quickly up to the corner I stopped waggon the second; and the driver, slow to find an excuse for proceeding, turned towards the College. So did waggon the third, and by this time the children were running up from the gate, with the Professor after them, looking after the precious commodity. He purchased the two loads or "cords" of wood at ten dollars each; two and a half, or three at most, being an ordinary price; and as Mrs. McGee had said, "the waggons have grown very short this year: the stems of the trees are not half their usual length for a cord."

While the wood lasted, the girls had their much-desired fires. There were times, however, when the supply ran so short that it was by no means certain that even the cook would have enough, and then the poor Professor hunted the town and country over, and came back fagged to death. How much anxiety they all suffered! what with the wish to make the pupils comfortable, and to find provisions, and fuel, to say nothing of the war! No wonder people watched anxiously for "recognition" as a means of stopping it. "England wants to see us both entirely crippled before she steps in," said the Professor. "When we are thoroughly weakened, she will urge us to submit to some compromise with her, by which she will assume a power over us, and claim the conquest." Frequently, of late, I had been pained by hearing sentiments of this kind, and what could be answered, except that England did not know the true state of things, nor the character of the Southern people; but that she would never be guilty of such meanness as that. "She respects herself too highly." When they saw it annoyed me to speak in such terms of my country, they forebore to do so, very kindly, but the Professor had often something on his lips to say, then glancing at me it ended in "Humph!" with a quaint sort of smile, as much as to say "I won't say it." All the newspapers went on just in the same way, watching every word and sentiment.

The good news arrived first through a Northern paper, that "the rebel steamer 'Theodora' had landed in safety at Havana, Messrs. Mason and Slidell, the rebel Commissioners to Europe, and that they had been received with the highest consideration by all the officials there."

All eyes were watching the destination of that "grand armada" also, that had been so long under a state of preparation in the North. It was wonderful on what a magnificent scale everything was prepared for that expedition. If they had been going to settle a colony, nothing more could be wanting. But in this, as on a former occasion, Providence seemed to thwart their efforts. The fleet was caught in a storm, and several of the vessels fell into the hands of the Confederates.

The Federal prisoners in Richmond enjoyed greater privileges than we poor British subjects. At one time 500 letters arrived for them, which were sent up from Fortress Monroe under flag of truce. They received letters regularly.

One of our favourite walks at Warrenton was to the Cemetery, from which the view was very beautiful. It was nevertheless a sad walk, for every time we went there we saw the row of the soldiers' graves increasing mournfully. Several of the churches had been turned into hospitals, so had the Court-house and all its offices, and also many other large houses and public buildings. Besides this, private families were devoting themselves to the cause. I heard of one lady who had eleven strangers living in her house at once. Her furniture was entirely ruined by them, and the philanthropy and patriotism displayed in nursing the wounded, were noble indeed. When the relatives of the Southern soldiers discovered their whereabouts, and knew that they were ill, several members of the family might unexpectedly arrive to assist in nursing. It may be supposed that all of these persons were not of the most refined class, and their careless habits were not a little trying to some of the benevolent and more gently reared families, who opened their houses to the sufferers. The Virginians, on their side, felt it their duty and privilege to act the part of the good Samaritan towards those who had forsaken their own States to protect the soil of "Old Virginny," and those same Southerners in many cases felt that they had a right to accept, or almost claim, that hospitality, because they had left their native State unprotected to fight the battles of another. Much diversity of opinion, as of character, one saw in all these things; but I used to mark with what careful impartiality the press would endeavour to award to each State its due share of credit; and to particularize the respective regiments that had distinguished themselves in engagements.

I think it was about this time that one saw more of those vexed sentiments regarding Dr. Russell, to whom was attributed a good deal of the non-recognition principle. The press has much weight among the sovereign people of America, much more so than in England; but why one conscientious individual, whose chief crime was impartiality, was treated so much as the aggressor, I never could discover. We must attribute it to "hope deferred," and the acerbity of accumulated sorrow. Since then the Southerners have enjoyed the means of knowing the truth; and I have not the least doubt but that open hands and doors would greet the London correspondents, were they to revisit the South forthwith.

And now came the report of an event which threw the whole Southern Confederacy into a state of excitement only inferior to that which raged during the attack on Fort Sumter; with this difference, *that* was the signal for war to commence—*this* raised hopes of its being brought to a conclusion.

[From the *Richmond Enquirer*, Nov. 19, 1861.]

"CAPTURE OF MESSRS. MASON AND SLIDELL.—The intelligence was officially received in this city yesterday, that Messrs. J. M. Mason and John Slidell, our ministers to England and France respectively, had been seized by a United States vessel, and are now prisoners in Fortress Monroe! The circumstances of the capture invest an event, important in itself, with extraordinary interest. * * * * * * * *

"This extraordinary act of the Lincoln Government must be followed by important consequences. It is impossible for the English Government, without disgrace, to fail to exact the fullest reparation. If Commodore Wilkes acted under orders, we do not see how Lincoln can possibly escape the most serious complications with the English Government. * * * * * * *

"Lincoln will have to apologize and restore the *status*, or fight. We see no other alternative."

For a time nothing else was thought of and talked of but this "unaccountable act." Whenever a guest arrived it was the first topic to be discussed; and the gentlemen stood rubbing their hands with glee to think that the "growl of the British Lion" would now be heard to frighten the "raving Yankees" into submission. "They have done for themselves entirely; nothing is left them but the choice of war or apology, and in either case they can never lift up their heads again."

"I cannot conceive how they will get out of such a scrape. Why, they might as well have walked into Queen Victoria's drawing-room to arrest them."

CHAPTER VI.

The Attack on Fairfax Court-house—The "Babies" Stand Alone—The Soldier's Wife in Action—Terrible Suspense—Florence and Francis—Novel Mode of Keeping Guard—The Question of National Dignity—Surgeons invited to run the Blockade—Invitations for Christmas—The Professor.

CAPTAIN JOHN QUINCY MARR was buried in that cemetery where we so often walked, and one day on our way thither, Mrs. McGee gave me the history of that first Virginia battle, at Fairfax Court-house on the 1st of June.

This lady was one of those active, practical and lively bodies whom everybody likes. She had been a resident of Warrenton for many years, and had an extensive acquaintance there. Though not particularly energetic themselves, the Southerners admire energy in others. I have often heard them enumerate the practical and useful qualities of their Yankee neighbours with a tranquil admiration, as if some unattainable virtue were exhibited, in the case of particular friends. "Do you remember how Mrs. A. used to do such a thing? how quick she was, and how 'smart!'" Or, "We had a teacher who used to do so and so. Oh! she did do it so quickly." One never perceived any signs of jealousy in such commendations, but simply the admiration of a quality which would appear to be either not in their power or their line of life to attain. Mrs. McGee was one of these busy, sensible little women. She loved the Southerners, and was a favourite among them, especially at the College, where Mrs. Latham's delicate health rendered such qualities highly appreciable.

But to return to the battle of Fairfax Court-house, which my readers will remember followed quickly upon the capture of Alexandria by the Federals; Fairfax Court-house being on one of those lines of road leading directly west from that city. It is quite a village, of perhaps a few hundred inhabitants, or was then, and is the county seat of Fairfax. There is another Fairfax in Culpepper County.

The reader will also remember that at that time it had been difficult to assemble troops and protect the places with sufficient celerity, while the great State of Virginia, with upwards of a thousand miles of exposed borders, including rivers and all, had been suddenly threatened by land and sea. It had not been known by the Federals that Fairfax Court-house was protected at all, but it chanced that the Warrenton Rifles, a company of Infantry belonging to the 17th Virginia, numbering however only eighty men, the rest being on the sick list or absent, had arrived there under Captain Marr the previous day. The Captain who "sustained the scratch," as his comrade jokingly said, on the 18th July, was then First

Lieutenant, and Dr. McGee was Second Lieutenant. The majority of that company were so young that their female relatives had given them the name of the "Warrenton Babies," many of them being only sixteen and seventeen years of age; one had attained his sixteenth year on the previous day. Two companies, the Rappahannock, and the King William Counties Cavalry, had lately arrived under the then Colonel Ewell, since General. The Warrenton Rifles had only reached the place late in the day before. Mrs. McGee, and another lady had gone to Centreville on the 31st May to see their husbands of the "Warrenton Rifles," and on finding they had just been ordered to Fairfax Courthouse, resolved to follow them there, six or seven miles further on the Alexandria road, and where they all had acquaintances, and where they arrived rather late in the evening. Dr. McGee and his wife stopped at the house of their friend Mrs. H. About two o'clock Mrs. McGee was aroused by the tramp of horses and firing of muskets in the village. Alarmed at the confusion that assailed her ears she awoke her husband.

At that moment their hostess rushed into the room, exclaiming, "The Federalists are coming in force, they have driven in our pickets (the cavalry companies), who are dashing through the town calling on us all to fly for our lives." A piece of advice not resting on precept alone, for they were setting the example in right good earnest.

"Where are the Warrenton Rifles?" exclaimed Mrs. McGee.

"Scattering in alarm," said Mrs. H.

In a twinkling Lieutenant McGee was apparelled and armed, and rushed out of the house to the quarters of his company, calling out as he proceeded, "Captain Marr! Captain Marr! where is Captain Marr?"

No one knew, and the few men already assembled were wavering in doubt and ignorance. It appeared that a large force of the Federal cavalry had pursued the cowardly companies of King William and Rappahannock counties through the village to the country beyond, and no one appeared, who was prepared to take the command of the few infantry still remaining there.

Therefore Colonel Ewell assumed the command of the forty-three members of the "Warrenton Babies," all who could be collected, and who were drawn up to receive the enemy on their return, and deployed behind a fence, preparing to make a stand. Colonel Ewell then advanced to receive the enemy, who were galloping back firing right and left in the darkness. "Are you friends or foes?" cried the Colonel, as he called upon them to halt. This gallant officer had rushed from his bed, without stopping to complete his attire, and even in the darkness of midnight, his white shirt was too sure a mark. A shot in the shoulder was the only reply he received. Thus for a time disabled, Colonel Smith ("Extra Billy,") took the command, being accidentally in the place at the time. A firing was kept up for about half an hour. Several times the Federal officers were heard to give the command to charge; but the men persisted in their refusal.

"*Charge*, I tell you, you —— cowards!" cried the Federal officer.

"I tell you we shan't do it; you won't catch us charging at that battery," said the cautious Yankees.

"I tell you they are only civilians; they have no batteries, you cowardly scoundrels!"

"You needn't tell us civilians can aim as they do, and our men falling like ten-pins."

Such was the conversation between the Federal officers and their sovereign men. Providence, so wonderfully displayed in those first actions, turned against them their own fears; the dreaded "battery" of their distorted vision was no more than a pair of old cartwheels, lying in the road by mere accident. Thus was the very darkness in which the enemy sought to disguise their own strength, turned against them; while they continually exclaimed, in order to terrify the invaded host,- "We are backed by 5000 men—you had better surrender at once." Be that as it may, their bravery lasted but a short half-hour. Their shots had been as usual quite too high, whereas the little band of forty-three were bringing to the ground an enemy with every bullet; until deceived in the numbers of the defenders, the Federal cavalry scampered off in their accustomed disorder, leaving the road strewed with muskets, hats, caps, coats and knapsacks.

Of course, the sudden appearance of the soldiers galloping home in the early dawn, created a great commotion among the country people, who reported that they had seen three waggon loads of dead and wounded men, counted fifteen horses galloping riderless, and several dead ones. Ten horses were captured near the village, but the precise number of killed and wounded was never ascertained.

Where was Mrs. McGee all this time? Shaking in her shoes, and weeping, with clasped hands, in her apartment? Not she, the wife of a Confederate soldier.

Following her husband to the street, she had cried out, "Where are the Warrenton Rifles?" and, regardless of self, entreated him not to leave his company. Then she made her way to the Court-house, where were the officers' quarters. In the darkness she groped about, feeling for matches; a box of them had been thrown on the floor by accident—they betrayed themselves as she rubbed them with her feet. Having lighted one, she next discovered a candle. Kindling this, she immediately set to work. The coat of Captain Marr rolled up for a pillow, told where he had been lying on the floor. This and the other officers' coats, and her husband's chattels, she rolled up in a compact bundle, and lay ready to be carried off. A quantity of new coats and other garments had just been brought for the use of the company, but not yet distributed. She was not going to leave such valuables in the hands of the invaders; no, indeed; for had she not helped to make them, and should she now lose them so easily? All were collected into the smallest compass. Next she went in search of the man in charge of the carriage, to order that, and have the clothes laid in it. She crossed the road to peer through the darkness in the direction from whence came the whizzing of musketry. A mounted trooper espied her, and cried out "Who's there? A woman, by Heaven!"

"It is I, Mrs. McGee," said the courageous woman.

"Mrs. who?" said the voice.

"Lieutenant McGee's wife, of the Warrenton Rifles."

"What in the world are you doing there?"

"I want to see what is going on."

"You had better go home, madam, than occupy such a dangerous position; you may be shot at any moment."

"I want to find out where my husband is; I must wait awhile."

"This is no place for a woman, madam! By Heaven! if you don't go into the house, I'll run this sword through your body," he added as she still lingered.

With this friendly threat to secure her safety, the courageous lady was compelled to obey; and she waited until the firing had ceased, and the noise of retreating troops told her that the fighting was over, at least for a time. Then day beginning to dawn she again ventured forth, and soon encountered some of the 'Warrenton Babies.'"

"Where is Dr. McGee?" exclaimed the anxious wife.

"I do not know," said one.

"I heard him give the command to fire," said another.

"But where is he *now*?" repeated the devoted wife, trembling violently.

"Oh, he's safe enough, I dare say."

"But where? tell me where you left him!" stammered she, becoming dreadfully alarmed.

"I don't know anything about him, madam," said one.

"I reckon he's all right," said a second.

"I have not seen him since the fight," said a third.

Poor Mrs. McGee, pale as a corpse, put out her hand to grasp the fence in self-support. A sort of stupor seized her; her lips quivered, and she tried in vain to speak again. Seeing her agitation several of the men continued to declare "he's all right," "safe enough," &c., and yet could give no definite information. Some of them undertook to return to make inquiries respecting him, when three or four men were seen to approach bearing a body into a house on the opposite side of the road. Those streets of the Virginia villages are very wide roads, with plenty of trees among them, looking more like what we should call "the village green." The wife and woman flew. Like a flash of light she was gone, and stood by the side of the body. On seeing it, she breathed afresh with hope revived; it was not her husband, but Colonel Ewell. The wound was only a flesh one, but he had neglected it until he felt faint from loss of blood, which in streaming over his shirt sleeve presented a terrible appearance. Her suspense again aroused was not much longer tried. Lieutenant McGee, at the head of ten men, had been ordered to the outposts to catch the stragglers who had been dismounted, and were prowling about in the neighbourhood, and his return was uncertain. "Thank God, he is safe!" exclaimed the wife, with a deep sigh of relief. None of the brave riflemen, or 'boys,' literally, were injured. Only Captain Marr, and where was he?

When those two terrified cavalry companies who had been on picket duty, came galloping through the town, incoherently giving notice of the approach of thousands of Federal troops, in accordance with their own statement, followed by the Federal soldiers yelling and shouting, and scouring the country in pursuit of the Confederates, Captain Marr had rallied his company, and having arranged as many as could be found, went forward to reconnoitre, saying he would endeavour to discover the force of the enemy; but he never returned. At eight o'clock the next morning his body was found lying in a field by the side of the road. He had not even taken time to buckle on his sword, both sword and belt being grasped tightly in the hand of death. It was supposed that one of the random shots fired in the darkness by the Federal cavalry had caused his death, because behind the trees it was scarcely possible that he had been distinguished. He died an honourable death, "the first hero on Virginian soil," as Mr. Quence had said. He was a single man, of about thirty-eight years of age, leaving a mother and two sisters who had depended on him for support. The whole town of Warrenton had attended his funeral and wept over his grave—a quiet unobtrusive grave, with a simple square marble slab to mark his remains. Ah! sad experiences of war! Five months from that time, and scores would not number the graves of the soldiers committed to the soil of the Warrenton cemetery.

There were two other heroes of that Fairfax skirmish, whose adventures were happily of a less melancholy character. Two of the Warrenton rifle company, named Florence and Francis, had been stationed half a mile from the village. When the retreating Confederate cavalry had gallopped past them announcing the approach of 5000 Federalists, Francis leaped over a fence into a field, and Florence turned with a rapid pace towards the town, and on being overtaken by the Federals cried out to them to halt. They did, but soon discovering that only one solitary foe was present, and he a foot soldier, a Federal horseman rode up and leaning forward, seized him by the arm, ordering him to surrender. Then the poor powerless prisoner was grasped by each hand between two horsemen, and dragged at a quick trot into the town, and on, between his captors in pursuit of the flying cavalry, through a back street to the country beyond.

Meanwhile Francis had run at the utmost extent of his speed, and reached the village, giving notice of their approach, which had enabled Captain Marr to collect and deploy his forty-three men.

And what became of the trotting Florence? Still held between his mounted enemies, was he going to stand and be shot at by his own friends and companions? No; watching his opportunity he dropped upon his hands and knees, having jerked himself from the grasp of his tyrants, and clutched at his cap to boot, which had felt of so attractive a form and texture, that it had been appropriated with his musket by one of his captors. Crawling and leaping in the darkness, dodging among the horses, away scampered Florence, but being too bold in his escape, he did not retreat to a sufficiently safe distance, and being pursued, he was again "grabbed" by the collar of his coat; slipping like an eel from his covering, and leaving his coat in the soldier's hands, a second time he got away, and to a safe distance now. The next morning, when the "fun" was over, he strolled along the road which the retreaters had taken. It was early day, and he was seeking for spoil to solace himself for his strained limbs and lost garments, when by good luck he espied and picked up, first his cap, then his own precious musket, and lastly his coat; all of which had been dropped in the flight of the Federalists.

Thus the little band of forty-three infantry, with Lieutenant McGee at their head, won their first laurels. None of them had ever been in action before; nearly all were young, and had only just enlisted. Eighty-seven mounted troopers, of well-armed, and well-drilled regular troops, had been dispersed and half annihilated. The very darkness seemed to have protected them, while their cowardly companions had scattered over the country. One excuse was made for those two cavalry companies: they were armed with sabres only, and had been deceived by the darkness, and the assertion of the enemy as to his real force.

On the death of their Captain, the Lieutenants were promoted; Dr. McGee, by another accident, continuing to bear the honours of succeeding actions. These were the gallant men who had entertained us so hospitably in the camp at Centreville.

As Mrs. McGee was returning home the next day, she met one of the truant riflemen who had fled at the approach of danger. It was quite evident that he had run away, although when she asked him, "Why, how is it that you are here, away from your company?" he answered, "Oh, I am keeping guard here." Guard! Six miles in the wrong direction.

Some excessively cold weather set in about that time. In our high regions thick ice covered the ground for several weeks. Ponds were frozen, and plenty of ice might have been collected for the following summer; but the good Virginians are not prone to be too much in a hurry. It was "only November," "time enough yet;" therefore none was collected. The unfortunate result of procrastination, was a very mild winter; and but little steady frost caused a second summer of serious deprivation for want of that important commodity.

"All the South will depend on Virginia for ice," said Dr. Butler. "I wish our people would learn to 'take time by the forelock.'"

The capture of Messrs. Mason and Slidell drove all the heads of the Confederacy to their law books. One got quite tired of reading long law articles about international and naval rights and privileges, "high seas," and the "dignity of flags." In the interim of waiting for that "onward movement" of the army at Centreville, that was to surprise Washington, Philadelphia, and New York, or if from the "Grand Army of the Potomac," to result in the capture of Richmond, Petersburg, and Lynchburg, and with a temporary lull in Kentucky and Missouri, quotations from legal treatises filled up the columns of the papers. The English feeling was watched with more intensity than ever, and every indication of public sentiment was transcribed only to replace quotations from law books. When it was seen, on the arrival of news from England, that the leading London papers were "violently resenting the outrage," and that "the blood of all England was roused by the intelligence," it was taken as another indication that nothing short of a war with England could result; excepting the most humiliating apologies of Seward, who was looked upon as the chief agent of the Federal Government.

It was not often one saw the Northern President to be very severely abused by the Southern press. There were members of the Federal cabinet who came in for a very large share of contumely, but President Lincoln was spoken of in terms of quiet contempt, as a person of no particular consequence one way or another.

One day Sallie, Bettie, and little Lizzie McGee went with me on a shopping expedition in the town. One of the desired articles we hoped to procure at a druggist's, of whom there had been three in Warrenton. One store was closed, being quite "sold out;" another had just sold the last ounce of the article to the hospitals: and the third promised to send to Nashville "next week" for the required medicine. Next we went to the shoemaker's. Poor man! what with his workmen all enlisted, and his materials so scarce, it was a slow process to get shoes, or even to have them repaired. He said he had been waiting, I forget how long, for shoe-thread. "That stuff they make here is of no use at all; our people have not got into the way of it yet." He said that a British brig had just come into a port in North Carolina with a cargo almost entirely of shoe-thread, and that it had all been "bought up" by one man, who had given so many dollars a pound for it—three, if I remember rightly. However, the captain had cleared $9000 on his cargo. I felt rather ashamed of my captain countryman who drove such unmerciful bargains with an oppressed and striving country. A soldier came into the store while we were there, and took up a pair of boots, asking the price. "Thirteen dollars, Cap'n," said the shoemaker. The "Cap'n" was a poor private, to judge by his appearance. "Thirteen dollars!" he muttered to himself, with a wistful look at the boots; "that is just my month's pay." And the boots were replaced with a sigh. Great inducements were being made to persuade people to collect and tan the hides that had been allowed to lie about the fields in the vicinity of the camps. We had passed repulsive heaps of them, engendering disease where health was so indispensable. For a long time it was nobody's business, and the Southerners were untrained to saving anything. Then persons were appointed to collect them, and so many country people commenced the operation of tanning, that after a time the army became abundantly supplied with shoes, not perhaps of so excellent a form and finish as they had been accustomed to wear: still they served the purpose.

Warrenton, Culpepper Court-house, Gordonsville, Charlotteville, Fredericksburg, in fact, every town and village throughout the north of Virginia, was a collection of hospitals. Oh! how I used to wish a ship-load of European doctors would find their way through the blockade; Never was a better opening for young surgeons, or, indeed, for any enterprise. It was frightful to walk through the town, and see within the open doors rows of pallets containing so many scores of sufferers. During that autumn the deaths in Warrenton alone amounted to six or seven a day. The soldiers were sometimes brought dying from the camps. The men were averse to yield to sickness, and fought against it, till an aggravated form endangered them before they were aware of it. Then so many had to be conveyed away, with so few accommodations to convey them in, that in certain cases they were brought to the hospitals merely to breathe their last. Other evils, in the lack of wholesome arrangements and ample medicines caused life to hang upon a very feeble thread; every regulation had to go through the hands of Government, and this caused other delays. Never did a Government work so hard and untiringly. That Judge Baker of Florida, whom I had known in Richmond, was once speaking of the difference he observed in the loyalty displayed by the clerks in his office. He said he knew directly who were true Southerners, by their zeal and contentment. Those who were aiming at the highest salaries he felt sure were not true to their situation. "It is of no use to apply to us if you are not willing to work," he said. A good many of the government offices were just opposite to the American Hotel, and I have seen the lights burning in them at all times in the night, and known that the devoted servants of the Confederacy were labouring in untiring zeal. Such a difference in that respect existed between the two Governments! No perquisites, no money-making contracts and frauds were heard of in the South, but such as were traced to Jews or Yankees.

It happened one day that a German professor of music, who had been giving lessons at Culpepper, came to the College to enlist the Doctor's and the Professor's interest and influence to recommend pupils to him in Warrenton, for he said nearly all the families had left Culpepper, "and I have no more de sc*o*-lars daar." Some of my pupils had taken lessons of him, and did him much credit; and although a lady musician was preferred by the majority, the Doctor thought it as well to engage *Mein Herr* to take my place, which would at once set me free at Christmas, according to our stipulation.

This change of plans was not made known to the pupils, in order not to interrupt their application. They all "took" a holiday at Christmas, and several of them, thinking I should spend that period at the College, invited me to go home with them.

"Oh *do*, Miss Jones," said Bessie of Rappahannock; "our house is mighty high up on the mountains, you will enjoy the view so much."

"I know mamma will be very glad for you to go home with me," said Allie.

Poor dear affectionate children! perhaps this year they have no homes to go to themselves!

So I summoned courage to leave these new and kind friends, though not without many scruples of conscience and hesitations of judgment, and I wrote to Mrs. Ayres and Mrs. Henningsen, to tell them I should see them *en route*. It would be necessary to stay a day or two in going through Richmond, and as Mrs. Este had again written to remind me of the Christmas engagement, it was arranged that I should leave Warrenton on the 24th, which would give me time to take the journey quietly, and enable me to spend a few days at Charleston and Savannah, two places I had greatly desired to visit, particularly as at the former city I had several friends, or who soon proved themselves such.

My short stay at Warrenton had been productive of great pleasure, and benefit as well. My health had been wonderfully strengthened, and the cheerful, agreeable society and cultivated minds of the Doctor, Professor Latham and his wife, had been a source of both entertainment and instruction. Besides these advantages, I had seen a battle-field, and visited the grand army at Centreville; had not once been doubted or suspected, but on the contrary, had been entrusted with some important revelations, out of which who knows what mischief might not have been made! I liked and respected the people all the more from having done them injustice in my first prejudices; and what conversation we did engage in, on the subject of baptisms and immersions, so won me over, that I told Dr. Bacon that had I not been already baptized, I would now be so, by *immersion*. In his own mind he did not consider that first baptism as a rite at all, so that my reason or excuse no doubt appeared to him to be null and void!

I bade adieu to Mrs. Latham in her chamber; she was quite an invalid, suffering from great debility too; and already it had become almost impossible to procure the stimulants she required. Her bright face had sunken sadly within a few weeks, but she was trusting in the frost to brace her up again.

Warrenton has since that time fallen into the hands of the Federals. The fine college building, with its beautiful meadow, so full of rare trees and shrubs of the Doctor's own planting, was really seized and appropriated as a hospital, but not by friends. What became of the family I know not, with one exception, and I may as well say here, that the Professor, driven from his home and occupation, the following spring, enlisted, fell a victim to camp fever, and died a few weeks afterwards! As for his poor lonely wife and their three little darling children, I have never learned their fate, nor that of their kind and excellent father and his other daughters. Oh! little did we think of such a future when the Professor, on that fine, frosty, lovely morning, conducted me to the railroad, and took such a hopeful leave. I had brightened them all up, he said. How kind they were! He was going home to write school-books, grammars, and theories, all of which were "sold out," and no longer to be procured in the South. One of his sensible speeches I well remember, on speaking of the lack of new books, and that was, "If it will lead people to read up all they already have upon their shelves, and to make themselves thoroughly acquainted with the standard authors, it will be of great advantage to them to be without new books for some time to come." He so often said, "We are saving a great deal by the blockade. As soon as it is raised, our people will spend large sums of money for articles that they are now doing very well without, or learning to make for themselves. Necessaries we have at home, or shall soon produce: luxuries we can easily dispense with."

All the Bessies, and Kitties, and Mollies, and Allies went off in the best of spirits for their Christmas holidays. Excepting when any danger threatened their near relatives, the war did not weigh very heavily on their young buoyant spirits.

Dr. Bacon took great care to remunerate me in funds that would present no difficulties in travelling, paying me in full, and even more than I expected, for my pleasant stay at Warrenton. Nothing but kindness had I received there, none but friends were left behind, nor did one of us then anticipate the sad fate of Warrenton!

CHAPTER VII.

Fellow-Travellers—A state of Uncertainty—Finding an Escort—Christmas Day.

THE moment one entered a railway-carriage in those days, one was surrounded by sad scenes. In the present case my fellow-travellers comprised both killed and wounded, as well as hospital patients. Several seats were occupied by the 'maimed and the halt," by those who were propped by pillows, and by those who were led or supported on the shoulders of their friends. There were some only just able to be moved, who had lain at Warrenton ever since the battle of Manassas; and one man sat near me who had his arm in a sling; and I heard him give an account of the skirmish at Dranesville that had just taken place, where the Federals had stretched a wire across the road, and lay in ambush to attack the pickets, who were thus unexpectedly brought to a stand.

On the platform at the Junction I saw several

coffin-like cases, with a name, address, and the age of the individual marked upon each, generally having also the name of the regiment of which the enclosed corpse had been a member,—the mortal remains of some dear one being conveyed to his last resting-place!

A strange porter handed me up to the old familiar reception-room at the American Hotel; strange faces greeted me; a stranger showed me my room—the very next one to that I had occupied the preceding summer, and next also to Mrs. Ayres' apartment: that at least was pleasant. Soon I ran down to Mrs. Henningsen's room on the floor below.

"Come in," said a very faint voice in answer to my tap on the door,—and there lay my poor friend, so changed, and thin, and wan, just recovering from a dangerous fit of illness. She had devoted herself to the invalid soldiers and hospitals, sitting up so frequently all night long, that her own constitution had given way, and she had been for several weeks confined to her bed. As is the case with many who are most zealous and self-sacrificing in health, no sooner does sickness or misfortune befall them than they are left alone. She who had been the centre of a brilliant circle when adorned with health and smiles, was now lying on her couch of suffering without a friend at hand.

"Where was Mrs. Ayres?"

"She comes to see me when she can; but she is incessantly occupied with the cares of the house and family, and with so many sick soldiers."

"Where was Mrs. ——, that lady from Pennsylvania?"

"Oh, do you not remember what you thought of her? Well she has been discovered sending letters to the North; she was seen about the places where the prisoners are, and was watched. She and her husband managed to find out a great many of the Government plans, which they communicated to the North; they are still in the city however!"

All the summer visitors had gone home to the South, and quite "a new set" had come, of whom, owing to Mrs. Henningsen's illness, she knew nothing. Poor lady! how glad she seemed to see me and keep me with her, until warned by the hour that the last cup of tea might be undrinkable.

The first thing the next day was to seek Judge Baker. He had not heard from the Governor, neither had he received any remittance for my journey. Was I sure that the engagement was conclusive, and that the Governor expected me? I showed him His Excellency's letter; which he agreed was quite decisive, and added, "Perhaps we shall hear from him in a day or two." I did not particularly object to wait "a day or two," as it would give me an opportunity of seeing the Castletons and other friends, and, above all things, of preparing another goodly packet of letters to run the blockade at Charleston, which I intended, or rather hoped to get accomplished through the influence of some friends. Then, as I was proceeding to such a warm climate, I had been very busy knitting up every scrap of wool, and converting other warm materials into little comforts for Mrs. Henningsen to distribute among her *protégés*, until people had asked me, "Do you never intend to be cold again?" Never mind, I had brought an ample supply of items from England last year, and it was not probable that these things would be needed by me, as I intended to go home if the war should continue; and if it did not, we could all procure whatever we might require. It was satisfactory even in such insignificant actions, to let the people know that one humble British subject sympathised in their deprivations.

It was a great pleasure to see the Castleton family again, and to hear of their friends in the war. Rebelfield was also in Richmond, and he accomplished some arrangements for me to be a Florida correspondent of one of the Richmond papers, which engagement, my residence in the Governor's family at the capital, would enable me to meet without any difficulty.

Still the Governor neither wrote nor sent remittances, and how could I be in Florida by the 1st of January? 'Tis true I had sufficient funds to travel with, but it was embarrassing not to know how to proceed, and again I consulted Judge Baker. This extremely cautious gentleman did not venture to advise me; therefore after consulting others of my friends who were more willing to give an opinion, I decided to wait no longer. What with the continued irregularity of the mails, the winter floods of Florida, and the Governor's unbusiness method of forming engagements, I might wait at the hotel till my "purse of *paper*," this time, was once more empty.

Of course I saw the British Consul, Mr. Cridland, who was deeper than ever in the pressure of unconsular business, spending his days in convincing crowds of applicants that he could not assist them to send letters, nor to obtain remittances; and a great part of his nights in his real consular business of writing. So he told me, and his looks bore witness to his labours. English friends were then too valuable to be neglected,—and he gave me a letter of introduction to Mr. Bunch, the Consul at Charleston, already partially known as a correspondent.

Travelling was so interrupted, dangerous, and disagreeable at that time, that my friends had made inquiries to find a pleasant escort for me. A Doctor Johnston, a Virginian gentleman in the Ordnance department, was going to Florida, and was introduced to me; after which he was prevented from leaving so soon; Major Yancey, a brother of the W. L. Yancey, Commissioner to England, was going as far as Alabama, and he was also stopping at the hotel, intending to leave on the same day I had fixed upon. Better than all, Captain Simkins was going all the way to the Florida Convention, and through Charleston, therefore he would be quite the right person. "Such a very fine man," my friends informed me; "fine" being a quality referring only to mental not personal perfections, and used in the same signification as "estimable".

in England. Captain Simkins was introduced, and undertook the "honour" of taking charge of me with a great many polite expressions, as if he, not I, were the obliged party. It must appear strange to English ladies, with the delicate reserve implanted by education and association, to read of a fellow-countrywoman undertaking a journey of hundreds of miles under the care of an entire stranger. In those war times the confusion and probable delays rendered it impossible for a lady to travel alone. I had also both confidence in those friends who selected the escort, and in the correct deportment of a Southern gentleman; and it would have been much more inconsistent for a lady to travel alone at a time when only those who were really compelled to do so, travelled at all, the army monopolizing roads, hotels, officials, and every other convenience. Nevertheless, it was a long dreary journey to contemplate, with such an uncertain destiny in view. Virginia had given me so many kind friends that it was like leaving home again to go so far away, though far as it was, I was encouraged with the hope of seeing several Richmond people at Tallahassee. Colonel Este was going down there on business shortly, and Mrs. Este promised to send by him all sorts of good things of her own preparation, to remind me of the Christmas party at her house. Judge Baker thought of going home soon, and perhaps he would not be quite so over-cautious when we met again.

Thus passed a second Christmas week at Richmond. A year ago the inhabitants had been trying to realize the possibility of war, and the gloom was even greater then than now. Again were the slaves running wild on their holiday excursions, and their masters and mistresses were driven to their wits' ends to provide them their accustomed and expected presents, or to procure a sufficient supply of small notes, and coin, to meet the never-failing demand of "Christmas Gif," which assailed one at every turn. Our "Egg Nog," handed round the first thing on Christmas morning, savoured strongly of the blockade; good brandy being substituted by vile whiskey. We also missed our organist, who had "gone North," and our Christmas anthem at St. Paul's church; but, on the whole, the week passed as happily as one dared hope, under the circumstances of war and exile.

CHAPTER VIII.

Southwards—Watching for the Palmetto—Curiosity to behold a Slave-driver—Southern Indifference—Arrival at the hot-bed of Secession—The Conflagration at Charleston—The Battery and Churches—Reverence for England—The Mill's Hotel—"Forsaken" Slaves—Escape of the "Ella Warley"—Fort Sumter.

On a first glance at the travellers who were proceeding southwards, one might have thought that the campaign in Virginia was over. The second look informed one that the majority were merely going home to be nursed, some probably to be buried, who had not much hope of surviving even the journey; some certainly to be buried, for there were the same coffin-like looking cases standing on the platforms, three in one place, two at another, with a melancholy sad-looking friend, who kept near and watched over his case with a solemn care. Sad scenes and sorrow wherever we go.

In the same carriage or "car" in which Captain Simkins and I were riding, was another officer, attended by a young and fragile-looking lady, and apparently her family of several small children, with a negro nurse. My escort recognized him thus: "Parkhill! Halloo! what are *you* deserting too?" The gentleman addressed came forward, and was introduced to me as Captain Parkhill of Florida. He said to his friend, "The truth is, I am tired of staying there doing nothing. We have had our batteries in trim I do not know how long, and cannot get those cowardly 'Yankees' to attack us. They won't venture close enough even for a shot. Just a few small craft pass by, hugging the Maryland shore, and that's all." Then I found out that Captain Parkhill had had command of the batteries at Evansport, on the Potomac, and he added, "If there had been any chance of fighting, you would not have seen me here, so I am going down to that Convention, and to take my wife home, for she finds it too cold in Virginia." It was the 2nd of January, 1862, when I set out on my journey to Florida. Our route lay directly south from Richmond. Already a great change was perceptible in the temperature. The last few weeks at Warrenton had been dry and frosty. At Richmond the frost had turned to slush, and by the time we reached Wilmington, in North Carolina, the end of the first day's journey, the frost had turned to rain. I had friends at Wilmington, an English lady married to a German physician, whom I had met frequently in Richmond during the summer, and with whom I had corresponded occasionally since. They had invited me to visit them, and I much wished to stay at least one day to see Wilmington, and the present lion of the town, which was a sword and bayonet factory lately established there. Could one have avoided travelling all night by stopping, I should certainly have done so, but the Southern train ran only once in twenty-four hours. It was nine o'clock when we arrived at Wilmington, and it would be necessary to proceed at the same hour the next night, besides which one must undergo the inconvenience of changing tickets, losing my escort, and probably my luggage into the bargain; therefore I was induced to give up the pleasure of seeing Wilmington, and we proceeded to cross the river by a ferry in the dark, when I almost *felt* the interesting scenery, without being able to behold it. Those night journeys were so provoking.

After leaving Wilmington we soon crossed the borders into South Carolina, the Palmetto State, the "hotbed of Secession," the "source of the rebellion," the everything that was bad; and one felt a singular kind of conscience struggling against a perverseness which made me rejoice to be in the Palmetto State at last, where, sad to confess, I knew so many nice people who had been in Virginia of late.

There is not much comfort in sleeping in a railway carriage, particularly if it be so crowded that one must sit erect, as if in a stiff straight chair; and I was growing much too impatient to see palmetto trees to sleep, even had the seat been more comfortable. Already the softened temperature admitted of the window being opened, and I was peering through the darkness, watching the outlines of the trees against the sky, to catch the first feathery form of the veritable palmetto. Not much variety could I detect in the uncertain glimmer, and the approach of dawn revealed only the same thick woods of pine that had, without intermission, lined the road all through the "Old North State," the name by which North Carolina is known. Pines, pines, nothing but pines —when shall we behold the now historical palmetto?

Major Yancey had come into our car. Everybody appeared to know each other, or soon to become acquainted. Every one spoke of the war, of course, and of the late lull in the Virginian engagements, and these were the constant remarks I heard:—"There is no prospect of fighting up there, so I concluded I would come home and attend to my business for a while." "I have resigned because it isn't worth while to be doing nothing in camp while my plantation needs looking after." "Just as soon as I hear they're going to fight I'll go back." "Any prospect of an attack up your way?" "No; you wouldn't have seen me here if there had been." And so on. "I didn't give up my business, or leave my family to go and get chills and fever in the camps; I went up there to fight, and if they are not going to fight I may as well be at home."

Major Yancey had been on the Peninsula. He had not heard from his brother in England for many months, and could not conjecture when he should be able to do so. He entertained me with some very amusing anecdotes of his own experiences regarding English prejudice, one or two of which may be mentioned here. The Major was once returning from a European trip, and met on board the "Persia" a young lady, who, with her mother and brother, was about to make a tour through the States. The young lady was pronounced a *belle*; she was accomplished and wealthy, and possessed of all those qualities which render such persons popular in a mixed company. Major Yancey, among others, made her acquaintance, and by the time they had been a week on board, had become on somewhat friendly terms. One day she said to him, "Oh, Mr. Yancey, they tell me there is a 'slave-driver' on board. I have heard so much of slave-drivers that I am most anxious to see one."

The Major asked her what she expected to see in a "slave-driver" that caused her to be so "anxious" about it.

She recounted the various qualities in which slave-holders are supposed to shine, much to the amusement of her companion, who then informed her that he was acquainted with the person to whom she alluded, and he wished her to look round among the passengers, and endeavour to detect those enumerated qualities in one of the guests, and see if she could discover the "slave-driver." She was a long time in deciding; but at last selected a heavy-browed, dark-eyed, bushy-haired man, and pointed him out to Major Yancey as approaching the most nearly to her estimate of the "slave-driver." She had selected a plodding, phlegmatic, metaphysical German, about the last man on board to whom the qualities she had mentioned were likely to be applicable. The Major told her she had mistaken the individual, and persuaded her to scrutinize her travelling companions a little more closely. She soon gave up the search as hopeless, and told her friend he must point out the man to her.

"Madam, he has the honour to address you at this moment," said Major Yancey, with a low bow, at the same time quietly turning away.

Now it happens that Major Yancey has a particularly mild, quiet, guileless expression of countenance, what I can only define as a Southern expression, seen nearly always in Southerners of mature years. Dr. W. of Essex, the Hon. R. M. T. Hunter, Mr. Bledsoe, Dr. Bacon, Professor Latham, and many of my friends had that same expression of face, which at first I used to think of as "the Virginia expression," but found it was not confined to Virginia, therefore my readers will permit me to call it the "Southern expression;" and when they travel through the Confederacy, they will judge for themselves of what it is like.

Our *belle* tried to recall all she had said, in a most disconcerted frame of mind, and took the first opportunity to ask forgiveness.

"My dear young lady," returned the slaveholder, "do not for one moment distress yourself, we are so accustomed to hear ourselves spoken of in this manner, that we take no notice of it at all. It is of no consequence to us what people choose to call us; we understand ourselves, and that is enough."

He then said that as she and her mother were intending to visit New Orleans, they must pass within no very great distance of his plantation, and that if they would honour him by a visit he should have great pleasure in showing her the home and servants of the "slave-driver."

The trio did subsequently visit Mr. Yancey's plantation in Alabama, and probably gave their own impressions to their English friends.

As a proof of the indifference of the Southerners to popular opinion, which has been more than ever to be lamented within the last few years, Major Yancey related another circumstance, of which I regret that I can only recall the outlines, but it was a *ruse* that went the round of both Northern and English papers at the time, and may probably be recalled by many of my readers.

Two young English gentlemen were *en route* from one city to another in the South,—Charleston to Savannah, if I remember right. They had just arrived, and knew of the slaveholders only through educational prejudice. With as little caution as that displayed by our fair friend, and perhaps with some tinge of that superciliousness not uncommon in Young England abroad, they entered into conversation with a travelling companion, whom they questioned concerning the Southern character, asking if it were true that slaveholders were so passionate that they always carried loaded revolvers and bowie-knives, and stabbed people on the slightest provocation?* The person addressed chanced to be both a Southerner and a slaveholder, and, seizing the capital opportunity for a joke, replied in a grave undertone—

"Yes, indeed; such is the awful state of society in the South, that we cannot feel ourselves safe from hour to hour. Let me advise you to be very careful not to provoke these people. I see you are strangers, and perhaps you have not heard of a dreadful affair that took place on this very road a week or two ago. Two slaveholders were travelling together, one of whom had his wife and child with him. The men got to quarrelling, and became so excited that at last A seized B's child by the feet, dashed its head against the wall, and threw it out of the window. The mother, screaming and frantic, rushed to the door, and B in an instant presented his pistol and shot A dead on the spot. The confusion was awful; I never heard of such a scene in my life."

The young Englishmen resolved to get through their

* Some travellers may have had reason to believe that this condition of society still prevails in the South, and the reader is carried away with that impression; not being aware that in the recently settled, and more Western States, the inhabitants have been inured to a life of almost lawless ferocity, engendered in them by living within dangerous proximity of savage Indians, wild animals, and the refuse of society who have repaired to those far-off States to fly from justice, or prosecute their roving pursuits as hunters and trappers. Parts of Mississippi, Arkansas, Western Missouri, and Texas are still in this pioneer condition.

business and escape with all speed from such a dangerous people; and when they arrived at home, related the circumstance, which was forthwith published in the London newspapers. Another Englishman who knew more of the South, and doubted the whole story, wrote to a friend of his in Savannah to ascertain the truth of it: it so happened that this same individual had heard of the joke, and, greatly amused that his English friend should think it necessary to make any inquiries about such a Munchausen affair, promptly replied in corroboration of the circumstances; adding, mendaciously, that he knew all the parties. Mr. Yancey said he believed that the story is credited by those who had read it, to the present day.

We arrived in Charleston towards afternoon of the second day, without having seen one Palmetto!

The Mill's House was the hotel that had been recommended to me, and I was glad to have selected that on reaching it, as it commanded a fine view of the city, and particularly of the effects of the late fire, though this part of the view was only another sad scene to contemplate.

The first thing was to despatch my letters of introduction, and to apprise my friends of my arrival. Mr. Bunch, the British Consul, wrote immediately to propose an hour when he and Mrs. Bunch would call. It was a great pleasure to think of seeing another fellow-countryman.

Mrs. Castleton's brother-in-law, a colonel in the Confederate army, answered his note in person, very quickly. He regretted that a call to join his regiment, on account of some sudden movements of the enemy, was taking him from the city immediately, which would prevent him from showing me those attentions that he otherwise would like to have done, &c. My third friend was also an Englishman, Mr. Frederick, a resident of Charleston, who hastened to welcome me to the "most delightful city of the Confederacy."

Thus passed the first evening at the "hot-bed of Secession," where an array of "gunboats" outside the harbour, and the recent capture of Beaufort, Edisto, Pocotaligo, and a great part of the coast, with the Federal army almost surrounding the city, kept the people on the *qui vive*, and in daily expectation of a battle there.

Mr. Bunch, the British Consul, in his official capacity, was one of the very few who enjoyed intercourse with the outer world, though even this privilege was rare and limited. He told me that when our Government ships were off the bar he went out in a boat to receive the despatches, delivering up his own without exchanging one word with a person on board, so strict was the neutrality.

Mr. Bunch kindly, intelligently, and patiently endeavoured to explain the law and justice of all these things, but no law and justice could be discovered by his rebellious listener, who certainly had never studied international laws, and blockades, or any other such very distressing and inconsistent arrangements, and therefore it was not likely that she should discern the justice of them.

Mr. Frederick called to show me some of the lions, and in the reception-room he saw a lady, one of the guests at the hotel, whom he knew, and introduced to me. He then invited me to go and see where the fire had first broken out. It was at a window-blind factory near the river, from whence, sweeping through the town, it had not ceased its work of destruction until stayed by the waters of the other river, Charleston being built upon the confluence of two rivers, the Ashley and the Cooper, names which have taken the place of the original Indian appellations.

The terrible calamity was met with a fortitude and resignation that did honour to the people of the South. The news had been received in Virginia like the shock of an earthquake. People gazed silently at each other on hearing it. There had been no loud cry of sorrow or vexation, no reproaches, abuses, or suspicions. For a long time no one could believe, nor would they suppose, that it had been the work of an incendiary. Cruel as the enemy had shown themselves to be, such an act was not deemed possible, even for them. I saw a quiet tear in many an eye, that such an affliction at such a time should have befallen them. And then immediate steps had been taken to relieve the sufferers. The Government had promptly appropriated $250,000, Tennessee and Georgia each $100,000, and the other States large sums; besides which contributions were made at nearly every church the two Sundays following the disaster; and many devices were set on foot in all parts of the Confederacy to raise money. When I was at Charleston not many weeks after the occurrence, $200,000 had been contributed by these minor measures alone, besides articles of clothing and other necessaries. In all, upwards of one million of dollars had been amassed in that short period, and subscriptions were continually pouring in. Charleston, the pride of the South, "our beautiful city;" "so like an English town, more so than any other we have." And so it struck me. It was one of the most finished, substantial, and well-kept towns in the American States. There was an air of refinement and exclusiveness that distinguished Charleston. The buildings reminded me strongly of dear old England. The public edifices were both numerous and handsome, with massive (for America) stone pillars, porticoes, and flights of steps, and also several substantial colonnades, that I had not seen elsewhere.

The Charlestonians pride themselves upon the neatness of their streets, which are well paved and even; and the pavements, slightly sloping towards the edge, are always dry and clean. Stone walls or handsome iron railings surround many of the private residences, with gateways and carriage drives through gardens, that, even in the beginning of January, were crowded with evergreens of Southern luxuriance and variety. Amongst them one saw roses, camellias, and other native beauties in full bloom. These and the ample piazzas, generally reaching from the ground to the upper floor, like an addition of open chambers on one side of the house, with walls of Venetian blinds, gave the foreign aspect to the otherwise "English city." In the summer these piazzas are lined with flowers and covered with luxuriant climbing plants.

We walked on the celebrated "Battery," which one might describe as an esplanade. The lawn was covered with evergreens, the merry mocking-birds were chirping, and the insects buzzing, the waves of the bay were rippling, and the sunshine dazzling one's eyes, which, with the mild and genial air, made it difficult to realize that we were in January instead of June.

There were thirty-one churches in Charleston before the fire, eleven of which were episcopal churches. In Richmond there are only four episcopal churches, with a somewhat larger population, and this fact speaks loudly for the orthodox principles of the Palmetto city. The church of St. Michael in Charleston was designed by Sir Christopher Wren, on the plan of St. Martin's-in-the-Fields in London. The pews are high, some of them square, which, with galleries and pulpit, are all of polished cedar and cypress wood. A handsomely-carved sounding-board over the pulpit, and a couple of ecclesiastical-looking chairs in the chancel, with a rich altar-cloth upon the communion table, completed the home effect. And this was the only church in the States where I remember to have seen the font in its orthodox place by the entrance; but of course there are hundreds of churches in America whose doors I have never entered.

Another English feature in these Charleston churches was the monuments on the walls. In the Huguenot church one saw inscribed the names of the ancient French families who escaped at the Edict of Nantes, and became the ancestors of the chivalrous South Carolinians, the De Sausures, the Ravenels, the Hugers, the Porchers, and the Gourdins, &c. Here one reads of those whose sons fought and died in the revolutionary wars, and whose great-grandsons are now again, for the third time in two hundred years, struggling for liberty and independence. No wonder these people are brave; they belong to a race of heroes. Their ancestors, through much tribulation, established their homes in that land of teeming wealth, and were but just reaping the reward of their labours when fresh troubles aroused their combativeness. The history of their endurances in the last revolution is well known to the reader, "and this," they say, "this present revolution is but a continuance of the former, which was never thoroughly completed. We ought to have separated then; we are two peoples, and always have been."

Mr. Frederic pointed out some very handsome monuments, which he said the people were proud to exhibit, with this introduction: "That came from

London." It was common to hear it said, "That house was built by an English architect," "These bricks were brought from England." Strange, yet true, one never detected in the Southerner that lingering spirit of envy and ill-will that might be almost expected in a people who fought so hard and suffered so much from the parent country; but on the contrary, a sort of veneration and affection remained for everything English. To be English was almost a passport to society. When Mr. Frederick introduced me to that lady in the reception-room, whom I shall here call Mrs. Alabri, and who was a refugee from Edisto, she said to me, "I fear you must have thought me very unpolite this morning, when you asked me the name of that church. Had I known you were English I should have made myself more agreeable; but to tell the truth, I took you for a Yankee." This was a very doubtful compliment. Was I to feel flattered most at being mistaken for a "Yankee," or at commanding attentions as an English woman? The reader must decide.

"Tribulation worketh patience," forbearance, hope; and "hope maketh not ashamed."

There was, without doubt, a fortitude, philosophy, and Christian temper about these people one could but respect and admire. The bravery with which they bore their losses from the fire was equal only to that with which they bore the loss of home and riches for the sake of liberty. Gravity one did perceive; much more at Charleston than in cosmopolitan Richmond, but cheerfulness also. I allude now more particularly to the ladies, who might be pardoned readily if they did bemoan the loss of every item—every loved relic and reminiscence—both by fire and sword. But so far from it, one met Mrs. B. or Miss S., who, when asked if they saved anything from the fire, replied in a tone approaching to gaiety, "Oh nothing, nothing; we began to move our things, but the flames travelled so quickly that we barely escaped with our lives." Another would tell you, laughing at her poverty, "Mrs. E. gave me this dress, Mrs. F. gave me this cloak; even these shoes were given me." And the luxurious homes of those very ladies had been swept away before the devouring flames, so that not one stone was left upon another. Some of them have summer residences on their plantations to retire to, and which they will occupy until happier times permit them to rebuild their town mansions.

The hotel at which I was stopping, called the Mill's House, is an extremely large building, covering a good deal of ground, situated at the corner of two streets, and about six stories high.

The fire raged all round it, and within two hours from the time of its first breaking out, nearly half a mile off, the flames were sweeping towards it with such violence that very little hopes of saving it were entertained. The majority of the guests remained in the building during the whole time—for the entire city seemed enveloped in flames—and many of them, homeless from the recent Federal captures, had no other roof to cover them. A high wind was raging, and men from the balconies, the roof, and windows, suspended wet blankets, scorched as they stood in their perilous position, while also saturated with water. Gentlemen and negroes were all at work together. For four hours the Mill's House was in the utmost danger. The then closed windows were so heated that it was almost impossible to remain in the rooms; panes of glass were cracked and the shutters blistered as they yet remained in the room I occupied. The house itself peeled (it was brick with a stucco composition over it), and was singed and cracked in several parts, but saved at last. And by saving this, at the sacrifice of three hundred blankets, which the landlord told me he had used on the occasion, one half the city was preserved; for this broad high building formed an important screen to a number of combustible tenements at the back. Yet the fire passed on each side of it, and continued its ravages until stopped by the river, and nothing more remained to be burned! At one time the British Consulate, at the residence of Mr. Bunch, was in so much danger that the public documents were removed.

The next time I met Mrs. Alabri she made herself very agreeable to the English lady, and also gave me some extremely interesting accounts of the capture of Edisto Island, and of Beaufort, which latter town had been attacked so unexpectedly by that "Grand

Armada" that the inhabitants had fled in the utmost speed. It may be remembered that Beaufort was not occupied by the Federals immediately after it was captured; and several of the gentlemen who had left there, afterwards made stealthy reconnoissances to see how matters were proceeding.

One officer with ten men, who ventured back into the town, found the negroes all drunk with the wines and liquors, to which they had been helping themselves from their masters' cellars. The women were dressed up in their mistresses' clothes, and were dancing and scampering all over the place. A splendid piano was found standing in the middle of the road—and it was a very foggy day—guitars, violins, and other musical instruments were lying about in fragments; so were ladies' and children's dresses, and many beautiful, expensive articles, smashed, defaced, or destroyed. A gentleman saw one of his own servants, and called to him. The man, though scarcely sober, recognized his master and attempted to slink away. Not coming upon the repetition of his name, the master rode up to him and caught hold of his arm. The poor wretch, conscious of his misdemeanour, trembled in every limb; his teeth chattered and his head shook as if he had the palsy; but his master pitied him, in his friendless condition, too much to hurt him. The master was homeless—what could he do with his negroes? He asked the man if he would go with him, or stay with the Yankees; but the half-drunken wretch had not the sense to reply. Many of the negroes when thus asked or sent for, said they would stay in their cabins and take care of their children, and if the Yankees came they would hide in the woods.

Generally the negroes have a great dislike to leave the localities where they "b'long to," and their pigs and chickens. Some few went willingly to the Federal camps, more were bribed; and more still went by force. But the aged, the feeble, and infants were neither bribed nor stolen, but left to take care of themselves.

Mrs. Alabri told me that her cousin, who was in the army, had returned to the island and found one of the negresses dressed in the most heterogeneous collection of stolen finery, loaded down with ribbons and trinkets, sitting at a piano, with her head thrown about, and her arms spread out, her great black hands sprawling over the keys, and her voice in full pitch, giving an entertainment to a circle of other black beauties who were all in full evening costume, playing the mistress and her guests. On this island, where were some beautiful residences, another gentleman found his house burned to the ground, some elegant furniture broken to fragments and lying about the fields and roads, together with a valuable library, many of the books having been thrown into a pond, and some costly statuary scattered about in the woods, fractured and ruined, of course.

Whether this wanton destruction was the work of drunken soldiers, drunken negroes, or both, it was impossible to state. Negroes, with their monkey propensities, are likely enough to perform such feats, particularly the young ones ; and their parents, ignorant of the value of the articles, would not arrest their spoliation. "I ain't got no use for it," is the negro's estimate of an article, and his sentence to destruction. Those scenes at Edisto and Beaufort were however a sad instance of what a negro is, and ever will be, when removed from a superior influence and authority.

Early the next morning a note was brought to me from Mr. Frederick, to say that if I wished to prepare letters for England, no time was to be lost—they must be ready at once, because a possibility of sending them had been found ; the means being both secret and sudden ; also that a trip to Fort Sumter had been arranged, and that he would bring some ladies, who were to be of the party, to call for me at such a time.

Fort Sumter is known to all the world by this time, both from pen and pencil, so are Charleston harbour and the neighbouring islands. Therefore I shall only relate that the weather still remained like June in England, that parasols were indispensable, that the sea was blue and beautiful, and the whole trip charming.

Our party was composed of Mr., Mrs., and two Miss Beauforts, Mons. François, Mr. Frederick, and another fellow-countryman, who had that very morning run the blockade and arrived from England in the "Ella Warley," and who, Mr. Frederick thought, could get my letters off through a prominent Firm in Charleston.

Oh, what a dreadful trio of "neutral British subjects," violating "law and order," blockade, and the Queen's proclamation *in toto!*

Mr. "Warley," as I shall call him, gave us a very exciting account of the escape of the ship in which he had run the blockade. A thick fog had enveloped them the evening before, and rendered it unsafe to pass those intricate channels during the night. The next morning found them in full face of the Federal gunboats. A race ensued—such a race! the cannon-balls whizzed past them, and for a time the poor little devoted "Ella" was in the greatest danger. She distanced her adversaries however, and, in the treble peril of capture, cannon-balls, and of bursting her own boiler by the force of steam under which she was going, at length arrived in shallow water and was safe. How could one help rejoicing at such an escape? I am sure I feel very sorry to have exulted over such unlawful doings, and as soon as the war is over I hope to be just as friendly with the North as ever; but it was impossible not to be glad under the circumstances.

Mr. and Mrs. Beaufort were, like so many others, refugees from their beautiful homes. The gentleman was rather past the age for the army, but he thanked God his purse was open to them; "For the last ten years," he said, "I have spent about a thousand dollars every summer with my family at Saratoga, and it is more agreeable to give this sum towards the independence of my country, than to squander it among the people who are endeavouring to subjugate us."

The conversation, as we sailed along, ran upon the defences of Charleston, the prospect of battles, &c. We passed some of those singular iron-clad gunboats, that looked like huge black, one-sided, round-topped trunks floating on the water; I could not see how people got into them, nor out of them, how they sailed, or could be steered. They were neither houses, nor boats, nor barges, nor boxes, but a compound of each.

The unanimous opinion with respect to the invasion of that part of the country appeared to be, that it would be impossible for an enemy to penetrate into the interior very far. "We know our own roads, and where to waylay an invader; they will be cut to pieces by guerillas, and never escape to get back again: our swamps are impassable," &c., &c. With regard to the recognition and intervention, which then began to be mooted in the English papers, Mr. Beaufort said, "We have now overcome our first difficulties, and are unwilling to lose the credit of gaining our own victories, and achieving our own independence. As for the blockade, we are saving by it." Thus one heard a diversity of opinions; the chivalrous South Carolinian preferring to gain independence with long suffering, rather than lose his laurels, or share them with others.

To an inexperienced person like myself, it did not

seem possible that Fort Sumter could be battered to pieces with any description of cannon-balls. Some of our party declared they would not be afraid to stand during a battle under those crypt-like looking archways where the artillery was placed, so completely protected did they appear to be; though one could comprehend how injurious to life would be the smoke of a fire when rolling through those arched galleries. From the battlements, with the aid of telescopes, we had the gratification of seeing the blockading fleet outside the harbour. Bales upon bales of cotton were piled up for breastworks. It was sad to see such a sacrifice of the staple for which my country was already suffering. England was reckoning her bales by the number of weeks they would afford employment for her people, and here was a winter's supply devoted to the prosecution of a fruitless warfare!

A small tablet, inserted in the pavement towards the centre of the court, bore the name of the man who fell a victim to the salutes, fired on the capture of the Fort, the previous April.

Over the chief entrance General Ripley had caused to be carved the following motto—

"*Lasciate ogni speranza, voi che entrate.*"

It was productive of a strange mingling of painful reflections, regrets, and enjoyment, that lovely afternoon at Fort Sumter.

On landing we walked home through the Market, which is really one of the finest public buildings in

Charleston. It is a straight colonnade of more than a quarter of a mile in length, with stalls on each side, divided into compartments for meats, poultry, fruits, vegetables, dairy produce, fish, &c. The effect of this long vista of an evening, when lighted up with three rows of gas-lights, is very fine. There did not appear to be much prospect of the South Carolinians being "starved out" at that time. Such a profusion of "all-the-year-round" vegetables and fruits I never saw before. Besides our usual English winter vegetables, there were radishes, salads, spinach, and many Southern productions I knew neither by sight nor name; abundance of eggs—and they were on table daily at the hotel—poultry and game; in fact one could not realize the month of January in any way. The negresses presiding over these delicacies were the most dignified and picturesque I had as yet seen; their snowy turbans were arranged in a pompous and complicated manner, some of them of a sufficient height to remind one of the peasantry of "*La Normandie*."

Mr. Warley not only despatched my budget, but brought a kind message from the Firm, that they would forward letters to England for me "whenever I pleased," with the astonishing assurance, "We send regularly every week." Mr. Warley said, "We only laugh at the stone fleet, and the blockade."

Mr. Bunch did not approve of my sending letters in this way, and was more inclined to be angry, than to congratulate me on my good fortune, of which it seemed so hard not to avail myself.

CHAPTER IX.

The One Palmetto — From Charleston to Savannah — The Northern Population in the South—Winter in Savannah—A short stay.

In taking leave of the clean, pretty, pleasant city of Charleston, one felt that of all the places in the American States one had hitherto visited, none promised so many attractions as that "hot-bed of the rebellion."

I have forgotten to say that there is one particular palmetto tree in Charleston. It is opposite to the office of the "Courier" newspaper, which, by the way, with the "Richmond Enquirer," were two of the most loyal papers in the Confederacy.

There may be a few other palmettos in Charleston, small specimens in private gardens, for they flourish chiefly on the sandy sea coast and islands; but one day in passing along a street, suddenly I came upon this significant tree, after all not a very large one, but fenced around, there it stood, not to be mistaken; the now historical emblem of the second American revolution, and an object that may in consequence be considered one of the lions of Charleston.

My new escort was a very gentlemanly and rather

taciturn personage, but there was quite enough to amuse and interest one along a line of road affording sufficient novelty and adventure. Whom should I perceive on entering the railway carriage but that Captain Parkhill with his wife and family, who had left Richmond on the same day with myself. Captain Simkins had continued his journey without interruption, but this family had been staying with friends near Charleston until to-day. I was glad to meet them again, and they were able to give me the desired information for the journey beyond Savannah, about which no one else appeared to know anything.

The entire road from Charleston to Savannah passes over rivers, cane brakes, and rice swamps, with but little intermission of solid ground. At that time, when the Federal fleets and army had possession of the whole line of coast to the east of our route, and when the enemy was having recourse to all manner of cruel and revengeful schemes to perplex the rebels; when incendiarisms and bridge-burnings were so frequent, it was a line of road replete with danger. Great caution had to be observed along every mile of it, as the continuous tressle work was almost as perilous as the bridges.

We passed small encampments and detachments of troops stationed at every bridge and cross road: for at any moment flat boats could have landed the enemy's troops from the rivers, though, as Mr. Beaufort had said, the character of the country was so against an invader that no great result or disaster need be feared. Tangled swamps of fallen timber presented an extensive natural abbatis, and the "cane brakes" are such a network of *impassabilities*, that one shuddered at the very idea of an army attempting to traverse them. Nature has done her own part in fortifying that line of coast, therefore to guard the roads and bridges was all that was necessary. The principal rivers we crossed were the North and South Edĭsto, the Cŏmbaheé, the Pocotăligo, the Coosawhatchie, and the Savannah, the two latter of great width, and the tressle bridges so high and dangerous, that the train crept along at a slow walking pace.

There was another Confederate officer in the train with us, who seemed to be well acquainted with the Parkhills. My new escort told me he was also a Floridian, of the name of McClellan, but he was not introduced to me.

It was exactly a day's journey to Savannah in those slow times. It was just dusk when we arrived; but not too dark to prevent my seeing that we drew up in a very fine railway depôt, one of the handsomest in the States.

The gentleman who accompanied me from Charleston was about to join his regiment, and while he was wishing me good evening preparatory to leaving the hotel, General Lee came into the reception-room, and was about to throw himself upon a seat, apparently much fatigued, when he recognized, and approached to greet, my last new friend. After the salutation he was introduced to me, and I was just congratulating myself upon the circumstance of making the acquaintance of so distinguished a personage, when another gentleman entered the room with a roll of charts and plans, and spreading them upon the centre table, engrossed the General's undivided attention until they left the room together. Everybody still occupied to the utmost with the one great business!

I could not help remarking the unsuspicious and incautious manner in which things in the South were conducted. At Charleston I do not know how many Northern people, and particularly Bostonians, were to be met with, even then. The landlord of the hotel and his partner were both Massachusetts men. The railroad conductors were generally Northern men. In several stores one found Northern men, and at the very time that General Lee was giving audible instructions about the form and position of breastworks and fortifications, that were to command such an inlet, or point in such a direction, there was a Northern lady, in that public room, listening eagerly. She had been sitting near me, and perhaps, seeing that I was alone, had entered into conversation, telling me how much trouble she was experiencing in vain endeavours to reach her home, and how many miles she had travelled here and there to try to run the blockade, or procure a permission to go under flag of truce. She was then on her way to Fernandino, Florida, where she had relatives, and was still persevering in her endeavours to leave the Confederacy. Before commencing the conversation she had asked me if I were a Southerner, and on my replying in the negative, but not telling her I was an Englishwoman, she had changed her tone in a striking manner, being incautious enough to betray to me without any doubt that she was far from being a "Southern sympathiser." Mr. Warley might have forwarded to Europe any amount of information of a very injurious nature in that great packet of mine, which could have been easily transmitted back to the North; and I observed in many other instances this same display of unsuspicious confidence towards people once introduced by a mutual friend; while towards an entire stranger perhaps no people on earth are more distant and reserved than those same confiding Southerners.

Savannah is like no other town in the American States. It is laid out in squares, or rather oblongs, not arranged in chequered fashion, but interlinked in a chain-like form, a short street connecting each, every alternate square being filled with evergreen trees and shrubs, so that which ever way you look a mass of foliage meets your eye. The principal streets are very wide, with a double row of trees along the middle as well as the edge, and between the centre rows a narrow strip of grass where seats are placed; every arrangement told you it was made for summer only.

I resolved to take one day more for this beautiful

city, particularly as the next stretch of journey would involve a long day, probably the following night as well, and the great change of temperature added to the fatigue of the last two weeks had deprived me already of much of the valued stock of health imparted by the mountain air.

The "Park" of Savannah consists of some, perhaps sixty acres, laid out in grass and walks, thickly planted with pines and other evergreens.; the whole surrounded by a very light and almost invisible iron railing. In the centre is a more substantial palisade around a circle of flower border which encloses a large basin of water, from which rises an extremely handsome stone fountain, in the form of two salver-shaped basins one above another, surmounted by a figure holding a jet. Four other figures of Neptune, each holding a jet, were rising from the water. The gardener, in a little skiff, was cleaning these jets. Roses, camellias, geraniums, verbenas, and other summer flowers were in bloom, over which gay butterflies and humming insects were hovering, as if they knew no winter, and thought it not worth while to die. The delicate tillansia, or "long moss," hung in festoons and tassels from the tall pine trees. A few ladies were strolling about, nurses with their young charges were sitting on the grass, soldiers from their adjoining encampment were leaning over the iron railing, in apparent enjoyment of the tranquillity of the scene. Flights of pigeons were whirling over head, violets and stellarias were sprouting beneath the feet, and such was the January of Savannah.

The private gardens belonging to the residences possessed even greater attractions than those of Charleston in the way of novelties. Giant ferns and tropical specimens indicated the taste of their owners. In passing along one of the private streets I was all at once arrested by a perfume; it was of no flower or fruit that I remembered ever to have inhaled, but of such peculiar fragrance, combining all that one could conceive of the most delicious odours, that one was feign to "sniff the air," and stop to seek the cause. On turning the corner of the wall, behold, there was an orange-tree laden with fruit; large, dark, rich fruit unlike what one had ever seen before, as also was the fragrance, so rich and full, that the remembrance of that first orange-tree, in its native soil, will be always associated with the charms of Savannah.

There is an exceedingly handsome and well-finished monument standing in the centre of the street leading to the park. It is to the memory of Count Pulaski, one of the heroes of the last revolution. The inscription is as follows:—

PULASKI,

THE HEROIC POLE,

Who fell mortally Wounded,

Fighting for American Liberty at the Siege of Savannah,

9th October, 1779:

Robert E. Lanitz,

New York, A.D., 1854.

The attitude and expression of the figure are strikingly beautiful. It is of white marble, a noble work of art, and one could but wonder that a people so full of admiration for liberty as those who designed and inaugurated this emblem, a liberty which has hitherto been the boast of the American Republic, should now be prosecuting with such savage fury, a war to quench that very freedom and independence, for which in their own case they fought so hard and long.

Savannah is built upon a bluff much above the level of the broad-stretching river. A wide street, bordered by a parade and grass walks under rows of trees, runs parallel with the river for a long distance. It commands a fine view of the wide-spreading rice lands on the opposite shore, where huge mills rise up on the flat plains like those great flour-mills of Richmond, making everything else small by comparison. That beautiful parade was now defaced by bristling cannon. In the distance one could just distinguish the position of Fort Pulaski. Under the cliff in the river lay Commodore Tatnall's fleet of gun-boats, and the Fingall that had just run the blockade; along the shore were extensive warehouses, wharfs, and docks, which, like those of Charleston, were now closed and useless, where was wont to flourish some of the busiest commerce of the world!

Everything in Savannah has relation to the Hero Pulaski. The best hotel is the Pulaski House. There are Pulaski streets, and a Pulaski county in Georgia.

My stay was too short to avail myself of introductory letters, and kind proffers of hospitality; and I set out on the tedious remainder of the Southern journey quite alone. We were leaving war behind us, and my fellow-travellers were few, not very prepossessing individuals.

CHAPTER X.

An Unexpected Friend—The Governor—A Solitary Journey—Ten in Family.

FOR some miles the road was of the same character as that between Savannah and Charleston. More rice lands, swamps, cane brakes, and rivers to cross. Then our course lay westward; we entered pine woods, and remained in pine woods without variety or intermission, except when one stopped for a few minutes at the little wayside station, which generally consisted of a low rough shanty, with a broad overhanging roof, and a deep porch for shade. As the banks were for the most part high, you must mount an ample flight of wooden steps to reach this "station," around which was a plentiful litter of old casks and wooden cases, planks and prostrate trees, litter, sand, rubbish, and soldiers. Very barren, desolate-looking places.

By-and-by we stopped again at a shabby little village, and then a gentleman got into the car whom I remembered to have seen before, He was past middle-age, and looked like a Virginian. I was trying to recall where I could have seen this gentleman, when he caught sight of me, and approaching, introduced himself as Dr. Johnston, from Richmond. Then I remembered that it was he who had promised Mrs. Ayres to take charge of me "down to Florida," but that he had been prevented from leaving the city at the time that I had done so.

He had just come across the State of Georgia by a different route, my detention at Charleston having caused us to meet again in this singular manner.

It was like greeting a friend to see a Virginian all that way from civilization, out in those dreary pine woods, travelling day and night. Dr. Johnston held a responsible trust under Government; he knew every road, and almost every person of any consequence; and the meeting with him was the most *à propos* that could happen. The whole of that day our journey continued through the pine woods, without passing a single town. In the evening Dr. Johnston, myself, and two other persons left the railroad, and got into a stage-coach on the borders of Middle Florida, continuing the journey till about two o'clock as far as Madison.

We were no sooner in the State of Florida than one perceived the effect of the remarkably salubrious climate. The warmth of the temperature was not of that heavy oppressive description that one experiences in those suddenly mild days of mid-winter; but it seemed quite pleasant and natural for the atmosphere to be warm; perfectly right, so to speak, to sit out in the piazza the first thing in the morning, and inhale the perfume of oranges, jasmine, and evergreens, without a thought of hat or shawl.

Dr. Johnston was on his way to Fernandino, where he expected to meet General Lee, who had left Savannah in the morning by an earlier train than that on which I travelled, and by a different route. He, it will be remembered, commanded all the line of coast from Charleston to Fernandino at that time. Dr. Johnston intended to be at Tallahassee soon, on business for the Government, and as he knew the Governor, he said he should certainly see me again. He was so kind and fatherly that this was quite a pleasure to anticipate, so far away from everybody. Madison, a pretty little "town," is on the Middle Florida Railway, running through the state from Jacksonville to beyond Tallahassee. On parting with Dr. Johnston he put me safely into the train, with plain directions for the rest of the journey, which would be only a few hours more.

As no one knew when I should arrive at Tallahassee, of course there was no one to meet me at the end of the journey, and I repaired bag and baggage to the "best hotel," and forthwith addressed a note to Governor Milton to apprize His Excellency of my arrival. The Capitol, a tidy-looking "frame" building, with flights of steps and a portico, was just opposite the hotel.

A negro servant soon appeared, to say that the Governor would "be over in a few minutes," which were passed in as great a flurry of wonderment as when I had watched over the side of the boat on the Rappahannock River, for the approach of the Slaveholder.

A very carefully-dressed gentleman was not long in making his appearance. His manner was not particularly cordial; and my courage vanished like a spark. His words were few; he had "a great press of business on hand." He did not make any inquiries about my journey, excepting to say that he had received my letter from Charleston, and thought, perhaps, that being there, I might have been tempted to run the blockade and leave the country. I heartily wished I had done so; but replied that such a step had not entered my mind, as I had promised to keep my engagement with him. How little the people seemed to be in the habit of depending on promises!

In the absence of anything else to talk about, he asked concerning my acquirements. Did I teach this, that, and the other? Could I play? glancing at an odd sort of chattel in the room, presumed to be a piano, as if expecting me to perform on it before even my gloves were off. I had heard that his family was very musical. Soon he rose to depart, without mentioning his wife and daughters, until leaving the room, when he said, Would I prefer to continue the journey immediately, wait till after dinner, or rest, and proceed the next day?

Continue the journey!—what could he mean? I looked the question, when he replied—

"My family is at my place in Jackson County; I have not brought them here, because the city is not so agreeable as the country, where they have everything they require. In case of an expected attack at St. Mark's they are safer there. My wife and daughters are accustomed to be where they have plenty to eat and drink from our own plantation; and as it is now very difficult to obtain provisions here, I think you will all enjoy yourselves better in the country."

With such tedious journeys of late, the night-travelling, and excitement, I felt so much worn out, that I proposed to proceed the next morning, and rest at Tallahassee until then. It was now about noon; the Governor said he would come again before dinner to conduct me to the dining-room, and would desire his servant to "look in occasionally," and bring the carriage to drive me over the town.

Tallahassee is built on rather high ground and hilly. There is not the slightest appearance of "city," scarcely even village, for the roads are very wide, bordered with trees, and with trees also along the centre, in some parts. A few adjoining stores are on one street, with another or two scattered here and there. There are two or three churches surrounded with trees, and some very pretty residences in gardens of trees. Groves of trees, thickly planted, are everywhere. Many evergreen oaks, cedars, pines and holly, and the warm weather and open windows, again made you forget it was January. It is a pretty place, though not a "city," according to our ideas.

The next morning I felt a little nervous to find that I was to take two days' journey through a nearly uninhabited country, with only a negro driver as a companion; but the Governor said, on handing me into the carriage—

"William will take good care of you, Miss Jones; he is my body servant, and has served me faithfully for many years; I would trust my own daughters with him." Then he added, more cheerfully and kindly, no doubt observing a very wo-begone face, "Do you love flowers? If you have any taste for gardening, I will hire an English gardener to lay out my place, and you can take him under your management." To which I gladly assented, in having some amusement to look forward to in the place of society.

The weather was lovely, only very warm, with the thermometer at 80°.

We arrived at Quincy towards the afternoon, where I was kindly entertained by a lady and her daughter, who started me off the next morning with an abundant supply of cold chicken, ham, and "breads," as all the variety of corn cakes, waffles, hot rolls, and hominy are called.

The country we passed over was, in some places, very interesting, and at others, through sandy pine woods, very tedious. The lower lands and swamps in the vicinity of rivers afforded beautiful wild flowers even in January. The fragrant yellow jessamine, which I think was the "*Gelsemium sempervirens*" of Dr. Asa Gray, climbed the trees and hung in festoons among roses and evergreens, which, with the peculiar softness and charm of the atmosphere, furnished some enjoyment, even in those two lonely days of tedious travelling.

William was a very respectable-looking and well-behaved servant, with patronizing manners, proceeding from his own sense of responsibility, and the usual pomposity of negroes in that case. He was accustomed to be trusted and consulted, and I learned that he had travelled a good deal with his master, and had formerly belonged to a gentleman in New Orleans; and he had not seen so much variety without improving his intelligence and observation. He knew the names of most of the trees and plants that we met with, was always obliging in stopping to gather specimens for me, and gave me, on the whole, quite a stock of useful information concerning the country we passed.

We were travelling in a sort of half-open carriage, with a top for shade, and two seats, both facing the horses; and a splendid pair they were, that did not change their pace nor cease to step together for hours at a time. Thus William, sitting on the front seat, could reply to my inquiries and attend to his beautiful greys at the same time. The Governor had not found time even to tell me the number and age of his children, therefore judge of my surprise, on asking William, to hear, "Ten, all at home." Ten children! And one son married, besides several who had died! Six were to be my pupils, William said.

Ten children are all very well, but where an inmate

in a family is concerned, experience had shown that, as a general thing, comforts naturally diminish in proportion as à family increases. Children monopolize the servants, children fill up the carriages, children share all the luxuries. It is quite proper that it should be so; still the ten children foretold much for me. About dusk on the second day of our journey, we arrived at a gate.

"Governor's residence, ma'am," said William, as he alighted to open it.

CHAPTER XI.

The Bright Eyes of Sylvania—The New Pupils—The McClellans —Life in the Woods—The Killing Season—Products of Florida.

It was just light enough to distinguish a long, low dwelling, surrounded by a deep piazza reached by steps extending along the whole front. A very pretty style of building, quite Southern, and in the midst of a wood. Excepting the drive to the house, and a cleared space in front, it was literally in a wood, and was therefore appropriately called "Sylvania."

Several of the ten children, who were sitting upon the steps as the carriage drew up, exclaimed, "William! here's William! Howdy, William? How's pa?"

They all ran down the steps to shake hands with William, without taking the slightest notice of me until the greeting with the favourite slave was over; then their attention was turned for a moment towards myself—a mere glance they gave—after which they resumed their play and tittering, as if no such person as Miss Jones existed. A girl of about fourteen, a pretty lady-like looking child, approached, and led me up the steps, through a French window, into a sitting-room, thence into a bed-room beyond, where she left me to doff my bonnet and cloak. Presently she returned with a candle, and gave me to understand that her mamma was not at home, but that she was expected soon.

I preferred to remain there quietly and wait. Before long the sound of carriage-wheels announced an arrival, and a tall, handsome, motherly-looking lady entered, and cordially greeted me, expressing no surprise either at my coming now, or at my not having come sooner; for of course she had not just then expected me.

A fire was soon blazing in the sitting-room, called the parlour, the evenings being chilly; but the doors remained open, and I heard steps and voices on the piazza, and saw by the light of the blazing fire, splendid black eyes peeping in at the windows, and popping away on meeting mine, and I knew that some of the ten were ascertaining what sort of a looking body "the new teacher, Miss Jones," might be.

At the tea-table some half-dozen of the ten appeared, and I never saw such a collection of eyes in my life. They were all dark, and all beautiful, and all like their mother's, but no two pairs alike. Pretty girls, and amiable, evidently; manners perhaps a little uncouth, listless, and inexpressive; temper easy, mind undeveloped, and character also expressionless. Such were my pupils in Florida;

not only the Governor's daughters, but sundry cousins who dropped in, as unexpectedly as I had done myself, in the course of the next month, to join the others in their studies.

Talents, manners, disposition, and character wholly untrained and undeveloped. Perfectly easy, always smiling, amiable and obliging; but never thinking of anything themselves; never reflecting one moment. Just like their negro servants, they came when called, and did what was asked of them, but never on any account *unless* asked. They were as pretty and amiable a set of girls as one could desire to see, but a type of Southern girls generally, who have fortunes spent upon their education, or rather upon the routine of getting "through" books, but who rarely are *educated* at all, in the true sense of the word.

The next day two or three vanished, and two or three more appeared; the carriage was going and returning continually, bringing and fetching young ladies; and though no one thought it necessary to tell me what was going on, I found that they were exchanging visits with other young ladies in the neighbourhood; going to stay for a day and a night, and bringing home friends who in their turn spent a day and night, and again carried off another pair of black eyes. The eldest daughter was seventeen, the youngest, "Jeff Davis," only a few months old.

As no sound of the word *study* was heard, I began to suggest some sort of commencement, but

Mrs. Milton said, "The girls have had so little time to themselves, that they don't feel inclined to begin this week;" and that my predecessor had not long departed. Five girls, and a boy of about the age of Johnny Quence, also called Johnny, were to be my pupils. The rest were too young. We had our school-house across the "yard," as that trodden portion of the woods was called; it was a large room with seven windows and two doors, not one of which had a fastening. Books, slates, torn fragments and old covers were littered all over this apartment, in which were some old shabby ricketty desks, an antique piano, and benches.

For a time I laboured hard to establish some system of order and tidiness, but in spite of blockade and scarcity, torn, worn, scribbled books, broken slates and lost pencils were of every-day occurrence. A great long row of books that I had arranged on the old piano, was one morning missing entirely; no one knew what had become of them, no one had touched them or seen them, but they were gone!

"I bet a dollar that Jim (a negro boy) has carried them off into the woods," said Johnny.

"Why should he do that?"

"Oh, just for mischief. I left my violin here one evening, and the next day it was gone. A long time afterwards, when I was hunting in the woods, I found it smashed up under the trees; and I know Jim broke it up, just for mischief." Thus the row of books vanished, their loss borne amiably and unconcernedly, without an effort to recover them.

I tried hard to get locks or some kind of fastenings put upon the doors, which should "certainly be done;" but every time any one went into town the locks were forgotten, and as each week produced a greater scarcity and a higher price for articles, they were "quite forgot" until not procurable at all.

Necessarily immense patience and some very grave faces required to be summoned over all these baneful habits. The pleasantest smiles and readiest promises responded to my expostulations, and there the responsibilities of the young ladies ceased. Their mother thanked me frequently for endeavouring to make her children orderly and systematic, which she said none of their governesses had ever troubled themselves to do, excepting one English lady, who she was so very sorry had gone away. She had tried very much herself, she said, to enforce these things upon her children, but she could not induce them to pay attention. No; Southern parents who have been reared on the same principles do not understand the discipline necessary to *enforce* any system. They are too indulgent, too much accustomed to control an inferior class, and to allow their children to control that class, to reconcile to themselves the idea of compelling obedience in their own children when once past infancy, which would perhaps be placing them too much on a par with the negroes.

Our post town was ten miles off, and the mail was

carried and fetched generally once, sometimes twice a week, when the weather permitted. All that winter very heavy rains occurred; after which the river Chipola, that we crossed to reach Marianna, the name of the pretty little rural town which was the capital of Jackson County, overflowed its banks, and rendered the roads impassable. At such times we were often three weeks without a possibility of knowing what was going on, either of war or peace, and a postmaster of some of the branch lines, thinking stale news was unprofitable, considerately sent us only the *very last* newspapers that had arrived, in order perhaps to save us the trouble of wading through the three weeks' information of which we knew nothing, and of which, therefore, we might continue to know nothing. Mrs. Milton was ever too much occupied by her ten children at home, to mourn over this abridgment of despatches, and the younger members of the family never seemed to know that such events as war and blockade were existing. Always perfectly happy, contented, and smiling, accustomed to gratify every wish, with no thought of care or sorrow, and no sense of responsibility.

I had not been many days at Sylvania before I heard some one say, "Captain McClellan has come home," and the name, recalled to mind my journey from Charleston to Savannah. Soon afterwards I heard that "Captain and Mrs. McClellan and the children are coming to see us." If it should prove to be the same Captain McClellan whom I had seen in the train, he was a very intelligent, gentlemanly person, and one might perhaps enjoy the opportunity of learning what was going on in the world beyond the limits of the woods.

They came; he was the same person, and remembered to have seen me in conversation with the Parkhills. We had both lately arrived from Virginia, we had both seen the sad realities of war, and soon found enough to talk about. His wife was an exceedingly lady-like, intelligent person, and a very intimate friend of the Miltons. She seemed, from the first hour of our acquaintance, to sympathise with the isolation of my position at Sylvania, in being so far removed from all family ties, and even those friends in Virginia, from whom I was now separated, more effectually so, by the uncertainty and ill-arrangements of the mails; aggravated as this was by the frequent inundations. Excepting Mrs. Milton herself, Mrs. McClellan was almost the only person with whom I became really acquainted in Florida, and a lady whose agreeable society and friendly manners were always productive of real pleasure whenever we met. Captain McClellan was intending to return almost immediately to the Peninsula, where his regiment was stationed.

A very important step was now occupying the attention of all the cotton State authorities, namely, the necessity of providing food throughout the country, and of suspending the plantation of cotton until the resumption of commerce should render the labour profitable,

Meetings of some of the largest planters in the Gulf States were held, at which they promised to set the example, and use their influence to limit the cotton crops of 1862.

One heard of several large nitre caves that were being worked in Alabama, and of improvements in many factories recently established in that State.

Several weeks elapsed without the receipt of a single letter either from Richmond, Warrenton, or Charleston; my friends at each of those places having promised to keep me apprised of events; neither did my regular newspapers arrive, nor from these woods could my promised contributions to Richmond be supplied. Probably my letters had been addressed to Tallahassee, which by mail route was nearly a week's journey from our locality, in which case Mrs. Milton undertook to instruct the Governor to forward them to Sylvania, but not one did I receive. I persevered in writing but without replies. Whether the letters reached their destination, and whether the answers were sent and lost, or not written at all, was vague and uncertain. The Governor was expected at home, and he "perhaps would bring the letters and papers." He did not appear when expected, nor until the week following. Like my own advent, no one knew whether he would or would not arrive until he came withinside of the gate. When his Excellency did appear, neither letters nor papers came with him; and so entirely absorbed did he seem to be under the weight of his gubernatorial functions, that I had not the courage to trouble him about such trifles as the loss of Miss Jones' friends and correspondence.

As for the English gardener, he was never more mentioned, and I do not think was ever more thought of. Johnny and I managed to lay out a few garden beds, but William, the head and chief, as well as the chief head of the domestic establishment, was required by His Excellency at Tallahassee ; and as for "Jim," and any of the other mischievous negro children, one could never secure them when wanted. The elder negroes were too busy planting, or ploughing, or chopping wood, or doing something else to render any assistance. When the weather permitted, I worked harder on those garden beds than the united labour of any three slaves on the place, while Johnny and the girls stood and watched me in astonishment, entreating me not to take so much trouble. I endeavoured in vain to persuade them to come and help, and that it was a delightful amusement. None of them could comprehend the delights of any kind of labour. Even Johnny called to a negro boy to hold his spade or to carry a root, and at last for want of physical strength myself, and finding it impossible to create a taste for exertion in any one else, the garden was almost abandoned.

Another impediment was the climate, and in this respect Southern ladies must be pardoned for much of that inaptitude for exercise which we of Northern constitutions can but ill appreciate. In February the temperature was often at 80° in the shade, and then would follow the whole routine of calm, oppressive heat, wind, rain, hail, thunder and lightning, succeeded by calm again, and terminating in excessive chilliness for a day or two. The process of the storm would not occupy perhaps half an hour, during which time I have observed the thermometer to fall twenty degrees in three minutes, and forty degrees in a few hours afterwards. On one or two occasions I suffered more severely from cold in Florida than I had done even in Virginia the winter before, so trying are those changes. The houses are only built for summer weather; the doors and windows do not close by several inches, and indeed are only closed at all during the night, let the weather be what it may.

The winter of 1861-62 was so mild, that in addition to other difficulties, great losses of meat were sustained during the killing and salting season. When I first arrived in Florida the people were watching anxiously for weather to be cool enough "to kill." Those killing days were horrible. You could not look out of a door or window without beholding cart-loads of slaughtered pigs being carried to the yard to be cut up. Then you could not venture a step beyond the threshold without perceiving this cutting-up process, when all sorts of appendages were strung upon lines to be dried, and a whole row of negroes were engaged before boards and benches in salting, packing, and drying these portions of pigs, which made one feel one never wished to behold a porcine dish in one's life again.

These are the times when Southern families luxuriate over the delicacies of "fresh meat," as every fragment of yesterday's and this morning's slaughtered pig is called. Mrs. W., of Essex county, Virginia, had told me that from thirty to forty hogs besides oxen were salted down every winter at Forest Rill for home consumption. The number at Sylvania I did not ascertain, but no doubt it was much greater, because the diet is confined more entirely to salt food as you proceed southwards, and a great deal of the trade of Florida consists in these kinds of provisions. In the vast woods of Florida people turn their cattle adrift to take care of themselves. They are branded with the owner's name, and then turned loose to wander for miles and months together. When required, the owners or the negroes, probably both, go in search of the vagrants, which may be hunted up some fifty miles from home.

Dr. Johnston told me that one man alone in Florida paid taxes on 18,000 head of cattle, and that the markets of Charleston and Savannah were chiefly supplied from this State. No country furnishes greater advantages for "squatters" than Florida. The probability is that a man may go and settle himself in the woods and never be disturbed. A few active enterprising families might establish themselves there, cut down the timber, build themselves houses, and raise the most yielding crops of a score of things as yet uncultivated, and almost unknown to be indigenous. I am alluding not to the staples of cotton, rice, sugar, and tobacco, all of which are grown successfully in Florida, but to a variety of fruits and valuable medicines. Oranges, lemons, pomegranates, limes, and citrons grow wild, but are, scarcely eatable for want of cultivation. Excepting in East Florida one rarely saw an orange tree, and as for lemons they were not to be procured for love or money in our neighbourhood, while they were decaying under the trees in the groves of East Florida for want of sufficient enterprise or labour to collect and send them away, and this at a time when as much as half a dollar was given for one lemon in Richmond, where the hospital necessities would have proved an excellent market for such fruit. It is in these things that the evil effects of slavery appear. Did any of those rough farmers I saw, not think it beneath his dignity to "put his hand to the plough," and to turn his attention to other things than raising cotton, he need not depend on foreign countries for either medicines or luxuries. The resources of the South are not even half known, much less developed. Near the Gulf were growing large groves of oranges, lemons, citrons, wholly uncultivated, besides other wild fruits in profusion; dyes, drugs, woods, ores, the castor-oil plant, and the most beautiful vegetation seen without the tropics, are almost ignored; while sugar, cotton, &c., alone are cultivated, and many of the most wealthy and influential families, living with their hundreds of negroes and thousands of acres, do not possess one square yard of garden plot! living literally in the woods, with an ordinary diet of corn bread in all its varieties, and hard salted meats, with cabbages and sweet potatoes for vegetables, and poultry for variety; they have plenty of horses and carriages, plenty of ready money in return for their productive and easily raised crops; but slovenliness, disorder, incompleteness, and discomfort may be witnessed everywhere. The negroes are too indolent and stupid to do anything unless compelled. The masters and mistresses tolerate any amount of confusion rather than exert themselves to remedy it, and indeed, having been reared in this same confusion, they do not often observe it. The further southward one goes, the more this is seen to be the case, where the relaxing and enervating influences of climate are also more perceptible.

CHAPTER XII.

A new Evil, and how it was overcome—Ladies' Gun-boat Funds—The Whipping—The Phantom—Changes of Temperature—Exposed Position of Florida—An Unpardonable Offence—Sudden Inundations—An artifice to procure Specimens.

I FELT my health fast giving way under the influence of the isolation, the temperature, and the diet. In vain I struggled against this new and worst evil of all. God help me! should my health fail, where would be my only protection. Day after day my strength decreased, until I had not energy to hold a pen or pencil, and could not walk ten paces without fatigue; then followed some cooler weather, cool enough "to kill;" another score of hogs was slaughtered, and I believe that put the finishing stroke to my indisposition.

The girls were very amiable, the elder ones said "Don't trouble yourself about the lessons," and undertook to instruct the younger ones; and they all seemed in the height of enjoyment with the idea of it. When at last I was confined to my room Mrs. Milton brought her work up to sit with me, and the noisy troublesome Flora sometimes came bouncing in with the pretty little Jeff Davis, who just began to know me. I fell back upon reading novels to draw away my thoughts from frightful subjects, but in spite of all, began to fear my bones would rest under the climbing roses and Cape jasmine in the little family graveyard of Sylvania, and, as in the case of the poor Marylanders in Western Virginia, my friends might never know where I was buried. Mrs. Milton sent for a doctor. The best physician in the neighbourhood had just gone to North Carolina to be near the army, but there was another one, she said. He came, and looked at me, and went away again, forgetting to leave the medicines, or to send them; he lived eight miles off. Mrs. Milton then prescribed for me, and tried every means to procure me suitable diet, but diet was unnecessary, I could eat nothing. If I could have received one letter it seemed as if I should feel better; but the reflection that friends might write, and even a letter from England might arrive, through those kind people at Charelston, and be lost by carelessness at the post-office, was not very consolatory. I will not teaze the reader with more of that illness, the most alarming and unhappy one of my life. Of course I recovered, as I live to tell the tale; but I shall always believe that, with the blessing of the Almighty, I was enabled to struggle against it, and keep alive by mere force of will. The idea of dying out there in the blockaded country, away from every human tie, was so terrible, that I exerted myself to keep alive, more than I ever exerted myself to do anything in my life before. Medicines there were none, of any consequence. Stimulants there were none; neither delicacies, or any kind of diet that an English invalid would require; but as soon as I was able to eat anything at all, Johnny went out to shoot birds and catch fish, and Aunt Peggy exerted her best skill in preparing the dishes to suit my taste; and at last I managed to get down stairs to take a drive.

The last time I had looked out at the woods none of the deciduous trees had shown a sign of buds. It had been within three weeks, and now the dogwood was in bloom. Also several species of plum, sassafras, and many flowering trees and shrubs quite new to me. The "live oaks" and some other trees were in full foliage, and among wild flowers I saw a very handsome verbena, like our garden varieties, oxalis, violets, white lilies, azaleas, and several strange plants all in bloom. This was the end of February. Uncle Steph, who drove me, was not so obliging as William. He wanted "to be home to give my pigs dere supper, and couldn't stop for no weeds." The girls enjoyed a drive into town, or to visit their young friends; but merely to pass along the road to look at the trees and inhale the pure breath of Heaven, did not possess many attractions; so I went alone.

An occasional newspaper from Richmond did begin to arrive at Sylvania, and the first letter I received was from Dr. Bacon. It had been three weeks in coming. Good, kind old gentleman! what a treat it was to receive his long, closely-written letter, telling me of all the things worthy of notice in my botanical rambles, and philosophising on making the most of my opportunities, "seeing you were intent on going," he said. The number of pupils at the College had increased, and the house was full. The number of soldiers at the hospitals was diminished, and the general health of the army improved. "The great" onward movement "to Richmond has not yet been made by the Federals, nor will it be this winter certainly," (the date of his letter was 7th February and this was the end of the month,) "for McClellan's army of the Potomac is effectually locked up by the roads for the next sixty or ninety days. They cannot move a mile, and yet they talk loudly of an advance from all quarters. Our troops have gone into winter quarters, and are making themselves happy in log huts with mud chimneys. Dr. McGee has got up a musical club in his regiment, and they are enjoying themselves finely.

"General Beauregard has just left us for Kentucky. This we all regret, but are glad to know he will return when his presence is needed. Nothing can be done here this winter, and it is scarcely worth while to keep two such Generals as Beauregard and Johnston at this point, when there is more to be done in Kentucky," &c. &c.—Then he spoke of the Georgians defending Savannah, and of the failure of the great "Burnside expedition," and of the continued "brag" of the Federals, who were "not any nearer to their object than they were a year ago, nor so near, if the expression may be allowed." He wound up his famously long letter by saying that "we are all anxiously watching the course that England and France may pursue, for by the latest news the probability of their intervention seems to be increasing. I have little doubt myself that in less than sixty days our independence will be acknowledged, and that in less than three months this odious blockade will be raised. Europe, I think, cannot stand it much longer. May God speed the day, for it is a sore oppression to us!"

This writer was a man of solid judgment, a scholar, a divine, and an example of Christian virtues.

At this time there was a perfect *furore* throughout the Confederacy for "Ladies gun-boat funds." Having supplied their soldiers with winter clothing, and used up all the flannels, cloths, and wools that were then procurable, in adding to their wants, their attention was turned to the gun-boats. In Charleston, Savannah, New Orleans, Mobile, and Richmond, as well as other places, ladies were forming societies for this object. One saw columns and columns of names and subscriptions acknowledged in the papers. Those who had money gave it, those who had not, gave plate and jewelry; the wealthy not only gave money themselves, but purchased, by raffling, the gifts of others, so that thus double assistance was rendered to the object.

The negro girl appointed to attend to my room and wait upon me, was not the property of the Governor, but had been hired, since Christmas, to take the place of one of his own slaves, who had not strong health. Jane was even uglier and more stupid than Barnes of Milbank. I never saw such a hideous picture of sullen, dogged stupidity. She was a sort of supernumerary in the dining-room in the absence of William, and her other duties were to serve me, and do needlework for the family. Mrs. Milton, one of the most good-tempered people in the Confederacy, got sorely tried with Jane, whose black looks (morally) were worse than her stupidity.

At last Mrs. Milton threatened to have her whipped by the overseer. This was the first case of private whipping I had ever known or heard of, during my residence in the South. Jane had some days more given her for trial, without effect, and then Mrs. Milton told me she had sent Uncle Steph with her to the overseer, to receive the threatened punishment. Now Mrs. Milton was a lady who devoutly believed in flagellations, according to the precepts of the wisest of men. There was one of the ten with fair curls, and another of the ten with dark curls, and a third younger still; and scarcely a day passed but one or other of these *petites espiègles* did not come in for a little "switching." Flora, also, Jeff Davis' especial attendant, and the most troublesome, impudent specimen of African blood that could be found, came in for her "switchings" with the rest of the juveniles, none of which created an impression more lasting than ten minutes. But Jane was beyond switchings.

The first time the culprit appeared in my room after her punishment, feeling very sorry for her, and expecting to see traces of tears or suffering, I was surprised to see her just as stolid and sullen as ever; but contrary to my principle, I could not resist enticing her into a conversation, until the subject was approached thus:

"What a pity, Jane, you won't try to do right without being obliged to be punished like one of the mules, who cannot understand as you can."

An indistinct growl was the only reply.

"You won't be whipped any more, will you?"

Another growl something about "d' know."

"Did the overseer hurt you much?"

No answer; only a shadow of mortification in her looks.

"Where did he whip you?"

"*I*'d 'no whar 'hooped me: d'no noffin 'bout 'en"; in a voice as if from under the floor.

Whether she really had been whipped, and how much she had suffered, it was clear she did not intend to confess. She was certainly ashamed at the very idea of it, and I respected her the more for that. Afterwards I found out she had received two or three "cuts" over her dress, but I do not believe the "cuts" had made any more impression on her person than on her manners, for I saw no improvement.

During my illness a visitor had arrived at Sylvania, in the person of a nephew of the governor, a soldier of course, Major Brown from Texas. Until I was well enough to resume my seat in the school-room, the advent of this cousin, a young gentleman of about twenty-four, did not tend to improve the application of my pupils. Great doings were going on in the parlour beneath. The piano was giving forth the liveliest airs, while merry steps kept time to the music, and scarcely a day passed, that some other cousin did not arrive to add to the group. The girls were all excellent musicians, and there were two good pianos in the house, often both in use at the same time.

When I was able to join the family, I found this young soldier, Milton Brown, to be a very agreeable addition to our circle. The rides into town became a little more regular, and we were kept better informed of the news, although it was rarely less than of two weeks' date when it did reach us.

The first time Major Brown and Johnny went to Marianna they brought back that accumulation of depressing news that came like a thunder-clap upon the nerves of the people. The disasters at Fort Donnelson, Fort Henry, Nashville, Columbus, Bowling Green, the death of General Zollicoffer, and the inroads on the eastern coast of North Carolina besides.

In nothing had the evil effects of slavery been more apparent—to me at least, so far as I was capable of judging—than in this succession of reverses. And another great drawback to the Southerners were their hopefulness and confidence. Their successes at first gave them too reliant an opinion of their own prowess and of Yankee cowardice. While the latter were drilling, and improving rapidly in the art of war, the Southerners became lax; foolishly watching every item of European news, counting by weeks and days when the anticipated "recognition" would take place; dwelling on the disaffection of the Federals, their inability to carry out their programme, and their want of funds, and prolonging too late the all-important action—practical laborious action—which unfortunately is so unwelcome to the Southerner. Neither courage nor determination was wanting, but you cannot persuade a Southerner to be in a hurry.

Thus, this easy indifference, this slowness and incompleteness, were visible on a larger scale when the time came for the whole South to exert itself as one man. And yet, for such men, they had done wonders, for they had everything to learn.

The victories which the Federalists gained in Tennessee and North Carolina, had now the effect of rousing the Southerners to still greater exertions. Several of the governors—Alabama, Mississippi, and Georgia—issued immediate calls for more troops, and private individuals again exerted themselves to form companies. The government of Virginia even proposed drafting, but it was not then necessary. The proposition was made as a stimulant, and there seemed but little doubt that a larger army than ever would soon reassemble where needed.

All those impediments in travelling, and the consequent deficiencies of the postal arrangements, added to the difficulties to be overcome in a country of few railroads, few inhabitants, vast forests, and rapid rivers; where after every heavy rain the country was inundated, and traffic stopped; and among a people wholly unused to active life, and with very little of the Northern business capacities.

Strange as it seemed, at that very time the South was swarming with Northern men. They professed to be "friends," of course, and the too confiding Southerners believed them, and were averse to turn them off. They had established themselves in business, and found it to their interest to stay. Nearly all the telegraph workers were Northern men, until a school was established in Charleston, for the instruction of Southern youths in the method of telegraphic communication. It was wonderful that the Federals had not gained more rapid access to the country, and that the Confederates had been so successful in protecting themselves, when one discovered so many Northern people in places of trust. The telegraph clerk at Marianna was a "Yankee," and there were even "Yankee" editors in Florida, but if a Southerner in the North had ventured to say one-half as much as they did, or to show the same partiality, he would have been quickly handed off to Fort Warren.

The weather at the beginning of March was as warm as an English August. In the middle of the day the thermometer was often at 85°. The evenings, however, were always cool enough to render a few blazing logs agreeable, and a blanket at night could not well be dispensed with. I never found that scarcity of blankets in the South, that our Federal cousins seemed to think must prevail, when it was reported that President Davis had issued a proclamation to "press" (into service) all the blankets in the Confederacy. I read the papers with tolerable constancy, and never saw or heard of such a step; nor did it seem necessary, as far as I could judge; for the Southern ladies, not so handy in their quiltings and contrivings as their Northern relatives, were in the habit of purchasing blankets, while the latter substituted the quilted coverlets called "comforts,"—a wadded counterpane, in fact. In spite of so large a number being volunteered and given to the army, I found more blankets in the South in one house, than I had seen in any three in the North.

But I was going to mention our storms in March. There was one particularly on the 7th, after an excessive and steady heat; in twenty-four hours afterwards the weather turned so cold that a heavy night frost ensued, destroying roses, killing the buds and peach blossoms, oranges, pomegranates, and many vegetables. It was a very unusual occurrence, and having anticipated such feasts among the flowers and fruits of Florida, to *me* it was a grand disappointment. Those "cold spells" were very trying. The wind was cutting, dry, and ungenial, like an exaggerated English March. The negroes went shivering about completely benumbed, mind and body, while such weather lasted.

After this particular storm followed more heavy rains. "Oh, me!" with all that suspense about Nashville, Savannah, Charleston, and Corinth; to which latter place every one was going now, as they had gone to Manassas last year; to know that more freshets would again deprive us of our letters and papers, was another grievous disappointment. Richmond began to be threatened too, and if that place and Charleston should be lost, the Consuls, who I now felt to be my only protectors, would be irremediably separated from me. I used to rush to my desk, and begin letters, only to reflect that they could not be sent, or might never reach their destination. Sometimes some were written, and at length despatched to town; where a week afterwards I heard they were still lying, waiting for the river to subside. That river, that was so often overflowing its banks, and blocking up the roads, was the Chattahoochie, which, in conjunction with the Flint River, forms the Apalachicŏla, which empties itself at the town of the same name on the Gulf of Mexico. Our nearest and most important large town was Columbus, Georgia, and in addition to our fears for other parts of the Confederacy, we lived in constant apprehension, after the evacuation of Apalachicola, that the Federal gun-boats would ascend the Chattahoochie, and thus cut us off entirely from Northern communication. When the Governor came home now and then for a day or two, his mind was wholly engrossed for the safety of the State: with as much despatch as possible obstructions were to be placed in the river, and defences to be erected along its banks. A very fine piece of ordnance had sunk in the river mud, owing to the inundations; this had to be recovered and placed in position, and the safety of Florida, with its fifteen hundred miles of coast to protect, and very sparse population, gave his Excellency much uneasiness: Fernandino had been captured, also Jacksonville, in East Florida, and a large portion of the coast; the eastern termination of the Middle Florida railway was in possession of the Federals, who at any moment could have advanced upon Tallahassee both by east and south. St. Marks, where boats of light draft could approach the shore, was twenty miles south of the capital. Pensacola was evacuated about that time, and many of the inhabitants, who had fled from there, were living in tents in the woods, suffering great deprivations.

Though able to resume my duties, it was with great effort and fatigue that they were accomplished, for there was scarcely a chance of recovering my strength. The woods presented fresh charms in the way of floral beauties, but my rambles could only be extremely short.

In all deference to Southern hospitality and the

"efficient blockade," I must confess that I had made sure of an arrival in town of "a few choice bottles of brandy," to purchase one. Now under any other circumstances, this step would have been an insult to the kind people who make you welcome to all and every luxury their house affords; but I had seen how long a bottle of brandy, or a gallon of wine lasted, where the latter was left on the side-board for every one, young or old, to help themselves without any reflection about its scarcity; and where every negro who chose to have a "spassum" was to be supplied with brandy as long as it lasted. Therefore I not only procured a bottle of this choice drug, for three dollars, but a bottle of a still choicer drug, a half-poisonous distillation called "whiskey," in which was to be steeped some bitter bark, and taken as a tonic, recommended by Mrs. Milton. The brandy by various means had greatly diminished, when, one morning, Jane came to the school-house to say that Mrs. Miller, a neighbour, had sent over to see if Mrs. Milton could give her some brandy, for a negro child in a high fever. Mrs. Milton knowing that I had some, had sent to ask me to give the desired dose.

This was an embarrassing sort of message. The improbability of being able to procure any more on account of the blockade, the doubtful remedy for a child in a fever, and my own health, one after the other presented themselves to my mind, and at last I sent the unfortunate message, "Tell Mrs. Milton the brandy is nearly all gone, but will the whiskey do as well? No Jane appeared again, and at dinner-time Mrs. Milton was more silent and distant than I had ever seen her before.

After the children had left the table, I tried to invite conversation, and asked if any bad news had arrived. She said no, excepting that she was sorry to find that her neighbour Mrs. Miller was likely to lose her little negro girl, to whom she was very much attached: and that she had felt quite hurt at my message this morning.

"Message? What was it?"

"Why that you thought brandy too good to give to a nigger. We don't consider anything too good for our niggers, and give them whatever we have ourselves, when they are sick, and need it."

Explanation was useless, and as the truth was, I really had thought so, under the doubtful propriety of giving a child "in a high fever" brandy, when that article might be required under less hazardous circumstances, my excuses were very lame. Whether the stupid Jane in her ill-temper or obtuseness had conveyed the impression, or whether either of the children had misrepresented the message, it mattered little; the fact was clear that the slave was thought to require the stimulant, which the country has hunted over to procure.

There was a little church out in the woods near Sylvania, that the Governor had built for the accommodation of the neighbourhood, and where service was held about once a month. The Miltons were all Episcopalians, but the only Episcopal church was in Marianna, and it was very occasionally that a service was held there, because at that time there was no regular clergyman.

The little church in the woods was generally served by a Methodist minister, but the family at Sylvania made it a rule to attend there. For two or three weeks in the spring an Episcopal clergyman, visiting at Marianna, offered to serve that church; and though it was ten miles off, we were glad to avail ourselves of the opportunity of going.

I had been once or twice into the little town to visit Mrs. McClellan, and to purchase books for the studies, or rather to seek them, and not find them; another *manque* involving extra fatigue on the instructress, as the lessons became almost entirely *vivâ voce*. "I wish you would buy *all* these books, madam," said the storekeeper; "you had better make sure of them, for now Nashville has gone, we are not likely to get any more." As they were not such as I either required or approved, it was impossible to comply with this moderate request.

To continue the drive to Marianna. There was a swamp, most productive of beautiful wild flower that we passed on the road, and every time I had gone to town, it had been my wish and endeavour to stop there for a few specimens. Various excuses had caused the stopping to be postponed from week to week, until one day when William was at home for a week or two, and I was going myself to town, there seemed a better chance of success. There had been a storm the night before, and the sandy roads were delightful for driving. Only one of the girls was with me; and William was talking of the heavy rains that had fallen. "I 'member the time when you could stan' on the bridge, and reach down your hand into the water an' I shouldn't wonder it was to be so agin," said William. The rain certainly had been tremendous the previous night. Such showers one had seen and heard for a few minutes at a time, but through the livelong night those showers had fallen not in rain, but torrents, rivers, floods, falling only to cease a moment to pour down with fresh fury. It was as if the hosts of heaven were letting loose the water courses, which fell not in drops, but rivers.

When we arrived at the swamp near the Chipola, which flows into the Chattahoochie, the water was up to the spokes of the wheels, and when we returned, less than two hours afterwards, the water had risen more than half a foot. "It is just nine days since any mail left this place," said the postmaster, "and the river is rising now, so there will be no chance of sending for a week or two." And no chance of obtaining the mail either!

I have wandered away from the Episcopal church in a very irreverent manner, and also from those much-coveted flowers. After trying to coax people who "quite forgot," and striving to obtain some of the specimens, I noticed on that Sunday, when we were driving into town to church, several very beautiful sprays of blossoms on shrubs peculiar to that locality. Many plants had already gone too far, and ceased to bloom, but there was a constant succession in the swamps. The first Sunday, as we were returning home, a pouring rain prevented us from stopping, but Miss Milton said they should send to town again on Tuesday, when she would try to think of them for me.

As Uncle Steph was driving off, I thought there might be some hopes of getting the beautiful specimens. "Now Uncle Steph, do be sure to bring me some of those flowers that you pass, by the swamp, as you come back.

"No, missus. Can't stop for no flowers to-day. Wants to git home quick."

I knew well enough it was altogether useless to coax him, which perhaps would have made him more stubborn. The next Sunday as we were returning home from church, I tried again. "Oh Uncle Steph, do stop and let me gather that flower."

"No stoppin' to-day; no scamperin' roun' on de Sabbaff."

"But I can admire the works of God, on the Sabbath, Uncle Steph; don't you think so?"

"Can't say, missus. I goes to prayer-meetin' and sings 'Praise de Lord,' an' feeds my pigs, an' kips straight; an' don't go no scrummaging after weeds on de Lord's day."

"Uncle Steph, it was on the Lord's day that I first learnt to love his works, when my father took me into the fields and showed me the flowers and insects; and when I see the beautiful things that the Lord has created for our enjoyment I love Him all the more. I can pray to Him and praise Him with my hands full of flowers, and never feel that it makes me love Him and serve Him the less."

"Can't say, missus," said the imperturbable uncle, who was determined not to agree with any such philosophy; "my pigs is a-waitin' for their suppers now, an' my horses wants to git back to their stables on de Lord's day."

The Englishwoman was about as determined to have her way as the old coachman, and in no mood to be baffled by him. Very soon other irresistible clusters hang by the road-side, and out of the window falls the fan.

"Oh, Uncle Steph, Uncle Steph! stop—stop the horses! my fan is out of the window!"

Poor shallow old negro, so unsuspecting of the imposition; the horses were checked immediately, and he was proceeding in his deliberate manner to secure the reins, preparatory to descending for the fan, when I hastily reached out my hand to turn the handle of the carriage door, and was on the ground before he had half twisted them up. It was not a minute's business to break off an armful of the beautiful sprays; old Steph showing no signs of impatience when he saw I was not going to detain his horses and hungry pigs: perhaps he was too much surprised to grumble; but determined to know best, he exclaimed, "Them's pisun—mighty hard pisun! I wouldn't go to take them ar into de carriage, no how." Hearing which, the girls looked excessively alarmed, but I promised not to allow the flowers to go near them, and finally succeeded in carrying home my much coveted and beautiful specimens.

CHAPTER XIII.

The Texas Rangers—The Phantom Dispelled—The Domestic Institution in Reality.

MAJOR MILTON BROWN had been in one of the State regiments of Texas, but his service there was not active enough to satisfy his zeal; for the population of Texas was considered so true to the Southern Confederacy, and the coast was so well guarded at that time, that the country was deemed safe; and he had therefore come to offer his services to his uncle, the Governor, who was also *General* Milton, having been in active service both in Texas, and the Florida wars of some twenty to thirty years back.

Major Brown entertained us frequently with accounts of the Rangers' life in Texas, and their daily exploits of killing the wild animals. Wolves, panthers, bears, wild cats, jaguars, deer, and foxes, are the adversaries that the Texan hunter exercises his skill in obtaining, or exterminating. So accustomed to encounter these animals are the sturdy Texans, and so on the alert at all times, that they acquire a courage and bravery unequalled in any other State. A Texan will attack a bear with his pocket-knife if he have no other weapon, and will, with this implement, succeed in killing him, too; and he is so reckless, that even to save a favourite dog, he has been known to risk his own life. It is by such training, foresight, skill and courage, that the Texans have become the daring soldiers whose feats have been frequently recounted, since the commencement of the war.

Besides the excitement raging on account of the "concerted movement" of the enemy, "the decisive blow," which would effectually "crush the rebellion," and the fresh routes for "onward movements," the Queen's Message on the opening of Parliament, and the intentions of Europe, were anticipated with almost palsied eagerness. That England had professed not to recognize an inefficient blockade, and that the blockade was wholly inefficient, every one knew; and on this fact placed their dependence. Not only at Charleston, where were published a daily list of vessels in port, under the heads of "Arrivals," "Departures," and "Waiting," as if no blockade existed, but Mr. Yancey had lately arrived in New Orleans, from England; the Nashville had arrived at a North Carolina port, and succeeded in getting off again, under the command of two boys, while the Burnside expedition was off the coast; and along the Gulf, from Florida to Texas, not a week elapsed without an arrival at some port being announced. Knowing these things, and trusting implicitly to the *integrity* of England, judge of the blank astonishment, the dismay, the disappointment, which fell like a pall over the hopes of the people, on receiving the intimation that Earl Russell had pronounced the blockade *efficient*, and that a strict neutrality would still be maintained! For a few days they staggered. It was like that depression, too deep for utterance, that had witnessed the election of Lincoln. The newspapers even ceased their abuse, and the people received the tidings in comparative silence. A momentary silence only. The Southerners are a proud people, a self-respecting, and a self-reliant people. Immediately after the first shock, the cloud rolled away, they took fresh breath and courage, and, as one man, said—

"*Henceforward we will depend on ourselves alone.*"

And it was surprising to witness them from that time put their shoulders to the wheel. Their papers were for a time filled with exhortations for exertion, with recommendations for enterprise, with receipts, and instructions, and lists of new inventions. How to make saltpetre, and all other war materials; how to practise economy, to save rags for paper, old iron for foundries; how to extract salt from the earth, under the floors of the meat-houses; and how to make candles with various ingredients, and vegetable productions. With instructions for preserving health and avoiding the necessity for expensive medicines; with simple remedies for common ailments; with plans for raising a navy, and increased lists of contributions, and lists of manufactures already established, to stimulate to fresh enterprise.

In fact, the luxurious, agricultural Southerners were learning to become a practical people; and in such families as the Miltons, and the W.'s of Virginia, and all that class of society, who had never learned the meaning of economy, you saw it practised without a murmur; they abridged themselves of their usual luxuries without even seeming to miss them. The daily papers were now all reduced to half sheets. The few advertisements required, related to war necessities, and the news was condensed. Many newspapers were discontinued entirely, for want of hands and materials.

At our own table we had long contented ourselves without mustard, black pepper, and many other trifles (red pepper is indigenous), we often had no rice, even in a rice-growing State, no white sugar, very little molasses (an every-day item of consumption), no more tea, and no more imported fruits. The cook was limited in her baking for want of soda, so largely used in the "breads;" Mrs. Milton was in perpetual dread of illness on account of the scarcity of medicines. Quinine, twenty dollars an ounce; castor oil, twenty dollars a gallon, a gallon at a time being the usual purchase; a reel of cotton, half a dollar; common cotton cloths, that one would scarcely make up for a poor person in England, half a dollar a yard; children's shoes, and very inferior ones, from three dollars upwards; full-sized shoes from five to ten dollars a pair; and other things in proportion.

Even the negroes thought proper to make high charges for the fish they caught in their leisure time, and for their poultry and eggs; the latter, no doubt, chiefly belonging to their mistress in the first place; for the lady, with her ten children to work for, and her sewing-machine out of repair, found it quite a task to keep the servants in order while the master was away. The hen-houses were left open or broken, the hens laid astray in the woods, and we scarcely ever got an egg without buying it. The garden fence was down, and the cows ate up the vegetables; another fence was down, and the calves got all the milk from the cows: butter became a luxury; and Uncle Steph, as we have seen, was quite his own master, though a good and faithful servant. William, the only tractable one, was away, and what with her servants, her ten children, her absent husband, the war and blockade, Mrs. Milton's life was no *sinecure*.

But kind, indeed, was she to me. If there was a pound of tea within twenty miles, she would endeavour to procure it; and flour, at twenty and twenty-five dollars a barrel, she sent for, that I should have my "English loaf," "Miss Jones' loaf," because my appetite was dainty, and I was so reduced in strength. It made me feel dreadfully selfish and greedy, when they tried to provide dainty dinners for me, to entice me to eat. "Now Miss Jones, you can have a broiled bird for breakfast, and a squirrel for dinner; I have shot you two or three," Johnny would come and tell me. Squirrels are excellent eating, and it seemed a pity to kill them. Though they cared too little about game to hunt for themselves, it was often shot on purpose for me.

CHAPTER XIV.

Jane, and her Notions of Freedom—The Incorrigible Chattel—Another Specimen—Corporeal Discipline—A Letter from the Peninsula.

VEGETATION seemed on the whole to be about a month in advance of Virginia but those March frosts had caused this spring to be unusually backward. Although the average range of the thermometer was 80° to 85° until May, in the middle of the day, fires in the evening and in rainy weather were indispensable.

Jane did not improve; I tried to talk her into good-humour, particularly after I found out that her father and mother had been taken by the Federals on the capture of Beaufort. Mrs. Milton was contemplating a visit to the capital, and said that if Jane would behave better she would take her as an attendant, when she would be able to see her own mistress, who, a refugee, had brought her to Florida. I said: "Shall you not be glad to go and see your mistress, Jane?"

"Ef I goes to see my missus I'll want to stay wiv her. I wants to go whar my muvver is."

"But the Yankees have taken your mother. I dare say she would be very glad to get back, if she could."

"Yankees treats coloured folks well. They don't make 'em work. Jes' does noffin, and have a good time."

"Oh yes, indeed you would have to work; everybody, who is good for anything, works in this world. God did not make any one to be idle."

"Folks don't have to work when they're free; coloured folks don't."

"Yes, they do; and if you go to see your mother, the Yankees will take you, and make you work."

"I'd 'know.' Ef they wanted to take me, they'd a took me when I was in Charleston. They ain't agoin' to take *me*."

"What did you do in Charleston?"

"I jes' walk out wiv de children, an' sometimes take a ride. Most every day missus gives us half a dollar to go to the 'fectioners (confectioners) to get ice cream, and she allers say, 'Jane, you have some too.'"

"Well, I'm sure that was very kind."

"My missus allers *was* very kind; she *like* me, she did. She say, 'Jane, I don't want you to go away.'"

Poor Jane! no wonder she was so doleful always, so far away by herself. She went to a sewing school in Charleston, she told me, but she didn't want to learn to read, which she could have done, saying, "I ain't got no use for it;" but she liked needlework, and had learned to do it beautifully. Nevertheless, Jane was truly a most aggravating piece of goods. She never would bring in firewood before a storm came on, and after keeping one waiting shivering in the sudden change of temperature, she invariably brought in three wet, straight logs, which she lay in a compact bundle on the andirons, with a few ignited pine-wood chips, spread half a foot below on the bricks. Of course, by the time she got down stairs the fire was out, and call as I might I could not induce her to bring any more. One of the young ladies, or her mistress, on hearing my voice, made her come back, which she never would do at my summons. Time after time I showed her how to lay the logs loosely, with the pine chips between them; but no, always just the same three wet, straight pieces compactly placed. Mrs. Milton thanked me more for doing my own scolding, than for troubling her to do it, and had even said, "Why don't you cuff her, Miss Jones?" I "cuff" a negro!

The incorrigible chattel was, however, so very aggravating and stubborn one day about those three wet, straight, un-ignitable logs, while she persisted in burning up all the little dry pieces of pine wood, without arriving any nearer at a fire, that I thought I would try the effect of cuffing, and I got my hand quite ready, doubled my fist up, and began to study where the "cuff" could be applied most effectually. Then I moved a little so as to aim very straight, and while she remained sprawling there, playing with the chips in a most provoking manner, I gave her two great blows, just as hard as ever I could, upon her shoulder. I had so little physical strength just then that the exertion put me dreadfully out of breath, and I do not believe she would have known what touched her, if she had not turned round and caught sight of my hand still doubled up. It seemed to dawn upon her mind that she had been struck, and getting up and fixing her black eyes on me with a terrible scowl, holding up her arm, as if to defend herself from a pugilist, she growled out in her underground voice, "My missus never hooped (whipped) *me*." Of the two, I was by far the more terrified, and the more injured; but still kept my eyes on her as one would on a wild animal. I did not know whether she was going to strike me, and she certainly thought I was going to renew the "cuffing," the first having been scarcely perceptible; but it was much too fatiguing a process, and I said, "Why don't you do right without obliging me to do so?"

"My missus never hooped *me-e-e*," was repeated, with the eyes still frowning at me.

The result was that my "cuffing" was wholly ineffectual. The negro was more dogged, stolid, and stubborn than ever; and I found that it would be best to let her alone until she had quite forgotten the insult offered her, and then to seize the first opportunity of healing the wound, and henceforth try to "overcome evil with good."

That girl, in spite of her temper, respected herself, and was really unhappy, from loneliness and want of sympathy.

Some time afterwards, when very warm weather had brought on the summer tornadoes, my second case of corporeal discipline occurred.

Little Jeff's nurse, Flora, was one of the most troublesome, impudent negro specimens I ever met with. It was pleasant enough to have Jeff Davis (the baby) with Flora in my room—a beautiful apartment, with a piazza opening from it, all to myself; and there were many kinds of toys to entice little Jeff, which Flora scattered all over the floor, where Jeff crawled about to play with them.

When the room was completely covered, until there was not a stepping place left, and Flora felt inclined for a change, she had a plan of exclaiming suddenly, "Missus calls;" and snatching up the child, quick as an arrow away she darted, in spite of my calling and screaming, leaving every scrap on the floor for me to pick up.

The next time she came, pretending Jeff wanted very much to come and see me, (intelligent baby of six months old!) she promised to put away the toys if I would allow them to be on the floor for Jeff. Perhaps she would collect one or two, and then contrive an excuse to run off with the baby, saying she would be "back directly," and that was the last of her.

One sultry afternoon, I was sitting by the door

opening upon the piazza, opposite the room door, and between two open windows. Suddenly a summer tornado came on, and before I had time to collect my brushes, for I was copying a flower, the curtains were flapping, one chair was blown half across the room, the little table at which I sat would have been upset by the gale had I not leant heavily upon it, and my papers were whirling like feathers about the floor.

Flora was in the hall outside, and I called to her to come quickly to shut the windows, while I held the table, and kept my arms over the things upon it. Flora came as leisurely as a person walking in her sleep. "Quick, Flora! shut the door!" She was not quick by any means, and gave the door a little push, the wind instantly dashing it open as if to tear it off its hinges.

"*Shut* it, Flora!" (another little push.) "Shut it firmly—*latch* it!" No, she would not; and I was pinned to the table, to keep paint-box, glasses, flowers, and papers together.

About the fourth or fifth time of trying, she latched the door, and then advanced in the same slow, impudent manner, staring about her without an effort to close the window, which, by this time had admitted the rain and hail two or three yards into the room, in a large pool, with everything saturated near it. The door once secured, the current of air was checked, and my hands released. As the "she imp of darkness" sauntered past me to stare at what was on the table, instead of going directly to close the window, I gave her a tremendous (to *me*) slap on the side of her head, and said, "Quick! shut the window."

"Oh, laws-a-me, Miss Jones! see what mighty big hail!"

Was I sleeping or waking? The latter; for my hand was tingling dreadfully, and my wrist was nearly dislocated by the force I had used. I was trembling all over with the effort, and she was not aware of the blow! I don't believe the creature had even felt me.

Those were the two instances in my Southern experience of punishing negroes. In both cases I came off so much the greater sufferer, that I concluded the means did not answer the purpose; and if I lived twenty years more in the South, nothing would ever induce me to strike a negro again.

Just before the Peninsula battles, Mrs. McClellan gave me to read the following letter from her husband, Captain McClellan, of the Second Florida Regiment. She knew I copied it, because some of the statements are very interesting, and it is one of many similar epistles I used to read from soldier relatives. As the events referred to have become a matter of history, I hope I am not abusing confidence by introducing it here.

Dated, "York Town, Va.," it commenced:

"*12th April*, 1862.

"We are all well. A week ago this morning the enemy appeared before us here, with General McClellan at their head,

100,000 strong, and we only 13,000. Now we are 50,000. All the week there has been more or less of cannonading and skirmishes on both sides, to the detriment of the Yankees. Yesterday, p.m., we had a brilliant skirmish in front of our fortifications. Just in front, about 600 yards, was a peach orchard fenced round, and some houses beyond the fence. Behind the houses were 1000 of the enemy's sharp-shooters, and they have been for seven days annoying us, by killing a man or so every day, and wounding others. So yesterday, p.m., the Mississippi battalion of Rifles were thrown out, supported by the Second Floridá (mine), and forward we went, and routed the sharp-shooters, killing some twenty, wounding many, and burning the houses and fences; while we had only three men wounded.

"Colonel Ward had command of the force, and behaved very gallantly. The balls whistled thick and fast around, but on we went. They struck close to me, but none took effect. After you get into the line, you go on as if nothing were occurring. It is all in the providence of God, and to his care you commit yourself, to abide his will.

"I do not think we shall have a fight here, and think McClellan will retreat. If he fights us we shall whip him.

"Yesterday I received Judge Finlay's letter, of 16th March, in which he says you were all well. This is all I have heard of you since 16th February. (She had written four times.) We are well prepared for the fight here, with artillery, having over 100 pieces. Do not be uneasy, but trust in God. I think I am a better man since I have been in battle, and if I live, trust I shall show it in my works. We hear that Beauregard has destroyed the Lincoln army in Tennessee. I believe that, in the providence of God, we shall yet maintain ourselves and free our country. May I live to see it! We have sent off everything from here. Kiss the children for me, and tell the servants 'Howdy.' Many kisses for you, my dear Addie. I am better in mind about you since Judge Finlay's letter. I suppose yours must have miscarried.

"I remain,

"Your truly affectionate husband,

"P. F. McClellan."

This McClellan is of the same family with the Gen. George B. McClellan, and the two fighting face to face were cousins. He alluded to the battles of Corinth and Shiloh, in his mention of the "Lincoln army."

CHAPTER XV.

Arrival of the "Florida"—The Natural Ally—The South becomes Practical — Battles of Yorktown and Williamsburg—Capture of New Orleans.

ONE morning while we were all busily occupied by the studies, a gentleman was seen riding quickly up the road to Sylvania. An arrival was usually followed by so much whispering and watching among my curious flock, that my best policy was to allow them to ascertain who the fresh comer might be, and then resume the business of the day. In the present instance the news proved highly exciting, as I saw by the contact of heads, and renewed whisperings, when Jenny returned to the schoolroom.

"What news?" was a natural question.

"Oh, Miss Jones, a ship has run the blockade at St. Andrew's Bay, loaded with muskets; and Mr. Miller has come to ask mamma to send down a waggon directly, to help bring up the cargo before the Yankees chase her. They did see her come in; and the people expect every minute to have a battle down there. Everybody is sending their waggons to bring away the ammunition directly."

Such news, of course, created an entire suspension of studies for the time being, and for the next quarter of an hour the only study was to see who could talk the fastest.

"St. Andrew's Bay? How far is it?" I asked.

"Oh! it is about seventy or eighty miles from Marianna. They go down the river to get there."

"Mamma doesn't know what in the world to do," said Jenny. "Papa has the carriage-horses, with William, at Tallahassee: Uncle Steph has gone to the mill with one waggon and the other horses, and all the mules are on the farm."

"I suppose our boys will be ordered off down there directly," said Matty.

"Our boys" were the Marianna "Dragoons," a company lately organized; among whom was Matty's (one of my pupils) young brother of sixteen, who preferred volunteering to studying; and several other brothers and cousins of all the girls in the county, were members of the company. They had, during the spring, been encamped within a few miles of Sylvania, and had been constant visitors, in twos, threes, and half-dozens at a time.

"Our boys" did set off in "double quick" to the bay, to protect the valuable cargo, which, with the assistance of many citizens and their waggons within eighty miles, was brought safely to the Arsenal. Though within reach of the Yankees, they had laboured unmolested, and the Marianna Dragoons came back quite disappointed at such an unaccountable fact.

The "Florida" brought some other useful articles besides muskets; which for a time occupied all the ladies, and all their horses and carriages within many miles, as they seized the opportunity of making purchases until the new stock was quite exhausted. For some weeks cotton bales were being conveyed across the country to reload the 'Florida,' which, although she had got so safely into port, was not allowed to escape again; but the shrewd Yankees had prudently determined to capture not only the ship, but her cargo of cotton too, and had postponed their attack until her rich freight presented a more tempting prize. Half the crew volunteered to go with the captors; the other half were, if I remember correctly, put on shore; but the pilot would not surrender, nor accept a bribe of 500 dollars to guide the ship out of Bear Creek. The consequence was she ran aground, and had to be lightened of a large portion of her cotton bales, which floated up the stream again, to the infinite amusement of the inhabitants.

Public affairs at that time were pregnant with impending battles and solemn events. In addition to the losses on the North Carolina coast, New Orleans, Mobile, and Richmond were threatened.

Island No. 10 in the Mississippi, Fort Pulaski, and other places on the eastern coast had surrendered. Manassas was evacuated, which movement exposed the whole of that portion of Virginia, where I had so many friends.

The reader knows how, ever since those fearful slaughters around Richmond, all that section of the country has been torn by battles and skirmishes, and how it is now one vast devastated wilderness, producing food for neither man nor beast.

We saw by the papers that President Davis's Message had been received and read with lengthy comments by the English press; the laudatory tone of which was viewed with much gratification by the Confederate journals. I observed also that in adverse ratio as Dr. W. H. Russell became *du trop* in the North, he grew in favour with the South; and as a letter from Mr. Phillips Day, explaining the treatment of the Federal prisoners in Richmond had lately found its way into the Southern journals, "our own" and the "specials" were permitted to keep "the even tenour of their way" without further comment or abuse.

Public attention was turned much more towards France after the blockade had been pronounced "efficient" by the British Parliament; neither should I be surprised at any day to find that an alliance between that nation and the Confederates has been formed. This is an extremely presumptuous assertion of the Author, who, it is seen, has not enjoyed the confidence of one single person in the Confederacy able or willing to impart such an idea. I am no politician, no diplomatist, only an observer; and have no other reasons in the world for asserting such an idea, excepting on my own responsibility and surmises. I have seen England loved, respected, trusted, and copied by the Southern population; I have received much attention from the mere fact of being *English;* and I have seen the right hand of fellowship held out to England, with sincerity and a yearning for her friendship, as "a natural ally." And I know also that from simple humanity the Southerners will stop this horrible war as soon as honourable means of doing so can be found. England received the first overtures, "but seeing ye put it from you"—— "lo! we turn to" another.

The *practical* class, both old and young, were becoming daily more appreciated in the Confederacy.

Manufactories in Virginia, were for envelopes, blacking, lucifer matches, hats, caps, tanneries, shoes for the Government, and iron. Cotton and woollen goods, sword factories, saddles and harnesses, agricultural machines, oil-cloth, foundries for engines, &c., sash, door, and blind factories, gun carriages, waggons, wheelbarrows, camp stools, tents, tent-poles, &c., and every kind of implement of war.

In North Carolina—candles, lamp-oil, salt, cutlery; nearly all from recent invention and natural products. Gunpowder, bayonets, sewing-machines, and a repetition of many of those articles made in Virginia. Also jeans, cotton-prints—called "calicoes" in America—for dresses; linseys, blankets, cloths, and a variety of things too numerous to mention.

General Beauregard's beautiful and pathetic appeal to the country to spare their church and plantation bells, to be moulded into cannon, is among the most touching events of the war. It is scarcely necessary to state that it met with ready response. Mrs. Milton, and all the people in our neighbourhood, had their old bells, copper kettles, brass door knobs, lead and iron fragments collected, and forwarded to Columbus, Georgia—another very enterprising and flourishing town.

Horticulture was more encouraged, and the practice of saving seeds adopted, and notices published by those who had plenty, to invite applications from those who had few. In fact the Confederacy became one united family.

Poor Mrs. McClellan, our friend, did not hear from her husband for a long time after the receipt of that last letter, when he intimated the probability of a speedy engagement; neither after the evacuation of Yorktown, and the battle of Williamsburg did he write. Reports of killed and wounded arrived, but not a word of her husband. Then it was whispered that *he* was wounded, and coming home; then that he was a prisoner. A telegraphic message arrived for a neighbour, from Richmond, with some particulars of the engagement, but containing not one mention of his name. Poor devoted wife! She came to stay at Sylvania with her children, for comfort and change of air, and we really trembled for her life, as she had a naturally delicate constitution.

At last a despatch arrived, merely a few words to say: "Send the carriage to the river for me on such a day."

"Oh! he is—he must be badly wounded!" she cried; "he never orders the carriage when he is well; he *always* prefers to ride." Many days of suspense, but in time he came; not wounded, only ill.

"Just a little done up," he said.

"Done up!" To hear the account of those battles, one would think so indeed. "Mud, rocks, fallen trees, bushes, swamps. Of all the most difficult and horrible countries to fight battles in, that beats them," said the Captain. Oh! what a description of those battles and retreats did we hear from the rebel soldier! How they marched and turned to fight, and marched again; and "double quicked," they called it; thirty miles a day. One man died "double quicking," Captain McClellan said. The mud of the swamps through which they marched was so deep that the skirts of the captain's coat were clogged, too heavy to permit him to proceed; and he cut them off, not to be impeded in his progress. He was very ill at the time, and it was with the greatest difficulty that he marched at all; weak with fasting besides, not having tasted a morsel of food for forty-eight hours, with the exception of a castaway scrap of bacon he had gladly picked up upon the road! Some of the enemy were lying in ambush, and fired upon them, and the captain heard their bullets whistle past him. The enemy was marking his pace, and he felt each shot come nearer and nearer. He was too weak to give the word of command while marching, and stopped to do so. At that moment a ball went through the collar of his coat: the accidental stopping had saved his life; one inch more, and it would have entered his throat.

As the main body of the Federal army had recourse to their boats to ascend the York River, the Confederates found them once more drawn up to receive them at Williamsburg after this fatiguing march, and again gave them battle and dispersed them. It was in this manner that the Peninsula was evacuated, and the Southern army collected about Richmond, previous to those heartrending and desperate encounters of the seven days' battles. Many, many such incidents did one learn of those Peninsula engagements, of which the reader has already heard so much, that I will not weary him with a repetition of them. Captain McClellan had come home on a furlough, at the end of his first year's campaign.

Major Brown had lately visited Tallahassee, and there being no prospect of active service in that place, he became impatient to be on duty again: therefore, having friends among the Texans in the army at Corinth, he resolved to repair thither, and volunteer afresh. He would resign his majorship and enter as private. This sort of thing one heard of frequently: on the other hand, some of the young gentlemen were ambitious of being officers only, insomuch that many good jokes were published at their expense, about getting up a company composed of *all officers.*

Not only did the free market at Charleston and New Orleans continue to be liberally supplied, and the gun-boat funds increase astonishingly, but every now and then a fresh object for public sympathy presented itself. When the "Hero of Shiloh," General Albert Sydney Johnston, fell, contributions were immediately set on foot for the support of his widow and family, and were promptly met. One could not doubt the wealth of the South by these various proofs.

Letters from Richmond indicated an anxious state of the public mind for the safety of the capital. The Federal gun-boats had ascended to Drury's bluff and had been repulsed, yet the inhabitants were impatient for more effectual protection, and many of the families were leaving the city. Federal ships had again ascended the Rappahannock, and for the second time attempted a landing at Acquia Creek, for the "On to Richmond" *viâ* Fredericksburg.

Of all the Southern disasters, none fell so heavily upon the public mind as the loss of New Orleans, a city upon which so much dependence had been placed, and from which such important assistance was derived. The sacrifices of property on that occasion were something frightful to read of, at such a time of want and scarcity. The river was positively coloured with the barrels of molasses and sugar; and the burning of cotton was enormous. Then the papers began to teem with Butler's proclamations and his tyrannies; and the people buckled on their armour tighter than ever. The emancipation proclamations only had the effect of turning into sound Secessionists those who had before been wavering. It seemed that from the first commencement of hostilities, nay from the very day of Lincoln's election, events had been crowding thicker and faster to the approaching "climax," a climax which drew no nearer, because events of still greater magnitude rolled rapidly on the heels of those that had passed, till a climax seemed unattainable, and the end was hidden in the complicated web that obscured the vision of the North, but only stimulated the South to more unyielding and determined courage. It seemed that all the skill of the Federal Government was exerted to make bad matters worse, while they pursued a policy that even children and servants were known to laugh at. "They will have enough of their own poor on their hands without our servants; and do they think we will ever permit our negroes to walk off *alive*, should they attempt to escape?" "But our servants know when they are well off: it is very few who love the Yankees well enough to go to *them* for protection."

CHAPTER XVI.

My Courage Wavers — The Route is Doubtful — The Plum Orchard — My Estate in Florida — Excellent Openings for Enterprise—The St. Andrew's Bay Salt-works—The Battles of Seven Pines, and Chickahominy—The "On to Richmond."

Mrs. Milton did not go to Tallahassee, neither did any of us. We were kept in a state of preparation for the move for many weeks, and the Governor hired the largest house in the place for his wife and ten children. It had a good piano in it besides, with three already at Sylvania. Every time his Excellency returned home for a few days' rest, he seemed to think we were all so much safer, and better supplied with comforts there, provisions continuing to be extremely scarce at Tallahassee, so that again he wavered. Some lady friends were going to visit there, and they persuaded Miss Milton to accompany them. Jenny was a sweet girl, every one loved her, and I had been taking great pains to give her a training that would fit her to instruct her younger sisters, because I had determined, one way or another, to make my way out of the Confederacy while life remained in me. Therefore I felt that it would be a serious interruption to Jenny's studies to leave home just before the expiration of our "term" of five months; and thought it best to suggest to her mother that my health, and the condition of the country, would oblige me to make every effort to leave, when the summer vacation commenced. Mrs. Milton expressed much regret at the admitted necessity, while she thanked me for the interest evinced for her children, and my timely explanations, which, on pointing out to Jenny, the latter willingly postponed her anticipated pleasure.

The next time the Governor came home he was apprized of my intentions. At first he was very much disappointed, and quite inclined to be angry. I felt almost as if I ought not to have gone to Florida for so short a time; but we had all thought that the blockade would surely have been raised, and that, in consequence, the war would have been over in the spring; in which case I should not have objected to remain for the year. I pointed out to him the injury that anxiety and deprivations were causing to my health, and the increased difficulties that were threatening the country; and also explained my confidence in his elder daughters, who would superintend the education of the younger ones, until a cessation of the war enabled him to engage the most accomplished ladies that either France or England presented to his choice. His Excellency saw the reason of all these things; and while admitting them, promised to make inquiries in good time, as to the best route for me to take, and to make all other necessary preparations.

That was just at the time when the Federal authorities were announcing, that the ports of New Orleans, Beaufort in South Carolina, Norfolk, and one in North Carolina, were to be opened; and the Governor did not apprehend the least difficulty in my getting away, recommending New Orleans in particular. His Excellency was acquainted with the British Consul at Mobile, and kindly volunteered to write and ask him what chances there were of a "neutral British subject" being able to sail from that port.

Much as I had desired to visit New Orleans under happier circumstances, I rather shrank from doing so at this time; for the "tyranny" of General Butler was a constant theme, and the lawlessness of the Federal troops there, with martial law proclaimed, daily fears of incendiarisms, revolts, and outbreaks, were enough to terrify a less venturesome personage than myself. "Our boys" had been gone to Mobile some weeks, and no tidings received from them. That route, and from thence to New Orleans, was a very indirect one, involving many changes of boats, trains, and coaches, and the chances were, that when I arrived near the lines of the armies, I might not have been permitted to pass. Indeed the hazard seemed too great, and the success too doubtful to think of such an expedition, without being well assured of its certainty and safety. As several weeks must of necessity elapse before any information could be received, I resolved to trouble my good and reliable friend, Mr. Bunch, once more, and also wrote a letter, left open, to the Consul at New Orleans, trusting to the kindness of whatever authorities into whose hands it might fall, to forward it. I also wrote to the Consul of Mobile, that place still belonging to the Confederates.

Mr. Bunch from Charleston wrote on the 21st May that he saw no chance of my proceeding to England; but in case of my procuring a safe conduct, he warned me against carrying letters, pamphlets, drawings, or any other matters that might compromise me with either combatant.

It stood to reason no prudent woman (alone) would attempt such uncertain journeys as those, either to New Orleans or Mobile, with the prospect of catching yellow fever, or at best, of spending all one's finances in trying to get there; and under such very doubtful circumstances! Possibly one might escape through a Florida port by running the blockade, or, better still, as a "neutral British, &c.," because the Federals had possession of Jacksonville, the St. John's River, and other parts of East and South Florida. It was reported that great friendliness existed between the Northern officers and the rebel young ladies of those localities; the relatives of the latter, however, came out strongly in newspaper articles to the contrary soon afterwards, indignantly rejecting the idea. I saw that Florida had 10,000 men in the field, in the service of the Confederate States, without a draft and without conscription, out of a voting population of 12,250.

In spite of the idea that General McClellan's great "concerted movement" was intended to be made at the time when the twelve months' volunteers resigned, the majority had re-enlisted without furloughs at all, many for the war; and only those whose constitutions required rest took furloughs.

Florida, in proportion to her population, exceeded all the other States in the number of her volunteers. Still it seemed probable, in spite of these things, which did not concern me in any way, that I might be permitted to pass the lines in Florida; and Captain McClellan, who was going to Tallahassee, undertook to inquire of the Governor, and also of the Confederate General commanding that section. The replies were equally discouraging. The lower part of "our river," the Chattahoochie, had been obstructed in order to prevent an incursion into Georgia, through West Florida; so the Gulf route was equally impracticable. Patience was all that was left to me.

President Davis set apart another day of fasting and prayer, the third since the outbreak of the war. It was responded to with the usual reverence; even to the suspension of the all-absorbing "news."

The evacuation of Corinth was the next great public event, which again set all the Milton family wondering what had become of their cousin, Milton Brown, from whom no letter had been received.

Several influential citizens fell under the displeasure of General Butler at New Orleans at that time, among whom was the lady, Mrs. Phillips, whose case has since elicited so much of the public sympathy.

The spring of 1862 was remarkable for changes of temperature and the "late season." I remember on the 7th April, after the thermometer had reached 92° for several days, a thunder-storm cooled the air so suddenly that towards morning there was almost a frost.

With so much warm weather as we had had, fruit seemed natural, but not a sign of it appeared until May, when a wild plum was ripe. It was strange that a plum should be the firstfruits of the season, but strawberries could be eaten in February by those who took the trouble to raise them. Little Fanny brought me in a great plateful of those plums, saying, "Now, Miss Jones, you will have plenty of fruit; the orchard is full of plums, and the blackberries and mulberries are very nearly ripe." The two latter were quite an inferior kind, but the plums were delicious. They were yellowish, about as large as a full-sized gooseberry, partaking of the flavour of that fruit combined with a cherry and plum; they were small stoned, and luscious when ripe; but only one more plateful was brought to me. When Mrs. Milton sent up to the orchard the first time, every ripe plum had been appropriated by the negroes on their way home from work. "There will be plenty more in a few days," said the girls; "mamma has told Uncle Steph not to let the servants help themselves until we have had some. They are very plentiful, and the servants always have what they like from the orchard."

In a few days more, another expedition of baskets was despatched to the plum-orchard. The trees were entirely cleared, but "the hogs" had done it this time. The porcine genus is certainly provided with remarkably long legs in Florida, though scarcely long enough to help themselves from the trees, one would think. Still that was the first fruit and the last that I tasted in Florida, until water-melons came into season.

We soon revelled in abundance of vegetables, however. I have seen ten or twelve kinds on the table at once, several of which, such as okra, are peculiar to the South.

The wild flowers rivalled even those of Virginia. Splendid phloxes, œnotheras, mimosas, cassias, and climbing plants that crowded upon the trees so thickly that you could not distinguish the branches. There was not a space unfilled with vegetation; that under the trees, and in copses being, in fact, the most luxurious. I have frequently found oak, hickory, and walnut saplings throwing out leaves of ten, twelve, or sixteen inches in length, or diameter. I counted at least twelve species of oak near Sylvania, many of which are evergreens.

The Governor was one day, when at home, speaking of some land to be purchased at ten cents an acre. "Ten cents an acre" for *good* land in the beautiful luxuriant State of Florida! One could scarcely credit the fact.

Captain McClellan took a journey to look at it, with the intention of making a purchase, and the idea of possessing two or three hundred acres of land in Florida was so irresistible, that I sent a message to him to buy some of it for me, should he think it advisable to do so. Even if lost, ten or twenty dollars would be well worth risking.

The claim could be easily made out for a "neutral British subject." The fact of possessing a fertile estate in Florida, which I could go home and rent to some enterprising Englishman—a horticulturist, for instance—would be so very charming. To be sure, people reckoned their estates by thousands of acres in the South. The Governor had about fourteen thousand near us, besides estates in Georgia and Texas. But in England hundreds would do very well. Unfortunately the messenger "quite forgot" to give my note to Captain McClellan, and he came back, having secured a most promising lot for himself, and, of course, had never thought of me. It was a pity, as nothing would have been so interesting as to persuade some English people to run the blockade, and go and cultivate my estate in Florida. During the war the Southerners have not time, and the negroes are too stupid, but there never was such an opportunity for enterprise as the Southern Confederacy now affords.

The various springs in the mountain regions speak for themselves, of the minerals, from which they are named. There are also nitre caves, coal, lead, and iron-mines, with supplies for ages. The working of some of these, together with the gold mines, has been temporarily suspended by the war. But besides the gold that has already been dug in North Carolina, Georgia and Virginia, there is but little doubt that much exists, as yet unknown, in the latter State. The quantity of quartz, in what are called the Piedmont regions of the Blue Ridge, may be taken as a sure indication of its presence.

The castor-oil plant is indigenous in Louisiana, Alabama, and Florida, and may be made a valuable article of commerce. Indigo, and hops also, which flourish everywhere. Cochineal is found in South Carolina, Georgia, and Alabama, and might be turned to valuable account. Fustic, and copal, with other dyes and varnishes, only require to be collected and prepared for trade.

Next to cotton, rice, sugar, tobacco, and the cereals, there are fruits, dyes, drugs, hides, horn, vellum, kid, and other kinds of leather; metals, minerals, valuable timber, such as live oak, cedar, teak, and pine; sweet potatoes, honey, and other articles innumerable.

While so many of our English poor are being supported in idleness, and doing incalculable moral harm to the country, *there* is a land where all that is required is labour, and intelligence combined with it.

And what an opening there is for emigrants. In their present mood to discourage "Yankees" any more among them, many vacancies are to be filled. Artisans of every kind might immediately find work and encouragement there. A little English enterprise and capital would succeed in almost any trade. The Southerners have no taste to be other than an agricultural people, as they have always been. Engravers, artists, educationists, millwrights, gardeners, engineers, telegraph workers, and business men of all kinds, will be welcome, if their appearance be not postponed until too late a day.

In spite of the vaunt of "all the South" being supplied with ice from Virginia, the want of it was severely felt on the approach of summer. A little for the hospitals was valued beyond price.

The Governor wrote to say that Mobile would be my best route. In the mean time the Consul had informed me that there was no egress from Mobile, and immediately I wrote to inform His Excellency of this. Three weeks more, at least, must elapse before his reply, before which he might himself leave for Richmond, which he was intending to do.

On his last visit I had suggested the prudence of settling our pecuniary matters, in case I might hear of some sudden opportunity of travelling; or we might find ourselves in some unforeseen danger, when it would be necessary to be prepared. The Governor had quite forgotten that he had promised to defray my travelling expenses, and quite forgotten that he had pledged himself to pay me in specie; but on showing him his letters, he assured me it should be "all right;" but that he did not think it would be possible to procure specie at all. He said, however, that money was due to him in England for cotton, that he would ascertain the name of the parties, and write me a draft for the amount over and above what I should require for passing out of the Confederacy; he would also send an order by me that the overplus should be devoted by his agents to the purchase of muskets and necessaries for his own State. That would be a very satisfactory arrangement, saving me the necessity of purchasing exchange, or of encountering on the journey any of those kinds of inconveniences. So things were to remain for a few weeks longer.

A resident of Marianna had gone down to St. Andrew's Bay to fit up temporary salt-works, in order to make enough for his own family use. Such practices were becoming common wherever persons lived in the neighbourhood of the coast. Another gentleman contemplated establishing works, large enough to supply one of the midland towns, where he had been offered as much as ninety dollars a barrel!

Our Marianna adventurer's salt-works became known to the enemy, parties of whom were in the habit of landing for predatory excursions along the coast. One day a skirmishing party arrived on the shore, and coming up to the place, asked him what he was doing there.

Mr. More told them.

"How much are you making?" asked the captain, "and for whom? Is it for sale? Is it for the Government? Is any one else making salt about here? Who? How far off? How long have they been making it? How long have you been engaged in this business?"

All of which questions were replied to by the salt-maker.

The Federal captain then expressed a wish to see the other works, but Mr. More hesitated, and made some excuses about the distance, and so forth.

"But I want to see them—I insist on it; or I will order my men to destroy these works of yours immediately," said the captain.

The prudent salt-maker still hesitated, and pleaded the inconvenience of leaving his business; but upon the Federal captain becoming furious, and threatening to shoot him down on the spot, he changed his tone, and said in a sort of confidential manner, "Well, to tell the truth, there is a horse company (cavalry) not far from here, and I thought, may be, you'd rather not tumble up against them."

The captain suddenly recollected that he had an engagement which compelled his immediate return, and cried out, "Turn about, boys!—march!" to his men; adding to the family salt-maker, "Well, well!

I have not time to go so far to-day; but mind you do not make any salt for the rebel Government. I do not object to your making a little for yourself, but you must be very quick about; it we shall not permit you to be here long."

By this pardonable *ruse*, Mr. More saved not only his own, but his neighbour's salt-works, both of them making the most of the time their Federal masters allowed to their sovereign subjects. Since my return to England I have, with deep regret, seen that those very salt-works have been destroyed, as threatened.

By-and-by, towards the end of June, his Excellency wrote to me, to say that he regretted extremely that all his attempts to procure specie were in vain; and that he had failed to ascertain the address of the parties in Liverpool to whom his cotton had been consigned, as his agent in Florida was now in the army; but if I would inform him what route I intended to take, he would be happy to render me every possible assistance.

Oh, dear! "what route?" That was the very thing that was so puzzling. After the letters from Mr. Bunch, and the Mobile Consul, and knowing the Federal army was pressing on Richmond, what route could I take while troubles were thickening on everyside? In vain I had written to Mr. Cridland, who had promised to keep me apprized of the prospects there; but neither he, Mrs. Henningsen, Mrs. Ayres, nor the Castletons had written to me, and all I could do was to decide to get as far as Charleston, and trust to circumstances to proceed in some way or other; for day by day I grew more timid and out of health, and the horror of being attacked by some of the Southern diseases, and dying so far away from home, seized possession of my mind, and I felt that every mile eastward and northward would be so far towards recovery. Then came the news of those terrific, those appalling slaughters of the 31st May and the 1st June, known by the names of the battles of Chickahominy, Fair Oaks, and Seven Pines. Then did the poor Floridians begin most terribly to realize the horrors of war, for their regiments had been engaged in them throughout, and were most frightfully reduced in numbers. Mr. Miller's two sons were wounded, and were coming home as soon as they could be moved; one had already fallen a sacrifice. Of another neighbour's sons, one was killed and one wounded. Captain Parkhill, my fellow-traveller, was killed; also Col. Ward, a highly esteemed citizen of Florida; the people of Marianna were all cast into mourning, and Mrs. McClellan congratulated herself with heartfelt thankfulness for her husband's timely safety.

Soon the two young Millers returned to their home, about a mile and a half from Sylvania. We all went to see them, for they were not too ill to converse quietly, after recovering from the fatigue of their journey. One of them was shot in the left arm, but he told me he thought he could manage to load his musket at the time, and as they were making a charge, he did not wish to give up in the middle of it. He had been so long in loading, that the captain discovered his wound, and ordered him off the field. He still thought he could do something with his right arm, and did not obey the order. By-and-by the captain ordered him off again, but not until four hours after his being disabled. He had not been able to find his brother, nor to hear of him for nearly a week after the battles. The wound of the latter was a shot in the neck, just above the left clavicle, passing out at the back of his shoulder, injuring the lung. He was still feeble, and could only speak in a low voice, and at intervals; but his parents could not prevail on him to be silent, so that his energy caused his life to be despaired of. He had fallen on his face when wounded, and had been lying nearly twenty-four hours among the dead and dying. He said, that had he fallen on his back he must have died of suffocation, as every report of cannon caused his wound to burst out bleeding afresh. After he had lain many hours and recovered the first shock, he had tried to lift his head, and found himself surrounded by prostrate forms; not a sound nor a groan was to be heard, and he thought himself the only living one among them. He lay all night, and until the next afternoon, when he was discovered to be alive, and was carried off to the city. Those were fearful days indeed! soldier brothers and relatives not knowing whom of their friends were living or dead. One might be carried off to one hospital or private house, and another to a different one; while anxious relatives were hunting everywhere, advertising for names and sometimes passing many days in searching for their missing sons or brothers. These scenes are too harrowing to dwell upon; the case of those two young Millers is only one of the mildest and least painful of the scores one heard of.

The general opinion seemed to be that a temporary cessation of hostilities would take place, as it always had done after the severest battles. The great "On to Richmond" had received one more check, and if ever an opportunity would present itself of being able to get away, it might be now, when the prisoners would no doubt be exchanged, and flags of truce again granted for a time. I became more and more alarmed and impatient; the remembrance of the last summer's delays, and their consequences weighed heavily on my mind, and once more I wrote to the Governor to have our business settled, and my route decided upon.

CHAPTER XVII.

The Cotton-field in Bloom—An instance of Negro Ambition—Final Arrangements—General Beauregard's Furlough.

THE Conscription Act had at last been passed, for the purpose of enrolling all between the ages of eighteen and thirty-five. This step was deemed necessary, that the Conscripts might embrace the great number of "Northern men with Southern sympathies," who persisted in remaining in the South for the purposes of trade, but who seldom volunteered; and also many foreigners, who had taken the oath of allegiance, but abstained from joining the Confederate army; which was composed almost entirely of landholders and slaveholders.

The "thrilling" (as Americans call them) contents of the newspapers kept one's sympathies on a perpetual rack.

The well-known "Appeal" of the daughters of New Orleans to their countrymen was published, which incited the Southerners, and especially the

Louisianians, to a savage fury against the tyrant Butler, whose very name sufficed to stimulate them on the battle-field. I was assured that "Butler, boys! Butler!" was used as a command to advance.

Once more the Governor re-appeared at home. We had already taken leave of each other, and Jenny had gone to Tallahassee and returned again. She and I had parted to meet no more, but in the delays of the times had, nevertheless, met once again.

Our school had been dispersed nearly a month, but that made no difference in my stay, as far as the family were concerned; for their efforts to study my comforts were, if possible, rather increased than diminished towards me as a visitor.

I had enjoyed leisure to rest, and to stroll about with little Fanny, collecting and exploring; and we had been to see some of the beautiful springs and caves with which Florida abounds.

There was one part of the plantation where a very short walk through the woods brought us to a large cotton-field, belonging to the adjoining estate. It was extremely interesting to watch the progress of the all-important plant, in its different stages of bud, blossom, and boll; not unmixed with anxiety, for fear the pods should not ripen, and burst in time for me to gather some of them.

There was very frequently a gang of negroes, some twenty or thirty, at work in this field; for the cotton requires a vast deal of weeding, and hoeing; but I never saw a white man with them, nor do I think the owner kept an overseer; and they afforded me one proof that the negro is not altogether devoid of ambition, and this even in Florida, where the race is not seen to the best advantage.

My first acquaintance with these people was as follows. Walking one day in a road that ran along the edge of another part of the field, I beheld a large herd of cattle approaching in no very tractable mood. These creatures, semi-wild with their woodland life, are not always safe to meet *vis-à-vis* in that manner; besides which they were creating a suffocating cloud of dust; there was no alternative but to mount a "snake-fence," ten feet high, with a view to escape into the cotton-field, just then rendered doubly attractive by the splendid masses of asclepias, (tuberosa) phloxes, and commelyna, &c., in bloom.

Having achieved the feat of reaching the very top rail, with one foot just ready to begin the descent, my ears were assailed by a furious barking, and behold a large rough dog stood guard over the cotton-field, flowers and all. Of the two, this last foe was the most to be feared; the cattle were not likely to leap upon the fence; but the dog might; and I must own to considerable cowardice on that occassion; but pretending to look defiantly at the noisy brute, I called aloud to the negroes, who were so far off, that I almost despaired of my voice reaching their ears. The barking of the dog caused them to look towards us, and by dint of beckoning and screaming, two of them were induced to approach, who comforted me with the assurance that "he warn't a goin' to trouble yer," which had already dawned upon me, or he would not have waited so patiently while I was perched up there in terror.

Of course the negroes, an uncle and an aunt, were curious to know where I lived, and what I was doing "all that way from home," a short half mile; as they can never understand a person moving for mere pleasure. They were hoeing up the beautiful phloxes most mercilessly, and I pointed to some other flowers not yet in bloom in a corner of the fence, begging the negroes to allow them to remain there until I came again, and then made my way to Sylvania, by the shorter cut across the field.

I suppose that man must have been the "boss," as they call any one placed over them. Whether by appointment or choice, he appeared to take the lead, and it was very amusing to hear the arguments carried on between him and his fellow-labourers, who always resent any usurped authority of "coloured folk."

These people, whom I used to come upon quite suddenly, on emerging from our little path in the woods upon the cotton-field, evinced the same fearless freedom of manner towards "white folk" that was so remarkable in Virginia. Whether I noticed them or not, a salutation was not long in greeting me.

"You be allers a hunting weeds, arn't you, missus? What's the use an' them?" On seeing me examine the cotton plants, and no doubt investing me with the qualities of a connoisseur, the "boss" uncle asked, "How's Muster Milton's cotton crop a comin' on, mistis?"

"It is very fine indeed—already in bloom."

That was the beginning of June, and the news did not appear very welcome to the man.

"Well! I reckon there isn't many that can beat *us* at making cotton. We can make more out o' one piece o' land than most folks, *I* reckon."

"Your field looks very fine, but General Milton's is nearly two weeks forwarder. It has been in blossom more than a week, and some of it is nearly in boll."

That was worse news still, and the man became quite self-important as he replied, "I allers likes what *I* do, to be just about the best as can be done. I don't like for no other hands to get a head of ours. That's what I allers aim at," he added, as he took a self-satisfied survey of his crop. That negro was one of ten thousand: such emulation is very rare among them.

Fanny assisted me in the all-important business of packing up, and never was there such a packing to achieve as that. In spite of Mr. Bunch, I resolved to sacrifice neither "papers, pamphlets, nor drawings," but to trust to the well-known politeness of the Northern gentlemen, to permit me to transport to neutral shores those innocent, yet treasured relics of the country and the war.

I could procure no suitable paper for my herbarium, and was obliged to substitute all the Confederate newspapers that I could lay my hands upon. Surely they would not object to this; and the heterogeneous collection of animal, vegetable, and mineral *inutilities*, amassed in some six or eight years' wanderings, it was probable that the Federal authorities, with so much on their hands, would soon be tired of examining.

The Governor had succeeded in procuring specie for a large portion of my salary. I am sure he must have paid an enormous premium for it, although he did not hint at such a thing; for when I reached Richmond, gold was at 95 per cent. His Excellency did not mention this fact, nor make any favour of the payment; on the contrary, he regretted that his utmost endeavours had been so far unsuccessful as to prevent his paying me the whole amount in gold. I had however enough to take me home, and that was all I cared about. The Confederate notes did very well for my long and expensive journey to the borders.

The expenses of the first journey the Governor defrayed, notwithstanding my short stay, as he had stipulated to do so; and paid a large sum besides for some delayed luggage, which had caused him and his secretary much writing and sending after, and freightage was exorbitantly high, because the army monopolized all the railroads. But no favour was made of this either; and, in fact, I had every reason to believe that, under any other circumstances, a person in my position would soon realize a comfortable stipend among the very liberal and generous Southerners.

As soon as I had decided to attempt the journey to Richmond *viâ* Charleston, Captain McClellan tried to persuade me to go *viâ* Tennessee. He was going to look after some property there, and Maggie was to visit some relatives in Alabama, and would proceed a great part of the way. Mrs. McClellan thought this would be an agreeable arrangement for both of us, and Maggie was an intelligent, pleasant little girl. The Captain said, "I can get you through Bragg's army," then at Chattanooga; and the Governor would give me a letter of introduction to the General. The Eastern route, however, seemed less hazardous; but it was finally settled that I should go up the Chattahoochie River, and across Georgia, as being a more direct route to Charleston; which would afford me the protection and company of Captain McClellan and Maggie a great part of the way. Those long, lonely journeys were so depressing at such a time, that this arrangement promised to be most fortunate for me.

Further delays had yet to be endured. One of the cousins, who had been my pupil, had forgotten to tell her father that I wished to leave Florida as soon as I could make the necessary preparations, and therefore his indebtedness for my instructions was not forthcoming. Mr. Miller also was from home, and he must be waited for, for the same reason, his two little girls having been my pupils. The people in the South never appear to think anything of weeks. Whether a thing is done one week or another is all the same to them, neither can they comprehend such a thing as *haste* in any one else; scarcely even of punctuality, as their life has not been passed in the kind of business that demands it.

My next fear, therefore, was, that the Captain would start on his journey without me; for he happened to be one of the active, energetic Tennesseans; and his business did require punctuality.

At the very time the wife of General W. Scott died, it was reported that Beauregard had also become a widower. His wife was very ill, certainly, but happily she recovered. After the evacuation of Corinth, the General's health was so impaired by his long and trying campaign, that he had a six-months' furlough, and proceeded to the mountain springs in Middle Alabama, with Madame Beauregard. As a proof of the wear and tear of mind this devoted servant of the Confederacy had suffered, I need only say that his hair is now perfectly white; turned in one short year from the rich colour it had worn, in a man who had scarcely attained the prime of life.

In the middle of June, the important victory at James Island, South Carolina, by the Confederates, ensured the safety of Charleston for another season.

The bombardment of Vicksburg in the opposite direction was going on furiously at the same time.

More, and yet more terrific battles were again raging round Richmond, the details of which came in slow and tedious scraps of information; until the day at last broke once more with a clearer horizon, and the confirmed good tidings that Richmond was safe, gave new life and vigour to the remotest bounds of the Confederacy. The reader knows too well the horrors of those seven days' battles, when Richmond was in an almost state of siege, with not much short of famine staring the inhabitants in the face; how the result was the retreat of the "grand army" about thirty miles; that is from their right wing to the James River, or rather in the remarkable "change of base," accomplished by the General McClellan under such a new and singular strategy!

CHAPTER XVIII.

Parting Gifts—The Steamboat on the Chattahoochie—Public Sentiments—Motives for wishing to be Free—Landing at Eufalla—The Hotel Waiting-maid—Macon, Georgia—A fellow-traveller from Chattanooga—Another from New Orleans—Charleston in a state of Repose—Effects of Martial Law in Richmond—The Honourable Secretaries—The Passport obtained—The Hospitals—Changes and Chances—Treatment of Federal Prisoners—Popular Names.

At last both Mr. Miller and Matty's father returned. The former still delayed the payment, under excuse of trying to procure *specie;* but Mrs. Milton advised me to make sure of whatever money I could obtain, as the Millers were "not the most reliable people." The other gentleman told me frankly that gold was "not to be found," which ended the matter, as far as he was concerned. The Millers would "send to morrow," and "call the next day," and all that sort of thing; till I declared, money or no money, go I must, and the good Captain had already postponed his journey till the very last moment.

It was with peculiar and painful feelings that I prepared to take leave of all these kind Southern people—these "rebels;" even neutral Sarah Jones rebelled against that appellation; I almost felt that

I was acting a cowardly part, in leaving friends in trouble, to seek enjoyment independent of them.

Had there been hopes of corresponding with them, the parting would not have proved so difficult; but to know that I must leave them to their fate, and such a fate, without a prospect of ever learning what that fate might be, this was indeed a trial to endure.

Even sable Jane seemed sorry, for I had at last succeeded in winning her smile, if not her heart; and found that she had a most splendid set of teeth behind those sausage lips, which improved her looks amazingly. Poor Jane! Some of the mischievous negroes had destroyed the best dress she had, and I promised her one of mine, "if she would behave herself civilly."

"Whether I haves de dress or not, I 'hāves (behaves) *my*self all de same," said Jane, indignantly.

"But if you were not so 'ugly' you would have a good many things given to you." ('Ugly' in the States is usually applied to manners, in the way of being unamiable, but Jane took it in its literal sense, personally.)

"If I *is* ugly, I is as God made me,—I didn't make myself."

"No, I was not speaking of your *looks*, they are well enough—I mean your temper; *you* make that so ugly: God did not make that, you know."

"I 'spects God made me to please His fancy. Ef I'd a made myself, I'd made myself a heap prettier den I *is*."

Poor Jane! I had not intended to hurt her feelings regarding her doubtful beauty, and promised her one of my trunks, that she might lock up all her clothes in it, and not be robbed any more. My chattels had been replenished only in the way of 'specimens,' therefore I could easily spare her this. A lady in the house happened to hear of Jane's acquisition, which did win her heart to me, I do believe; but the lady said, "How I wish I had known you were going to give Jane that nice trunk, I should have been glad to buy it of you!" *That*, from a Southern lady! Blockade, cruel blockade! it positively brought tears to my eyes, to think of her expressing such a wish.

"The dearest friends, alas! must part," but I hope never to part with dear friends under such circumstances again; and to think how many of their own friends are being separated under these painful trials, is far worse to reflect upon.

The Governor and Mrs. Milton presented me with two large and handsome volumes from their library; and just as I was leaving, one of my dark-eyed pupils, a picturesque and noble girl, brought me a much-prized treasure, saying, "Miss Jones, will you keep this for my sake, and excuse its not being new? for there is nothing I can find in town worth your acceptance." Poor darling Kico! (she had a queer Greek name,) it was as painful to take, as to reject her gift.

We were all out on the piazza to postpone to the last moment those strangely painful partings. The Captain and Maggie had already arrived in their own carriage, and were waiting. How many friends there were to leave, and perhaps not even to *hear* of them again!

Little Jeff Davis had the last kiss; little laughing Jeff—*he* knew nothing of those sorrows.

Captain McClellan had heard about the tardiness of the Millers, and insisted on stopping as we passed their house. The lame excuse now made by the old gentleman—made me feel quite sorry for his meanness; but it would be strange indeed not to find some mean inhabitants of the Southern Confederacy, as elsewhere. Had it not been for the Captain, I should never have obtained even as much as I did of those dues, which, with such a long and doubtful journey before me, I could ill afford to lose.

We had started at dawn of day, and the first few hours of our drive were delightful. It was about eighteen miles to the river, over a tolerable road through woods—pine woods chiefly—under which a perfect garden of gorgeous flowers and luxuriant vegetation flourished.

We repaired to a house, or "hotel," on the river banks, to wait for the boat, which started from the ferry near the Arsenal, where we had crossed in coming from Tallahassee. In ordinary times the boats ran regularly from Apalachicōla, Florida, to Columbus, Georgia, a trip occupying no particular time; dependent on the amount of business, the number of passengers, and the punctuality of the latter. In the present instance, we were first told that the boat would not be "along" till to-morrow morning, then that it was expected at two or three o'clock, and another person was sure that it might "be two or three o'clock at *night* then." All we had to do in such a case was to be ready, and the boat happened to arrive at half-past five, P.M., precisely.

This river steamer was so crowded that Maggie and I thought we should be obliged to sit up all night, every state-room being occupied. There were, among the passengers, refugees from Pensacōla and Apalachicōla, relatives going to Richmond to visit their wounded brothers and husbands, and several country doctors going to offer their services to the army, who perhaps had never extracted a bullet in their lives, nor dressed a fractured limb.

At last it was arranged for some of the gentlemen to rest in the saloon, so that the ladies should appropriate the berths. We need not dwell on the accommodations of the river steamer, more than to say that on the next morning all the female passengers waited most amiably for the only hand-basin on board to be passed from one room to another, before they could make their toilet. I coaxed the stewardess to bring me a good-sized, broad tin bucket full of river water, and I do not believe any one else was so favoured. This was another effect of war and blockade, for I was told by those who knew the boat, that it had always been famous for the convenience and elegance of its fittings. People were getting accustomed to these things, and made no complaints at all.

Never shall I forget the heat—the burning, scorching heat—of that day, on the Chattahoochie River. Just at that time great cotton speculations were being carried on. Every planter was sending his cotton to the interior, where it was being bought up by speculators for fifteen cents per pound. This caused many tedious stoppages at the landings. The banks of this river are uniformly steep, and it was melancholy to see the cotton bales sent tumbling down the rugged precipices, with the casing worn and torn away, and the cords broken: the precious staple, for which so many of my countrymen were suffering in penury, floating down the river in large masses, whitening the muddy stream as they wasted away! Had any of us been at all poetical, we might have written some very appropriate stanzas about that unattainable path of cotton on the rebel waters, floating far away, until hidden from sight by the distant windings of the river.

While these much to be regretted sacrifices were going on—for in some places the sacking was so torn that scarcely half a bale was put on board—we, the passengers, were roasting under the intensity of the sun's heat. Every article on board was burning; every fragment seemed to absorb and retain the heat till it was absolutely *hot* to the touch of even my broiling fingers. How we managed ever to survive that roasting, is, and ever will be, a marvel. At dinner time the plates fairly burnt my hand, and as hot plates and dishes are a luxury one has never known even in the coldest weather in the South, I was surprised indeed at the strange season to commence such a custom; until my other hand got burnt with the handle of my fork, and then I found that everything was burning equally, excepting the eatables.

The foliage on the banks surpassed in luxuriance all I had ever imagined of vegetation. The tecoma and scarlet lonicera, with vines and other climbers, reached the tops of the tallest trees, and covered them with their brilliant clusters of blossom. Vines hung in festoons or fell in perpendicular branches, which were again caught up and twisted amongst other pendants, all crowded with foliage, until the form of a tree was lost entirely, and changed into a solid mass, like an ivy-covered ruin, or sometimes a cross, or a piece of statuary, arrayed in foliage.

Others have seen and described these things when there was no war or blockade; therefore I will recall some of the conversations of my fellow-passengers, that belong more peculiarly to the present time.

Captain McClellan found several acquaintances on board; Maggie also met with a friend; and as, under these circumstances, introductions are usual, and as the war made of the scattered inhabitants of "Dixie's Land" one mutually sympathising family, very little reserve was perceptible.

One sad lady was introduced to me, who soon informed me that she was going to the neighbourhood of Chattanooga, where her husband was, that they might enjoy better opportunities of meeting. She had been married about a year, having been a wife only two months when her husband joined the army, and she had never seen him since. "Oh, this is a hard, a cruel war!" she cried; "there never was a war so cruel as this!" She felt that if she could only have her husband home again she would be willing to make any sacrifices for peace. All this time she had lived alone on her plantation, and she said the trouble and responsibility was so great that she had not been able to endure it any longer, and had now left everything to the care of the overseer. She said that when her husband had first left her, (she lived in Florida,) she had felt timid regarding the faithfulness of her slaves, eighteen of whom were strong, stout men; and in the neighbourhood of Pensacōla, where she lived, there were several Northern people who had been known to bribe the negroes to do mischief. Therefore her overseer had taken the pains to inform himself of the negro sentiment, by listening, and hiding himself behind their cabins, which are always loosely built in those hot climates. One night there was a gathering of negroes at one of the shanties; and he secreted himself to discover whether mischief were brewing. Nothing transpired for a time, more than general conversation, dancing, and frolics, as usual. The war and "Yankees," came accidentally on the (not) *tapis*, and they began to argue upon the delights of freedom; attractions, nevertheless, appreciated by only two of the whole of the party, who said they should like to be free "because they knew all about cards, and could get a good deal of money by gambling, without doing any work." None of the rest expressed the least desire to be free, and the lady said, "I felt much easier when I found they were so contented." "No work,"—that is the charm to a negro.

While I was sitting on the shady side of the boat, watching the beautiful bends of the river, and the enchanting vegetation on its banks, of course I could not help hearing the conversation of some of the gentlemen; and though I cannot repeat their precise words, the following was the sum and substance of their opinions.

European news was, as ever, predominant, and one gentleman said he had just seen some extracts from the London press, in which an immediate recognition of the Confederacy was urged.

"Ay, ay," said another, "the sympathy of England for the cause of the South, increases each day, and the daily aggravation of the distress in Lancashire will compel interference before three months."

"It is slavery that sticks in their throats," said another. "But when they discover that the *name* of slavery is its worst enemy, and that slavery, with all its evils, is not so bad as it has been represented to be, that need not withhold their interference."

"The worst of it is that Europe can't get at the

truth. The Yankees have the *say* all to themselves; they know too late the spirit of the South; they find they can no longer live upon the South as they have done; so with "envy, hatred, malice, and all uncharitableness," as my little girl says in her catechism, they are revenging themselves in this terrible way," said Captain McClellan.

Captain McClellan had a friend on board who was going to stop at Eufaula, a little town in Alabama, on the banks of the Chattahoochie, and from thence would proceed to Macon, in Georgia; a city it was necessary for me to pass. My good adviser said that by stopping at this little town it would save me distance, time, and expense, as nothing would be gained by making the angle at Columbus, excepting to see the place, and to enjoy each other's company some twenty-four hours longer.

He said that on reaching Macon I should find such a crowd and confusion on the railroads, caused by the immense rush of people at that important junction, both of relatives going to Richmond to nurse their wounded, and of the latter returning home, that a protector would be absolutely necessary; and his friend would see me safely "on board" the train for Augusta, whence the road to Charleston would be more agreeable.

Such experience was too useful to be slighted. We should arrive at Eufaula at dusk, and set off early in the morning, reaching Macon at dusk on the following day. I was always glad to avoid the night travelling; therefore these arrangements would be quite *à propos.*

Captain McClellan had been one of my first Florida acquaintances. We had come on the same train six months ago, and were now leaving together, and I could not have had a pleasanter escort. "Don't forget to give me your English address," he said; "because when the war is over I mean to take Maggie to Europe to be educated, and I shall want you to recommend a school, either in London or Paris."

On many of the Southern rivers there are wooden landings, with a flight of steps for passengers, and "shoots," or long wooden slides for the cotton to be passed down the banks to the boat. The Chattahoochie river is remarkable for its sudden and excessive rises, so that the warehouses on its banks are built with four, five, or even six floors, to be used according to the height of the water. I saw watermarks on the trees and warehouses as high as sixty and eighty feet above the level of the river at that time. The bridge at Eufaula, a wooden one, on foundations of strong brick buttresses, is eighty feet above the average summer level; but once the water was so high, that even there a steamboat passed round the side of the bridge, over what was, when I landed, high banks and fields. It seemed surprising that the inhabitants had no ambition to make a flight of wooden steps to ascend and descend this high bank; but no, not a path nor a step was there.

By leaping, sliding, and being lifted, I had descended to the river; and now, by springing, climbing, and being pulled, I must be dragged up the rough, precipitous bank. If there were only two men in town, one would think they would remedy such inconveniences; but there were plenty of idle men there, as everywhere else, though in no way troubled about them.

Another adieu must now be made to the Captain and his intelligent little daughter!

Eufalla, or Eufaula (the pronunciation the same in both words), is a pretty village with the usual wide roads, and abundance of trees, that hide up the houses, so that, until close to them, you cannot perceive what has "lately been incorporated as a *city*." A small daily sheet is published there, called "The Spirit of the South;" that for the day, contained the, to the Confederates, gratifying intelligence that "the 'Nashville' had just arrived at a Confederate port, with a valuable cargo; among which was a present from the Liverpool merchants of so many pieces of artillery; that she had been chased and fired at, but arrived safely, with *just one ton of coal left!*"

The "Nashville" had carried one of my great packets of letters for me, and I could not help feeling glad she was safe again.

A postscript was added to the "good news," stating that "the boys in the streets of Liverpool were lustily hurrahing for Jeff Davis and the Southern Confederacy," which seemed to be highly gratifying.

Early the next morning I took a little stroll round the town, where were to be seen the same melancholy effects of war and blockade. "Drug stores" with broken windows, open doors, and a few dirty bottles in the front of two or three out of the whole set of shelves. There was no attempt at renewal or repairs, everything was going to decay; nature alone was vigorous. Nearly all the shops were closed, and excepting groups around the hotels inquiring "What news your way?" the place seemed almost deserted. But the people were cheerful as ever. No despondency was to be seen. They charged me, at the hotel, three dollars for a supper, room, and breakfast; the general price would have been two dollars for twenty-four hours. I must have been a profitable "guest," for excepting a glass of milk, all I ate could have been easily packed in an egg-shell.

A very magnificently attired negress, in an evening dress, *décoltée*, and short-sleeved, but an ugly person withal, was the independent chambermaid of this establishment. She lives, unwillingly, in my memory, because while she was in my room, she three times ejected from her hideous mouth the consequences of tobacco,—down on the floor, too, before my very face; and in less than as many minutes. Those creatures chew, if they do not smoke.

At all the best hotels in the South you meet with European servants. The proprietors quite understand that negroes are not to be relied on; nor is it possible to appoint a person to look after each one; without which, nothing is properly done. I could fill pages with stories of slaves that I knew during my two years' residence in the South; and I am quite sure that the quickest and surest way of putting an end to slavery, or at least of improving the condition of slaves, is for the Southerners to be thrown more amongst the educated and refined nations of Europe. You find even now, that those persons who have travelled most, and who have experienced the difference that exists between the finished and highly cultivated farms of other countries, and their own thousands of wild rough acres, and between the orderly, systematic, and efficient white servants of England, and their own dirty, disgusting negroes, are by far the most ready to give up their slaves, "if we could only get the land cultivated without them." Intercourse with Europe will do more, and more rapidly, to advance this vast and fertile country, than a lifetime of speeches and harangues against the evils of slavery.

Only one circumstance of the Sunday's journey from Eufalla to Macon is worth recording, and that is one never to be forgotten at such a time.

Necessity compelled me to continue my journey on the Sabbath-day; and what did I see throughout that Sunday journey? Crowds of slaves in gayest attire, both men and women, getting on and off the train at every country "stopping place;" more particularly at Americus and Cuthbert, two towns of Georgia. Where were they going, in dresses more expensive than many of their own masters and mistresses, in those times of blockade and economy? Some to a distant church, some to exchange visits at a neighbouring plantation, and some merely to enjoy the ride—merry, noisy, loquacious creatures, wholly unconscious of care or anxiety; while on the platform at the road-side station stood groups of grave-looking thoughtful men, who only lifted their eyes from the ground to give a nod to the negro slave, who persisted in attracting the attention of "massa." My heart grew sick at the contrast, while I reflected that it is these very slaves for whom the whole world is now being brought into calamity. I took particular notice of the dresses of some of the negro *belles*, which were not only expensive, but in excellent taste; and so were those of their *beaux*, who sported heavy gold rings and chains, tasteful neck-ties, and who held the fans and parasols of their companions, assisted them into the carriages, and treated them to water-melons, with all the dignity of New York, or Washington.

The Governor had given me letters to families at Macon. His Excellency was related to the Cobbs and the Lamars of Georgia—the Hon. William Howell Cobb* being the brother of his first wife. Every person of consequence was at Richmond, or their families "in the mountains," excepting one gentleman, who on receiving my letter, sent a note of apologies that lame-

* This highly esteemed gentleman, a General of the Confederate army, was killed at the battle of Fredericksburg, 13th December, 1862.

ness would prevent his calling on me, but offering the hospitalities of his house and carriage, &c. As the lady members were in the country, and my stay would be for only one day, I merely accepted the use of the carriage, being glad of such an opportunity of seeing the town.

It looked like life again to pass through the streets of Macon, which is now becoming one of the most important cities in the Confederacy. Manufactories of all kinds are springing up there. Government stores, arsenals, and the recent presents from the Liverpool merchants just arrived, (the lions of the town for the time being,) were all to be seen. The railway depôt is a large commodious structure of iron arches and roofing; the streets are well paved, the stores stylish; in fact it did one's heart good to see so flourishing a place as Macon. It is beautifully situated; the private residences on hills, from which extensive views over a luxuriantly-wooded country are obtained. Some of the most elegant private residences I have seen in the American States were in Macon.

The hotel prices there remained the same as in ordinary times. A first-class, delightful hotel, at two dollars and a half per day of twenty-four hours. Quantities of delicious fruits we enjoyed there—peaches, figs and melons, quite reasonable, and most grateful in a temperature of 95°.

One could be nowhere for ten minutes without hearing of the war; and while resting in the reception-room, I met a young lady of about twenty years of age. The war or the weather was sufficient introduction, and she soon began to be communicative. She had just come from Chattanooga, where she said she had "done as much nursing and dressing of wounds as any woman of five-and-twenty." She spoke of the large army recently collected there, and the importance of the place, where so many roads branched off, to "our people." "But there have been too many Unionists there, that is the worst of it," she said. The population may be some 2000 or 3000. She described the illness and deaths in the army as frightful, from want of water: every spare building, churches, Court-house, private houses, and empty stores, had been all turned into hospitals.

This girl had had three cousins killed in the recent battles of Richmond, whose deaths she described to me; then she said, "I have a young brother in the army, not seventeen, and such a little fellow. That boy has been in four hard battles, and never got a scratch. After the battle of Corinth one of the legs of his pants was torn completely off. There are the holes of three bullets, one above another. I suppose the force of them wrenched away the cloth. We have the pants now at home; and the child went with one leg bare all the rest of the battle. Another ball cut in two the strap of his cartridge-box across his shoulder, and never hurt him. It seems as if a special Providence was guarding him, poor little fellow!" Poor girl, too! for she could scarcely command her voice to finish the narrative. "Now he is at Vicksburg, and they are shelling the town;" she added, bursting into tears, and hiding her face in her handkerchief.

There were three thousand prisoners taken to Chattanooga after the battles of Corinth and Shiloh. Like many other places I heard of, "the Yankees could have taken the town easily at one time, but now we are well protected," she told me, after recovering her composure.

On the road to Augusta, from Macon, the crowds, and the wounded soldiers reminded me of the journeys in Virginia. The train was indeed, as Captain M'Clellan had foretold, crowded to the utmost. Some passengers had got on at Macon for the North, others for the South—Macon and Augusta being both two important junctions.

A lady sat near me with two small children and a negro nurse. The lady looked pale, careworn, and *distraite;* the children were fagged and wearied, as if they were teazed, and had no enjoyment of their existence. The mother was a stylish-looking person, but, like the children, wearing a hopeless, melancholy expression.

I soon won the smiles of one pretty child by presenting a peach, and then the mother turned round, apologizing for her child's fretfulness by saying she had been travelling for many days. This soon led to her telling me she had just escaped from New

Orleans, having been trying for a long time to get away, and at last through the influence of a friend, had been permitted to do so, on giving eighty-five dollars for her passport. Butler had been raising the price of passports daily, in order to prevent persons from leaving, and one gentleman had paid as much as five hundred dollars for his; "all of which money was pocketed by the Federal officers," she said.

She assured me that hundreds were trying to get away, who could not afford to pay for the passports, and that the negroes were becoming so unruly that people were in the greatest state of alarm. Much more she told me concerning the fearful condition of things there, and the tyrannical rule under which the people were living, so much of which has since then been made known to the English reader, that it need not be here repeated. To add to her troubles, her husband was in the Confederate army, and she had heard nothing of him, or from him; and did not know whether she should find him living, wounded, or not at all, when she arrived at Richmond. God of mercy! what a state for a young wife to be in!

Augusta, as far as I saw of it, is another city honourable to the enterprise of Georgia. A very fine railway depôt and about a mile of beautiful streets, I passed, in walking from one station to another. I was alone here, and what with the difficulty of hunting up my luggage, and finding out how to dispose of it, and the usual inconvenience of no one knowing anything one wished to ascertain, the stage went off without me; my only resource being to walk as fast as my feet could carry me, with the thermometer about 90°, to the Charleston station. I had been travelling all night, and did not object to the pleasant morning air, but it was a terrible walk; and after all, there was plenty of time had I only known it.

Charleston—pleasant, welcome Charleston—was reached the same afternoon.

Mr. Bunch gave me some excellent, though rather unpalatable, advice and cautions about obedience to the Queen, and being sure not to take any letters or papers, &c.,—when I had even aspired to carrying despatches; and certainly hoped to accommodate many friends by carrying *letters*.

Mr. Frederick and his friends had lately escaped through the blockade to Europe; and the Firm who, through them, had so kindly forwarded letters for me, now offered me a passage in a ship just about to sail; but Mr. Bunch strongly discountenanced such a breach of loyalty, and I was induced to discard the idea and proceed to Richmond. Those new friends therefore gave me letters of introduction to the Secretaries of State, and of War; thus rendering the doubtful journey to obtain a passport a little more hopeful, and greatly faciliating my success.

While arranging for my departure, the landlord of the Mill's House thoughtfully came to inform me that Major Pendleton and his son were going to Richmond the next morning, and would take charge of me on the journey; so with scarcely one adieu, I turned my back once more on that interesting city.

It was a pleasure to see the soldiers—what few there were in Charleston—with such an air of comfort, sitting about in groups, after their toilsome campaign. They looked as if an immense weight had been removed from their minds, in having so lately secured the safety of their city. The Federal army had been dispersed, James Island once more was cleared of the enemy, and the greater part of their own men had been recalled to Virginia. Charleston looked as if it were taking a holiday, and feasting on melons, figs, and peaches. Three times a-day, was abundance of fruit on table at the hotel, and the very last thing that I did before leaving the depôt, was to buy as much fruit as could be stowed away, in order to carry some to Richmond. A fine cantalupe melon, at five cents, would certainly remain good, and several dozen figs at ten cents a dozen; the same for peaches and pears. I collected enough for the journey, and to give to my Richmond friends besides, who, I found on arriving, were paying ten, fifteen, and twenty cents *each* for peaches and pears, not half so good as those I had bought by the dozen, for the same price.

We reached Wilmington, North Carolina, at night again, and thence through Goldsborough and Weldon, two towns being rapidly protected against anticipated attacks from the coast; both important localities of branch routes, and easily accessible by rivers. The next evening we arrived in the capital of the Confederate States, still honoured with the presence of its beloved and respected President, and the Government.

Here we quickly verified that we were at the seat of war. The depôt was crowded with soldiers, who had just come from Petersburg, and were waiting to be quartered. They were lying about on the side walks in heavy slumbers, so that it was impossible to pass them. At Petersburg we had been delayed several hours because the trains were engaged in transporting troops. The next impending battle was in the valley where General Jackson commanded. Not long before, that General had resigned, it was whispered, but his resignation not having been accepted, he afterwards began those independent, daring, and successful movements, that have been attended with such singular success. "Send me 10,000 men, and ask no questions," had been one of his messages, and the commencement of his mysterious and almost ubiquitous advances. Martial law existed at Richmond and Petersburg, and no one knew anything; but in spite of that, many thousands of troops were going somewhere; and what with the business of getting passports for ourselves, at Petersburg, and waiting with a crowd of passengers for trains to carry us on, the continuation of my journey would have been hopeless without the assistance of Major Pendleton. At last, through him, and with him, I arrived in Richmond, many people having been waiting at Petersburg for several days, without being able to proceed.

The Major sent his son to attend to the luggage, and remained by me in the darkness and crowd. His son was gone some time, and the confusion being very great, the Major asked me to wait in a certain spot, while he went to seek and assist in collecting the luggage.

There were no carriages, all the horses and waggons having been "pressed;" no porters, none but crowds of soldiers, and an approaching engine warned me that I was standing on the track. Major Pendleton must have sought me and passed on, just as I retreated out of the way of the engine, for I waited and waited in that crowd and darkness until nearly fainting with the heat and fatigue, and thought it best at last to make my way to the American Hotel, while I had strength yet remaining.

No sooner was my name sent down to the office, than my arrival became known, and Mr. Ayres appeared to tell me that Major Pendleton had been inquiring for me, and, in great alarm for my safety, had retraced his steps to the depôt to seek me. It was very kind of him, for the confusion was dreadful.

The hotel was crowded with strangers, and had become very dirty and shabby in these few months. Mrs. Henningsen was not there, nor was there a single face I knew. Mrs. Ayres only came to welcome me.

Major Pendleton sought me out in the course of the evening, and came to take leave, saying he was ordered on immediately to the valley; so that he could not assist me in getting a passport, which he had promised to do. Judge Baker had just set off for Florida, or he would have helped me, for with all his caution he was a reliable friend. Judge Wright had become a colonel in the army, and was in North Carolina. No one else whom I knew could help me, therefore I must depend upon myself. I went, the first thing in the morning, to see Mr. Cridland, at what the "blockaded British subjects" used to call "*anything but the Consolation Office.*" On the present occasion I found the Consul in such a crowd of English, Scotch, and Irish, applying for papers, that he could only say to me, "See the life I lead! If you knew how I have been occupied since you left, you would quite excuse me for not having written to you, according to promise. It is useless to apply for a passport; it will certainly not be granted you at this time."

The Governor had given me a letter to the Secretary of War, so that I hoped at least to be admitted to his presence. Having also two letters to the Secretary of State, to him I first presented myself. He was polite, but evidently deep in important business. He endorsed the letter with a few words of his own, and recommended me to Secretary Randolph. That personage was exceedingly stiff and reserved, in spite of my two letters, and said it was impossible to issue any more passports, so much harm had been done by people going under flags of truce. I pleaded my nationality, and urged my case, to an inexorable, cold Secretary of War, who only said in reply, "General Winder attends to these things."

I had heard enough of the crowds of applicants at General Winder's office, to know that it was impossible for a lady to venture there; and in much tribulation I repaired next to the office of Mr. Mallory, Secretary of the Navy, who, being an intimate friend of the Governor's, (and to whom I had also a letter,) I thought might at least advise me. He received me, after I had waited about an hour in an ante-room, with more cordiality; but the maps and papers, charts, plans, models of gun-boats, and clerks, who did not cease to bring fresh business, told too plainly his ear was not for me. He continued to read his letters while I addressed him, and this mark of indifference, not to say rudeness, added to my utterly hopeless endeavours, with the remembrance of a year ago, so pressed upon my wearied spirit, that Miss Jones entirely lost her self-control, and shed a plentiful shower of tears in the presence of the Hon. Secretary of the Confederate navy. He pointed to a tankard containing a little tepid water, and perused his letters while I recovered myself. Afterwards he somewhat relented, and sent a note to General Winder, to save me that annoyance; and promising to apprize me of the answer, bowed me out of his presence. It must have been "martial law," for both Mr. Randolph and Mr. Mallory had the reputation of being remarkably amiable and excellent men. I never knew the Southerners so imperturbable and uncompromising before, while I was sympathising so deeply with them all, and wishing I could take messages and letters to England for them, and feeling worthy of being trusted even with the gravest secrets.

In deep depression I was finding my way out, and passed the office of the President, who was sitting at a table before the open door. At another time I should have walked straight in, to shake hands with the Hon. Jefferson Davis, but martial law had frightened away my courage; and what would he think of such a fagged and red-eyed individual as I must have looked, with my nights of travelling and days of anxiety? I was glad I did not stop, for on descending the stairs, whom should I meet but Mr. Bledsoe, with his kind, genial, placid face. He seemed surprised and glad to see me, and opened his office door to invite me in.

All these Government offices were under one roof, of what had been the large public Lecture Hall and galleries of the Mechanics' Institute, at Richmond; refitted, and divided into apartments when the Government had first made that city the capital.

The meeting of one pleasant friend at such a time let loose the saline tears again: and no doubt caused all the clerks to wonder who upon earth Mr. Bledsoe could have brought into his office. I soon told him of all my troubles and difficulties, and he promised to see what could be done, and to call at the hotel to inform me. He did so that evening; and between them all I obtained my passport. It ran thus:—

"Pass Miss Sarah L. Jones, a British subject, beyond the lines, by flag of truce. Subject to the military control of the General in command.

"(Signed) J. H. WINDER,

"By order of the Secretary of War.

"*Richmond Va., July 26th*, 1862."

Even that did not seem so very certain. What could "subject to the control of the General" mean? And which way was I to go? Mr. Cridland could not inform me, nor could any one else. No one knew anything. All owing to martial law, no doubt.

Once more did I venture to appear at the Government departments. Mr. Bledsoe was not to be found, and everybody else was "too much occupied," with their compliments, to see me, of course. Was it to be expected that any Honourable Secretary, with such a press of business, could be interrupted by such a silly Niobe?

Mrs. Henningsen had devoted herself to a hospital, and had removed her lodgings to its vicinity. The passport so far secured, she might, I thought, be able to advise me, and I went to see her. Ah me! only a repetition of sufferings were to be recounted, whichever way one turned.

She had written to me in Florida several times, and wondered why I had not replied to her letters. I had written to her, and had expressed the same thing. The letters both ways had been lost.

She and several others were surprised that the Government persisted in granting passports, while so much harm was being done by communication with the North; therefore my success received from her and her friends neither congratulation nor sympathy. "As for Europe—what do we care?" they said: "when it suits their own selfish ends, they will acknowledge us; and as for the blockade, our people would never have done what they have for themselves, had they been able to trade with Europe. Now we are making everything we want, and saving all the money that otherwise would have been spent in folly, had the blockade been raised."

Mrs. Henningsen asked me if I had been to call on Mrs. Greenough.

No, I had neither strength nor spirit to call on any one.

"Oh, you ought to go and see her; she has just been released from Washington, after her year's imprisonment. She is staying at the Spottswood Hotel, and everybody is calling on her. She is quite the lion of the city just now. Here is one of her *cartes de visites:* you really ought to get one, to show to your friends in England."

The expression of her face was one of steady suffering, resignation, and determination.

When the wrath of my friend, and her friends, had somewhat subsided, she became a little more civil, and insisted on my remaining to dinner. "You *must* see what our hospital dinners are. You need not be afraid of starving, we are so well supplied by Government, and have everything you can desire." But they had been suffering seriously during the siege, when Richmond was supplied only from one section, and by one line of travel.

"You need not be afraid of seeing the wounded soldiers; only those that are armed come down to table; the others remain up stairs. They have their dinners first; and afterwards, we (the nurses) and the doctors dine at a separate table."

"Those that are 'armed!'—to what do you allude?"

"Those that *have* arms—those that can help themselves without being fed."

What a horrible picture did that one word convey!

It would be too harrowing to human sympathies to relate some of the details of those times, of which doctors, nurses, and relatives became cognizant, and of which one heard only too many. Of these, the caprices of bullets in passing round the skull under the skin of a man's head, and only creating a slight flesh wound; or of passing half round his neck or shoulder in the same manner; of entering the arm and travelling down close to the bone into his hand, and being retained there, are among merely the curiosities and escapes of the battle-field, of which army surgeons can recount enough. But of other horrors, such as a man having the whole of his face, excepting his eyes, shot away, (and Mrs. Henningsen had such a patient), or of another entirely limbless mortal; of waggon-loads of wounded arriving more quickly than it was possible for stores and houses to be cleared for their reception; while people were stopping women on the street, and entreating them to come and help to nurse; and poor young dying soldier lads were whining piteously for their mothers: while broken and torn limbs, neglected for days and weeks for want of sufficient medical attendance, were causing the death of the sufferers from mortification, in that fearful temperature; while some were going mad from suffering, and some from thirst; all these things are too dreadful to be told, though no doubt they are the experiences of every battle-field, particularly in hot climates.

Amidst the tales of sufferings, one heard of other circumstances that display the bravery and fortitude of the devoted Southern soldiers. A doctor told me that during amputation of some of the limbs, the soldiers frequently lay and smoked their cigars, and kept up a conversation with their fellow-sufferers. One man who had just had his arm cut off, said to an attendant, "Hand that old friend to me if you please, I have not quite done with it." Then he quietly took a ring from the finger of the severed limb, saying, "that was a keepsake nothing could induce him to part with;" after which he tossed the discarded arm back into the basket, full of other severed members.

Poor fellows! "those that were armed," and not too much disfigured, came down to an excellent dinner of several varieties of meat, with abundance of vegetables.

Afterwards, a still daintier fare was laid for us; but I had heard of too many horrors to appreciate it.

My departure being uncertain, I did not then take leave of Mrs. Henningsen.

I could hear nothing of Colonel and Mrs. Este, who lived too far off for me to walk to their house in the day time, and in the evening, one could not venture out.

The Castletons were in town, but I had no strength even to reach their house; my first, and ever kind friends. I met a gentleman, whose relatives belonged to Warrenton, and from him, learned of the afflictions of that excellent family at the College, and the death of Professor Latham: of the rest he could inform me nothing! Rebelfield was in town, but I did not know where, neither was he aware of my arrival. T. H. W. called, on receiving a message from me; he had entered upon a new and urgent business for the Government, and was working night and day. His wife and daughter were in North Carolina; he promised to endeavour to send me some newspapers to England occasionally; but that was more easy to promise than to accomplish.

Of the W.'s of Essex, and the Quences, nothing could be learned.

Mrs. Smith and her daughters were still at the Wharneford House, and kindly exerting themselves for the sick and wounded; I was sorry to be unable to go and take leave of them. The Rev. Doctor Woodbridge was not at home; I did manage to get as far as his house; the Rev. Mr. Hogue had joined the army. The Rev. Doctor Minnegerode, of St. Paul's Church, was in the country with his family. His health was always delicate, and he was frequently absent. The whole body of clergymen, remaining in the city, had enough to do in visiting the hospitals.

I heard a great deal about the prisoners, and saw numerous extracts from the Northern papers, complaining of the treatment they received, which seemed, to me, to originate greatly in misunderstanding the condition of things in the South, because the Northern people do not realize the privations that a blockade brings on a country.

While the Confederates were contentedly resigning every description of luxury, and paying almost fabulous prices for even home-produce, when brought from a distance, could the prisoners expect to be fed upon the fat of the land? While their own soldiers were hurried into their graves from inefficient medicines and imperfect treatment, could the very men who brought all this sorrow upon them, expect the first and best of medical attention?

The truth is, however, that they did share whatever comforts their captors had it in their power to bestow. The people who enforced the blockade complained loudly of its consequences, when visited on themselves.

I know that Mrs. General Pegram, Mrs. General Henningsen, Mrs. Ayres, the clergymen, and many others, frequently visited the prisoners; and I may be permitted to declare, that as long as any comforts and luxuries were to be had, whatever medicines or attendance, or what not was required, I know also that they had it. When tea, coffee, sugar (the latter owing to difficulty of transportation), and other provisions became scarce—the prisoners were necessarily deprived of these comforts. Nevertheless, it is to be much regretted that subsequently many of the prisoners were annoyed by vermin. I was told it was their own fault, and their own want of cleanliness; that they could have as much water as they wished, and bathe in the river whenever they desired it, under guard, of course. There is no doubt but the tobacco factories are filthy places, and that if there had been any other accommodation they would have had it; but Richmond, crowded with soldiers, politicians, and all the government-officers and their families, besides more visitors than it ever had before; to say nothing of sick and wounded soldiers in every other house, with every available place fitted up for a hospital, could provide no better prisons.

Of one thing I am sure, and that is, that a Southerner, for the sake of self-respect, and in accordance with his naturally humane disposition, would shrink from imposing undue punishment and restrictions upon helpless prisoners. Richmond is a dirty place. Negroes are dirty people. The Southerners are indifferent concerning their own comforts, and one can scarcely expect they would make any extraordinary exertions for their prisoners that they would not for themselves.

At the time of my final visit to Richmond, General McCall, taken at the late battle, was among the prisoners, and I heard two or three anecdotes of him, which I may be permitted to repeat as they were related to me. He requested his guard to make certain purchases for him, which was done, but when the General was informed of the price of the things, he could not believe but that the man was imposing upon him, and refused to pay such exorbitant sums. The Southerner, indignant at the implied insult, mentioned the blockade as the cause, which was little realized by the Federal General; who, however, continued to be so abusive to the man who had endeavoured to suit him in the purchases, that the latter took them back, and the angry General was obliged to content himself without them—at least for a time: he was not likely to remain long in want.

One of the clergymen at Richmond was visiting General McCall, who, in conversing about the late battles, and the "strategic movements" of General McClellan, said that the sudden "change of base" had been a part of his programme. "Indeed, General," said the clerical brother, rather cruelly, "and was it also a part of the programme that you should be here a prisoner?" The reply of General McCall was not stated; perhaps he made none.

As almost daily exchanges of prisoners were taking place, there seemed quite a possibility of my accomplishing my departure; excepting that, like the previous summer, it was impossible to decide which way to go. No one was able to afford the least advice, but each proposed a different route.

The table at the hotel was well supplied, although the charges were necessarily nearly twice as high as usual. I was congratulating Mrs. Ayres on her success in furnishing the table, although it was not in *her* province to attend to that. She said, "But you have no idea what we are obliged to pay for common necessaries. Even 'tea,' that is only the dried leaves of a shrub gathered in North Carolina, cost ten dollars a pound."

I had found no soap in my apartment, and told the chambermaid there was none.

"Soap!"

"Yes."

"No, nor hasn't been dis yeah long time."

"What do people do for soap, then?"

"Why folks 'jes goes out an' gits it to suit theirselves, jes whar ever they can fine any."

A very doubtful "suit" that, one would fancy. I passed a pretty little child, in its nurse's arms, on the stairs, and asked its name.

"Jeffersonia."

The last child's name I had asked was "Beauregard," a little negro baby. Another was "General Lee." There will be no want of "Generals" in the Confederacy for at least a generation to come, so far as names are concerned.

Although the papers were as full as ever of English quotations, there were not the same abuses and reproaches to introduce them. Even the North received a little bit of credit occasionally, as thus:

"Mrs. Lincoln, on her late visit to New York, visited the wounded soldiers and showed them many kindly attentions."

The Confederates began now to realize that the majority of the English, if not of the European population, comprehended the justness of their cause, and appreciated their efforts for independence, and that if a *vote* could be taken, it would be in their favour. Opinions concerning the cotton famine and all hopeful demonstrations continued to find a ready place in their journals. Also the "English opinion of Butler's atrocities."

CHAPTER XIX.

Discouragements — A Dark Farewell to Richmond — Another British Subject—An Oath of Allegiance—The Flag of Truce—Approaching my Federal Relations—We seek Permission to go Home—The Petition Granted—The James River Transformed—The Examination—The Verdicts—The Federal Pass—Another Concerted Movement in View—The Emancipation Question—Emancipation may be Extermination.

I HAD waited several days in much anxiety, and with many efforts to ascertain how I could get away, after obtaining the one thing needful—a passport. One person said, "Make haste before the next battle comes on," which did not help me at all. Another said, "It is of no use to try such a route, because this person or that went that way and came back again." Another said, "You must hire a carriage and go down to Harrison's Landing, and ask McClellan to let you pass." The next one said, "You cannot hire a conveyance for love or money." And again another added, "An English nobleman went to the river the other day, and McClellan would not permit him to pass, but retained his baggage." All this was not very encouraging, but I was resolved to go, even if I had to walk this time. Mr. Cridland explained about the English nobleman. It was Lord Seymour, whose "baggage" had been detained for examination, and I believe he had returned by choice, either to wait, or take another route.

The majority of my advisers said, "Try the Petersburg route;" and, almost despairing, I decided to go at least as far as there, and ascertain my chances of success in that quarter.

There were very few to take leave of, notwithstanding the number of acquaintances I had made in Richmond. To see them, or not to see them, was equally melancholy. Everything was sad, and tinged with "martial law." Go, one must, and better try to be callous.

Again I had recourse to Mr. Cridland, who was always ready to pardon the interruptions, and whom I invariably found working as hard as anybody in the Confederacy; and he always said, "You will excuse my not paying you any attention, and rendering you the assistance I would gladly do, if possible. I am no longer Consul; I don't know what I am. See these crowds, who come to me after they have been voting, and fighting; and then want me to make out their papers, or procure them passports. 'My good fellows,' I say, 'have you read the Queen's proclamation?' 'No, sir.' 'Be so kind as to step into the hall and read it, while I am attending to these others; and then tell me if you can answer the questions.' See here," continued the Consul, "look at the paper I am obliged to use, and glad to economize even this: a tailor would not send a message to his cobbler on such a piece, at home. And as for envelopes and seals—why, I cannot even find a piece of coloured paper in the city for my official stamp."

"If ever you come to Virginia again, you will come and see me at our own plantation," said Mrs. Ayres: "we shall give up this hotel very soon: I prefer the country."

"Keep this for my sake," said Mrs. Henningsen, hanging a memento on my chain.

Ah! those were sad partings, and yet the people were so hopeful.

The train to Petersburg left at three o'clock, A.M.! In the obscurity, confusion, and difficulty of finding porters, together with the hindrances at the ticket-office, where only certain notes were acceptable, the train was moving as I gained the platform. The cars were horrible; close, crowded, repulsive, and all in darkness. In the crowd my travelling-bag had been wrenched from its handle; and after obtaining a seat, I *felt* that much foreign substance had been amassed with its scattered contents, from the dust and darkness.

Day-light revealed a frightful and a motley collection of fellow-passengers. No wonder the cars were not agreeable. Soldiers, poor wounded soldiers, propped upon the seats, plaistered and bandaged! I leaned out of the open window, and studied the foliage all the way to Petersburg.

The hotel I knew best at Petersburg, was kept by

a relative of Mrs. Ayres. Her sister was wife to the proprietor, Colonel Carrington; with both of whom I was acquainted. That was some consolation, as they would advise me.

"A flag of truce goes every day to City Point whenever the prisoners arrive from Richmond," they said. The reader can imagine the comfort such news imparted.

Being sure of a few hours, I lay down to endeavour to procure a little sleep, but was soon aroused by a tap at my door, and a plaintive voice outside. A poor, thin, fragile little woman, with a miserable, puny little baby, came to say she had heard I was going "by the flag," and could I tell her anything about the trains. She had been here for two days, and no flag had gone, and she had heard that no one was to be allowed to go any more!

I pointed out to her that we should not have had our passports given us, under such circumstances; yet I resolved to go quickly and ascertain, somewhere.

She said she had been obliged to have a pass from the Provost Marshal at Petersburg, besides that of the Secretary of War, and that I must have one also. No time was to be lost. It was a long way to the Marshal's office; but I found it, and after considerable trouble, waiting, and explanation, with no place to sit down upon, excepting the very dirty, *tobaccoey* stairs, at last I was admitted. The official who had the management of the passes was a kind, pleasant old gentleman, a complete Mr Pickwick, excepting that he was a Virginian, from near Winchester. I was so glad I had visited him, for he explained that the reason the flags of truce had been suspended, was because the road was under repair, but that there would be another, "perhaps to-morrow, or the day after;" and he would certainly let me know. He said there was a "sickly English lady," with a baby, who was going at the same time; and I found out it was the unhappy little woman, who had disturbed my welcome slumbers. He promised to inform us both.

The poor creature was somewhat comforted at my explanations, and I then hinted to her that I should be glad to rest.

She came again and again for more advice. Poor thing! she was so glad of company, that I gave up all further hope of sleep, and sat and looked out of the window, while she gave me another list of troubles and horrors from her late experiences. I shall only relate the most amusing part of them.

Her husband was a mechanic, working for the Government. She was going to her friends in the North, because her health had failed, and there was "nothing to be bought in Richmond." Her husband had given nine dollars for a dozen small bottles of porter for her, and twenty-two dollars for a quart and a quarter-of-a-pint of brandy. He had bought all there was to be had, of some that had lately been smuggled in from Maryland. She had lived near the depôt, and near to some of the Government workshops, where she had been watching the mounting and polishing of the celebrated cannon, "Long Tom," taken at the battle of Manassas. She said that one Sunday morning, a number of men came post haste, and took away Long Tom by means of a dozen mules to drag him. He was brought back on Monday, broken down. Tuesday he was ready, and started off again. Wednesday, behold him back once more, again broken down, and covered with mud. They could not tell the colour of the mules for mud. From Wednesday to Sunday, Long Tom was being burnished up again, and remounted; and once more started off. On the following Tuesday, like an evil spirit, he reappeared, more muddy than ever, and there she had left him. He had been standing in the road for a long time, exposed to all weathers, and sometimes loaded. The children used to play upon him, and get inside of him, and our poor little Englishwoman had been terrified out of her wits, for fear he should go off and annihilate her and her baby as she stood in her doorway. One day she said to a negro workman, "Why don't you all wheel it away, and put it into some lock-up place. It isn't safe to stand there for every one to handle."

"De Lord *bress* you, missus! why, there ain't no place big 'nuff for him."

So Long Tom remained in the middle of the road, and there she had left him.

A lady in the reception-room had just escaped from

Suffolk County, then occupied by the Federals; and she had many tales to relate about the way in which the Yankees bribed away the negroes there, and paid them in bad money. One family of servants had been so terrified at the Yankees, that they all ran away in the night, *up* the country, not towards freedom, and when the gentleman rose in the morning, "there was not so much as a boy to hitch up a horse," she said.

There was also a family of German Jews in the reception-room, towards whom my attention had been attracted, because the father, on hearing that I was going by flag of truce, had asked me to show him my passport: a singular request, which had perplexed me whether to attribute it to suspicion, martial law, or mere curiosity. Then he compared mine with his own, the result seeming to cause him some uneasiness.

We were only twelve miles from General McClellan's "new base," just then, and Petersburg was being fast protected. An attack was anticipated; the low water in the river being just then its chief safeguard.

Our old gentleman did not appear, and I went a second time, to satisfy my nervous little countrywoman. He had not forgotten us, and thought that "to-morrow" would be the day.

During that second night nearly everyone else in the house, excepting myself, had been disturbed by reports of cannon, the smell of gunpowder, and a great glare of light towards the James River; which, we learned, was caused by a midnight cannonading on the Federal fleet, from a wooded hill called Coggin's Point. It lasted about two hours, resulting in the retreat of the chief part of the vessels several miles down the river. The previous day about 150 vessels had been observed by reconnoissances.

A party of Federals immediately landed to cut down the woods and burn all the buildings in the neighbourhood, among which was the family mansion of the Hon. Edmund Ruffin, the venerated Virginian who fired the first gun at Fort Sumter.

After their nocturnal exploits, the officers of this artillery skirmish came to breakfast at the Carrington Hotel. Mrs. Carrington was conversing with me in the reception-room when one of them entered, whom she knew, and who informed us that the celebrated Long Tom, had been one of the champions of this feat. Having lately heard of his unwieldy disposition, it was interesting to know that he had achieved some end at last; though I would rather have learned that he had been locked up as no longer required. The Captain invited Mrs. Carrington to see the monster; politely including me in the proposal to drive up to ———, where he was on his way. Mrs. Carrington promised to drive me up there after dinner, should the flag of truce not be previously announced. That was something worth waiting for.

At dinner-time Mrs. Carrington informed me that she was going to attend the funeral of the son of an old and respected friend; one of the first families in the county—the Meades.

"Meade! I know that name: which son was it?"

"Captain R. K. Meade, who was at the taking of Fort Sumter, and has been on the Peninsula so long."

(The same! the very one who had explained to me all about the battle of Bethel.)

"Did he die from wounds?"

"No, his health gave way; he has been ill for some time, and has just died. His loss is severely felt by his family. He was a most excellent young gentleman."

Oh, war! how many sorrows dost thou cause!

Mrs. Carrington could not therefore drive up to see Long Tom; but within half an hour a messenger arrived to say that the flag of truce would leave at 5 P.M.

"Now, I *am* glad I did not go back to Richmond," said my nervous little countrywoman.

Of course we were all ready, Jews and all, and I was surprised to find quite a number of others, about eighteen people, all with passports, going under "flag of truce."

Our pleasant old gentleman—I am so sorry I have forgotten his name—accompanied us, with his secretary, who carried an immense bundle of letters from the prisoners to their friends in the North, and also a quantity of newspapers to exchange for Northern ones.

Was there ever so strange a war!

The "flag of truce train," this time, consisted of only one car for passengers, besides the luggage car, engine and tender.

Our kind old gentleman, accompanied by his young son, sat near to me. He said, "My boy, here, is crazy to go into the army, but I want to keep him at school His cousin, a few months older than he is, has just gone off, and I have to hunt him up, as I am his guardian. He ran off without telling me, and enlisted; but I think I can trace him, and bring him back. He must wait a year or two, when he will do better service than he can now. We must take care of these youngsters, for the war has only just begun."

That was what so many people said, for they were determined to fight until there were not a hundred men left: and that hundred would entrench themselves in a valley in the mountains, and fight till they were exterminated. One never could imagine a people so determined.

Near to us sat a couple of young persons, whose voice and manner immediately betrayed their New England origin.

These young ladies were excessively garrulous, and in the highest spirits. We soon discovered that they had been working as milliners in Richmond, until the prospect of dollar-making had rather faded away; and now they were returning home.

They talked loudly of their sympathy with the South, "unless Washington were taken; *then*, &c., &c."

Two other ladies, in deep mourning, I had seen at the hotel, and we recognized each other merely by a slight inclination of the head. They were silent and reserved. The Jew's family were engaged in making signs, and nodding to each other, as if in a cautious warning to guard the unruly member.

Several other people were there, whose anxiety seemed to betray itself in their careful observance of their neighbours, in order to ascertain who were friends, and who were foes. It was singular to see so many of the company disguised as it were in masks, studying who could prove the most accomplished hypocrite, and hide from their neighbours the sentiments that oppressed themselves.

In passing the pickets we all had the form of showing passports to go through. Soon afterwards we were approaching the Federal army, encamped on the opposite side of James River, which their gunships also occupied.

My last Virginian friend made inquiries of his secretary about the flag. "They know we are coming—it is all safe," was the reply.

"I hope they will hold the flag up to display it well," I could not help saying; for my heart beat terribly at the idea of my "Federal relations" firing into the approaching rebel cars; a thing that had happened not unfrequently during the war. We had passed many rebel encampments, and even caught sight of Long Tom and all his mules, and some other immense pieces of artillery on their way back to Petersburg. It was very wrong indeed of a "neutral British subject," but I could not help feeling that I was leaving friends behind me; and was much nearer crying than rejoicing at the prospect of escaping beyond the blockade.

We drew up at last at City Point, the very place

where I had landed on coming up the James River, under far different circumstances. The wharf, the warehouses, every building, even the trees, excepting blackened stems, were burnt; only singed and ruined chimneys were standing of what had so recently been a place of business. The Federal ships, a few of them, stood off the shore, and a group of officers were on the banks, watching the train with an expression of contemptuous curiosity. I don't believe there was a more determined rebel in the Confederacy just then, than my disloyal self. Our good Pickwickian old gentleman, his secretary, and, I think, the conductor, or one other person, approached their enemies and held a short parley; soon they returned, and informed us that we must present our own requests to the Federal officer commanding.

We all alighted from the car, and remained hustled under its shadow, as if unwilling to leave its safe protection; at least that was what I felt. It would have been quite natural for the German Jew, and another gentleman who was among the passengers, to have undertaken the errand, and requested *permission to go home,* as representatives of the whole party.

But no; the Jew declined the mission, and so did the gentleman, who I was sure was a Southerner, and therefore his unwillingness to ask such a favour was easily accounted for. Why upon earth the party should select, and urge upon me to make the request in their united names, I could not conjecture; nevertheless they did so. Even the two reserved ladies in mourning, added their entreaties. "*You* go; *do*—please do." I knew by that they were Southerners also.

Why could not the two Yankee girls go and make such a natural request to their own people? Yankees never put themselves in any unpleasant position, if they can help it. Those two girls could talk fast and loudly, and there their courage ended. For an Englishwoman, a "neutral British subject," to have to ask *permission* to go to her own country, did appear the strangest and most unwelcome piece of strategy that could be invented. But the passengers were waiting, pushing and urging me, so I went, dragging with me the little timid woman with her baby, and feeling very like a culprit and a disgrace to my country, with my head down and my eyes on the poor, singed, yellow grass, that had been cruelly burnt so lately.

I was obliged to look up on approaching the Federal officers. How well they were all dressed! what nice new suits of dark-blue cloth they wore! and what a different expression of countenance to that of all those rebels I was leaving! Ah, those faces reveal much truth: your hearts are not in the cause; you are making a good thing of this war; you, who take care not to be killed, and are driving such a profitable trade. What cold, hard faces, and unyielding manners they had! One felt, at the moment, that it was meeting a different race of people.

I summoned all my little self-possession to speak civilly.

"We are wishing to proceed to the North."

"Are you a Northerner?"

"No; I am an Englishwoman by birth."

"What is your object in wishing to go to the North?"

"I am going home."

"Is your home in the North?"

"I have been living there for several years, until I came to the South."

"How long have you been in the South?"

"Since before the war commenced."

"Is this lady a friend of yours?" (looking towards the timid little woman.)

"Only a fellow-traveller."

"What, madam, is *your* purport in going to the North?" (addressing her.)

"My home is there, and the South does not agree with my health," she replied.

"Are all those persons going too?" inquired the officer, looking rather pleased at the idea.

"I believe so, I know nothing of them."

"Are they Unionists or rebels?"

("Rebels.") "I do not know."

"Well, I suppose we can accommodate you all. I will speak to the Provost Marshal." (How very gracious!)

So we two Englishwomen waited there, while all sorts of men were leaning over the sides of the boats, and ridiculing, with their heartless observations, the shabby railway carriages, and our good old gentleman.

It was a singular position for two respectable Englishwomen to be in—waiting for *permission* to go home.

After the lapse of some minutes, while we were waiting there in that humiliating situation, the officer returned, and said, "Tell the people they can come."

("Tell the people!" Did he think he was speaking to a "rebel" or a negro?)

This ridiculous farce over, we returned to obey the mandate. Then our old gentleman and his secretary conducted us all in a little crowd, and in due form presented us and our requests once more; the two Yankee girls, and some more Yankees, laughing and talking loudly, the two ladies in mourning sealing up their lips, and putting on the most expressionless face they could invent; the Jews not ceasing to say, "Hist!" to their children, who said nothing at all; and the Southerner wearing a more determined face then was quite prudent.

My last Virginian friend and his secretary began to shake hands with the Federal officers, and give them newspapers. In the name of mercy and humanity, why did they not shake hands all round, and vow not to fight any more! The great parcel of letters was delivered up, I forget how many hundreds there were, and all left open. I might have brought some too, had I only known it. Then they laughed and talked together, those *friendly enemies*. Oh, what a singular war!

We were wondering when and where our luggage was to be searched, the little Englishwoman and I. She didn't care, she said, she had so little, and there was nothing they might not see. I did not feel quite so happy about mine, as the packing had been a very troublesome business, requiring some skill and ingenuity, and once disturbed, all hope would be over of ever replacing the articles, many of which might have been pronounced *confiscatable*: how could one know? We saw our trunks all dragged on board and deposited somewhere, lost to sight; what if they should be examined when we were not present: that would be worse than all!

The time came to say good-bye to my last "rebel" friend; the civilities were exhausted, the flag of truce was about to return. Returned to be exchanged for the battle flag, and return to civil war!

We could only shake hands—the old Virginian gentleman and I. A "neutral British subject" could not even venture to wish well to him or his country. Many pairs of eyes were watching us, for we were now in the presence of people who think it their privilege to arrest and imprison women for doing less than shaking hands too kindly with a rebel. It was a silent parting, with that last "good old Virginian."

We now found "martial law" in its extremest sense. First we were handed up rank and file between armed soldiers, and told to go in a certain direction; suddenly to be stopped short by a man with a book, who, as we passed, took down each name. Then, between two other guards, we were ushered on to the open stern of the ship, where were seats all round, and a covered top. One would think we had been so many pickpockets, by the way in which we were watched; and we could scarcely turn round for the purpose of looking at the view, but a pair of Federal eyes were on us. The masks the people wore were thicker than ever, with the exception of the loquacious Yankee girls, whom nothing seemed to abash. I felt so desirous of exclaiming to those two silent ladies, "Open your lips, I am your friend!" or to the Southerner, "I sympathize with you;" but we were all hypocrites, and never did I so entirely realize the assertion that "language is used to disguise our thoughts."

It was a beautiful evening, and we were soon sailing down the James River. It was five o'clock when we had left Petersburg; the ride to City Point was not a long one, and the sun was yet half an hour high. Not many ships were at the landing, but we soon came in sight of dozens. The aspect of the quiet river was entirely changed. It was more like the Hudson, in its busy crowd of masts. Steamers and tugs were hurrying backwards and forwards, and large gun frigates were lying at anchor. We passed the "Monitor," and several other naval monstrosities; each one, I am sorry to confess, arousing very unbecoming sentiments in the mind of a "neutral British subject." I felt angry with myself for even admiring the scene, the hateful scene that was causing so much misery. I would rather that it had poured in torrents of rain, and shut out the prospect altogether, and that the weather should have imparted the same dull gloominess that oppressed my spirit. James River was, notwithstanding, as beautiful as before, provoking as it was to think so; but undulating hills, blue sky, rich foliage, water, dark hulks, lights, sails, sunset's glow, shadows and reflections—with all the beautiful contrast of tall masts, curved lines and angles—*will* make beautiful pictures, in whatever aspect you view them.

While we were sitting there, the Jew searched through his pocket-book nervously, and selected one or two small pieces of paper, that looked very much like the passports, tore them up carefully into very small fragments, and dropped them by degrees over the edge of the boat. I saved my passport in remembrance of the revolution.

Where I sat I could see through the glass partition that divided that part of the boat from a saloon, and perceived a circle of gentlemen, with very self-important manners, arrange themselves around a table, upon which were paper, ink, &c.; and a large official-looking book, of blank paper. All being seated in state, one of the officers appeared at the door, and called out, as if addressing so many prisoners, (and I felt very like one,) "One of the party will come before the Provost Marshal."

A little hesitation ensued as to who should go first, and a lady, between whom and the Yankee girls a great intimacy had already sprung up, made the advance. I could not hear, but saw that she was being questioned by the Provost Marshal, one of the others writing down her answers. By-and-by she was dismissed, and another passenger stepped forward to go through the ordeal.

Some were a long time being questioned, some were soon dismissed. Before my turn arrived, a Federal officer came, and seating himself by me, commenced a conversation.

Had I been in Richmond? How many troops were there? Where was "*Bew*regard" now? How many troops at Petersburg? how many boats? how high was the river? how many were killed in that night skirmish? and a full catechism of similar questions. All of which I answered in a very prudent and neutral manner. While we were talking, the Jew's turn came for examination, and as he entered the door, and took his seat, the gentleman by me, said, nodding towards him: "*That's* a thorough good Unionist; *he's* safe enough; I have had a long talk with him."

Could I believe my ears and eyes? And what reply could be made by me? Of course I said nothing, but I thought, those are the people who are offering such enormous sums for substitutes, and who are doing such injury to the South. He had shown me his passport, on which was plainly written, "having taken the oath of allegiance to the Southern Confederacy," &c., &c. *Now*, one could account for his nervous watching, and inquiries, and the tearing up of those papers. And that man had been all that time growing rich through the confiding, liberal Southerners, whom already he had begun to traduce.

My turn soon came. I will repeat the questions as faithfully as I can recall them, and they are tolerably impressed on my memory. Few of the answers only need be stated.

"Where were you born?"

"When did you come to this country?"

"Where did you land?"

"What ship did you come in?"

"For what purpose did you come?"

"What is your age?" (Very polite: I wondered what that had to do with it.)

"Are your parents living?"

"Have you any relatives in the South?"

"Any in the North?" "Where?"

"Where have you lived since you have been in the South?" Where else?"

"What was the name of the largest town near you in Florida?"

"There was no large town," I said. Upon which they all laughed as much as to say, "We don't think much of Florida."

"What was your object in going there?"

"What is your object in coming away?"

"Do you intend to return?" and several more questions. He did not ask me if I sympathised with the rebels, nor if I had been to Fort Sumter, or to the battle-grounds, or if I had any sketches of Rebeldom, nor with whom I had lived in Florida. The questions asked me happened to be easily answered, and also truthfully so, and I was *permitted to proceed.* By-and-by, we all had Federal passports given us, with the exception of four people. One lady who was going home to Kentucky, because she could proceed in no other direction, was pronounced a spy. The Southern gentleman who had been too ready to declare that he had taken the oath of allegiance to the Confederate Government, and "meant it," but who was going to bring home his two young orphaned sisters from the North, where they were alone and unprotected, having been at school, was not seen again. Whether sent back, or imprisoned, we could not discover.

Another person who acknowledged that he had taken the oath to the Southern Confederacy, was an Irishman; but he said he "did *not mean* it," and had made a "mental reservation at the time;" therefore his crime was not considered so great, and upon taking another oath to the Federal Government, he also was allowed to proceed.

The two ladies in mourning were sisters; one of whom was married, and a resident of Norfolk, Virginia. She had left four young children at home, and, in the absence of her husband in the Confederate army, had been compelled to repair to Richmond, on business. While there the recent battles had made the returning journey more difficult to accomplish, and she had been endeavouring for some time to find a safe method of proceeding, having even hired a conveyance at an enormous rate to pass through the country south of James River, and by way of Suffolk County; but had been compelled to retrace her road, rather than encounter the Federal army.

The same gentleman who spoke to me about the Jew, had also made himself acquainted with her story, and remarked, "It looks very suspicious for her to come *this* way to get to Norfolk; she cannot have any good reasons for doing so, excepting to watch our movements." It occurred to me that a person who so quickly discovered the intentions and destinations of the passengers, might have other motives than mere civility in making himself companionable to Miss Jones, who was, therefore, very much on her guard. In the course of conversation he discovered that some of my relatives lived where one of his fellow-officers had come from, and this gentleman happening to know my sister's husband to be a staunch Unionist, secured the confidence of the inquisitor towards myself; but the two unhappy Norfolk ladies were sent back to Petersburg.

My Federal passport was on a very tiny and tidy bit of paper, and ran thus :—

To all whom it may concern:

No. 182 **Head-quarters Provost Marshal General,**
Army of the Potomac,

August 2, 1862

KNOW YE, *that the Bearer,* Miss Sarah L. Jones *has permission to pass from* this landing *to* Baltimore, *for the purpose of* ....

This pass will expire August 5, 1862.

By command of A. PORTER, Brig.-Gen. U. S. A.,
Provost Marshal General, Army of the Potomac:

.........................., *Capt. & Adjt.*

[*Signature indistinct.*]

[*Reverse Side.*]

Age 30	*In availing myself of the benefits of the within Pass, I do solemnly affirm that I am a true and loyal citizen of the United States, and that I will give no aid, comfort, or information to the enemies of the United States Government in any manner whatsoever.**
Height 4 feet 17 inches	
Complexion Florid	
Hair Carroty	
Eyes Hazel	
Build Robuist	
Whiskers	....

* N.B.—*Not* "solemnly affirmed," by a British subject.

When all the party had gone through their examinations, a meal was prepared of coffee, tea, cold meats, vegetables, &c. There was abundance of everything, which I heartily wished could be shared by some of my rebel friends.

It was strange to see so many conveniences lavished upon the army as I observed on these boats. We had been of late so careful over every fragment of paper and other trifling things, the value of which these people did not appear to appreciate at all.

Everything was furnished to them, and, as one of the officers remarked to me,—"There never was any army so thoroughly equipped as ours; there is not a convenience that we have not got." No doubt it is so; the soldiers are fighting for a business, not because their homes are invaded; they are hired for pay, and make their own stipulations. I could pity the generals who had the control of such an army, composed of "sovereign men," who would not scruple to refuse to stir a step, unless extravagantly supplied with every comfort to start with; while the Southerners, with but one end in view, the defence of their country, have neither wish nor thought for luxuries.

It was almost midnight when we were transferred to a miserable kind of ferry-boat, which took us somewhere else among the shipping, and again transferred us to another passenger-boat, where berths and better accommodations awaited us.

It was a tedious business to accomplish all these changes, for at every door way and flight of steps were placed guards, to whom we must show our passports and tell our names: and at one place I only stepped forward a few paces to try to catch sight of my luggage, which I had not once seen nor heard of, when two soldiers planted their guns before me as a barrier, and sent me back in no very courteous manner, as if they thought I had been going, with a sly match, to set the boat on fire.

Long before day, the tramping of horses on ferry-boats, and the noise of soldiers, told me that important movements were going on. Hundreds of horses I counted as soon as daylight permitted; and at every landing, encampments and bustle prevailed. I heard them boasting of having burnt the house of Edmund Ruffin, the aged and honoured Virginian, after that midnight cannonading; and several other places near the river. A spirit of revenge seemed to possess them. "To gain all we can and damage the rest," seemed to be their only principle of action.

That Federal officer was nevertheless very polite to me, and assisted to collect my luggage, which after all was never examined; and I might have brought even despatches, and no one would have known it. He conversed a good deal about the war and the "rebellion," and said, among other things, "Much as it would have been against my feelings a year ago to harbour such a thought, I am now convinced that we must go on with this war until the country is cleared of them," (the Southerners).

"And you *must* annihilate them before you conquer them, for they will *never* come back to the Union," I told him.

"Oh, you need not tell us that. When we get possession of Richmond we shall bring them to their senses. We are now preparing to attack them by a concerted movement on all sides at once. Nothing can save them: look at our vastly superior numbers compared with theirs."

Just think of my listening to such things, and not being able to warn the "vastly" *in*ferior "numbers" of devoted rebels; though I knew they possessed one advantage that their enemies could not boast, which was a spirit and courage that made up for their deficiency of numbers. But I merely said, "Excuse me, you may possess Richmond and all Virginia; Charleston, Savannah, and Mobile besides, and it will make no difference."

I said that, and a great deal more, and was quite surprised at my own boldness; but I resolved that if I *could* do anything to convince them of the uselessness of prosecuting the war, I would do so. We also talked on the emancipation question, and he asked me what the "rebels" thought of it. I told him they thought that the Northern President in this, only gave fresh proof of his short-sightedness, and total misapprehension of Southern character.

"How will Lincoln's proclamation scheme affect these people?"

"Some will never know of it, God be thanked! Some will never leave their homes and masters, if they do hear of it. But some, no doubt, will hear of it, and also take advantage of it, as the negroes of New Orleans are doing."

"Do you not think that the greater part of them will rise, and try to escape to our people?"

"How can they escape to the borders from the far-off interior without the risk of discovery, which would be certain death, or else the risk of starvation and of suffering which they have never known before. Nothing but misery can result from such a scheme; misery to the slaves and grief to their masters, when compelled to resort to such fearful extremes as will be forced upon them."

"Well, to tell the truth there are very few of our people who approve of the scheme, nor yet that of arming the negroes to fight in the ranks. I believe three-fourths of us would resign if Lincoln persists in carrying it out."

"Besides, what right has Mr. Lincoln to send messages to the Southerners' servants any more than you have to give permission to your neighbour's coachman to take a trip in the 'Great Eastern?'"

"We don't really want to interfere with slavery, it isn't *that* we care so much about; but it's this thing of having the Union broken up: we can't allow *that*. I have been in the South myself, and I don't find so much fault with slavery; but you see the niggers stay at home and work while all the white men go and fight. Now if it were not for them, their masters would be obliged to stay at home and cultivate their own land, as our men do, or starve, and that would so reduce their army that there would be no chance for them. That's what our Government is up to."

"Supposing they do hear of the proclamation, as a few of them may, but with very confused notions of what it means; how are they to get away? Would any of the Southern army allow a band of negroes to pass their lines with the intention of escape without shooting them down, after such a proclamation as Lincoln's? It will simply drive the negroes to their destruction. Removed from authority the negro is a savage."

"They are so confounded proud, those Secessionists. The worst thing in slavery is, that labour is disgraced by it. Those slave-holding aristocrats look down upon us for the very thing that we pride ourselves most upon. We respect people all the more when they help themselves."

"That is very true and praiseworthy. I have observed with regret what you mention to be the case. Slavery is certainly an obstacle to progress, both of the white and the coloured race."

"They keep their negroes ignorant, to hide their degraded position from them."

"Excuse me, I think *not*. I have met with many very intelligent negroes, slaves, and feel convinced that when left entirely under the influence of their owners, they will be educated much more than at present. The Southerners choose to manage their own servants, and have been more rigorous of late years on account of the abolition rage. Slavery will wear itself out, and that is its only remedy."

I felt myself excessively presumptuous to venture to say all this, and a great deal more, to a Federal officer, and he certainly was very forbearing to listen to it.

There is not an unkind thing in this book that I have not said to themselves, both Northerners and Southerners. No doubt at the time they all thought, "We will let a woman talk; women must talk, you know." With regard to President Lincoln's emancipation proclamation, however, I do know that rebellion would result in the ruin, if not the extermination of the slaves; and are there not enough of the white race being sent to their last account through this war of pride and ambition, without visiting its vengeance on the innocent slave, whose disobedience in this case would, *must* result in his certain death. Grievous as it would be to the planter to massacre his own servants, towards whom exists a tie, a relationship, a self-imposed responsibility, impossible to comprehend by those who do not "possess" a human being, yet can he see them in their ignorance and infatuation rise against himself and his family, without visiting them with condign punishment?

I could not help noticing all the good firm landings the Federals had made, even in that short space of time while they had occupied the James River. The efficiency of white labour was certainly conspicuous directly one came in contact with it.

"All we want are Generals," admitted the Federal officer, in another conversation.

"General McClellan does not command the field in person as the Southern Generals do. Does he?" I asked.

"No, indeed; *he* is not going to put himself up for a target to be shot at."

Well, we steamed all down the James River, and then past Fortress Monroe, and at every turn came in sight of greater preparations for exterminating all my "rebel" friends. How could one feel happy!

CHAPTER XX.

Arrival in Baltimore—Dissimulations—Contrasts—Dangers in the Land of Freedom—A Civil War indeed—Colonel Corcoran's Ovation—Conversation on Neutral Ground—Impartial Views of the Slaves.

IT was even stranger to watch countenances in Baltimore, than it had been to try and read the secret sentiments of the people who had come by the flag of truce.

The first thing to be done was to send a telegraphic message to my sister in Indiana:—

"Arrived safely, viâ James River. Expect me immediately."

The clerk looked inquiringly. I believe he suspected from whence I had come. It was natural to speak of those who had engrossed every thought for so many months, and I said, "I have just come from Richmond."

"How did you manage to get away?"

That was what everybody asked, as if it were a thing impossible. I told the people that the flag of truce was bringing away almost daily those who had had no other tie in the South than their business;

and that prisoners, letters, and papers were daily being brought northwards with every means of communication.

At the hotel, the proprietor presented himself as usual to the "lady travelling alone." I was curious to see the effect of that little speech, "I have just come from Richmond," which scrap of information I managed to introduce in my inquiries about the western trains. The landlord only looked earnestly to examine my countenance, as if to read there what his answer ought to be. At last, the safe and uncompromising question, "How are things going on down there?" was uttered with apparent indifference, but with an unmistakable earnestness of eye, that aroused my instant sympathy. But the "neutral" subject was obliged to be as much on her guard as any of the Secession sympathizers in Baltimore, and she cautiously answered, "They say they will die to the last man before they will be subjugated."

The landlord's eyes shot forth a dart of enthusiasm, but still he expressed no opinion; therefore I continued: "People do not know whether they are addressing friends or foes in this city. Every one is in doubt as to what they may venture to say?" which was also very non-committal.

"It is so," said the proprietor, but—" and he looked still more intently to read my countenance —"I—I fancy you may speak out, Madam."

Poor man! I saw plainly where his sympathies were, and yet I was afraid, being alone in a place where women had been arrested for even the colours they wore, and for sympathizing with the "rebels." My Southern friends were all "rebels" now, and their honoured President was "Jeff," "the traitor Jeff Davis, hanging on an apple-tree." Such impertinences as these were not likely to keep one so very "*neutral*," because I happened to be much better acquainted with the character of the Honourable Jefferson Davis than the vulgar boys who were shouting such sentiments through the streets. But the proprietor of the hotel was waiting anxiously for a reply, which I was as anxiously trying to invent.

"I met a good many Marylanders in the South," I said, in another uncompromising speech.

He was still uncertain, and only replied, "Yes?"

"This is a dreadful war and it seems perfectly useless to continue it—I wish it were over; the Marylanders are suffering a great deal, away from all their friends."

"Are they, in*deed?*" said the "*Secessionist;*" for the truth revealed itself in the feeling with which he now spoke. "I see I may speak to you, madam," continued he; and gladly did he proceed to make inquiries, and listen eagerly to all the information I could give him of Secessia, every moment looking cautiously around, to discover if any person near might be listening to the conversation.

"If any of the Southern Generals were to appear in this city, we should rise as one man," he said. "We are only waiting our opportunity."

As I got into the carriage which was about to convey me to the station for my western journey, the proprietor re-appeared, and an old man was by his side, who after gazing earnestly at me in silence, suddenly put out his hand and caught at mine, while tears gushed from his eyelids. "God bless you, madam! God bless you! you feel for us, I know!"

"He has a son in the Confederate army, and cannot obtain any tidings of him," added the proprietor, in explanation of his actions.

"You have just come from there, and it does me good to look at you," said the old man.

How could one withstand such sorrow? That evening I arrived at Harrisburg, in Pennsylvania, and feeling too much fatigued and indisposed to travel all night, stopped at another hotel; but not to sleep, for the streets were uproarious with bands, and fifes, and processions, and a "public demonstration" on the square close by, consisting of shouts, hurrahs, and inflammatory speeches, which the open windows of the hot month of August forced upon my ears, and told me that recruiting was being vigorously pushed.

At every station we stopped at, flaming handbills were displayed; headed as follows:—

"DOWN WITH THE REBELS"
PROMPT ACTION."
"THE FINAL BLOW AND THE REBELLION CRUSHED."
"FREEMEN TO ARMS."
"DEATH ON SLAVERY."
"UNION AND FREEDOM," &c. &c. &c.

and ending in exciting addresses arousing the worst passions and most revengeful hatred, tempered with enormous bribes to "AVOID DRAFTING."

The next night I stopped on the summit of the Alleghany Mountains in Pennsylvania, to try to obtain one night's repose, after the recent fatigues and painful excitement of the journey from the rebel South.

"Cressons Springs" is a summer resort, and was crowded with fashionable visitors. One seemed to have fallen all at once upon a different planet. Such a thing as war or suffering never entered the minds of those gay groups of butterflies. Gentlemen of all ages were pursuing their several routines of smoking, lounging, and flirting, the elder ladies fanning and gossipping, and the younger ones promenading and coquetting.

After the evening meal, which consisted of every luxury, including the most delicious wild fruits of the mountains, the immense dining-hall was being cleared for theatricals. Several pianos in different parts of the house sounded through the open doors and windows, and the loud, light-hearted tones of the *cantatrices* rang through the lofty passages.

As I walked backwards and forwards on the terrace before the open windows, alone in that thoughtless crowd, it was impossible to convince oneself that in that very country a war—and such a horrible war—was raging. Had none of these people a relative engaged in it? Had they never heard of the suffering soldiers? of the thousands and thousands of deaths both by sickness and on the battle-field? I pressed my hands against my temples, and felt as if I must be walking in my sleep or dreaming, and recalled with an effort, in that din of merriment, the circumstances of the past week to assure myself of their reality.

It was twilight, and a glorious sunset was tinting up the wooded points of the mountains. I moved to a less crowded spot, and was leaning against a corner of a balcony to enjoy the beautiful scene, while my thoughts dwelt on the sad contrast of those I had so lately quitted. Inadvertently, for I scarcely knew that the sounds escaped my lips, I hummed the air "My Maryland," almost unconscious of the existence of any people near me, until the word "Secesh," in a loud whisper, recalled me to the fact, and also the very inopportune occasion of my careless act, which might draw upon me the unwelcome observations of the crowd. The hotel and neighbouring boarding-houses were all so thronged with visitors, that I was compelled to wait some time before accommodation could be furnished me, and during those two hours of sitting and pacing backwards and forwards among that talkative assemblage, not one syllable of war or sadness did I hear. They did not seem aware that such facts existed.

On arriving at my sister's home, it very soon became reported in the town that Mrs. Wilson's sister, Miss Jones, had just come from the rebels, and was a "rank Secesh;" but I found that I was far from being the only person of that title in the place.

Many old former friends came with eager curiosity to see me, and to hear the latest news from Rebeldom, asking so many questions, which I resolved to answer truly, that at last my sister's husband said, "Sarah, remember that you are now with loyal Unionists, and such remarks are very unwelcome." And my sister one day came home and said, "Sally, it is reported all over town that you are such a violent Secessionist that Judge B. and Mr. C. have asked me to request you not to say any more about the South, for they are really afraid the people will have you arrested."

On the other hand, they could not disguise the fact that a tremendous volcano was ready to burst under that very town, "to resist the draft;" and one gentleman said, "These streets will be running with blood in thirty days if they enforce this draft." Since I have returned to England I have learned that riots and arrests have occurred there. Two of the most prominent citizens were arrested for opposing the war as useless and fruitless, and the drafting was "indefinitely postponed."

Every newspaper one looked at contained conspicuous headings of "REBEL BARBARITIES;" "INCREDIBLE INHUMANITIES OF THE REBELS;" "THE WAY THEY TREAT OUR PRISONERS IN SECESSIA;" "MORE REBEL LIES." Southern women were represented as wreaking revenge by putting helpless and wounded prisoners to torturing deaths, by firing on unarmed men from windows and hiding-places, and by performing many other outrages no less unfeminine than untrue. Indeed, in passing through the North, I was astounded to find how entirely the public were blinded and deceived by their own newspapers, which they seemed to swear to as to gospel; and the remarkable efforts of the Unionists to keep up in the public mind a bitter and excited prejudice against the "rebels," and to present facts in a form so disguised that they rather claimed the romance of fiction than a true detail of circumstances. In vain I tried to convince my friends of their mistake, and to prove to them my opportunities of knowing the truth. "You are mistaken, you have been deceived and misled," they persisted in declaring; even going so far as to deny that women had been imprisoned, or that their own Government was anything otherwise than the most lenient and merciful Government in the world. It was common to hear men whom you had hitherto esteemed for social virtues, and women adorned by Christian graces, firmly and resolutely say of the Southerners, "We must annihilate them," with as little remorse as they have before displayed in destroying the Indians. Annihilate eight millions of people! Lay waste a country half the size of Europe! Is this to be permitted? Can it be that these were the inhabitants of a Christian country, among whom were my own blood relatives, who uttered such revolting sentiments through sheer revenge and malice, backed by their ambitious worship of their idol Union.

After such a long absence and endurances, was the civil war to be carried into the very heart of our own family by a simple statement of the *truth?* In this one fact was proved the violent and implacable hatred that exists between the combatants. And yet these rebels, whom they hate so furiously, are the people they think to persuade to come back and sit in their halls of Congress at Washington. No! every step they take only deepens the gulf that separates them. At first the Southerners would have continued their chief dealings with the North, and the world would have scarcely called Dis-Union the appointment of two, or even more Presidents over such a wide-spread territory. It had been a "glorious Union" indeed. Who but must regret the infuriate self-destruction that is making it the despised of all the world.

I was too much in danger of engendering strife amongst my own relatives to feel inclined to prolong my stay, and soon turned my face once more towards the East.

All the conversations one heard partook of these sentiments:—"We will cut off their supplies and starve them into submission;" "we shall soon have more gun-boats ready;" the rebels "far outnumbered us;" and "their loss exceeded ours," till one was surprised to think that any rebels at all were left, and yet I had seen only too many idle men wherever I had been. Those who questioned me asked, the first thing, where Stonewall Jackson and Beauregard were, and "How long will they hold out?"

Not the least of all the painful events of my last two years' experiences, was the fact of bidding adieu to the once United and enviable States of America under such sorrowful convictions. Many happy days had I passed in those United States; many dear friends had I left in the North whom now perhaps I may never meet again. I had been proud of the Union for their sakes, and for their sakes do I still mourn over its destruction.

As there was not one familiar face to give me a parting smile, nor one friendly hand to wave adieu as our ship was loosened from the wharf in the ever-beautiful harbour of New York, it was no little surprise and pleasure to greet the good-humoured face of an old acquaintance in the captain, and to be assisted with my luggage by the civil and obliging steward, who had been so careful of my little mocking-birds two years before.

Not five minutes had one been on board, before one felt the superlative comfort of being on a British steamer, and of witnessing the charms of freedom which, after all, is more enjoyed in England than in any other country.

The grand Corcoran ovation had just taken place in New York.

"What fools they are making of themselves

about that fellow, Corcoran!" I heard one gentleman say.

"They are only making a tool of him, to get up an Irish brigade," said another.

For a day or two there was a good deal more of the study of physiognomy being prosecuted, and by degrees we discovered that our fellow-passengers were composed of many representatives of different political parties as well as states and countries. Many conversations and arguments were of course overheard, all of which were remarkable for one thing—an extraordinary toleration and forbearance among those who took part in them. I doubt if there ever were so many persons, entertaining strong and opposing sentiments, who passed two weeks together amid exciting discussions, and preserved such friendly feelings.

Perhaps a repetition of parts of the conversations, as far as I can recall them, that occurred between some of the most intelligent of the passengers, may not be an unsuitable *finale* to my Southern experiences.

Colonel or General Corcoran was being upheld by a Northern gentleman, and was represented to have been imprisoned in the "Tombs," and to have been kept "over a dead-house"—no such places existing in the South, that I ever heard of.

An English gentleman who had not long since left the South, took up the subject, and warmly exclaimed, "I was in Richmond while Colonel Corcoran was imprisoned there, saw many persons who visited his prison, and know that this statement is entirely false, and that until his condition was changed, as a means of warning to the Federal Government that it should, by undue violence to Southern prisoners, be held responsible for his life, he was treated as a gentleman and prisoner of war, and amply furnished with whatever comforts Richmond itself afforded.

A Southerner added, "These things are written in order to deepen the hatred and stimulate the revenge with which the war is now being carried on."

"If the Union party in the North are firm in proclaiming 'Death rather than dismemberment,' the Southerners are much more determined in saying 'Extermination rather than submission,'" said a gentleman from New Orleans.

The former replied, "And as to union, it is not power we crave, but peace. It is to escape the contact of 'Yankees' altogether, under any and every circumstance; and if President Davis were appointed Military Dictator, King, or even Emperor of the North, I firmly believe he would decline the privilege of ruling Yankee subjects."

"The Yankees leave no stone unturned to weaken the power of the South; and one object is to lure away the negro labourers in order more easily to 'starve their masters into submission,'" rejoined the Louisianian.

"*Starve!* that's the old story again. Can they starve us in such a country as ours? Look at

Virginia and Tennessee, what large wheat-growing States they are; they would supply the English market as well as our own, so soon as our own ports are opened, as they have already done through Northern ports before the war. There will be no lack of 'bread stuffs' when peace and agriculture go hand in hand, not only for ourselves, but others. There is not much danger of our starving; we have only to plant corn instead of cotton."

"Exactly so," replied the gentleman from New Orleans; "but no cotton will be planted if there is no prospect of a sale, and another year of bloodshed, which is a disgrace to humanity, will ensue, and another year of suffering for your English factory hands."

"Let neutrality display itself in trading with all ports, or none, and then the war would soon be over, —that's what I think," said the Englishman from the South.

"But we should not permit you to open our ports: the raising of the blockade would be followed by war," said the Northern gentleman; "and what would be the use of your attempting to fight us? you would only get whipped again, as you were before."

"As to that, it was our blood that fought your battles," retorted John Bull; "the States were inhabited by people of different mettle then than they are now. You have too much on your hands already, and are going headlong to ruin. Recognition of the South would be more likely to bring your Government to its senses, with so large an anti-war party already rampant; and you find it too hard a matter to raise men and furnish artillery to conquer the South to attempt the conquest of England or Canada either; and what would you do between all three?"

"Excuse me, sir," said the Yankee, "you underrate our power; we have had upwards of a million in the field, and don't miss our men. We shall now raise 600,000 more, and as many more to back them when they are gone."

What a wholesale extermination way of talking, and how horrible that sounded! though it was but too true, as I had seen so lately, and where their armies were composed chiefly of foreigners; but I could not help wishing that they did miss their men much more, and realized the horrors of the war they were waging, which perhaps would have induced them to put an end to it without such reckless sacrifice of life. Yet I had heard the Northern people declare (among themselves) that the factories were losing their best hands; and out west, that the farmers offered three dollars a day for labourers.

Another day they were talking of slavery, and the Yankee gentleman was speaking of the Southerners leaving their negroes to take care of themselves, while they made good their own escape.

My fellow-countryman again took up the cudgels, and spoke of the sacrifice the owners were obliged to make when they had fled, with the Federal gun-boats firing on them. He said one lady had informed him that she had saved three negroes out of two hundred. Another had brought away one out of fifty, and so on. And these were carried away in preference to clothing, jewellery, or other valuables, which would have occupied less space, less care, and required no food and lodging. Valuables of all description were left to the enemy.

An English lady observed, "If the helpless and old ones were left behind, I am inclined to think that it was a sad consequence of the invasion, and not the neglect of owners."

I thought of sable Jane in Florida.

"The negro slaves are better off than our paupers," said the Englishman, "under ordinary times, but now are in a more enviable condition in every way, as they know not the want of food or clothing, while the state of our starving poor is only one of the frightful consequences of the war."

It did seem as if the whole world were being brought into trouble through the negroes, who, after all, were requiring so little sympathy.

Much as I had hesitated in going to the South, through a dread of witnessing the sufferings of the slaves, not once had I seen serious reason for pitying them. I had known them in houses and in fields, domestic servants and "plantation hands;" had come upon them unexpectedly and suddenly in the midst of their labour; and in the two years and a half between six of the slave States, exclusive of Maryland, I had never seen nor heard of corporeal punishment, excepting such as has been mentioned in these pages.

Yet, reader, English reader, do not for a moment suppose that your countrywoman approves of slavery, though she has been very careful to relate the exact truth, leaving it to others to decide, how far it is just to denounce a people, who preserve an institution entailed upon them by our own ancestors.

One has no right to expect perfection in the Southerners more than in any other people, but they are now known to be a nation worthy of the world's esteem: and the Author who has observed them, and their country struggling in its infant nationality amidst such cruel obstacles and injustice, will feel that she has not written in vain, if those, who have not before so thought of them, should be induced, through these imperfect pages, to regard with more leniency and justice the people of the

SOUTHERN CONFEDERACY.

THE END.

CPSIA information can be obtained
at www.ICGtesting.com
Printed in the USA
LVHW040350110522
718423LV00001B/212

9 783375 001087